D1571777

The Eighth Realm

MICHAEL CHATFIELD

Cover Art by Jan Becerikli Garrido
Jacket Design by Caitlin Greer
Interior Design by Caitlin Greer

eBook ISBN: 978-1-989377-91-8-
Paperback ISBN: 978-1-989377-92-5

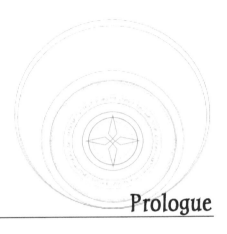

Prologue

The First Realm came into focus around Zen Old Hei's carriage and his personal guards. The defenses around the totem showed signs of fighting, the gates to the city half-sealed to slow the progress of people.

Fighters wearing the same open-faced helmets, fatigues, weapons, and slimmed down armor stood on the walls, weapons pointing at the totem, ready for use. They all wore hardened expressions. Among them were several with the face piece of their helmet sealing them away from the world.

"Keep moving. Those traveling by foot or with a mounted beast on the right, carriages on the left! Prepare your beast storage crates for inspection!"

The heavily enchanted carriage and powerful guards gained attention as they rolled over the pitted ground, following the procession of carts entering the city. Every beast storage crate was checked, and contracts descended in a golden light.

"Everyone that enters the Alvan Empire must adhere to the safety contract. If you do not, then please exit back through the totem!" another guard said.

The carriage reached the inspection station.

"I have to see everyone inside the carriage," a guard said.

Captain Khasar moved to the door and knocked. "Sir?"

Old Hei opened the door, noting the soldier's clothes and gear showed signs of fighting. "Zen Hei, from the Alchemist Association. I have been sent here to talk to Lord West."

The guard turned his head to the side, communicating through his sound transmission device. He held out a hand. "Identification?"

"Who do you think you are to ask *Master* Hei for his identification?" one of Zen Hai's guards sneered, placing his hand on his sword.

The Alvan's expression didn't twitch as he put his hand on his rifle and met the guard's eyes with an expression that said he had seen and dealt death so closely he had seen the Reaper on the other side. "Shut the fuck up or I will tear you down from that goddamn horse." It wasn't a boast, it was a flat iron truth.

The mana in the area became sluggish, drawn to the soldier. His skin hardened, showing faint red lines.

Earth and Fire tempering.

"Here we are." Old Hei smiled and held out a medallion.

The Alvan soldier looked away from the guard as if nothing had happened.

Khasar glared at the guard, quieting him.

The soldier took out a formation and pressed the medallion to it. It showed some light-projected words above the medallion.

"Just need to check your beast storage devices." A few minutes later and with a Ten Realms contract, the soldier waved them on.

"Welcome to Shida. A representative will meet you outside the totem processing facility."

Old Hei saw the true extent of the fighting when they passed through the gates. Buildings lay in ruins where barriers had failed. The people of Shida were clearing the rubble and trying to rebuild their homes. Mages worked together, repairing water and waste lines. Children ran in their new playground, not understanding what had happened, while a couple cried against one another at the front of what had once been their home.

Soldiers marched through the streets, carriages giving them right of way. Some wore the more traditional armor of the Ten Realms: gambesons, leather, and plate in some places, with swords on their hips, shields on their backs, and repeaters in their hands. Others, like the guards at the totem, wore thinned-down armor and updated helmets. *Looks like Rugrat and his fellow smiths have been busy. Never seen weapons like those before.*

Undead were working for the mages, each a juggernaut in their own right, clearing roads and moving materials through the city. Some had been recovered from Vuzgal and from the fighting dead. Bodies that could be used as tools were a boon in a world where they had little value.

A woman rode up on a panther. Her gear was more streamlined than most soldiers, radiating lethality. Old Hei couldn't see through her cultivation, nor that of her team members.

Khasar went to talk to her before returning to the carriage. "That's Roska. She's one of the people that led Erik's guards in the past. She will take us to him. She says that he's hidden from prying eyes and will need us to agree to not share information."

"Are you expecting me to have a conversation through my carriage window?" Old Hei sighed.

Khasar tried to thread warning into his voice, "This was a battlefield not so long ago, and it is my job to maintain your safety."

"I know, Khasar, but hiding in my carriage isn't safety. It's hiding."

Old Hei opened his door, feeling Khasar's defeat in the air as he stepped down and closed the door. Khasar walked behind him toward the trio.

Roska and the two others bowed their heads.

"I'm told that you can take me to see Erik, but there are stipulations?"

"Yes, your grand-student Delilah made them. She wants to see you as soon as possible to assist."

If Delilah needed his help, then it must be bad. As an Expert alchemist, she could make extremely powerful concoctions.

Roska offered Old Hei a piece of paper that he skimmed through. "The Association won't like my report. Going to have a few holes." He chuckled. "I agree on the Ten Realms to adhere to this contract."

He completed the second contract of the day. "Okay, now that's done."

"Guards as well," Roska said.

They all completed the contract and Roska and her people guided them through the broken city. A series of pillars jutted out of the city, landing platforms sticking out at their highest reaches, their peaks blurred by the thin mana mist.

"We will travel by Kestrel. It will be the fastest way," Roska said, leading them to the nearest pillar.

It was several minutes later, as they were riding up in a lift to the top of the pillar, that Old Hei couldn't take the silence anymore. "What is all this mist?"

"Mana, aggravated by the fighting and released by it. We'll have it cleared in a few days. Right now it's just a pain in the air."

"We tried to teleport to Chonglu City, but we couldn't find it listed as a location."

"The city was renamed Zahir. It was leveled by the United Sect Alliance," Roska said as they reached the top of the pillar.

They walked onto the flight platform and toward a Kestrel with a wooden cabin on its back. Once mounted, the rear ramp grew back together, and the Kestrel flapped its wings, then *dove* off the platform.

Hei grabbed onto the wall and chair. A few guards let a yell slip out as the Alvans glanced over and sat back, relaxing. The Kestrel's wings caught the air, sending them cruising over the countryside towards King's Hill.

Old Hei settled his beard and clothes, grinning with excitement. His smile faded as he looked out the window.

The ground was torn asunder in the fighting. Unnatural lines showed where barriers had blunted the blast in the midst of destruction. Fields had been churned up in the fighting, stone platforms grouped together, fresh new stone surrounded by scorch marks. Undead toiled endlessly, clearing the ground and repairing it.

There must be thousands of undead.

Old Hei swallowed as they reached the outposts standing outside the forests. The fighting had been fierce. The ground was cratered and blackened. Outposts stood tall as if untouched by the destruction around them.

"They never made it to the outposts?" He asked.

"They repair themselves, some were nearly torn in two." Roska said.

Crews of people were everywhere, clearing debris, repairing roads.

"Those are the ones that surrendered," Roska followed his gaze. "We pressed them into work, repairing what they broke."

That kind of mercy was nearly unheard of. With this many contract bound fighters from the higher realms as an unpaid force.

Zen Hei suppressed a shiver.

The mana fog lifted enough to reveal a corvette smashed against the ground. Sections lay along the scar that cut through the ground and forest.

Zen Hei saw carcasses of other corvettes and weapons of war. Bodies were turning to motes of light, adding to the mana fog over the battlefield.

Teams scavenged through the debris, loading carts that ran up and down the repaired roads toward the heart of the Beast Mountain Range.

"That's what we call the bunker-line." Roska pointed to the row of squat stone buildings that the scar stabbed into, thinning into a spearhead, and then breaking through.

"It…" Zen Hei had been trained in conversations, had talked to leaders of nations and sects, but seeing the devastation before him, he wondered how *anyone* could make it through all of this. He shook his head, words tumbling through his fingers as he stared at a tunnel that bored through the dirt and stone of a small hill. Undead and construction crews transformed it into a road. Twin towers stood on either side, squat, utilitarian and military in nature.

He looked at the broken frigate and corvettes again, trying to imagine the sheer power used here, the ferocity of the fighting.

The Kestrel rose in altitude.

Carved into the mountain was a light hangar. The Kestrel came in, flapping her wings before settling down halfway into the hangar.

Roska balanced with one grab rope, walking toward the rear as the ramp lowered. They followed her out, heading to a set of lifts. At the end of the hangar, there was a checkpoint.

"All maps here, please." The soldier manning the station held out a box. The Association members relieved themselves of their maps.

Roska guided them through several corridors before they arrived at an elevator that dropped into the depths of the mountain. At the bottom, they passed through several other lifts and along corridors.

They finally entered a medical area. There were rooms filled with pods containing people.

"Old Hei!" Delilah saw them as they turned a corridor. She bowed her head. There was a heaviness to every fiber of her being, a solemnity in her movements. Her skin was pale, bags around her eyes and, while shadows lingered in her eyes, determination shone through. "Please, come with me."

She guided him down the hall and into a room. Inside, there were several healers and alchemists tending to pods lined up on either side of the room. Guards at the door rose and opened it for Delilah. She stopped at the bottom of two pods. Inside lay Rugrat and Erik. They had been stripped to their underwear. Their bodies were covered in angry scars, the shrapnel glowing under their skin.

"You must be Master Hei." A woman approached. "I'm Jen. I'm in charge of this ward."

"How are they?"

"We have them sedated hard due to their poison resistance. They're okay-ish. Never seen anything like this before. We're monitoring them to see just what they did to themselves."

"What happened?"

5

Jen glanced at Delilah, who nodded.

"A dungeon core blew apart in their faces and some of the shards embedded in their bodies. They drew a massive amount of mana during the fighting and burned themselves out. The dungeon cores draw in ambient element mana, and elements, constantly harming them. If they weren't cultivation maniacs and had tempered their bodies, then there would have been no way to save them." Julie snorted and shook her head. "The dungeon core shards are all over their bodies. It's broken their cultivation systems, and they are in constant pain. With all that mana being forced into their mana systems, when casting a spell, they'd have to go against the flow. Like they're trying to wade against a constant stream pushing against them." Julie sighed and rubbed her dry eyes. "Their cultivation is effectively crippled; they can barely use eighty percent of their power, I would guess."

Alva's Intelligence Department Director Elan Silaz, put down the information book he was about to absorb with the knock at his door.

The door opened allowing Aureus, one of his agents inside.

"Sorry sir for interrupting you."

"I asked you to report back as soon as you finished clearing out that Willful Institute backup site."

"It was as we suspected, though things didn't exactly go to plan."

Elan sat up, his face hardening, they had lost so many people losing more was like a knife to the heart.

"When we go there, the fighters that were hiding there were dead. Instead we found a man half alive in the midst of them. It looks like he got there before us and killed his way through them."

"By himself?"

"Yes."

Elan raised a eyebrow.

"He was laughing through his wounds, said his name was Sage, Sage nightshade, looked at our weapons and said they were awfully familiar. We got him stabilized and healed up. Said he comes from Earth too and that he has a deal for us." Aureus waited for Elan's signal to go on. "He said that his best friend was killed by the bastards, ambushed on the road. He set his life's purpose to hunting them down and getting back to Earth. He said he knows where all the rest of the Willful Institute are hiding, he just wants us to promise him if we find a way back he gets a ride and that he is part of the teams that hunt down the Willful Institute."

"Is his information valid?"

"He gave us two locations. I checked them, they're both legit, Commander Glosil is preparing forces to attack both locations as we speak."

"How did he get this information?"

"After his friend died, he went around basically killing fighters from the Willful Institute. He learned how they worked, operated as a kind of assassin. Seems like when we found him, he'd taken on a group that was just too strong for him. These other places he knows he wouldn't be able to kill on his own."

"Taking on the whole Willful Institute on his own," Elan shook his head as his words trailed off.

"They killed his best friend, known him since they were kids, did nearly everything together. He wants to go home to tell his wife, to give her closure and to fulfill a promise to his fiancee. He's been working for years hunting them down."

"And any traces of the Institute?"

"These were the last, we've torn them out from the root."

Elan let out a sigh that came from his core.

"The Willful Institute defeated. I never thought I would see the day. Years ago I sent Domonos to join their ranks, a giant that I couldn't see the knee of. Now just another broken group." Elan shook his head.

"The future is not set." Aureus said.

Elan snorted. "Too true."

1

Behind the Times

Mid-afternoon mana-light revealed the shifting dust inside the lecture hall, the comfortable warmth, drawing eyes closed into sweet sleep. Pens scrawled across pages, the students' attention captured by the lecturer.

Erik rubbed his face, no notepad in front of him, as he rested his chin on his hand. He ran through a check on his notifications, past glories.

Quest Completed: Upgrade the First Realm
Well, it looks like you took the hammer route! For the greatness of the Ten Realms, you are forging ahead! With your contributions, we will all become stronger!
You have opened up the ley lines of the first realm
Rewards:
Receive a Four Star Hero Emblem; must be collected from the Tenth Imperium's Quartermaster
+10,000,000,000,000 EXP (Divided among all participants): +4,000,000 EXP

Skill: Marksman

Level: 98 (Expert)

Long-range weapons are familiar in your hands. When aiming, you can zoom in x2.0. 15% increased chance for a critical hit. When aiming your agility increases by 20%

Skill: Hand-to-Hand

Level: 73 (Journeyman)

Attacks cost 20% less Stamina. Agility is increased by 10%.

Skill: Throwables

Level: 67 (Journeyman)

Your throws gain 5% power
Stamina used for throwing is decreased by 15%

Quest Completed: Mana Cultivation 3

The path to cultivating one's mana is not easy. To stand at the top, one must forge their own path forward.

Requirements:

Reach Liquid Mana Core

Rewards:

+40 to Mana
+40 to Mana Regeneration
+500,000,000 EXP

Quest Completed: Mana Cultivation 4

The path to cultivating one's mana is not easy. To stand at the top, one must forge their own path forward.

Requirements:

Reach Solid Mana Core

Rewards:

+80 to Mana
+80 to Mana Regeneration
+5,000,000,000 EXP

Title: Mana Reborn IV

Your body has undergone a deep transformation, bringing you closer to

Mana, reborn with greater power and control over its forces.

Mana channels are transformed into mana veins. Your mana sense and control increases greatly.

You can now convert Stamina into mana and vice versa.

Quest: Mana Cultivation 5

The path to cultivating one's mana is not easy. To stand at the top, one must forge their own path forward.

Requirements:

Reach Mana Heart

Rewards:

+80 to Mana

+80 to Mana Regeneration

+50,000,000,000 EXP

123,013,359,527/128,249,000,000 EXP till you reach Level 86

Erik's level was so high compared to those that he'd been fighting that they barely registered as experience, only fighting the Hunters had increased his experience by a few thousand a chunk of experience had been taken back, losing his Dungeon Master V title.

Title: From the Grave III

You've died and come back to the land of the living not just once, but twice. You're a true survivor who has put one foot in the grave.

Rewards:

+1.0 modifier to Stamina and Mana Regeneration

+1.0 modifier to Mana and Stamina Regeneration

Name: Erik West

Level: 85

Race: Human-?

Titles:

From the Grave III

Blessed By Mana

Dungeon Master IV

Reverse Alchemist

Poison Body	
Fire Body	
Earth Soul	
Mana Reborn III	
Wandering Hero	
Metal Mind, Metal Body	
Earth Grade Bloodline	
Strength: (Base 90) +58 (-89)	1554
Agility: (Base 83) +110 (-101)	1109
Stamina: (Base 93) +35 (-112)	2016
Mana: (Base 157) +134 (-239)	2978
Mana Regeneration (Base 180) +71 (-201)	156.62
Stamina Regeneration: (Base 162) +99 (-237)	56.86

"Alchemy involves combining different ingredients into a concoction. Looking at the four different stages: growing, harvesting, preparing, and concocting, we can see a pattern emerge in relation to the elements. Ingredients grown in places with higher concentration of elements or mana, harvested and prepared in ways to maintain the elements and mana within the ingredients, have a higher efficacy." Delilah's words captured the room better than the late afternoon's warming rays trying to lull one into drowsiness.

"Elements and mana are the cornerstones of *all* concoctions. A spell made physical through ingredients. As we refine mana and elements within our bodies, so do the plants around us. We are merely using different methods of refining ingredients together with our skills. As we see in chemistry and with the practice of pure magic, it is possible to change one thing into another in different combinations."

Delilah's words settled throughout the room, her eyes carrying through the rows of students to where Erik sat. He pushed his frown into a semblance of a smile.

"Our own Lord West, through consuming different ingredients, and being placed in a cultivation pod, was able to turn his blood into a concoction for many. Changing the input to the ingredients, increasing the concentrations. We already know this makes better ingredients. I theorize that ingredients are just the vehicle, absorbing elements to be used in alchemy."

Erik rubbed his arm, trying not to scratch lest he upset the dungeon core shards embedded into it. *Ingredients have a chemical effect and mana enhances it.*

All drugs are based on chemical reactions. Elements only increase cultivation and the effects of those chemicals. Saying that they're all just based on elements... Erik stopped himself from grimacing.

"When looking at the pill refinement process, we know that pills can absorb elements and power from their surroundings after they are completed. This is similar to how one can cast a fire spell on a living floor and a fire floor, yet the spell will be much stronger on the fire floor. I like to call this Sympathetic Elemental Reaction."

She pushed a rolling chalkboard out of the way, showing an image.

"I will be undertaking a study to observe the effect of creating several pills and then introducing them to highly concentrated elemental parameters. It is my hope that with this we can make, say, a novice level pill, but through an incubation period, the pill's efficacy would increase, making it as strong as an apprentice or journeyman level pill!"

Murmurs ran through the students.

"I will also be studying the effects of one consuming a pill in different elemental environments. If the pill is tuned to an element or not, does it change the effects? Look at how people temper their body with the Fire element now. They consume a Fire-tempering pill, then they go into a cultivation pod where the Fire elements are slowly increased at the same time their vitals are stabilized with the pod's medical abilities. If we were to give them a pill that drew in more of the surrounding elements, could we decrease the cost of tempering? Could we speed up the process? I believe that concoctions are really just the spell circles of the human body. They ignite change and then draw upon the Ten Realms to complete the change. After all, isn't using external mana and elements one of the key ways to cast powerful spells? Why not have that with pills as well?"

Delilah smiled and bowed her head.

The room lifted in applause. Erik frowned and stood, clapping with them, pressing out a smile. People in the front row moved forward to talk with Delilah as the clapping died down, replaced with excited chatter as praise and debates filled the hall.

He grimaced upon seeing the press of people. His eyes hardened, taking in the badges on their chest that marked them as mid or high-level expert alchemists.

"'Scuse me," Erik said, moving past a few people coming towards him. He headed down through the throng of people. His security detail moved to surround him as he palmed off his alchemy badge and stuffed it into his storage ring.

Storbon, leading his Special Team, took them through a door to a hallway between the lecture halls.

Erik couldn't remember the last time he had lectured on anything of importance. He sighed and bent forward, taking out a healing pill and swallowing it as he leaned against the cold wall in the stark white mana-lit hall.

"Do you need a chair, sir?" Storbon asked.

Erik gritted his teeth and stood up straight, ignoring the flashes of pain through his body, forcing it to not catch in his voice. "No, I'm fine."

The low hum of conversation faded and moved away as people left the adjacent room. Erik looked at the door.

"Come on, Delilah." The ache in his chest moved to his legs and then his arms. The legs were the worst. A deep bone ache that, once settled in, took hours to get rid of. All he wanted to do was sit down again. *Where the hell is she?*

The minutes ticked by. Erik was of half a mind to go out there and call her back to the hallway. He ran his knuckles down his leg, trying to relieve the stiffness.

"Are you sure you don't want a seat, sir?" Storbon said.

"I'm fine," Erik growled, flicking his eyes over and back to the door. His thoughts swirled as deep muscle tremors kicked in.

The door let in a flood of noise as it opened.

"We'll figure out a time to chat. Sorry, I really need to go!"

Delilah passed through the door with her security detail, looking flushed. A smile spread across her face as she turned toward Erik. As it shut, the door closed off the sound of the lecture hall once again.

"Teacher." Her face dropped, watching him standing there, kneading his leg.

Erik felt a twinge of anger flare, adding an edge to his smile. "Didn't know you'd be so long."

Delilah schooled her expression and glanced down.

"Good lecture. A lot of people were interested in it. Though I don't think it's quite right." Erik turned and started walking, shaking his legs to get some life back into them.

She walked with him, a half-step back in the tight quarters as Storbon's Special Team led the way.

"I got the idea from the gardens you planted on the living floor and how you used your body with the cultivation pod to create the blood revival concoction," Delilah said.

"I study the interaction of chemicals that are enhanced by the elements or mana. It's those chemicals that create changes in the body."

"What if, because our bodies become closer to the elements, that they interact on a different level?"

"Then what you are proposing is a change to body and alchemy understanding. Bodies can be altered through chemicals. I wasn't looking at the elemental reactions of my body eating those ingredients. I was studying how my body digesting different chemicals would add those effects to my body."

"But what if the mixture of elements is stronger than the chemicals?"

"It's *not*. They are just chemicals. Enhanced, but still chemicals." Erik turned his head, glaring at her. She held up her hands and lowered her head.

Erik grimaced. "You're your own person, Delilah. Your path of Alchemy is still wide open." His fist tightened around his storage ring, feeling it dig into his skin, the image of his alchemist badge rising in his mind. *Just an expert. She's already further than I ever will be.*

He cleared his throat and slowed his pace, not turning around. "There's a group heading to the Eighth Realm to attempt the test. I wanted to let you know that Rugrat and I will be going." Erik turned his head.

"Teacher..." Delilah's face fell, her voice sounded strained.

"We were injured. We're not *invalids*." Erik shot her a look. He heard it in everyone's voice, and in their actions, as if the outside world was out to hurt them. Like they shouldn't be trusted with the cutlery.

"I never—"

"We're going. I wanted to tell you so you could organize things."

Delilah clamped her teeth together and raised her head, a hardness entering her expression. "We haven't sent any teams to the higher realms before. We don't even know what's up there. By all accounts, there is a question and a fight that happens."

"And how many realms have Rugrat and I been to? how many times have we scouted the way for Alva?" He glared at Delilah. "Do you think we can't do it?"

"You were both injured. At the very least, get checked out by the medical staff before you go," she said, as if surfacing from the deep.

Why? Do they know the situation within my body any better than I do? Others had surpassed him in their fighting ability. They had surpassed him in their alchemy. He still held onto his ability in healing above all others.

Erik turned away so he didn't have to suppress his snarl. "Storbon, we'll head to the hospital now. Jen should be around. I'll tell Rugrat to meet us there."

The group reached an intersection in the hallways. Erik schooled his features and looked at Delilah, who fumbled with her hands, her lips moving, but she held back the words behind them.

"Thank you for your time, Council Leader. Rugrat and I will be ready to leave with the team in two days' time." Erik rose to attention and bowed his head quickly.

"Good luck."

Erik grunted and turned down the intersection, more out of determination to get away, his stomach churning from acid. *Dammit, why am I so damn angry all the time now?*

He rubbed his face.

"Prisoner in my own home," he mumbled. *I've fought across the world, trained to heal and kill. Now everyone's treating me like a damn child. This coddling is suffocating.*

He rubbed his arm, absently trying to release the tension as he activated his sound transmission device.

Rugrat yelled as his conjured mana spear shot through the air. Lee Perrin dodged the attack as chains rattled out of the ground like a dropped anchor. When the dust had settled in the First Realm, Lee was one of the first people to arrive. He was interested in Alva and owed a debt to Erik and Rugrat. He saw Alva as a place to put down roots and share his knowledge, and had taken a post in Kanesh academy as a lecturer and combat trainer.

Lee jumped and walked across the sky toward Rugrat. He injected power into the thin bamboo fan in his hand, a flash of power striking the chains as they broke into shadows.

Dozens of chains broke free of their spell circles upon the ground and in the sky.

Lee waved his fan and shot backward, then turned, his eyes closed as his fan snapped out, glowing as it diverted the chains and their spiked ends. His body flowed like water, as if he had anticipated everything that was to come and had happened.

Rugrat hissed. The dungeon core fragments were like glass, his mana system a chaotic mess, pulled in a dozen different directions. A few minutes of walking left Rugrat sitting for nearly ten times as long to regain his stamina. Rugrat panted, his hooded eyes focused on Perrin. *He's showing off now.*

A guttural roar tore from Rugrat's throat as he pushed past the pain. His body glowed, mana traced through his body, causing the fragments to twist and open his wounds. He coughed, spitting blood to the side as he reached out with his hands. Spell circles appeared by the dozen as chains formed of crystal mana flew free from their shackles.

"See if you can escape those!" Rugrat coughed again. His protection detail moved forward, but chains appeared behind him like deadly flowers, watching them.

Rugrat felt the mana resonating through his body, the agitation from the shards embedded into his body, causing waves of pain. His power was slipping away, his mind becoming foggy from the pain. The fragments altered his spells, turning them chaotic.

No, you don't!

He poured more power into his spells to maintain their form, his eyes following Lee's flickering figure as he continued to advance.

Rugrat's back was covered in sweat as he coughed again, his power starting to escape him.

"No!"

His power went wild and forming chains exploded before they were complete. The backlash from the spell hit Rugrat. He groaned and bent forward. The spells shattered in the training square as Lee landed feet-first on the ground. His eyebrows rose, his relaxed expression peeled away.

Rugrat wanted to reach out, grab even a shred of mana and attack Lee as he reached him.

"Are you okay? Let go of the spells." Lee pulled out a concoction. "I pushed you too hard."

Rugrat set his jaw, baring his teeth in a way that wasn't brought on by the pain. "Nothing to worry about!" Rugrat looked away and pulled out his own concoction as if he hadn't noticed Lee's.

He gulped it down, panting, taking three more swigs before he finished off the potion. He leaned into the chair, the torn muscle threading together and tightening around the blade-like shards within his body. He forced himself to sit up.

Lee seemed to recognize the light in his eyes, stored the potion, took out his own seat, and sat down. "You are still using your power over technique. Even if your attacks are ten times stronger, they will have the same effect if they miss the enemy."

Rugrat grunted. It wasn't anything new compared to his last lessons.

"You're too reliant on your eyes and physical senses. You don't use your domain nearly enough. I wonder if this is because you are used to fighting while seeing the enemy with your eyes."

Rugrat breathed in and released it the next second, studying the floor. "That might be the case. So, how do I learn to use my domain more?"

"Trial and error. By closing off your other senses, you might listen with your newfound ones."

Rugrat ground his teeth together. "And learn new spells at the same time?"

"I think you might have too many spells, actually. Instead of learning more, consider combining them. Consider the last spell you called on, the mana chains. Combine your control over mana and the chain spell structure; they are stronger than your elemental versions. Right now, mana is the easiest form of power for you to use other than Fire element spells. If you can develop your domain and your mana spells, the results might surprise you."

"What about my Exploding Shot and the other spells I use on my rounds? Are you saying I should forget them?"

"No, not at all. Just look at what you have now and develop them. Techniques are simply spells that have been adapted by the user. Like how a smith makes a weapon that fits perfectly to the user," Lee said.

Rugrat's sound transmission device went off.

"Rugrat, got us into the trip to the Eighth. They need us to do a *medical.*" *As if they don't already know everything that's wrong with us,* Rugrat added Erik's unsaid words. "Get to the hospital as soon as you can."

"All right, I'm on my way." Rugrat put the sound transmission device away and waved to George, who was lying nearby.

George moved up next to him.

"You're going to the Eighth Realm?" Lee stood.

"That's the plan," Rugrat said, grunting as he got to his feet, glaring at the Special Team who had moved to help him.

"The fighting isn't the important part of the trial. One can only pass into the Ninth Realm if they are able to answer the question of the Eighth."

Rugrat grunted as he put his leg over George's back, grimacing as he felt the shards shift under his skin.

"There is a reason that the trial between the Seventh and Ninth is called a Realm. It is because few can pass its trial. For those that can, it is only a matter of time until they step onto the highest stage of the Ten Realms."

"A single question stumps so many. What is it, a math question?" Rugrat grinned.

"If only it were that simple. It is a question that strikes at the core of every person in the Ten Realms. A question that is rarely asked but always thought." Lee grabbed his arm. "Do not follow the stream. Follow your own path. One's own will is the strongest force inside and outside of the Realms. Will shapes and changes us in a million ways, both seen and invisible."

Lee must have seen his fading interest; he tilted his head and waved his fan. "I wish you luck on your travels. Even if you do not make it through the trial, you will take a step upon a path that few have tread."

He turned and walked away as George rose to his full height.

Rugrat frowned as George turned and padded toward the exit. They left the training grounds attached to the academy, heading for the hospital. He chewed on Lee's words as the Special Team rode with him. The city had gone through a round of building and alterations. The dungeon headquarters had been rebuilt and upgraded. Buildings destroyed in the fighting were repaired, or new buildings had risen in their place. The glaring hole to the outer world now had a gate installed in its mouth.

A constant stream of people passed through into Alva or to King's Hill and the empire that stretched out across the Beast Mountain Range and beyond.

Ah, he's just trying to sound like some mystical master. Rugrat cleared his thoughts of Lee's words and increased his pace, catching the pained expressions as people bowed along their path, their tense smiles.

Rugrat nudged George to go faster until he jumped into the sky and unfurled his wings.

He slouched in his saddle, looking over Alva without seeing it. The city had expanded again. Using the cores from the corvettes and looting the United Sect Alliance member's dungeons, they'd gained quite a lot of resources. People poured in from across the realms to join the empire. Even with the strict requirements, there were thousands joining the empire every day. Instead of having trouble finding people to join, they had too many.

Rugrat weaved through the towers. It seemed that they always got bigger. He glanced over to the new dungeon core headquarters, a grand tower three times wider and stretching high into the sky. The largest building in Alva, the beating heart of it all.

He looked down as they descended, seeing Erik and his special team on the hospital landing pad. George barked and yipped.

"You want Miss Woo's dumplings? There was a time you were happy with just some jerky! Wah!" George banked suddenly. Rugrat snatched at the reins. "Miss Woo's dumplings! Got it. That won't be a problem." He could swear George smiled at his correctly serious tone.

They came down, George landing gently.

"How's it going?" he asked Erik, easing himself off George's back, feeling his mana going in the wrong directions as the shards of dungeon core shifted painfully.

"Been better. Feel like I'm two hundred with bone spurs," Erik growled, turning his head to hide his frustration and anger. "You?"

Rugrat panted from dismounting. "Like I should have done more cardio in my youth. I think I need a nap." He was only half joking. He didn't have the body cultivation like Erik. While he could cast spells without too many problems, he was constantly tired as his body went through a persistent, slow tempering.

Erik barked out a laugh, waiting for Rugrat to join him before leading the way into the hospital. They walked in silence. Well, grunting and panting, forcing the Special team members to slow to their pace.

"When do we leave?" Rugrat tried to hide his labored breathing.

"Heading up in two days. Just need to get past the tests." Erik grimaced.

They fell into silence, moving and not expending mana. Rugrat kept up with Erik without any problems.

The hospital, like the rest of the city, had expanded and changed. Erik knew the place like a second home.

Rugrat glanced at Erik's scarred hands.

"You still looking into that cultivation and level imbalance?" Rugrat asked.

"Yeah, still don't know why. I think it has something to do with the environments of the different realms." Some people who had undergone cultivating but hadn't leveled up much or just hadn't gone to the higher realms had hit roadblocks in their cultivation. "Looks like people don't just need to increase their level. They have to go to the higher realms. If they don't, it creates issues, small at first, but they increase. It seems that even one trip to a higher realm can set things right."

"Huh, weird," Rugrat said as they walked on silently with their protection.

They soon reached a medical bay. Most were empty, but this one had several people inside, including Melissa Bouchard, the leader of the mana-gathering cultivation research team. Jen, the leading Alvan healer and previous director of the healing house in Vermire, and Rex, once a leading beast Trainer but now taking the lead spot of the Body Cultivation Research team, were also inside.

Rugrat didn't miss how the room stilled as they walked in.

"Looks like everyone's here. Let's get this over with as soon as possible. Momma Rodriguez is expecting us for dinner." Erik smiled.

Rugrat felt the chill behind the smile. He and Erik would spend most of the night going over gear prep and getting ready for the coming operation.

"Of course, this should be over quickly," Jen said.

"So, how are they?" Delilah asked. To her right sat Commander Glosil of the Alvan Military, and on her left, Lieutenant Colonel Niemm, commander of the Special Teams.

Jen took in a deep breath through her nose and released it through her mouth. "Not good."

Melissa's and Rex's expressions seemed to agree.

"They're getting better. We've removed as many fragments as we're comfortable with. Their bodies are constantly healing, which makes them tired and *irritable* at times," Jen said.

"They were trained to be at the peak of performance at all times. Now they're wounded and they think everyone else is passing them by," Niemm said. "Right now, the mental part of their wounds isn't pretty."

"The fact remains that they *are* getting better, and their bodies are adapting to the wounds and fragments. Their cultivation is limited because of their bodies' constant healing. They require time really, but how much is unknown," Melissa said.

"All of you, and Old Hei, have done outstanding work to get them mobile and on the road to repair. I'm still worried that they'll push themselves too hard and it will negatively affect them, though." Delilah looked between Rex, Jen and Melissa.

"Their main problem is that their own power is weak. They have a greater connection to the dungeon core and can draw upon it, but the power burns through the fragments in their bodies." Melissa shook her head, letting out her breath between her teeth.

"As much as we can try to stop them, we can't." Niemm cleared his throat. "This is Erik and Rugrat we're talking about. They channeled two dungeon cores through their bodies in the same day. They saved Alva because they are block-headed stubborn bastards. You think we can stop them by saying no? Do you even think we should?"

Glosil snorted, the corners of his mouth lifting. "Just a question of when not how, Delilah."

Delilah twisted her mouth.

"From what Lee Perrin has told us, if they pass the Eighth Realm Trial, their bodies will go through a change that could well reverse the damage." Jen shrugged. "It's a long shot, granted, but how many times have they pulled off the impossible?"

"So what are we really talking about?"

"Who's going with them," Niemm said.

2
To the Eighth Realm

Erik and Rugrat walked into the armory. Master Smith Taran and Formation masters Qin and Julilah had several items laid out on the tables in the middle of the room.

"What do we got here?" Erik asked, eyeing the armor plates, formations, and weapons.

"New loadout for the Eighth Realm," Taran said.

Erik grinned. "Well, hell, some new toys are always welcome."

"We've got you the newest armor plates." Taran tapped the inserts. "Got one Commander Conqueror's armor formation socket. The rest should help out. Rugrat, we've got you loaded with formations that will stop the elements from entering your body. It'll cut you off from tempering, but shouldn't cause any more problems. Erik, we've got a mana-storing formation in the armor. Also, each is fitted with a dungeon core." Taran opened what looked like a back pouch. "Link to the dungeon cores and you can use them as you want. Fully charged. They have a Sky grade mana cornerstone worth of mana each."

"Sweet," Rugrat said, patting the carrier and plates.

"And for guns, well, Rugrat, you got most of the toys." Taran smiled and waved to a production model version of Rugrat's own 20mm rifle, the Beast and the mobile machine gun platform.

The Beast

Damage:
Unknown

Weight:
14. 57 kg

Charge:
9,568/10,000

Durability:
124/124

Innate Effect:
Increase durability by 24%

Socket One:
Empty

Socket Two:
Empty

Integrated Enchantment
Silence - Silence weapon and attack

Heat Exchange - Remove heat from area

Dissipate - Expel Fire element

Range: Long range

Requires: 20mm rounds

Requirements:
Agility 60

Strength 50

The MG4311

Damage:
Unknown

Weight:
4.45 kg

Charge:
10,000/10,000

Durability:
135/135

Innate Effect:
Decreased thermal gain by 27%

Socket One:

Ammunition storage
Socket Two:
Empty
Integrated Enchantment
Heat Exchange - Remove heat from area
Dissipate - Expel Fire element
Range: Long range
Requires: 7.62 round
Requirements:
Agility 75
Strength 45

"Some people nickname it the Hell Raiser. Otherwise, grab what you need from the armorers." Taran waved to the two people at the counters. "Also, with the Hell Raiser, you'll need to pop out the ammo clip and put it into a pouch or pocket because it's a storage device. You can also use standard magazines, but they won't last long."

They checked over the weapons, figuring out how to maintain them and get familiar with them. No one tried to help them; no one coddled them. They were just left to do the job and learn by doing. It was refreshing.

Morning sunlight was just starting to spread across Alva as Rugrat smacked the last pin into place on the Beast. He pulled back on the cocking handle, hearing the scrape of metal on metal. He tested the rifle on safe and on fire, hearing a click.

"Good to go?" Erik said, walking in with the smell of coffee. He put one cup down on the living room table.

"Yeah, ready to see what the Eighth Realm has for us." He smacked a magazine into the rifle, loading it and placing it on safe, and storing it. He picked up the coffee and sat back in his chair as Erik pulled on his body armor.

He let out a sigh, either from the caffeine sparking his soul into life or the relieving effects of the carrier taking the load from his body. Rugrat thought the latter.

He hooked his hand into the top of his carrier, taking in a satisfying mouthful of coffee.

Erik secured his vest, checking the various magazines and medical pouches before he sat down and drank his coffee. "This could be it. Could fix us in one shot."

"A whole realm dedicated to one question, though. Seems a little much." Rugrat placed his cup on the table.

"Must not be an easy question." Erik tapped his cup, looking from the floor to Rugrat.

"Lee said that it's some internal question, no multiple choice, and kept talking about our will." Rugrat chased the question with the last of the coffee.

He smelled the food before Momma walked in with chalupas, his stomach twisting more than could be blamed on the coffee.

"Come on, you two. Can't start the day on an empty stomach. Give some to the Special Teams too," she said, her eyes red-rimmed and angry.

Rugrat stood up, holding onto the tray. "I got those, Momma. Please sit down."

She opened her mouth and then closed it in a shaky smile and sat on the couch. Rugrat offered them to Erik; he took one with a tight smile.

"Thanks, Momma. These look great! I'm gonna save it for lunch. Too much coffee."

"Same for me." Rugrat smiled and stored it.

"Oh, okay." She played with the edge of her apron, smiling at them before her gaze fell to her hands.

I should've just eaten it. His appetite had fled, and he glanced at Erik, who had his head lowered as well.

A knock at the front door broke the tense silence.

Momma R glanced at the door like a startled cat, stilling as the fear spread across her features.

"We'll be back in no time, Momma." Rugrat stood.

She hugged him tightly.

When was she this small? Rugrat took care to not use too much strength as he hugged her back.

"Don't take any risks, you two. When you're back, we'll have all your favorites." She put on a weak smile that broke Rugrat's heart.

She patted his chest and turned to Erik, hugging him.

Rugrat took a step away, remembering the chalupas. He grabbed them and opened the door to see Special Team Four and Three waiting with a convoy of beasts and carriages. Major Gong Jin, leading Special Team Three, and Major Storbon stood with Egbert at the front door.

"You think you can make it any less obvious?" Rugrat growled and pushed the tray towards them.

Gong Jin winced and took it.

Rugrat whistled and George jumped off the house and flared to his full size.

Erik came out of the house as well, sharing a look with Rugrat as he pulled out a helmet and put it on.

Rugrat got on George's back. The armor made him feel just like someone from Earth again. No extra strength. He tried to ignore the lingering pain from the shards as it started to build with his movements.

Momma Rodrgieuz had followed Erik to the door and stood in the doorway watching them.

"We'll be back soon," Rugrat said.

"Thank you for the food, Momma Rodriguez," Gong Jin said.

She smiled as the two Special Teams and Egbert moved out with Erik and Rugrat toward the totem.

People glanced at them and muttered as they passed. Rugrat was thankful for his face-covering helmet, finding peace in it as they moved on.

"You know we can get to the totem perfectly fine by ourselves," Rugrat said to Egbert, who was floating beside him.

"I'm coming with you."

"You can do that?"

Egbert opened his robe and tapped the mana stone that had grown through his rune-carved bones and around his central dungeon core. "I'm self-contained. I link to the dungeon cores here, but I can go anywhere and cast spells for as long as I have mana."

"Huh, neat! Might have to learn your secrets later. Been thinking about getting a return on this meat sack." Rugrat patted his chest and chuckled.

Their procession made it to the totem, gathering around it. Storbon pressed his hand to the totem.

You have reached Level 70, meeting the requirements to ascend to the Eighth Realm.
Do you wish to ascend? *YES/NO*

If we pass this, then we can heal ourselves. We can go back to the way things were. Stop having people treat us like we're children and cart us around and dive into our business.

Rugrat hit the yes and light surrounded them all.

Invitations to the Violet Sky Realm

Milo Leblanc walked through the halls of the Leblanc estate. Family members, guards, and servants bowed to him as he passed.

Instead of guards, golems of worked metals, wearing armor stood outside his office. They opened the doors for him.

"I am not to be interrupted."

"Understood." They sounded like the metal they were made from, sealing the doors behind him.

Milo glanced around the room. The chairs faced one another near the fireplace and his desk sat further back, with large windows showing the dungeon outside. The estate lay underneath Purkesh and the Sha clan's territory. He looked out at the carved pillars of the other white-washed estates, the gardens that could be seen behind gates and hanging between the pillars creating a multi-tiered growing area. They were the source of the Sha wealth, as they produced alchemical ingredients and plants for others.

He pressed a formation inset to the wall. Shutters closed off the outside light and mana light shined down from the painted ceiling.

Milo moved to the side of the room and pressed a piece of molding. A section of the wall pushed backwards and to the side, revealing a small recess the size of a hand. He took out part of a formation and put it into the recess, shifting it around until it dropped into place then turned it until it clicked.

Faint light emanated from the cubby and formation lines traced through the tiles underground toward a formation behind the couch, facing the fireplace.

The formation filled with power and then dimmed. Milo waited, looking at the formation expectantly. *Where is he?*

He clasped his hands behind his back, looking at the door and around the room, then started pulling at his embroidered suit sleeves, smoothing out his buttons, feeling his growing paunch.

The formation flared with power. Milo held his hands to his side, standing straight as a man wearing a red shirt and black suit and leggings with fine golden weaving stood upon the formation, wearing matchlock pistols on his hips that were as elegant as they were deadly. He had a tanned complexion from working near forges most of his life. His brown hair showed streaks of white and grey, pulled back into a ponytail at the base of his skull with ribbon. His sharp green eyes took the room in, resting on Milo.

"Grandmaster Crox." Milo bowed.

"Milo, we have known one another since you were learning to walk. There is no need for you to call me grandmaster." Crox smiled, waving his hand and walking around to the couch.

"Can I get you something to drink?"

"Your news is all the sustenance I require." He indicated to a chair opposite.

Milo rushed to sit, licking his lips. "Through negotiations, we were able to sway the Marshal." Milo's mouth twisted into a snarl at the mere mention of his name. "We invited the leaders of his closest allied sects to the Violet Sky Realm." Milo took a seat in one of the high-backed chairs off to the side of the couch.

"Will they come?"

"He rarely allies himself with someone that is stronger than the clans. They are all small groups. For them, this will be a great opportunity. They will not turn it down."

"What of the Alvans?" Crox's voice deepened.

"They have a lot of power in the lower realms, but they have no place here. They need to prove their position, and this would allow them to do so."

Crox sucked in a breath as his eyes brightened. "If we can remove their leadership in the same act, we will gain a greater position in the gun market."

"Grandmaster will dominate the newly formed market without peer. Finally, your craft will be free of the Sha contracts, and you can gain the acclaim you deserve across the realms."

"The Marshal blindsided me as a child, as he did with you, telling me that I would be the greatest gun smith the Realms had ever seen. How can they see if I can only make weapons for the clan? No room for innovation. No way to express myself to others. Gunsmiths! Bah! We should be called slave forgers. Unable to do anything else." Crox waved his hand.

"Grandmaster Crox, you were the one that showed me the truth. You showed me who the Marshal really is. I looked at him as an uncle, but no more." It was the Marshal who had killed his father, using his death to destabilize Milo's family and take control over the clans. He had closed any routes to wrestle power from him, keeping it to himself. "He enslaves us and uses us for his own means. Now his tyranny will come to an end, and we will lead the Sha into a better future."

"It is as it was supposed to be. Your father should have been the next Marshal. I do not know what magic Edmond Dujardin used on your sister to twist her mind, but I am glad that you, at least, have seen the truth."

"I will be eternally grateful to Grandmaster Crox." Milo bowed in his chair.

"I saw your father as a brother. While I do not have children, you are the closest heir I have." Crox smiled.

Milo's eyes shook and he bowed even deeper. "I... I am lost for words, Grandmaster."

"Ah, come on. Let us not dwell on that. Once we have removed the Marshal, then we might finally set the clans to their correct purpose. What of Louis Gerrard? Has he joined the cause?"

"He has been approached, but he has not made it clear which way he will go." Milo pursed his lips. "With your skill in gunsmithing and the crafters you have on your side, my legitimacy, and the Velten's trade contacts, we need a strong Clan like the Gerrards to secure our position. We have done well in pulling fighting clans to our cause, but they are all insignificant compared to the Gerrard clan and it will make things easier in the Violet Sky Realm."

"With the three strongest clans, the crafters backing them, and our old allies cut off, the other clans will have one choice: to stay with us or be cast aside. We will be free of all the restrictions Dujardin placed upon us. Has there been any change with the Black Phoenix Clan?"

"No, just as we have been conserving our strength for the Violet Sky Realm, they have focused their people in defending what lands they have remaining, upgrading and arming their ships for the last three months. Their losses this time were impressive."

"All the greater reason to pull Gerrard to our side. His clan was able to lead our forces in a number of decisive victories. We cannot lose him."

"Do not worry. My wife is working to pull him to our side as we speak."

Captain Stassov, sub-commander Branko and several other Captains of the Black Phoenix Clan and their aides stood around a table. Upon it was a rough map, showing the Violet Sky Realm.

Commander Novak stood opposite the captains and circled an area on the map with his finger. "This area is supposed to have a high density of Ilisa Fruits, each of which can be turned into a pill to temper one's body with the Earth Element. They are rare in the Ten Realms and if possible, we could add them to our gardens to help future generations." He tapped his pointer on a structure sticking out of the forests.

"This is called the Treasure Hall by many, but it is a land of death. Hundreds of creatures not normally seen in the Ten Realms sleep around it. If someone uses mana, then they will wake up and attack without regard for their injuries. Each of them is as strong as someone that has tempered their body with the Metal element, and each of their spells causes elemental poisoning which will corrupt your body and make your mana run wild. Many have tried to enter this treasure hall but have failed."

"What about ship emissions?" one captain asked.

"They will sense them and attack. They do not possess flight or mana as far as we can tell. They are just beasts with corrupted elements, but they use them with ease and can twist the air to their will and enter warships. Do not pass within two kilometers of this location unless you want to lose your ship."

"Can we not draw them away?" another asked.

"Once they move a certain distance away from the treasure hall, they will turn back and return. Their numbers do not increase, but they grow stronger each year."

Where did such creatures come from? Stassov held her tongue. She had barely made it into this meeting, having brought the scourge of Alvans upon their heads.

Novak looked around. "We must destroy or severely weaken the Sha forces that go to the Violet Sky Realm. Our very position is at risk. We need a win. If we can weaken them and gain enough prizes, we can divert attention toward the Sha and make other clans and sects think twice about attacking us. If we do not, then we will appear weak and be open to attacks. In a week, the

Violet Sky Realm will open. Make sure your crews are ready."

He nodded and stepped away from the table. The captains all bowed as he left the room.

Stassov turned and left the lecture hall. Her guards, headed up by Ranko, fell in around her as she left.

Ranko was the only surviving sub-commander that she had gone to Vuzgal with. She had lost Bela in that cursed place, while Gregor, her strongest, had fallen in the heart of the newly formed Alvan Empire. Gregor's brother, Goran, had taken Bela's place while Natalya Novak, one of Commander Novak's nieces, had defeated all comers to gain the position of dungeon hunter aboard the *Eternus*. Stassov was wary that she was only one step below herself.

Why place her aboard my ship? Is she a spy for the commander, or there to take my position in a moment of chaos?

"Will *they* be there?" Ranko asked.

"We do not know if the Sha have invited them. We will see when everyone assembles at the transition point."

"If you just let me—"

"I have lost two sub-commanders to the Alvans. I do not need to lose a third from his idiotic actions," she hissed, turning her gaze on him as the weight of her domain smashed him to his knees. "Listen to me, Ranko. We are related by blood, so I have given you leeway and freedoms. We are fighting for the existence of our clan. If you cannot do as you are ordered, then I have no use for you, and you'd best return to the clan so I can find a subcommander who will help me defeat the Sha clans." Her guards had moved around them to create a screen from passersby.

"I was hasty in my words, Captain."

She increased the pressure before removing it. "Gather yourself. When we enter the Violet Sky Realm, we go to war with the Sha once again and the commander doesn't want the Marshal coming out alive."

She turned around and marched onward, seeing him quickly pick himself up and hurry after the group.

The Black Phoenix Clan was on the ropes.

They had taken people from the First Realm, turning them into power houses of the Sky Realms, Expert smiths and alchemists, artisans of cloth and food. Formation masters that created weapons powerful enough to destroy cities and barriers strong enough to rebuff her own Phoenix Breath Cannons.

Their military appeared and disappeared just as quickly, and in their path, they created sweeping changes.

4

Why?

The light of the totem disappeared. Erik scanned the ruins around him, pulling out his rifle as he jumped from his panther.

The hell? A formation underneath his feet faded away as if it didn't exist. The rest of the convoy had disappeared, leaving him in what looked like a ruined cathedral covered in moss and weathered by time.

Everything was clear for several hundred meters around the ruin before reaching fog that hid the surrounding area. He only knew he was outside because the sun had turned the fog pure white, as if formed from cotton.

The panther growled as the raised section of the ruin shook. Stone and dirt formed into a golem as tall as Erik.

Erik shot it, scattering stone across the ground.

"Come here." The panther obeyed and Erik put her away in his beast storage crate.

He couldn't feel the movement of mana anymore with his armor on, but he could feel the elements like a fresh breeze across his skin.

"Why do you fight, Erik West?" The voice seemed to come from the world around him. Curious, bland, and with a timeless quality to it.

"It's what I'm good at."

"You will only pass this trial if you are true to yourself. Why do you fight?"

A section of the cathedral near the open arches tore free with the sound of cracking stone. Erik fired, hitting the golem's head back into the wall it had just stepped out from, but it took another step forward as a sword of stone assembled in its hand.

A second and third shot hit the creature's chest, turning it into rubble.

Erik ran for the arch beyond the creature, escaping the ruin.

"Why do you fight, Erik?"

A golem hand reached out of the ground and hauled itself up. Another formed from one of the stone roofs ribs, dropping to the ground below.

"For duty."

Erik fired into the golem coming from the ground. Another tore out the side of the cathedral.

"Because it's what I was trained to do."

He fired, his shots becoming frantic, feeling a pit in his stomach grow.

"Why do you fight?"

They're getting stronger.

Erik drew on the power of the elements, crying out in pain as his skin cracked, showing the veins of magma beneath, a metal sheen spreading over his skin as his reactions sped up.

"I fight for others, to protect them."

"Do not lie to yourself."

"You fucking voice! Come and face me!"

There were a dozen golems tearing free of the church, moving towards him, creating weapons of stone, and clawing their way out of the ground, pulling up the dirt and grass with them.

Erik fired as he advanced, feeling the pressure as they closed in on him.

"I am the trial, nothing more. Why do you fight?"

"For Alva!" He dodged to the side and grasped a spear heading for him. Turning, he threw it back, smashing apart a golem in mutual destruction.

Erik pulled out his machine gun, firing from the hip. The stream of tracers cut down several golems as he paused to throw grenades.

"Why do you fight?"

"I'm a soldier, and a medic! I fight to save my patients. I fight for the United States. I fight for the people I want to defend."

The grenades went off in a spray of stone and dirt, clearing the last of the golems.

"Why do you fight?"

The remains of the golems flowed back together, the ruins coming apart as golems made of a darker stone and metallic flecks appeared; two, then four, then eight.

Erik had given the damn voice his answer, as corny as it was. He'd gone to the depths!

"Truths and lies. Your damn question is rigged. I gave you your answer!"

"Search deeper. Why do you fight?"

"To kill annoying pricks like you!" The world was drowned out in a stream of tracers as it ate through the stone golems, tearing up the ground to reveal the stone square underneath.

Even as he cut them in half, the golems reformed, and more were coming.

Erik threw out grenades, buying time.

"I fight for those who stand on either side of me!"

The golems paused for a half-second.

"Close, but there is more. Why do you fight?"

Erik yelled, firing on the enemy.

The golems swarmed, closing in on him. He stored his machine gun and reached toward a golem, tearing hammers from it.

He swung the hammers, smashing arms out of the way in a stream of shards. He knocked a golem's head clean off as he jumped, calling on his dungeon core. A burst of air threw him across the ground. He hit the stone, rolling.

He came up to his feet as golems charged him. The pain and adrenaline warred with one another as the shrapnel shifted.

He gritted his teeth, welcoming the pain as he ran, calling the elements into his hammers before he hurled them.

"I fight because it's what I do! I fight to protect others! Fighting is my profession."

The hammers smashed into the first golem, taking it and three others out. His second followed afterwards as he formed and caught two more, crashing into a golem. He tried to dodge, but his reactions were too slow.

He transformed his left hammer, turning it into a shield to deflect a sword aimed at his head as he used his hammer to hit the golem in the stomach, lifting it off its feet. A sharp pain tore through his back.

Erik kicked the golem away with a shout. "I was born to fight! I fight against the Ten Realms and others who would harm my people and those I care for!"

He smashed arms apart, kicking and punching, launching his hammers as more golems piled in. Still, he heard that same voice, sounding tired and saddened.

"Why do you fight, Erik West?"

Erik was hit in the back, clubbed with the flat edge of a sword.

Is this it?

The pain from the beating was bad enough, but that question hung above him, tearing his heart through his stomach.

Light wrapped around him, and he found himself back in the cathedral. The ruins were once again whole, the grass flat over the hidden stone.

He dropped into a fighting stance, looking around and touching himself. He could no longer use Medical Scan on himself without control over mana. There were no broken bones or cuts.

"The golems are your doubts, your lies, the ones you tell yourself. More insidious than any lie another can tell you. As you propagate lies born of fears, truths, and others' goals, you become buried in them. They will multiply, creating layers of other ideas and truths. Once you know why you fight, you can change how you fight, and only then can you examine who you want to become. Truth of self. What do you fear that you fight so hard? Go back to why you started fighting."

Golden light surrounded Erik. As he glanced down, he swore he saw a complicated magical circle. It looked familiar as it passed over him and then he found himself back at a totem in the Seventh Realm, on his panther as if the Trial had never happened.

Quest: Why do you fight?
You have started the Eighth Realm Trial. Be true to yourself. Answer the question aloud. To gain control over yourself is to gain power over the Realms.
Rewards:
Reformation of Will
Entrance to the Ninth Realm once you reach level 80

Erik had shed his armor and sat in a bar. The only benefit to his injuries was they brought his body's tolerances down, meaning alcohol actually affected him again.

He rested his elbows on the table, looking around the bar. There were quite a few people around, even though it had barely passed midday. People traveling the realms came from all kinds of places and time zones.

He took another drink from his beer, examining the woodgrain in the table. *Said I wasn't a soldier, or a medic.* The fight had fled, leaving him tired.

"You want another?"

Erik tried to hide being startled.

The barman raised an eyebrow. "Maybe you want some food instead?"

"Nah, just tired. Uhh, yeah, I'll take another." Erik cleared his throat and finished off the remains of his beer.

The barman narrowed his eyes and shrugged, taking the old beer mug, rinsing it, and filling it from a keg.

"Much been going on around these parts?" Erik asked.

"Nah, some of the smaller groups are making moves against one another, but the ones who have their Violet Sky Realm Tokens have been quiet. Saving their strength, I expect. Heard that there are some schools having tournaments for students wanting to join the expedition. Rich people, huh? Got all the best cultivation resources." He snorted and cut the foam off the top of the beer and walked over, putting the glass on Erik's table.

"Thanks."

"No problem. Let me know if you need any food with that."

"Will do." Erik raised the tankard as the barman headed to the next table.

Erik held his drink up. *Trial said that I didn't fight for those beside me, didn't fight for those on either side.* He tapped the beer against the table and drank deep, trying to not curl his lip. He was prolonging the inevitable by not going back to Alva right away. He had stayed around the Totem for a while, but none of the other party members had shown up, so he had come to this bar to think upon what had happened.

"Why do you fight?" Erik's words contained heat, thinking about the voice talking down his reasons; each burnt into his soul.

When was it ever just a question? There had to be something he was missing. He had to defeat the golems. Perhaps if he learned some more fighting techniques, he could win against them. He remembered how they formed up out of the ground in a surge towards him.

He took out his stat sheet.

Name: Erik West	
Level: 85	
Race: Human-?	
Titles:	
From the Grave III	
Blessed By Mana	
Dungeon Master IV	
Reverse Alchemist	

Poison Body
Fire Body
Earth Soul
Mana Reborn III
Wandering Hero
Metal Mind, Metal Body
Earth Grade Bloodline

Strength: (Base 90) +58 (-89)	1554
Agility: (Base 83) +110 (-101)	1109
Stamina: (Base 93) +35 (-112)	2016
Mana: (Base 157) +134 (-239)	2978
Mana Regeneration (Base 180) +71 (-201)	156.62
Stamina Regeneration: (Base 162) +99 (-237)	56.86

"What a mess."

He dismissed the screen, drinking from his beer.

He sighed, peering into his glass.

"If I go back there..." *I'll fade into the woodwork, getting praise from everyone and being treated like some damn hero. I was just doing my job.*

He was scared to face them, to tell them he had failed the trial. If he told them that he wasn't strong enough, they'd insist on protecting him even more until he could no longer leave Alva to do anything.

"Haven't been a soldier in a long time I guess." He kept sitting there, drinking, trying to numb his thoughts and the pain.

With a grunt he stood up, paying out his tab with some mana stones and headed outside.

The smell of wet mud, wood homes, and sounds of carts and carriages passed through the streets with the same hubbub of the city's people going about their business.

Erik moved with them, heading in the direction of the Totem, enjoying the anonymity of being someone in a crowd, lost among it all. He gazed at the rising towers that rose to meet the city hanging from the dungeon ceiling.

The crowds thickened as he reached the totem; traders, fighters, disciples and masters on foot, mounted in carriages or riding carts. Erik moved along with the line. Reaching the totem all too soon, he entered his destination. The city disappeared, and the buildings above him were replaced with formation lines carved into Alva's ceiling.

Erik moved with the press of people from the totem to the custom's gates. *Looks like the southern totem.*

Another Totem had been built in King's Hill and transported to Alva, building a second for themselves. It linked them to the outer cities of the Empire, which each boasted one of their own.

Erik took out his identification medallion. *I should get a chain for these things. Starting to forget which ones are which.*

He pressed it to the formation reader.

The guard read the information, his eyes widening.

Erik pressed a finger to his lips and winked at the guard, walking past.

"N-next!" The guard tried to get his voice under control as Erik looked at Alva. He smiled at it all, moving, living.

"Excuse me, where is the teleportation pad?" Erik asked a passerby.

"Down there three blocks, take a left, then three more."

"Thanks." Erik walked in the direction the lady had indicated. He passed through the security around the pad and activated the formation, scrolling through the options that would take him across the Empire. Egbert and the Formation department had created them to connect every city, town, and village. Even when under attack, Alvans could move about freely. Erik activated it and appeared on another pad.

He tossed a mana stone into a collector, and it spit out smaller mana stones on the other side. Erik stuffed them into his storage ring. *Nice tidy money maker.*

He walked through the streets toward home, eager to put Momma Rodriguez's worries to rest.

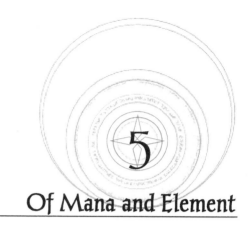

5

Of Mana and Element

The crafting stadiums, when not being used for testing or tournaments, were the site of various classes from the Academy and the Alvan military.

Erik sat in the stadium seating. The Special team fanned out through the area, watching the mages as they sparred. Lee walked among them, offering advice to the advanced members. Most Alvan military members wished to advance and hone their skills or prepare for the combat mage course.

There was sparring going on at one side, while others were focusing on set training, divided up throughout the remaining area.

"Form up!" a sergeant major hollered.

The fighting and training stopped as everyone gathered into rows in front of the sergeant major.

"Take a seat or organize yourselves how you want." Lee waved a hand. They spread out, some taking out chairs, all of them taking out notebooks as Lee Perrin moved to where the sergeant major had stood.

"What are elements?" he asked, holding his hands behind his back as he walked. He nodded to someone that raised their hand.

"They are impurities found in mana types."

"That is something they do, but what *are* they?" He pointed to another.

"They are the properties of spells."

"A type of energy like mana?"

"They are the building blocks of the realms?"

"Elements are a transforming thing?" People laughed at this answer as the man shrugged, lowering his head.

"There are no wrong answers and that is the closest anyone has come to it. See, elements are seen as things all around us. An abundant, frivolous, and mostly annoying *thing* that gets into our mana, makes it all messy and can screw up or enhance our spells. Like, who doesn't want a fire when you're on top of a mountain, but then it's ten times harder to cast a fire spell!" Lee smiled. "Elements are an ever-changing form."

Erik's brows pinched together, as did about every other person hearing the lecture.

Lee simply grinned at their expression.

"Fire, Earth, Metal, Water and Wood. All elements, all different sides of the same coin. Take a piece of wood. If you burn it, it will become fire, which becomes ash, which is Earth. If you leave Earth long enough, then it will layer up, compressing itself to such a point that it becomes Metal. Water is pushed out of the Metal, which then grows into a tree, or the Wood element.

"These elements create one another, and they also restrict one another. Wood breaks up the Earth and drains it of nutrients, commanding the power that was once its own. Water extinguishes fire while fire bends Metal to its will. Metal creates lightning that destroys forests. Each controls another, and is controlled by yet another in turn."

A soldier raised her hand.

Lee turned his head to her, pausing his pacing.

"So, are all the elements the same thing?"

Lee snapped his fingers and pointed at her.

"Bingo, like how water can be steam and ice, the elements are essentially the same thing, an ever-changing form." He pointed at someone else raising their hand.

"If that's the case, then why do we need to temper our bodies in all the elements?"

"*Great* question! While our bodies are made up of all the elements, tempering makes sure that we can *control* them. Otherwise, we would be burned by the Fire element, electrocuted when calling upon lightning, cause our bodies to break down under the effects of Earth, or drown ourselves and burst our cells with Water. Not pleasant! So, while these are different forms that can change into one another, our bodies must adapt to them. There are four stages to work with when talking about the elements. Assimilation, Integration, Manifestation and Projection. Can anyone guess what I mean by that?"

He pointed to a new hand.

"Assimilation is Tempering?"

"Yes, we must assimilate the element into our body. All of you have tempered your bodies with at least one element. Fire. Most people in the Ten Realms take months or years to draw in the Fire element to reach Body like Iron. This is why many of them do not temper their bodies to the Integration phase, where your body has been tempered to such a degree with the elements that you resonate with those around you. Now!" He stopped walking and looked at them. "Who is stronger, an Alvan that has assimilated with the Fire element or someone else from the Realms?"

The derisive chuckles and shifting feet told of their opinion.

"The person from the Realms." Their chuckles stilled as Erik shifted in his seat. Half-bored with the lecture. *I wonder what's for lunch.*

"See, in Alva you will only need a few hours, maybe a week, to temper your body with the Fire element. But how much have you *learned* about the element? Body cultivators that temper their bodies over years, even if they are only passively studying the Fire element, will have much more insight into the Fire element than someone who did it in an afternoon." He resumed his pacing.

"While Alvan tempering reaches the Integration phase, gaining a title and increasing the resonance you have with the elements, actually incorporating it into your body, you have less opportunity to grow your knowledge with your element. This is why you should take time to study and learn the abilities of the elements under your control.

"All of you, because you have achieved complete integration, can use Manifestation." Lee held out his arm. Magma veins ran down his arm, heat shimmering around it.

"Then there is Projection." Flames appeared around his hand, turning from deep red to blue then white, after which they faded away.

"Two things: manifestation is controlled by the strength of your elemental core—your bloodline, and the greater your control, the more lethal you will be."

Erik leaned forward, resting his chin on his hand.

Lee fired out some normal punches, letting out blasts of air. Magma threaded through his body, from his foot, through his legs, up his hip and through his stomach, chest, shoulder, upper arm, lower arm, and hand.

Erik was barely able to keep up with the tracing of lights as Lee's punches *cracked* in the air.

He slowed down, showing the elements coursing through his body.

"Now, this takes more control than just manifesting the element throughout my body, but I can use it for longer than someone using manifestation on their entire body." Lee began walking again. "Sergeant Major, when you are in a battle, what would be best?"

"A partial manifestation. It allows us to fight for longer and still be effective. Once you drain your elemental core's power, you'll be hit with a wave of fatigue, like when you use up all of your mana."

Lee manifested the Fire element through his body and fired out punches, with lighter cracks than before.

"It takes me nearly three times as long to call up full body manifestation. The stronger your elemental core is, the less time it will take for you to call up the elements that have reached a higher grade." He fired off a punch with fire igniting through his muscles.

"When you use your muscles, they create heat. Not much, but it is a natural occurrence of the Fire element. Using that heat in combination with the Fire element means that I can manifest it faster. You." Lee pointed at a raised hand.

"Won't it take longer though? You have to figure out the muscles that are moving, then target them with manifestation, and then through your body and up through your hand. Wouldn't that make it easier for someone to read your attack?"

Lee punched again and Erik could only see the magma veins on his hand.

"Did you read it?" Lee grinned and tucked his hand in his sleeves, continuing his pacing. "Clothes are pretty useful in hiding what you're doing with your elements." He smiled at the grins and snorts. people shifting around.

"Someone that has enough knowledge of elements will be able to see through your attacks. The less of an element you use, affecting *just* what you want enhanced, will decrease your elemental spend and increase your fighting ability. Though it will take you longer to master this, think about how you trained with your rifles. It took time, and now you could take them apart in your sleep. Training. Takes. Time."

Lee Perrin looked at them all. They seemed eager to try out what they had learned.

"All right, one last thing and you can get to working on your manifestation. This has to do with your spells." Lee turned to the side and raised his hand.

A small lightning bolt as big as a pencil shot out some ten meters and left a burn mark on the ground.

"Lightning Blast." The chanted spell sucked in the surrounding mana as it went fifteen meters and then hit the ground, making a larger burn mark.

His hand turned silver, and lightning played around it, shooting out a paltry spark. "Body like Diamond manifestation and Metal element projection." His hand returned to normal.

"What if I was to use my domain?" A larger lightning bolt shot out of his hand, landing thirty meters away. "I'm still using the same amount of mana in the spell, but the spell's enhancement by the elements and mana in the area can have a great effect."

Lightning shot out of his hand without warning, turning into a stream nearly fifty meters long. "Same elemental projection as before, but I linked it to the Metal and Water elements in the air, strengthening it and giving it greater reach. Now if I were to do that and add in mana, turning it into a spell, I could do this."

The lightning shot out nearly seventy meters and he shook his hand, using it like a whip for several seconds before it went out.

"Or this."

He punched forward and a compressed spear of lightning shot out of his fist and hit a target nearly a hundred meters away, destroying it in a blast of light.

The target's remains scattered and dropped to the ground.

"Learn your elements. In each form, what do they do? Play with them, test them, and get to know them as if they were another limb. I used the same amount of mana in each spell, and the same amount of Metal element." Lee drew himself up, holding his hands behind his back as he faced his silent class.

"Two major things: elemental spells require a base to work from. Yourself—or something within your elemental domain—to create a tether from where they're held to where they're going. So that whip of lightning? If someone were to blast through the middle of that spell, then the other end would fail. Spells, however, can work anywhere in your spell domain. Once cast, they can be broken, but they have little in the way of a tether. Most pillar spells are just the spell being cast continuously. The more you know about your elements, the stronger your spells will be."

"Any other questions?"

"Why is air not an element?"

"Good question. Air is a medium between the elements instead of an element itself. It carries them all, and it is made from many of them. Lightning will displace it. Wood will consume it and create it. Earth will do the same. Fire will burn brighter with it, or less without, while it will be heated in the process. It is formed easily by using heat, or one can use water."

Erik rose and left the stadium with his Special Team wearing thoughtful expressions.

Erik manifested surges of the Earth element; the shrapnel in his body shifted in the direction of the element, causing him to wince. His elemental capacity was pitiful in comparison to his previous level. The dungeon core shards consumed the elements coming into his body, taking even longer for him to recover once he had elementally fatigued himself.

They reached a carriage and Erik got inside. He held out his fingers and created a small flame on his forefinger. *I wonder?*

He rubbed his fingers together, feeling them warm, and called the Fire element to his finger. It appeared quicker and was about a half centimeter taller.

"An interesting trick." Erik muttered as he felt his elemental fatigue catching up. Maybe if his body weren't so broken, he would have been able to do more than conjure up a spark. As the carriage rode on, Erik's finger turned to stone, a small pillar poking from it.

Erik stared at the small bit of stone. He waved his hand, and it collapsed before his finger turned metallic and a smaller pillar of metal appeared on his finger.

He dismissed it, panting, and wiping away the sweat on his brow.

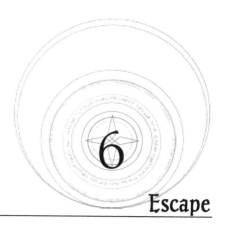

Escape

"Move out of the way!" a voice called out.

Erik turned to see a group of riders racing through the streets toward downtown.

Sha?

They wore fine red and blue cloaks with a golden weave, their armor as ornamental as it was functional, muskets in musket bags on their mounts or slung on their backs.

"Move, damn you!" one yelled at a trading cart that was trundling along. They used some spell of light and noise that went off next to the beast, startling it. The horse whinnied and ran toward the pavement as the driver blinked to try to clear his eyes.

The Sha riders laughed at their game as they continued.

Erik reached into the heart of the dungeon, drawing the power from the dungeon core. His power flooded back to him as his inhibitions washed away with the mana burning through his muscles. He threw out a calming powder, a wind spell pushing it into the beast's face and picking up the cart so it flew over the people on the sidewalk, clipping a building with its momentum.

His domain stretched out as he reached with the Earth element. Three hands extended from the ground, grabbing the running beasts from the ground, jolting the Sha riders as they shot backwards.

Trying to be low key.

Erik took off his hat as he settled the runaway cart down.

He glanced at a stunned girl nearby. "Get a police officer, please."

She looked at him with round eyes. He gave her a smile, making her blush as she hurriedly pulled out a sound transmission device.

The trio had come to a halt, the stone hands holding their mounts above the ground still.

"W-what!?"

"Are you okay?" He asked the cart driver, who was shakily getting down from his cart.

"M-my Lord!" He realized who was speaking to him and dropped to his knees.

"Woah." Erik held the older man's arm, wincing as he pulled him up.

"My Lord?" The man said, wanting to drop to his knees again, but Erik held him up, fighting the urge to punch the man for the pain running through his body. It was bad enough supporting the spells that burned through him.

Erik used the Medical Scan spell on the man. *High heart rate, but all okay.*

He turned to look at the trio held aloft. "And what brings three of the Sha Clan members into my city, creating havoc upon my roads?" Erik asked, drawing stone from the road to create steps that met his feet as he got close to them. Each creation felt like it was tearing a strip from his insides.

"L-lord West?" one of the men said. The other two's eyes widened, and their faces paled.

"We... carry an invitation for you," another said, more blue clothing than the others, pulling out a letter.

Erik hid his clenched teeth. Flames turned into a tiger the size of a mouse next to the man, grabbing the letter and returning to Erik's hand, disappearing in embers as Erik opened the letter.

He read it all, releasing his hold over the surrounding mana, allowing his body to rest and heal the damage he had incurred.

Police officers rounded the corner and came to a slow stop to talk with the girl that had called them.

An invitation to the Violet Sky Realm. Erik's excitement lifted. At the same time, he feared how long he could keep this charade up, and thought of the places nearby he could hide. He was quickly reaching his limits.

"I have received your invitation. There are rules in Alva. Officers." Erik nodded to the police officers and stepped into the sky on hardened mana, the density enough to put the lower Earth realms to shame, as he walked off into the distance.

Out of sight, he coughed and pulled out his sound transmission device, his hand shaking as he took out a revival needle and stabbed it into his leg.

"Matt, I need your help."

"Momma, Erik?" Rugrat yelled into the house as he opened the front door.

"In the living room," Matt said.

Rugrat frowned, closing the door, and walking in to find Erik laid up on a couch as Matt pulled an IV stand back out that he'd hurriedly hidden in his storage ring. Egbert sat in a corner reading a book, casting healing magic on Erik.

Rugrat looked in the hallway and closed the door to the room. "You okay?"

"Yeah, just had three Sha riders running through the city. Nearly drove a cart into the sidewalk." Erik let out a wet cough and pulled out a letter.

Rugrat took it and read it as Erik sighed, pulling out another potion and drinking it.

"Found him 'round the back of a bar. Burned himself out," Matt said.

"Did you--?" Rugrat glanced up from the letter, trailing off.

"Pass the trial?" Erik finished. "No." A shadow passed over his face. "You?"

"No," Rugrat said. "Just kept asking me why I fight. Thing is broken. Just beat on me with golems. Then I showed up in the Seventh Realm. No sign of George, you seen him?"

"Nope."

Rugrat glanced at Egbert.

"I entered the trial but appeared in the Ninth Realm. I took a look around and returned here." Egbert shrugged.

Rugrat was of half a mind to ask him about it. A stronger part wanted to *see* the ninth realm with his own eyes, not hear about it through someone else.

He lowered his eyes to the letter. "So, the Sha are inviting us to the Violet Sky Realm. What's the catch?"

"I dunno, want to show off or something?"

"Could be. Does Delilah know?"

"Nah, had some *problems.*" Erik waved his hand.

"I'll take it to her, see what she says."

"Get us on it. Delilah can't go up there. She doesn't have the fighting experience, but we do, and we have to send someone. If not Delilah, then Chonglu or Glosil, who are needed down here. Should be a cakewalk. We go do ambassador things, show we care about the Sha. Everyone that has jobs can focus on them."

"And staying cooped up here would suck."

"Bingo." Erik pointed at Rugrat.

"And keep your *problems* on the down low?"

"Just make them worry and they'll stick me in a healing tank when I can do just the same thing with my concoctions." Erik shrugged.

Rugrat looked at him, weighing his words.

"I'll be fine." Erik held his gaze.

"All right. Nice save, Matt." Rugrat patted him on the shoulder.

"Glad to be of help."

Rugrat pulled on a jacket. "Well, I'd best get to convincing. Egbert, you coming?"

"I'm already attending the meeting through the dungeon core, but it is nice to attend in person every so often."

They left the house. Rugrat could practically hear the questions in Egbert's head. "Out with it."

"Why do you really want to go?"

"Maybe the Violet Sky Realm can help. *Why do I fight?* What dumbass kind of question is that? *I* know the answer even if the damn test doesn't. Like it knows the answer better than I do." He hunched his shoulders as he walked. "I'm going to show the Eighth Realm its test is wrong."

Delilah sat at the head of the council table in the dungeon headquarters.

"Members of the alliance are still pushing for us to take aggressive action in the Fourth Realm and support their attacks. Lead a campaign to change the balance of power." Glosil sighed.

"Fighting has been ongoing around Vuzgal. The cities that supported the United Sects have either fallen or are under siege," Elan said. "No one has laid claim to Vuzgal. They are leaving it for us to take back."

"I think it would be best to go with the suggestion from the Associations here," Elise said. "If we push too much into the Fourth Realm, it will create greater friction, and we could face another war soon. If we wait, over time, the fighting could come to a halt on its own. Some are allies, some were our enemies, and most have nothing to do with either side. The Fourth realm is the battlefield realm. We could easily get trapped in a cycle of fighting. Easier to stop what we don't start. We need to rebuild. For that we need trade. We need builders. We need money. War is an expensive undertaking."

Delilah didn't like it. She wanted to bring an end to the fighting. But she knew that they were not Alvans and people could always go to a lower realm and find a happy existence.

"I agree. Let's table the discussion for the next three years. Make it clear to the forces in the Fourth Realm and our allies."

"In four years, it's possible that our allies will clear the realm by themselves," Glosil said.

"They are free to do as they want in that regard. It will bring stability in the long term. We must focus on fusing our efforts and combining our nations so the alliance is bound so tightly together it will be near impossible for it to unravel," Delilah said. "Too much expansion and they'll start to worry about the forces in the higher realms. We don't need to deal with a Seventh Realm family coming down on our heads."

Glosil nodded.

"What is our military situation otherwise?"

"We have five thousand in training. New limits have been placed upon entry. Reserves have a nearly constant turnover, so everything is fine there. The overall individual power of the soldiers has increased. I have a proposal to increase the minimum cultivation and level strength required of each soldier." Glosil took out a binder and passed it to an aide, who handed it to Delilah. "I talked to the researchers and with the dungeon managers and checked the cost of increasing their cultivation."

"Thank you. I'll take a look at it after our meeting. Anything else in regard to our alliances?"

Jia Feng raised her hand.

"Head mistress?"

"Of the six academies built, the consortium has finished its alterations and expanded into the First Realm. The academies in the Second and Third Realms are still under construction, but the main campuses have been completed. The academy in the Fifth Realm has been established as well. Each academy is in remote locations. We have hired and trained teachers as fast as possible, but have not yet met up with demand. We are hiring externally and adding them to our training rotations as well. Hopefully, in two months we will have all the teachers required to meet the academy's needs."

"That is great news, and I agree with your priorities. I know the students will be ecstatic. I hear that we are nearly full for this year's round of students?"

"Yes, even with the new testing, there are a great number of people wishing to join the academies as they want to join the Empire." Jia smiled at Lords Chonglu and Aditya. They looked well worn and tested, new lines added to their features.

"Well, as we are talking about the empire..." Delilah smiled at Aditya, who nodded.

"King's Hill has developed rapidly. We planned the next one hundred years of development in rough strokes, we hope. The city is swarming with people. The beast problems have greatly decreased. But with the increase in dungeons the various fighting guilds have remained. Trade is strong within the Empire. As we meet the demand internally, the external demand is only increasing." Aditya looked to his counterpart, Chonglu.

"Alva has grown rapidly. Each of the floors is populated. The living floor is bigger than ever. With the destruction of the dungeon core, we had to consume dungeon cores in remote locations and weaken the cores on the lower floors to make up the difference. The influx of citizens and people within the Empire has meant increasing the amount of mana we draw in, and the dungeon cores are rapidly expanding. Only Alvan Empire citizens are allowed within the city. Still, we have people trying to enter the city illegally. The number of non-Alvan citizens within the Empire has increased."

Egbert cleared his throat to speak.

Delilah indicated for him to continue.

"The changes don't stop there. The mana drill was like stabbing a needle into a dam. While it released a surge of elementally *dense* mana in the direction of the well we created, it shifted the plates around the world. Volcanoes became active once again, dungeon cores, mana stones that were buried deep beneath the planet's crust shifted and rose to the surface. Dungeons have appeared across the first realm, and the mana density increased. Mana stones are being actively mined now. Fragments of dungeon cores have come with the mana, joining with our own dungeon cores to speed up their rate of improvement."

Delilah nodded. "I should add that all the nations within the First Realm have made it clear they don't want to be on our bad side and have joined the alliance by whatever means possible. It may be because there are riches to be found in the First Realm and they want a strong partner to rely on if people from the higher realms try to apply pressure. Aditya, and then Chonglu, how is the clean up going?"

"The prisoner force is working on the southern fields and will be moving through the Empire on different projects. I have the city's leaders putting forward suggestions for updates. Looking at the numbers while we have gone through a lot of growth recently, things seem to be stabilizing. Everyone has done a great job."

Aditya sat back and turned to Chonglu.

"Repairs have been much quicker for us with the dungeon cores, and we have been assisting the rest of the Empire as we can, working together. There is a plan in place to increase the traffic between Alva Dungeon and the rest of the Empire to make sure that everyone feels connected."

"Thank you both." Delilah checked her notes. "Blaze, how are things with the Adventurer's Guild?"

"Council leader," he said, checking his papers, "the Guild has grown, even with losing a large number of members to the reserves or joining the Empire. We have re-established our guild halls across the higher realms alongside the Trader's Guild. Other guilds were hesitant to compete with us to start with, but now things are heating up in a good way. Trade routes are more secure than ever and most of my adventurers are searching for dungeons for the Special Teams to clear and control."

A knock came from the council chamber's door.

Delilah frowned, checking a seeing spell before she pressed a formation that unlocked the door.

Rugrat stood there. "Hey, everyone." He walked inside.

"I thought you were off to the Eighth Realm?" Blaze asked.

"It's as Lee said. That place is just a trial. Here." Rugrat handed Delilah a letter. "Message from the Sha. They're inviting us to go to the Violet Sky Realm. Asking for representatives of Alva to grace them with their presence. Erik and I know you're busy, so we'll go in your stead. No knowing what is in a realm like that."

"But Rugrat, are you—" *healed?* Delilah bit off the word. "Sure about this?"

"Well, you can't go. The council all has things to do. Erik and I can grow our asses or get out there, fly the flag, and all that. We'll be right beside the Marshal in the middle of his fleet. Give us a Special Team to come along for the ride. We'll be in and out in no time. The realm is only open for three months. Be good to get out and see the world a bit."

Delilah looked at Glosil, who shrugged.

"I'll have to read this and check it out."

"Okay, sounds good. Nice seeing you all." Rugrat turned and left the room, closing the door behind him.

"You think that he...?" Blaze asked.

"No, if they had made it through the trial, you think he'd be so down?" Glosil sighed and rubbed his face.

"They're hurting, understandably. Their cultivation has been crippled and they're sitting at the highest seat with nothing to do," Aditya said, rubbing his leg unconsciously.

"You ever think they were two people to sit back on their asses and watch other people get shit done?" Chonglu said.

"I wish there was more we could do for them." Jia Feng held her hands, her eyebrows pinching together.

"We can only help people who want help. They're stubborn mules and what we've tried hasn't worked. We can try to stop them from going on this trip. But like with the Eighth Realm, either we let them go with our blessing, or they'll do it themselves." Glosil shrugged.

I wish they would just get better. Delilah's hand tightened on the letter as guilt flooded her thoughts.

"Yeah," she exhaled. "Glosil, make the preparations. I hope it helps them." If only she could make a pill that was able to reverse the damage, to heal them. She knew that across Alva, alchemists and healers were working on similar concoctions, therapies, and treatments. She was also aware that Erik and Rugrat saw it as a burden instead of a help. Nothing she had said or done had changed their minds. *You can only help those who want to be helped.*

"Our ships are ready for the Violet Sky Realm. Our people have been confirmed and our supplies are loaded," Markus said.

Markus was from the Kalari Clan, a farming clan. He had worked with the Gerrard Clan as a fighter, becoming Louis' right-hand man. His tanned skin came from long hours spent working in the sun before he got the courage to join the fighters' ranks. The scars on his features, including the one that ran through his short grey and white hair, marked his time with the Gerrard Clan fighting under the Marshal for the Sha Clans.

Louis wasn't looking at him or the reports on his desk. Instead, he stared out the window to his left, just low enough for him to see Selma working on his uniform, repairing a small tear while his two daughters harassed his youngest son.

He let out a heavy sigh. His decisions wouldn't just change his future. They would affect the Sha and the clans under the Marshal's banner. "I heard that Marshal made a last-minute change?"

"Yes, he's invited his closest allies to join the force heading to the Violet Sky Realm."

"What is he thinking? We bled for every slot and he's giving it away to bottom feeders?" Louis snapped, glaring at Markus.

Markus opened his hands and shrugged.

"For too long, division and isolation have hurt our clans. We are falling apart at the seams; can he not see this!"

Even now, the clans huddled together. While they didn't erect gates or mount patrols against one another, the difficulty Markus had in joining the Gerard clan spoke to the divisions. Markus' own Kalari clan doubted he had gained a better position.

"Come, we both know the state of the ships heading to the Violet Sky Realm. There is no way the Marshal would allow us to head out with less than everything ready. I bet he's been hoarding ammunition and supplies from the gunsmiths for months, and if we had that ammunition, I bet we could have driven the Black Phoenix Clan out of their last redoubts."

"Extra ammunition?" Markus frowned.

Louis coughed and waved his hand. *Lily Velten had gotten that information through the gunsmiths themselves.* He couldn't give away his sources. Markus was loyal and had been there for the birth of all his children, but he had always supported the Marshal in his own quiet way. The Marshal held power over the rest of the clan through the gunsmiths. With them in his back pocket, the power of the rifles and pistols was under his complete control.

"Sorry, my mouth gets ahead of me. So, how much are the other clans going to decrease their pay once again?"

Markus sucked on his lips and pulled out the papers from his folder as if he needed to check the numbers again. "Ten percent."

"Ten percent, and seven percent last year, five the year before. They grow bolder. Three percent instead of a two percent decrease. That won't even pay for our people's training."

"If you go to the Marshal—"

"Go to him?" Louis hissed and looked away. "He already owns us!"

Louis stood, stabbing his finger into the desk. "He owns us through our weapons, our gear, our training. We fight with gunpowder and rifle. All the gunsmiths are under his thumb, every grain of powder and ball of shot is made at his request alone. He abolished us serving other groups as protection forces for fear our weapons would be stolen and copied. We can *only* serve our fellow Sha members." He stabbed his finger toward the door. "They know that we cannot take any more contracts, so they decrease the price every year! Only the Velten Clan hasn't decreased the protection fees they pay, and only because they value fighters."

"Louis," Markus started.

"Tell me which contracts you get requests for? Tell me how many people seek training in the rifle now?"

"The Velten Defense contracts are the most sought after," Markus ground out.

"And how many mothers and fathers that have served us faithfully have been telling their young to turn their eyes to the other clans? How few are allowed into other clans? How few people marry the Gerrards anymore? We're the defenders of the clan, but we're falling apart. Soon we won't have any fighters, maybe not in our generation or my sons', but my grandson's, I do not doubt!"

The silence closed in around them. Markus worked his jaw, looking to either side. Louis had him over a barrel without a way to exit. *Should I ask him? The clan will follow, but Markus, just how loyal are you, and to who?*

"You need to talk to the Marshal," Markus said. "You can figure this out. The clans are just trying to fix things themselves and it's making problems worse."

Louis' thoughts and hopes died.

"I would hope so, but he has his own path, and I cannot persuade him." Louis' voice was empty as he sank back down into his chair. "I want my people to be respected for their actions. I want them to do more than just fight, to be free to do as they want. They have learned other crafts, but the Marshal has made every clan their own entity. Even if we try to raise our own crafters or farmers, the other clans will work to shut it down. Sha Clans are supposed to work together but we're watching one another like hawks and fighting for scraps and extras while we die slowly."

The silence fell.

"Sorry, Markus, it was a long fight against the Black Phoenix Clan and all the stress of having to leave my family when I had just gotten back. I've barely had time to see them other than through windows because of all the meetings."

"I understand, Louis, I do. We're all trying to do our best."

"Thank you, my friend."

"How do you want me to deal with it?"

"Get us more for protection, lean on them hard. The rest of it, you know how to deal with it."

"Yes sir." Markus walked to the door, half opening and closing it. "Get some rest, Louis, and remember the Marshal is just a man too."

Louis looked up at his smile, giving him a weak one in reply.

"Say hi to Selma and the kids."

"I will." Louis' smile softened.

Markus left and closed the door behind him, leaving Louis to watch his family. The children laughed as they looped around their mother, using her as a screen in their game of tag before his son made a run for it. His other sister screamed around a pillar, running after him while his other sister ran for the other pillars.

I want them to be able to learn how to fight, or craft, or do whatever they want to do. We gained escape from slavery, but this is freedom by degrees.

With the Velten Clan, the main trading clan, the support of the Gerrards and the crafters, they could become a powerful sect of their own. That didn't include their own warships and bringing powerful weapons to the market, weapons that had never been seen before. *We could create our own future.*

Sound was cut off from his office as he pulled out his sound transmission device.

"Velten, you can count on my support. No more bloodshed than necessary. For the good of the clans."

He listened to the voice on the other end, hardening his features. He doubted that he would have any time to spend with his family before he departed. What weighed more on his mind was Markus.

When we are committed, he will have no option but to join me. He will see reason. That is why he has remained as my second-in-command for all these years. Sleepless nights lay in his future.

Joining the Party

Rugrat cleaned his rifle at the table. Matt had left and Rugrat took over checking on Erik, who had fallen asleep.

Egbert looked up from his book. "Interesting."

"Good part of the book?"

"The book is good, but no, our next guest."

"Guest?"

Egbert had a mysterious smile on his face as he returned his attention to his book.

"Fine, be the all-knowing skeleton in the corner." Rugrat started to assemble the rifle again, making sure to clean the table properly of any stains.

The door opened as Momma walked in with a tray.

"Momma." Rugrat stood to help her.

"No, don't you worry. I have plenty of strength to carry a tray now," she admonished with a smile and put down a pot of chili, bowls, and bread.

Erik blinked and sat up, rubbing his face.

"It can even raise the dead." Rugrat laughed.

"I wish I still had a stomach," Egbert said.

Everyone sat around the room with a bowl. Egbert muttered to himself and tried to get lost in his book, but Rugrat saw him looking over the top of his book, watching them.

A knock from the door made Momma move to stand.

"I've got it. You just sat down." Rugrat put down his bread and bowl.

He opened the door to an unfamiliar, fit young man. He wore a stained and torn pair of pants. Red runes dissipated from his skin, his hair, like flickering blue flame settling into red.

"Master!" the man said at the same time Rugrat heard him in his thoughts. He hugged Rugrat.

Rugrat's brain backfired, then clunked forward as he held out the man at arm's reach. "George?"

The man laughed and grinned.

"Y-you're human?"

"Mostly." George raised his hands as he flexed claws out from his fingers, grinning the entire time.

"What happened?"

"Who is it?" Momma asked.

"Is that chili?" George asked, his tongue falling out as he started panting.

"Uh, yeah, come in," Rugrat said, still thrown.

George walked past him and into the living room.

Rugrat closed the door slowly. He traced his link to George, and it clearly led to the young man heading into the living room.

Demi-human. He knew about demi-humans through Fred and his family, but he didn't think George would become one of them.

He walked into the living room. Everyone was looking at George.

"Welcome home, George. Can you still take on your other form?" Egbert asked.

"Oh yeah." George leaned forward. Fur sprouted across his body. His tail that had been hidden behind his back stretched out as his form altered, his nose extending into a muzzle, leaving him looking like the same old George, sized to fit into the room and with a pair of shorts around his back legs.

"Well I..." Momma stared at the fire wolf in the middle of the room, caught wordless with a raised eyebrow.

George reverted to his humanoid form, his ears retracting. His eyes remained the same and his tail shrunk while the fur disappeared. He grabbed onto his shorts to stop them from falling off, pulling the drawstring tight, looking at the floor.

"What happened?" Erik asked.

"I appeared on a glacier and a voice asked me why I fight. I gave it some answers and these ice golems appeared and started to chase me. I kept on giving answers. When I thought I was going to die, I said, 'I fight so I will have the strength to not be hurt again'. The golems faded and then the voice said I had found my will. Said that knowing one's motivations will allow you to change anything and everything. Then this power flowed into me, and it was as if my body was like those drawings Matt makes. I looked at it and saw flaws and I started thinking of humans. It was as if everything I've learned led up to that point. I used my will to guide my body into a new form: this form." He patted his chest.

"Becoming a demi-human," Rugrat said.

"Yeah, now that I think about it, I would have undergone the change by myself if I kept increasing my elemental cultivation. It just sped up the process. It felt like I was just picking from different Beast-kin forms. Like I had a plan in my head already." George shrugged, eyeing a bowl of chili.

"Help yourself," Rugrat said, pointing at his bowl.

"You sure, Master?"

"Rugrat is enough and go for it."

George grabbed the bowl and made to tilt it backwards.

Momma Rodriguez cleared her throat, stopping him mid-movement.

George hid in his shoulders.

"Spoon, young man. We're not—" She caught herself. "We don't eat with our hands. Sit down. Do you know how to use a spoon?"

"Ah, no, I'm not sure," George said.

"Well, let's start you off the right way." Her smile smoothed his shoulders as she moved next to him to show him how to use cutlery.

Rugrat hid a grin, glancing at Erik. They could hear the pain in George's voice. The bowl was so close!

Momma Rodriguez taught him how to use cutlery and he dove into the meal with relish.

"Did you answer the voice only once? Get it on the first try?" Erik asked.

"Nope, I don't know how many reasons I gave for why I fight. Kept saying that I was giving weak answers. That I needed to go deeper, search my fears. That damn voice kept bugging me." George shrugged. "Though I didn't think that was the reason I fought. Now that I know why I fight, I, well, I don't know. I feel like I have endless energy. Like there was a mental wall and what I saw as a wall was just some paper and there is so much more beyond it."

Then my answers were really wrong. So why do I fight?

"How did you get back here?" Egbert asked.

"The transformation took a few minutes, but then I appeared in the

Ninth Realm. There was a Beast-kin waiting for me. He tossed me these shorts and invited me to enter the Ninth Realm Academy. Said that if I was able to get a position in the Academy, I could join the Tenth Imperium or something. I declined and asked him if he could help me get back to the First Realm. That mana stone pincher. He sent me to the Mission Hall. Apparently, I have a Three-Star Hero rating. I was able to get a loan from them for a Celestial mana stone to return to the First Realm."

Rugrat winced. "Celestial?"

"It was the Ninth Realm," Egbert said.

"We'll get that figured out." Rugrat patted George on the shoulder.

"Did you answer the question Mas—Rugrat?" George grinned.

Rugrat sighed and interlinked his fingers. "No, I didn't have the answer."

"Well, I am sure that you will find the answer. Nothing can stop you."

Rugrat smiled and sat back in his chair. "Guess I just need some more time to think on it."

The same kind of answers started to float to the surface as he looked at the ceiling.

Egbert cleared his throat somehow. *Magic I guess?*

"I was just told by Delilah that you will be heading to the Violet Sky Realm. Special Team One will be going with us. Any more and it will seem like we don't trust our hosts."

"Us?" Erik said.

"I will be heading out with you as well. I'm the strongest mage that Alva has, and I'm a moving dungeon. Also, it's fun getting away from Alva. Don't get me wrong, I love Alva and its people but..."

"But now you have your freedom, you want to see the rest of the Realms. Doesn't mean that Alva isn't your home," Erik assured him.

"Oorah! Just getting stuck in one place sucks. We're made to roam. When are we heading out?"

"Three days to get the team together, then we can head to Purkesh and fly to the transition point. There is one week until the transition point opens," Egbert said.

"I heard that there should be all kinds of rare ingredients, ancient weapons, and technology," Erik said.

"Won't that stuff have fallen apart by now? Hasn't it been like a hundred years since it opened last?"

"Eighty years, but it is its own contained place. Some say that it used to be a city, but then beasts and plants took over the city. The whole place has nearly no mana in it, just elements, a perfect environment for ingredients. Most of the ancient gear will be broken, but the really strong stuff should be fine. As long as they have enough elements or mana charge, they should be fine. Storage rings don't fall apart for hundreds of years as long as they get some passive mana," Erik said.

"Sounds like you've been researching," Rugrat said.

"Well, I was hoping that they would send an invitation. It's a once in a lifetime experience. I'd be lying if I didn't think it could be fun."

Roska looked up from the mission packet with a bitter expression. "My team and I only just got back from our last mission and you're sending us out again?"

Niemm shrugged. "You know how it is. Even with us starting two new Special teams to bring us up to six, there are always more jobs than people."

"And you need someone who knows Erik and Rugrat to contain them, through words or strength." She groaned.

"You know what they're like."

"Yeah, I know. I get it. They saved Alva *again* and paid a huge price. Doesn't mean that they've changed."

"They just want to be treated with respect, left to do what they want. Everyone is scared they'll get hurt. That they'll hurt themselves in trying to prove they're fine."

"And that's the real reason they want to go to the Violet Sky Realm. They want people to stop looking at their limits, at what they can't do, or what they've lost, and be recognized for who they are." Roska leafed through the pages. "Still, that said, they're much weaker than they were before and they're trying to prove themselves to everyone. Ego can get a person killed."

"And who better to bring them down than the Special Teams leader they helped to train, have seen grown up, and has the strength to put both their asses down on the training mat?"

"Niemm—"

"I know, Roska, you see them like older brothers. And I get that you might feel bad about ordering them around and the rest of it. Your mission is to protect them from others and from themselves. I'm not telling you to hold them back, but support them. They do something that you know will be risky, it's your job to stop them. Doesn't mean you have to straight up deny them or patronize them. Give it to them straight. Hopefully, this can be the thing that brings them back to us, and they won't see everyone trying to help as coddling them."

"They're trying to act like nothing is different. You hear about the incident with the Sha riders?"

"Yeah, I did. The other part of your mission is to make sure that the others don't figure out that Erik's and Rugrat's cultivations have been affected. Everyone has heard how strong they are. They're a deterrent to others. If we can keep up that façade, then it is one more reason for people to not attack us."

"This is getting more complicated at each turn."

"Everything should be fine. This is the Sha's first time going into the Violet Sky Realm, but they have gathered a lot of information. They shouldn't be moving too aggressively. Check out some peripheral sites, increase the size of their dungeon cores and then come back. They'll be running protection. Basically, just be there to make Erik and Rugrat look good. Let them sort their shit out and protect them. If something does go wrong, I don't care if you have to lock them up. I need you to promise that you won't let your feelings get in the way of your mission."

Roska drew herself up in her seat. "Don't worry, sir. Even if I have to lock them up and bring them back in a beast storage crate and they hate me forever, I'll make sure they're safe."

"Good to hear it." Niemm rapped his knuckles on the counter and stood. Roska rose with him and shook his hand.

"Good luck, Major."

"Thank you, sir."

Niemm made for the door.

"Also, sir, I heard that some made it through the Trial? Did they?"

"Egbert reported that they failed the Trial, while George passed through it. It looks like they can pass the Trial if they answer a question. We have had some members of the Special Teams return, but others have disappeared. They have gone into the Ninth Realm and are completing their mission to gain information. The Trial doesn't sound like it would last more than a day. The ones that returned have a new quest. It looks like ascending to the Eighth unlocks it. Oh, one more thing, Egbert will be joining you as support."

"Understood."

Niemm nodded and left the room.

Roska sighed, holding the back of her head and stretching her neck. *Great. Running security on two stubborn, hurt idiots who act like nothing's wrong.*

She felt a rising ache in her neck.

"If I was in their position, I don't know if I'd do anything differently. Remind me to never become a hero or a public figure."

"I'm having a case of *deja vu*," Erik grumbled as he came out the front door, looking at the convoy that had been arrayed.

"It's a bit smaller than last time," Rugrat said.

George came out of the house. He stretched and yawned, transforming into his beast form as he landed next to Rugrat, and nudged him.

Rugrat paused for a half-second, frowned, and scratched George's neck.

I guess at the end of the day he's still a Fire Wolf and Rugrat has helped to raise him from a puppy to a demi-human.

Erik shook his head and greeted Roska, who was sitting on her mount.

"Morning!" She raised a hand.

"Breakfast for the road!" Momma Rodriguez said.

Special Team One was halfway out of their saddles as Roska coughed, causing a few red cheeks to appear.

"Might as well fill up." Erik smiled.

Roska sighed and shook her head, sliding down from her mount.

"So, what's the plan?" Erik moved closer as Rugrat walked up. George went to hang out with the panthers.

"Totem to Purkesh Sha compound. They have things laid out for us there. Then head to the transition point. Guess we find out what they'll be up to on the way. They haven't shared what their objectives will be in the sub-realm."

"Sub-realm? We have any more information on where this place is, really?" Rugrat asked.

Wind washed over them as Egbert landed and walked over.

"Sorry, I was just getting a top up and some reading material for the trip. So, sub-realms. Usually, they are areas that are far away from normal civilization and are hard to reach. Some are deep underground or underwater. Others are in lands with powerful elemental effects. There are teleportation systems that will allow groups to enter at certain times for a certain length before they close again. The majority of sub-realms, that is."

"Anything particularly interesting about this one?"

"It might have been a waystation between realms. Mana lights illuminate the realm, but stars can be seen in the sky and there is no sun. Also, there is no dungeon core in the realm, so the elements have only increased with time, while the mana is very low. High element areas, where they interact, create treacherous areas. This realm has many such dangerous areas. Extended stays in the realm could lead to elemental poisoning." Egbert took out a bottle of pills and tossed them to Erik and another to Rugrat.

"These pills will make sure that you don't succumb to such poisoning."

"What about you and your dungeon core?" Erik asked.

"The elements are so heavy, it's a perfect place to grow dungeon cores."

"And the real reason why he's coming comes out." Rugrat smirked.

Egbert raised his arms as if flexing and turned, imitating the pharaoh dance.

"Welcome to the gun show." Roska laughed as Davos handed her a breakfast burrito. "Thank you, Momma R!" She held up the burrito as the rest of the Special Team munched their breakfast and moved back to the convoy.

"Hope you have a safe trip. Look after my boys!" She smiled.

Erik turned away, seeing the same shadow in her eyes that had been there since he and Rugrat had come out of the cultivation pods.

"See you later, Momma. Look after yourself!" Rugrat waved.

"Bye!" Erik pushed a smile onto his face, and they boarded the carriage.

They waved as the Special Team pulled away from the house.

Erik didn't miss the tears in Momma R's eyes just before they passed out of sight.

Silence weighed heavily in the carriage between Rugrat and Erik.

"You think we're doing the right thing?" Rugrat asked.

"Someone needs to represent Alva."

"Not that. You know." Rugrat held his eyes.

"This is the Ten Realms. There has to be something that can heal us."

"You spent months researching in the libraries, talking to the doctors, the alchemists."

"Just because we haven't found it doesn't mean there isn't a way. Look at George; he became a demi-human. From my research and the information Lee gave me, we know it's possible for people to change their bodies after the trial by gaining their will."

"Most of the techniques and ways that change our bodies are with our cultivation and we're too imbalanced now. The systems are interlinked. Mana and elements, they work together. If we increase one, then the other will increase as well. We're both far away from making any breakthroughs."

"I know, but when your mana channels were shattered, Old Hei made a master level pill to deal with it."

"And what did he say when you asked him about our conditions?"

Erik grimaced at Rugrat's dry voice. "He said we needed someone of the star level to create a concoction that *might* have an effect. We would likely need to be treated over a long period of time."

"Right." Rugrat sat back against the cushioned bench.

"He also said that if we can't increase our body or mana cultivation, that it doesn't mean that we can't increase our overall level. All three work together." Erik frowned at the words.

"And the Eighth Realm is a trial that we didn't pass." Rugrat spoke through his clenched teeth. "Christ on a crutch, we're..."

"We're what Rugrat? What are we?" Erik let out a snort of a laugh. "Has beens? Broken fools that can barely fight anymore? Useless idiots? Two nobodies acting like we're something? I know, I *know!*" Erik cut him off. "We lost our damn cultivation. Shit, I can see it in black and white on my stat sheet. I can feel the constant fatigue, the fucking dungeon core fragments that make my muscles ache and my bones itch. I can feel how powerless we are." Erik's voice lowered. "I wonder... I wonder what if we didn't that day."

"Erik..." Rugrat spoke with steel.

Erik met his brother's eyes, cutting him off. "I don't. Not for a minute do I wish we had done anything differently. I accept it. And you know what, I would do it again in a fucking heartbeat, but..." Erik's voice softened as he clenched his hands, wetting his lips. "Fuck, dude. I'm scared."

He grabbed his forehead, feeling the betraying tears in his eyes. Rugrat sat there silently, waiting on him.

"I'm scared that if we stop looking, we'll fade away. Not the fame and all that shit." Erik made a throwing gesture, glancing out the window as he felt the tears running down his face, his mouth full of spit. He swallowed hard. "I'm scared that if we stop pushing, we'll lose who we are. Stop being us. That we'll be two broken guys who let the world run us down and burn us out."

Rugrat nodded, his lips pressed together, his knuckles white, tightening over one another as he ground his jaw. "If we give up, take it easy, take some time off, relax... What about our edge? What about who we are? I like who I am, who I *was*. I don't want to let this turn me into someone I don't recognize."

Erik wiped his face, sniffing. "That's the short and skinny of it."

Rugrat took a deep breath, running his hand through the short cropped hair on the back of his head. "I hate feeling like a burden, seeing Momma that way, taking up everyone's time as they work on me, healing, training and so on when I don't even know if things will get better. I feel like I have to put on a front for everyone hopeful that we will get better, but I don't know if we will. If we're broken and we can't be fixed, I don't want to be the man who broke his mana channels by not listening to others. I don't want to push so far and turn into a little rage monster. I don't want to let everyone else down. They're trying so hard, but I see how it tears them up when we put ourselves in harm's way."

He threw his hand forward, letting out a sigh that didn't know whether to be defeated or angry.

"Really, I wanted to go to the Eighth and to the Violet Sky Realm, not because I think that we can get past this. I just want to get away from everyone. They're all trying so hard for us, and I feel like a fraud. You know, when George came back, I was stunned. He made me realize that there must be a way to fix this. It scared me some because I knew that it would firm others' ideas that they can help me."

"And 'cause he came back as a human." Erik laughed.

"And 'cause he came back as a human. Dude, I'm not gonna lie. It's kind of weird. He transforms into his wolf form and it's like everything is normal. Then he'll go all human and help out Momma with the dishes."

"He just wants to lick them clean."

"Yeah, but you know, it's kind of weird that if I'm flying on his back, I'm sitting on him. Like he's a wolf, but a demi-human at the same time?"

"You'll get used to it. Has he said that he doesn't like flying you?"

"No, but you know what I mean."

"He's a beast first and a human second. Just ask him, man."

Rugrat grunted and sat back.

They looked outside the carriage.

"Thank you."

"What for?" Erik asked.

"I didn't know how to bring it up. Been dancing around it for months. Good to know what you think about it and let me say my piece. I feel guilty saying it out loud. I know they're trying their best."

"But it feels bad taking up all their time and hopes for something that we're not sure will work," Erik finished.

"Yeah, and thank you for sharing; glad you trust me that way."

"You're my brother, aren't you?"

"To hell and back. Oorah." They bumped fists as Erik sat back against his bench. "Okay, just a vacation to a sub-realm to see if we can find anything to fix us."

"Who knows? Maybe we'll find an answer to the Eighth's question." Erik smirked.

Rugrat snorted. "Yeah, Ten Realms riddles. Sounds like a good time."

They chuckled together, a weight lifted from both their shoulders.

Erik shook the sleep away as Rugrat called his name and tapped his boot. "We're here."

Erik nodded, moving his tongue around in his mouth. He stretched in his seat to get rid of the last vestiges of sleep.

The door opened and Rugrat stepped out. Erik rolled his shoulders one more time and followed him out.

The Special Team had dismounted and fanned out. They wore their armor openly, their rifles stored away as they scanned the palace and surrounding grounds.

A lady wearing a fine white-haired wig, a thick layer of makeup, and a slimmed-down version of a dress that belonged in the seventeenth century stepped forward from the Sha guards who stood at attention at the entrance of the palace, creating a pathway.

"Lords West and Rodriguez of the Alvan Empire, it is my honor to greet you." She curtsied as Erik and Rugrat strode up to the palace.

Davos and Tully were a half-step behind, while Roska moved among the rest of the team. Egbert snapped his book closed and stood behind Davos and Tully, staring at everything. He had chosen to go for a muted shirt of bright orange and white flowers covered in his purple interior and black exterior casting robe. He also wore pants and shoes, but his rune carved head was still visible. George hung out back with him in his beast form.

Bet you just want to find the buffet table instead of meeting all the high and mighty people.

The lady took them in through the main entrance into a grand ballroom. People flaunted their finery, guards dotting around wearing high level gear. Refreshments that would be seen as potions in the lower realms were finger food. Groups greeted one another, sized them up. The groups flowed between one another, a hundred styles of dress. Sect leaders and elders talked to one another and the various Sha Clan leaders.

"Lord West and Lord Rodriguez of the Alvan Empire and leaders of the Fair-Trade Alliance," a man announced.

Conversations dimmed and people glanced at the duo as they entered.

The woman who had greeted them led them into the ballroom. People wore suits and dresses woven from expensive materials, finished with mana enhanced materials that shone or gave of various effects. Such blatant extravagance showed off their positions.

By contrast, Erik and Rugrat wore cargo pants, boots, large duster jackets and their armored carriers. He looked at Roska, who shrugged. The Special Teams detail wore their face covering helmets.

Erik felt their judgements, but they slid off. *Nothing compared to a drill sergeant's rants.*

"When do we leave for the Violet Sky Realm?" he asked as they walked down the stairs to the crowd. Already, some were peeling off from their conversations to talk to them.

"We will be setting off tomorrow morning." The lady smiled even in the face of Erik's falling expression.

He glanced at Rugrat. "Oh look, a bar."

Erik heard Davos groan, warming his cold heart with a smile.

"Don't worry. See if we can steal a bottle," Erik muttered.

Davos snorted and looked around, the consummate professional. Erik wondered what his expression must look like under his helmet.

Erik's smile grew as Davos shook his head, grumbling. Even under his helmet, Erik could feel his smile.

They greeted several sect leaders and elders, deflecting them by directing them to the Alvan council. Erik and Rugrat were resting by the bar as Egbert wandered around the room, floating food from the tables and down to George without anyone being any the wiser.

Egbert reached behind a table and picked up Davin, who was holding a platter in mid-air. His mouth was frozen open to receive the rolled meats. In a single move, the fire imp tilted the platter, expanded his head to fit them all in his mouth and closed it.

"Hhi, Eg-urt! An-cy eet-ing ew- err," he tried to say around the meats.

Egbert muttered something about gluttonous imps, cast a spell on him, and walked off, holding the still chewing imp by the scruff of his shirt.

"George," Rugrat said under his breath. He snapped his fingers as George looked around the room, standing very still at the scene of the incident. The party's eyes were all on the skeleton and fire imp as George's head snapped down, hoovering up the meat that had missed the Imp's mouth.

"Seems that you two bring entertainment everywhere you go," a woman snorted from Erik's side.

"Esther." Erik nodded to her as she raised her glass in salute.

"George," Rugrat repeated, trying to call him over as the wolf eyed the next platter of food, a clear debate in his brain. *Guess some things don't change.*

"I like your style." Esther's eyes ran down Erik's armor.

"I see we have the same designer."

She laughed and glanced down at her black pants and shirt. She'd pulled a coat on, but there was no hiding the pistol holsters on her shirt and the two that rested on her hips.

It wasn't odd to see people with weapons at hand. Everyone in the Seventh Realm knew at least several spells that could be used against others. Everyone in the room had a weapon of some kind on their hips, even if they were wearing finery.

"So, what brings you two on this trip? Certainly, you've got enough toys down in your Empire?"

"Still tons to see in the Realm, and who could give up the chance to see something new?" Rugrat said.

"Uh-huh, well, let me give you some advice; keep your eyes about you. The Violet Sky Realm has been mostly mapped out, but there are all kinds of oddities inside." Three men and a woman walked in through one of the side doors. Esther waved them over, diverting their path from the buffet.

A middle-aged woman wearing a lavender headdress with golden thread and a deeper purple silk dress walked forward, threads of fine silver tattoos showing on her hands. She led two men who could not be more opposed. One, a heavyset man, wore various items that seemed to have been hammered into submission to fit his large frame. A squashed nose and scarred face with half burnt sections of hair and eyebrows that framed his animated eyes. Erik would swear his clothes had singe marks. He gestured to a journal with a pencil, explaining something to the final member of their group, a pale man that looked like he was carved from marble. He had gray eyes. Earrings hung from one ear, and his golden hair showed grays and silvers that added to his appearance instead of detracting. He wore a silver suit, classy instead of gaudy, with a green vest underneath. Even in such finery, he had a relaxed, almost bored air.

He listened and replied to the big man with the practice of a long-acquainted friend as his eyes passed over several women and a few men in the room with interest.

"So, if you were to loop it through the third input here—" The big man pointed to an image with his pencil. "—you could increase the output by fifteen percent!"

"And having it just a hair away from the power output formation, it would take only a small fluctuation to breach the formation, and then it could all go up."

"We just need to reinforce it a little, and it didn't happen that much in the simulations!"

"Harrod, didn't you have more hair this morning?" the woman asked the big man.

The large man patted a burnt bald patch of hair, other hairs falling to dust. "I guess I did." He immediately forgot continuing his conversation with the man. "But that's not the point. A minor error! Think of the possibilities, Rob!"

The gray-eyed man pinched his brow and sighed.

Esther greeted the woman with a hug. "Aunty Kameela, seems you were able to drag them out."

"Someone has to get them out of their bedrooms."

"Hey, it's a workshop," Harrod grumbled, smiling as Kameela and Esther disengaged, stepping in front of Rob. "Hey, little one." Harrod opened his arms wide with a smile to match.

"Uncle." She grinned and hugged him, too.

"A workshop that happens to have your bed in it?"

"Convenience," Harrod said as he released Esther. She went to hug Rob, but he caught her hand and bowed to her.

"Niece." He winked and kissed her hand.

"No hug?"

"Not after hugging him and I can smell the powder on you. Needed some shooting practice? At least you have been listening to my advice on drinking. A nice twenty-year wine." He indicated to the glass by her side. "Needed some incentive to play nice with others?"

His eyes danced in amusement as Esther grimaced. "Things are easier and more fun at the range. Your nose doesn't fail you, Uncle."

"All so he can smell an interested lady from across the continent, " Kameela huffed.

Rob grinned as he stood, releasing Esther's hand, familiar amusement in their eyes.

All three looked at Erik and Rugrat with various expressions of amusement.

"My face is here," Rugrat said.

Harrod was actually drooling staring at Rugrat's chest plate. "Hmm, oh, what?"

"Stop staring at the armor, Harrod." Kameela sighed, looking to Esther.

"Lords Erik West and Jimmy Rodriguez."

"I go by Rugrat."

"This is my aunt Kameela and my uncles, Harrod and Robert Larionvich."

"Hi," Robert said, using the corner of his eyes to look at the ladies in the room, paying no attention to Kameela or Esther.

"There's someone that you haven't met before?" Esther muttered.

"Yes, great to meet you. See you in the sub-realm." Rob shook Erik's and Rugrat's hands, smiled, and walked toward a group of ladies.

"Some things never change," Kameela said. "Harrod is our front-liner, and he's also a little interested in formations, some alchemy, and smithing."

"And you are?" Rugrat asked.

"The one that keeps them out of trouble."

Erik felt the room shift as the Marshal walked in through a side door. He scanned the room, smiling as he greeted those closest to the door.

His gaze stilled on the group with Erik.

Kameela turned around just as the Marshal looked away, talking to another person. He laughed and disengaged, heading for the group.

"Lords West and Rodriguez," said the Marshal, taking a few more seconds to look at Rugrat as they shook hands.

"Marshal Dujardin, good to see you."

"And you. I have been hearing about the Alvan Empire constantly. Your little Empire has done much!"

"Ah, that would be the council. We just sit around training," Erik smiled.

Rugrat grunted.

"I see you have met my old team members."

"Ah, once a team member always a team member," Harrod said, patting Edmond on the back with a gap-tooth grin.

Kameela coughed out a laugh as Edmond looked at her bitterly.

A captain behind Edmond coughed, signaling for him to move on.

"Sorry, there is still much to plan and do before we leave for the sub-realm. I'll see you aboard the *Le Glaive.*"

"Look forward to it. We'll be in your care." Rugrat said.

"Kameela, niece," Edmond tilted his head, and they curtsied before he was ushered over to another group.

Esther had called him her uncle in the past, but they weren't related by blood.

"Team members?" Erik asked.

"Before all of this." Kameela waved at the rich chandeliers and artful raised ceilings. "We were just a group of people fighting together for one another. Edmond, Harrod, myself, Zala—Esther's mother—and Bartan, her father." Esther hid her grimace behind her cup. "Even Robert was part of the same party. We came together in the Third Realm. Zala, Robert, Edmond and Bartan pulled together different Clans to form the Sha."

"Sounds like one hell of a story."

"Ah, it is a long one, and still ongoing." Kameela chuckled.

"Are you going to the Violet Sky Realm as well?" Rugrat asked.

"Yes, a last-minute change. Not often that they allow us to go out," Harrod said, wrapping his arms around Esther and Kameela, leaning down to put his head between them. He chuckled and went back to looking at Rugrat and Erik's armor and writing something on his notepad.

Roska gestured to Erik and Rugrat from the side.

"Well, we'll see you later. Hope you have a good night," Rugrat said.

Erik waved to them and left, their special team guards moving around them as Roska led them away from the party with a Sha clan servant in the lead.

"Thought I'd heard that the Marshal was in a party before. Didn't think that they were still around."

"You interested in Kameela?" Erik asked.

"No, why?"

"'Cause the Marshal definitely has a thing for her."

"He's the leader of the Sha Clans. Why hasn't he done anything? Haven't the clans been around for like hundreds of years now?"

"Well, not like our relationships are the best," Erik said.

"You've been looking at the marriage proposals coming in again?" Rugrat muttered.

"Didn't think that people still married off their sons and daughters." Erik shook his head.

"Sons? You didn't, did you?" Rugrat snorted.

"You must not have been checking your mail. I should make sure it gets directed to Momma."

"You wouldn't."

"Come on, she's always saying that you need to bring back a new lady.

She's looking for grand-kids." Erik's grin stiffened, and he rubbed his leg as they walked.

"Don't need to remind me. Though you're pretty bad at picking out a good lady yourself. Who knows? Momma might pick you the right one!"

Erik nudged Rugrat. He just laughed as they walked onto a teleportation pad and vanished.

"Please use this manor for the duration of your stay. The staff will see to your every need. Here is an itinerary of everything happening 'til the launch." Roska accepted the letter from the servant.

"Thank you. Where are the sleeping quarters?" she asked.

"This way."

"You think it could be bigger?" Erik asked as they rode an open top carriage, showing off *Le Glaive,* the flagship of the Sha warships. The ship was covered in formations with sealed cannon ports running down the length of the massive ship.

"Most of them are smaller than they could be. Need to match their formation lift to the weight of the ship, thickness of the armor, and such, and then there are the barriers and the mana gathering range of the dungeon core to charge up the core constantly. Too big of a ship and they'd drop out of the sky. The higher the realm, the greater mass the ship can support because it can draw in more mana to the formations," Rugrat explained.

"I thought you were a Marine, not a ship builder."

"Eh, I got to reading."

"The designs are based on warships from Earth. The Sha utilize sails to increase their velocity and turning speed, as well as gunpowder-based cannons that allow them to divert more power to their mana barriers and internal formations instead of their weaponry," Egbert added.

Erik looked around at the shipyard. Aerial beasts moved in formation across the open air. Warships glowed with power, mana distorting the air with the emanations.

Last-minute preparations were underway as supplies were loaded into the warship. Their carriage came to a halt at a red carpet leading up a gangway into the warship.

"This way, please." A Sha officer took them up the gangplank onto the ship.

"First time on a ship and we're not fighting," Rugrat muttered.

Erik opened his mouth and cocked his head to the side. "Shit, I think you're right."

"Try to not break this one." Roska passed like a ghost, moving with her people as they covered Erik and Rugrat entering the ship.

"Wood?" Rugrat said.

Inside, mana lights illuminated the halls of the ship. Wooden beams crossed overhead.

"It's all made from wood?"

"Sha ships utilize wood over stone and metal. They grow it in their farms. The different kinds of treated woods are as strong as enhanced iron, and they allow for greater flexibility. It has an outer casement of enhanced and compressed iron of the Sky grade. You could call it ironclad. They require very little metal, reducing the weight. Oh, this is interesting." Egbert's eyes rolled around in his skull as he inspected the ship. He reached out, grabbing Davin without looking, pulling him away from the wall and casting a spell upon the imp.

"Ah! No more ice spells!"

"Makes it look like those old warships back on Earth. Ships of sail," Rugrat said.

"But wood, isn't it flammable?"

"Everything is with enough flame." Rugrat rubbed his fingers on a wall and smelled them, holding them out to Erik.

Erik sniffed it, triggering his Reverse Alchemist skill. He closed his eyes reviewing the ingredients.

"A base of Blackwood. When chilled it becomes flexible. When heated, it hardens. Very strong. Resins are mixed to increase the strength of the wood and reduce changes due to temperature."

"They must have laid down all the wood, treated it beforehand, and then used resin on it to harden it into form. Instead of being brittle and rigid, the ship can shift and move."

"Interesting," Erik said.

They walked through the warship. Teleportation formations allowed them to skip through the ship, seeing men and women in overalls, pants and shirts going about their tasks.

It wasn't long before they arrived at the bridge.

"You have guests." Captain Adamus looked over Marshal Edmond's shoulder at the arriving sects and clan leaders.

"Oh joy." Edmond rolled his eyes, quickly checking his attire with his hands.

He turned from the main map to see the different sect leaders and elders walk out onto the bridge. It hadn't been his idea to invite them. He would have been happy with just having the Sha. Through the different clan leaders, they pressed the importance of bringing their allies to cement their ties in these uncertain times. *They were really focused on the Alvans.*

He glanced at Erik and Rugrat, resting on Rugrat for a bit longer. He could sense nothing from them, as if they didn't have a cultivation. Their guards, twelve in total not including their mounts, similarly didn't reveal their cultivation.

A life of fighting had taught him that it would be a grave mistake to challenge them. He looked between them and Kameela, his eyes thinning. *They better not be interested in Kameela.*

He hid his frown, clearing his throat and glancing to where his old teammates were sitting off to the side of his throne at the rear of the bridge. Robert was asleep from his late night. Harrod had a potion between his lips that he tilted up occasionally, writing down notes or looking to the ceiling in thought. Kameela was pointing out something on her rifle to Esther.

Things were so much easier when it was just us.

He turned back to his guests. "Welcome aboard *Le Glaive*. Seats have been prepared for you. Please, make yourselves comfortable. we will be lifting clear of Purkesh in ten minutes."

They moved to the seats on the other side of his throne. Attendants guided them to the food and drink tables and introduced them to the second map console.

Others moved up to look through the glass windows that provided views over the warship. The Marshal's gardens and his manor rested on the top deck of the warship in the shadow of the bridge that allowed clear views over the front of the ship, sides, and the rear of the ship.

A forecastle rose beyond his manor and gardens. Capped cannon batteries pointed skyward.

As he looked down on the sides of the ship, the batteries traversed, checking their arcs, formations flared and died, the last checks being carried out by the crew below-decks.

Erik and Rugrat walked up to the windows with two of their security detail.

"Impressive," Rugrat said.

"Big," Erik said.

"All about how you use it."

One of the security detail coughed, hiding her grin.

"You know I don't get that, or the bridge," Erik said.

"Why?"

"Think about it. You can get hit from everywhere: above, below, left, right, backwards, forward. Wouldn't a submarine form work better?"

The Marshal moved closer. "The manor will drop into the heart of the warship when we are fighting and the bridge collapses so it's closer to the deck too. What's this submarine?"

"Morning, Marshal-Edmond." Erik grinned at his glare. "Submarines are vessels on Earth that fight underwater instead of on top of it."

"Interesting, like fish?"

"Yeah."

"How do they not sink?"

"Uhh," Erik looked at Rugrat.

"I dunno. I didn't want to go into those propellor missiles."

"Technology I guess?" Erik grinned.

"Sir," Adamus moved closer.

"Ah, sorry."

"Do what you gotta," Erik said.

The Marshal moved to his command chair, opulent to the extreme. He thought it too much, but he could not deny the artisans.

He activated the formations within the chair that resonated through the formations in the ship. "Attention all ships, readiness report."

"The *Aquilion* stands ready," Captain Louis Gerard reported.

"The *Méduse* stands ready," Captain Fredrick Gerard reported.

"The *Amazone* stands ready," Captain Kline Adamus reported.

"The *Tourville* stands ready," Captain Danielle Boudet reported.

"The *Le Glaive* stands ready," Captain Alex Adamus said.

"Launch all ships."

The crew standing ready by their stations sat down and started going through launch procedures. The manor and gardens dropped below the upper deck. Metal bars created a lattice as wooden beams grew into place. Plating spread out over the top of the still descending home, covering it as casting platforms and gunnery mounts dotted where the manor had once been, and the surrounding mana density increased.

Le Glaive creaked and rumbled as it freed its bulk from the ground and rose into the sky.

Around the Sha's Purkesh compound, the four other ships rose also. Aerial forces patrolled the limit of the compound as secondary warships. Corvettes and frigates moved around in the sky in a display of military might.

"With entry to the Violet Sky Realm, we can only bring five ships with us. Any more and they will not be able to enter the sub-realm."

"How will we exit?" a sect leader asked.

"There are transition points inside the sub-realm much like how we use totems to transfer across the realms. We can use these transition points to return to the Seventh Realm. While only a certain number of ships are allowed to enter per rune card, as long as one reaches a transition point before the three months are up, you can leave. Raise the sails."

The ships formed up; the four Destroyers arrayed in a diamond formation off the Cruiser *Le Glaive.*

Sail masts pushed out around the ship, tilting into the wind as the sails opened as one. Their white sheets snapped outward, catching the wind, causing the ship to lurch forward as the captured air dragged them forth.

The formation moved out and away from Purkesh. Cannon-fire rumbled from their fellow ships, saluting them as they turned back to Purkesh and their berths.

Edmond took in a breath, leaving the shackles of marshalship behind and becoming a commander leading his forces on a trip into foreign skies. "We will sail to the transition point. There will be a small gathering of forces that have gained a rune card. Then we will transition to the Violet Sky Realm. When we do, we will split up. We'll simply regroup and traverse the Realm to see what gains we can make. After three months, we'll transition back to the Seventh Realm with our holds stuffed with loot."

Time passed quickly as they bypassed different controlled territories and elemental storms. The fleet was left unmolested as they entered the mountain range. The transition point was located within. The Marshal held a telescope to his eye as he checked the markings of other warships visible in the distance, heading in the same direction.

He closed the telescope, a sound-canceling formation covering Kameela, Adamus, and himself.

"Keep an eye out for the Black Phoenix Clan. They have an additional Cruiser. They're in a precarious situation. If they can hurt us, they will."

"Are we still carrying out the Treasure Hall plan?" Kameela asked.

"I know you want to use this as an opportunity to gain information and then come back later to loot the place. We need the resources to sway the other clans and bring the Sha together. To stop the in-fighting that's started up again."

"More resources will not always help. We have carved out a place in the Seventh Realm and still they desire more," Kameela said.

Adamus had a sour look but nodded in agreement.

"It is my duty. So many gave their lives for this. Dedicating my life to protecting the clans, their dreams, and their descendants, it is the very least I can do to honor them."

"Is it your burden alone?" she asked in a sharp voice, turned, and left as Edmond grimaced.

Adamus bowed and moved away, leaving Edmond. Edmond's eyes followed Kameela's trail.

Kameela. His chin dropped as he released his hands. However much he wanted to cross that final wall, to ask her the questions he had held inside for so long, he walked a lonely and daring path. *Any that are connected to me are under threat.* His memories turned to the day Bartan Leblanc died, a man he called his brother and was to name as his successor. *Killed with a Sha weapon. How could I bring children or a lover into this viper's nest?*

He stiffened, feeling the breeze. In the distance, he saw the first group of airships gathering at the transition point.

Stassov looked out of her windows as the Black Phoenix Clan formation came to a halt. The three destroyers created an inverted arrow behind the two cruisers leading the formation.

Ranko stared out of the windows, glaring at the Sha formation. If wishes could cast spells, he would have destroyed their formation several times over.

Stassov moved from her chair to the map table, studying the different formations. Only eighteen groups had been able to find rune cards for this opening of the sub-realm. The Black Phoenix Clan and Sha were the weaker of the two.

A group of Sha attacked Black Phoenix Clan miners, and it had escalated into a war. Stassov didn't know if that story was correct, but it gave the two groups an excuse to attack one another in an attempt to weaken the other force and steal their rune cards.

In a meeting of giants, we're but a footnote.

There were clans and sects here that had several rune cards. Forces that had lasted for hundreds of years and had entered the sub-realm on foot before the era of dungeon core-ships.

Cruisers, the larger battleships, and dreadnaught mana hogs were all on display.

"Three dreadnaughts." Goran shook his head.

"They boast powerful weapons and armor, but their weakness is in their fuel. Each minute they are in the air they burn through countless mana stones. Each shot from their cannons evaporates Sky grade mana stones. They really are only weapons of war. To take them out, they must be assured that the benefits outweigh the costs."

"Most of the time, they rest in claimed territories of those clans, clearing out elemental storms, creating high grade mana stones. They just can't be supported in the Sky realms with our lack of mana density. They would have to go to the celestial or divine realms to support them," Natalya added from her other side.

"They are groups that we cannot draw ire from."

"One hour from transition!" an officer called out on the bridge.

Stassov turned and walked over to where Ranko stood, her sound-canceling formation surrounding them.

"Once we make it into the sub-realm, you have one mission. You and your people are to find the Sha forces and follow them." Ranko's head snapped over. "If there is an opportunity, you will inform me, and I will pass it on to the commander."

"The Alvans?"

"It would be best if they fell with the Sha."

"Transition in ten, nine, eight…"

The bridge had retracted into *Le Glaive's* protection, and everyone was wearing their weapons and armor. The drinks and food had been cleared away as the elders and leaders kept out of the Sha's path.

Ships disappeared from the sky in their groups.

A massive formation looked to have been pressed into the middle of the mountain range, flattening as it glowed with a dull white-silver light.

"Transition!"

The sky filled with a violet tint. Bands of metal, like ribs covering the sky flickered randomly, some with mana lights, others without.

"Stars," Erik said, looking at the night sky. He stood up, feeling heavy elemental mana press against his skin. His armor stopped the elements from entering his mana gates as predicted.

"The elements here are so thick," Egbert said, moving his hands around. His runes lit up as he gathered a ball of purple gas that revolved quickly. It emitted heat and lightning before turning to rain, then stone, then a piece of metal, shifting between them before Egbert released his hand.

"When compressed or in high densities—" Egbert shook his head. "—that would be unpleasant. It would be best to not stir up the elements in this place."

The rest of the ship was in action as Adamus and the Marshal talked to their people.

Erik felt the ship shifting.

"Ah, very smart. The ship is drawing in the elements of the sub-realm. It will rapidly increase the level of the dungeon core. That is why it is best to bring one's strongest ships here." Egbert nodded in understanding.

I miss my domain.

"The density of mana here is minimal; the elements are so thick," Rugrat added. "I can see why elemental poisoning is possible."

Marshal turned to his allies. "Welcome to the Violet Sky Realm. We're coordinating with our other ships, we'll—" A siren interrupted him as cannons on the main deck fired into the sky, illuminating the darkness above, revealing black and purple tinged darts that dropped from the sky. They hit the deck of the warship, piercing it. The black and purple outer layer folded like a sheet, revealing a gray backing and several dozen eyes.

Their bodies contorted like an octopus, trying to get through the points they'd hammered themselves into, gaining access to gun turrets and mounts. They looked like grey squids with four thin tentacles over a grey apron that hid their penetrator undersides. Their aprons wiggled, allowing them to move across the ground freely.

Acid on their underside melted the mana-tempered and alchemically treated wood of the upper deck, leaving thin grooves

They gathered the purple mist within their tentacles, releasing lighting bolts to strike the protrusions on the ship. Others worked together, hammering their dart-like undersides into the deck to try to breakthrough.

More of the creatures dropped from the sky and were greeted with cannon fire and spells.

Erik looked at the command staff and took his thumb off his storage ring. The crew were well prepared and showed no sign of panic. *They've been well trained.*

Cannon teams pulled together, and illumination spells of light revealed the dropping squids.

"Seems we have run into one of the first races that call this place home. They are called Piercers or droppers by some, and can be found in caverns. They drop from above, drive their piercers into their targets, inject a poison to liquify, then swallow their prey and fly back to their perches to wait for the next victim," Egbert said.

"Where do you get this all from?" Rugrat asked.

Egbert looked at him. "Books."

Erik schooled his features, stretching his shoulders from the tightness in his chest, trying to not slouch to ease his discomfort.

"They're leaving," one of the sect leaders said.

"If they cannot kill their foe rapidly, they leave them alone. The blood and scents from the Piercers will ward off others," Marshal said.

The ship's formations activated as the warship headed deeper into the Violet Sky Realm. Below was a thick forest of different colors. Here and there buildings jutted out of the ground, the forest slowly subsuming them.

The warship gradually grew silent, and shutters opened as crews moved to clean up the Piercer bodies.

"With airships, we can bypass most of the creatures in the realm. Otherwise, we would have to fight through the forests and buried cities. Down there, there's little light, and creatures of all kinds jump out," The Marshal said, watching the last of the Piercers fled.

"Those Piercers, they were able to use lightning spells. They didn't look higher than level seventy."

"Every beast in the Violet Sky Realm has a variant beast core, attuning them with an element." The Marshal had to raise his voice over the excited elders and leaders. "Most of them have a few elemental attacks. Did you see how their dark undersides shone as they reached the ship? They were using the elements to harden their penetrator."

The mana density aboard the ship decreased suddenly, causing the leaders to mutter.

"Do not worry. We are decreasing the ambient mana around the ship to avoid attracting more beasts. They are strong in an environment without mana.

If they could fight in a mana rich environment, it would increase their attack's power many times over," Captain Adamus said.

It's as Delilah was saying in her lecture. Mix elements together, and add in mana to enhance and stabilize the effects.

"Well, I feel safer already," Rugrat said.

Erik looked at the Special Team and their grim expressions.

The Piercer's blood was cleared away. The creatures would be dissected and stored.

"Refined by the Metal elements, their piercers could be forged into weapons and armor, their lower apron appendages could be turned into robes, and tentacles into lightning attribute staves and wands. They'll make a nice profit," Egbert said, using a sound-canceling spell.

"I wonder what they taste like," Davin said.

George raised his head in interest.

"You'd both... well, I guess you'd be fine to cultivate other elements now, George. Davin, you'd need to partition your elemental core," Egbert said.

Erik looked away, feeling a familiar itch to train and not waste a second. *Would do more harm than help now.*

"Urggh, I should have gone to the Eighth Realm as well."

Erik set his jaw and shifted in his chair while Rugrat rubbed his knuckles down his arm, grimacing as he loosened up some tightness around a fragment.

Marshal Edmond and Captain Adamus checked the map tables, adjusting their heading and coordinating with the other ships.

A few minutes later, the cannons lit up the sky again, killing Piercers as they dropped.

"I thought you said others wouldn't drop?" an Elder asked.

"Yes, if we'd left the blood on the decks, they wouldn't. Attacks on this level, it is like mana stones falling from the heavens." The Marshal smiled.

8

Usurper

"Looks like that is the last of them," Markus said.

"Damn crazy beasts," Louis muttered, looking at the mana lights above. *I wonder how many of them are hiding up there. This is their third attack.*

"Ship spotted!"

The bridge shifted to look in the direction of the spotter.

"Markings of the Farelli Family. They are going in another direction."

"Make sure to keep an eye on them. Make no aggressive maneuvers. Keep your eyes open for other airships," Markus said.

The bridge settled down.

"This place is massive. Nearly a hundred airships in here and we've only spotted three," Markus said.

"Yeah." Louis leaned forward on his armrests, resting his chin on his clasped hands.

"Ship spotted. It looks like the *Amazone!*"

Louis felt his stomach shift and drop. He rubbed his hands to regain some warmth. A cold sweat trickled down his back.

"Good job. I'll contact Captain Kline Adamus myself." Louis activated his sound-canceling formation and sound transmission device.

"Captain Gerrard."

"Kline, how are things on your side?"

"I have secured my ship. Only loyal crew remain. Yourself?"

"I am sending them the order now. When we next meet, we'll be free from the Marshal's control."

"Yes, sir."

Louis closed the sound transmission channel. He pulled out a device from his storage ring, a small formation the size of a pocket watch.

For freedom, for the Sha Clan's future.

He pushed the formation together with a metallic click. It flashed with light and then dissipated. He forced himself to not touch the white and blue flower broach on his chest that vibrated in response.

Louis stood up, catching the eye of his cousin. A guard standing behind his chair tapped his chest. A blue and white flower held by a broach.

"Markus, Kline had some new details for us, if you'd join me in the meeting room?"

"Ah, certainly. Samara, you have command."

"Yes, sir."

Louis walked ahead of Markus into the meeting room, steeling himself.

The door closed and a sound-canceling formation closed them off from the rest of the ship. *Already across the ship my people will be moving to subdue the loyalists. By the time we step out, it should be complete.* Louis sighed, gripping the back of a chair with both hands.

"You okay, Louis?"

Louis just let out a dry laugh and shook his head. He leaned on the back of a chair.

"I didn't think you were the sentimental type, flower brooches for good luck." Markus grinned. "Wish we had more. I think I would have looked pretty good with one."

Louis twisted the stalk, looking at the flower. "Oh, how I wish I could give you one." He pushed up to standing with an exhale and walked a few steps down the table, looking to the ceiling for strength.

"What do you mean? What's weighing on you?"

"There is nothing new from Kline. This is a coup, Markus." Louis clasped his hands behind him, and turned to face Markus, playing with his ring behind his back, straightening.

"Wait, what?" Markus's brows pinched together.

Louis gripped the chair tighter, but he didn't feel it. "Right now, those who seek to better the future of the Sha Clans are rising up within the Violet Sky Fleet."

Markus stood up, his chair falling to the floor. "What have you done, Louis?"

"I did what I had to." Louis glowered at Markus. "The Marshal is an egotistical tyrant. He dictates what we should do and when we should do it. He keeps the clans separate so he can play us against one another and weaken us to maintain his power over us all. This time, we will not let him divide us. We will unite and drive him out. We will take the power of the Sha Clans and forge it into one. We will become one clan instead of many!"

"Louis, what you're talking about? It will lead to death! It will mean civil war within the clans. You might win here, but what about when you return to Purkesh?"

"Others are taking care of that. Milo Leblanc, with the support of the Velten and Gerrard Clans, will rise to the position of Marshal."

"A puppet! The Veltens are foxes! They will turn on you if they can profit!"

"Markus, it is *done*!"

"You will lose the guns and powder from the crafters! This is doomed, Louis!"

"The crafters have been caged for too long. They stand with us."

"You will break the Sha. You will tear out its heart. There will be no coming back from this! Listen to yourself! It isn't perfect, but it is stable and safe. What can be said about the rest of the realms?"

"If the Sha's heart is the Marshal, then we must cut it and its pollution out. It is only then that the body can be whole!" Louis yelled.

"He binds us together. Yes, he controls all the Sha, but he is the source of our strength. Without him, our clans would not be what they are."

"The past is the past. We cannot let it create our future blindly, Markus! I *need* your answer. Where do you stand?" Gerrard demanded.

Markus shook his head, his face devoid of color, drawing his sword. "I stand for my oath. Please, Louis, I don't want to hurt you.

"And if I say I stand on the side of a man trying to do his best to hold us together? A man you call tyrant and I call a poor soul. What would you do with me? Would you kill me?"

Louis ground his teeth, smacking the chair before resting his hand on his sword. "Can you not see it, Markus? There is no future with him!"

"How can you know when you do not reach out to talk to him? How many times have you held your words instead of talking to him? How many plans have you made without asking others? Did you create this plan after asking everyone in your clan their thoughts or did you decide for them? How is that any different from him?" Markus gestured with his hands, gaining movement and force with each question.

"He dismisses anything that goes against him. He allows no one to advise him. He only listens to his teammates, all strangers that do not have a clan!" Louis yelled, stepping towards Markus.

"He might not make the best decisions, but he is making the best ones that he can. I fight for the Sha, I fight for the Marshal, for this will tear apart the clans." Markus drew himself up.

"Milo is the rightful heir!" Louis stabbed his finger down.

"That little brat?" Markus' face contorted. "Do you hear yourself? The Marshal raised him as a nephew, even if they do not share blood, and Milo turned on him. He blames the Marshal for his father's death!"

"His father died from a Sha weapon." Louis' words stopped Markus cold. "This I swear."

"You think the Marshal killed the man he called brother? How many times has he dueled people honorably?"

"It was a Sha weapon, and Edmond took that opportunity to take control over the clans. There was no one that could ask him to step to the side. He was the one and only Marshal."

"Where are your facts? Where is the weapon?"

"The details are clear. Markus, stand beside me. Join me. Join my clan officially. Do me the honor of taking up the name Gerrard."

Markus raised his sword in salute. "I would have been honored, but I cannot pledge myself to one while betraying another."

The door to the room opened. Louis felt the hairs on the back of his scalp raise as his guard looked from Markus' raised blade and Louis.

His pistol was covered in a cloud of smoke.

"No!" Louis turned to Markus, who had been thrown backward, his blood painting the wall as he looked at the bloody stain spreading across his chest.

The guard dropped his first pistol and drew the second, pointing it at Markus' head.

"Hold your fire!"

The guard twitched, still aiming.

Louis ran to Markus' side and pressed his hand over the wound as

Markus's mouth opened and closed. "Not what I expected."

He coughed blood as Louis picked him up off the floor and used his leg to support him, his hand doing little to stem the flow of blood. "You stubborn bastard. What were you trying to do?" He took out healing potions and poured them on Markus' wounds.

"Ah, shit." Markus coughed again, blood staining his teeth. "Not nearly as stubborn as you." He gripped Louis' arm, looking into his eyes. "Don't lose yourself to the blood. Don't confuse—" He coughed again. "—confuse killing as righteousness. The Marshal didn't kill others for having different opinions. If he did, would there be a clan left?"

Markus was wracked with coughing. His wound was too severe to be healed by Louis' potions. Blood foamed on his lips before sudden stillness as his body slackened.

"Markus!" Louis' body trembled as Markus' tombstone appeared. He pinched his eyes together at the Ten Realm's merciless ways. It took a power of will to control his emotions, to hold his tongue against his guard. *Oh, Markus, why couldn't you just let your foolish blind trust go?* Something felt rotten and broken within him.

Louis held his second-in-command, his closest friend and godfather to his children. He closed his eyes carefully.

"You stubborn fool." He bowed his head, standing and gently laying Markus on the floor.

"Clean his tombstone." Louis's voice was rough as he exited the room, passing two of his guards. They bowed their heads, moving toward Markus' body when he left.

Louis stepped forward to his command chair. Several people sporting bruises were bound and escorted away from the bridge. They'd been gagged as others came in and took their places.

"Sir." Samara handed him a wet towel, her voice tight as her gaze flitted to the meeting room and back out over the bridge, unshed tears filling her eyes.

Louis looked at his hands staining the white towel red.

He rubbed the blood from his hands. It spread down his shirt and pants. A clean spell released red flakes from his clothes. He scrubbed his face with the towel, hiding his tear-filled eyes. He stored it away, spells clearing bloodstains from various stations on his bridge where the scuffles had gotten heated.

There is no going back now. The Marshal did this. His lies and tyranny blinded many. He clung to anger like a lifeline as Markus' words stayed with him. The Marshal didn't kill others for having different opinions.

"I want a report from each department as soon as possible. We have only a few hours until we meet up with *Le Glaive*. Prepare all boarding parties."

Edmond checked the milling leaders at the map table they'd effectively taken over. The bridge ran with its usual professional air.

"The *Meduse* has taken up around *Le Glaive*.

"That's better," Edmond said.

"The captains are on their way over," Adamus said.

The Marshal nodded, checking the map table.

So close. The Treasure Hall was a few hours away from where they'd gather, but the other captains had spotted other ships scouting the area, each checking to see if the Treasure Hall's guards were still alive.

The Marshal pulled up markers on the map, locations of interest based on their element readings and what they could gather through various intelligence networks. He plotted out a route around the Treasure Hall. *Close enough for teams to reach the hall, and for the fleet to support them if needed.* He'd brought multiple spiders, small ships that were nearly impossible to detect and could give positional data to the main ships.

Each location he marked was a place where they could find rewards, plants, elemental storms to harvest, and different ruins with resources worth gathering.

He looked up as Captain Danielle Boudet and her guards walked into the command center. He raised a hand in greeting but kept working on the map.

Captain Louis Gerrard followed with Captain Kline Adamus.

Fredrick Gerard was the last captain to join them.

Edmond stood at the head of the rectangular map team. Robert, Harrod, Kameela and Esther stood behind him. To the left was the open space where the elders and leaders rested with their own map table.

The Sha guards waited near the doorway on that side of the bridge.

Le Glaive's Captain Ross Adamus moved to Edmond's right side, his cousin standing beside him. Louis Gerrard stood at the other end of the table.

"Okay, so I've plotted out our route," Edmond said, pointing to the different markers. "Thoughts?"

No one said anything, looking at one another instead.

"It is time for this to come to an end!" Louis raised his eyes from the map. "Come peacefully and I will let you live."

Edmond looked at the other captains. Only *Le Glaive's* Adamus stared back at them. The rest were all focused on Edmond.

"What is this?" Edmond stiffened, suddenly aware of where every guard was located. He put his hand behind him, signalling to his team members and hoping they saw his signs as different scenarios ran through his mind.

"This is a coup, Marshal," Captain Boudet said.

"You would betray the clans?" Edmond hissed.

"*You* betrayed the clans!" Louis yelled, silencing the bridge. "You pit us against one another, you hold power in a vice. You offered my clan freedom. Instead, we are nothing more than your hunting dogs."

"Run, sir!" Ross raised his pistol. His cousin's blade stabbed through his ribs twice and cut deep across his neck.

Edmond hit a formation on his hip. A barrier snapped around him, the round shattering against it. Grenades detonated, killing the allied leaders and throwing Edmond to the side.

The Alvan skeleton glowed as Edmond slammed into a wall. He shook his head, trying to focus. A large, scarred hand grabbed him.

Harrod?

Gun smoke billowed around Esther's hands when she fired.

Robert pulled him backward as he threw fireballs among the captain's guards. Edmond looked back. Landing craft and aerial beasts lifted off from the other ships, covered in Piercer blood, and headed for *Le Glaive.*

Robert led Edmund to the doors behind his chair, and he kicked them open. Edmond's vision started to clear as the Alvans exchanged fire with the other captain's guards.

Two team members pulled Erik and Rugrat away, guiding them to the rear as they pulled on their helmets.

Egbert created a barrier from floor-to-ceiling as they drew back. The Alvans sported smoking, stained armor.

"We can turn this around," Edmond insisted.

"Shut up, Edmond," Robert growled as Kameela and Esther joined the group.

The Alvan special team tossed out grenades that went off in a flash of light and noise. They fired into a bridge that had turned to chaos, hitting the barriers thrown up by the captains. Guards rushed onto the bridge as Egbert maintained his barrier, covering the last of the Alvans through the doorway.

"Seal those doors!" Roska yelled.

They snapped shut. The metal of the wall twisted and melded to the doors.

"We need a way off this ship," Roska yelled.

"This way," Kameela said, turning and running into the rooms beyond. They passed bedrooms, a grand meeting room, and arrived in the library.

The doors rattled behind them as they sealed them shut.

"If we can cut down the captains, we can turn this around," The Marshal said.

"Uncle, Louis is leading them, the second highest ranked man in your fleet. Has he ever done anything that he was not confident about?" Esther asked.

Edmond ground his teeth.

"Now that I think about it, someone must have moved the strings to get me here," Kameela said.

"All the sects and clans that were invited were the ones you were closest to," Harrod said.

Only the Alvans and his own team remained.

Edmond gritted his teeth. *I'll make them pay for this. I'll tear them apart!*

Kameela went through the books on a shelf, throwing them to the side.

Erik watched Kameela tossing books onto the floor, clearing an entire shelf. She pulled out a formation and inserted it into a recess in the wood.

He, Rugrat, and Roska had their heads together in a corner of the room under a privacy spell.

"Okay, so the Marshal got betrayed, and it looks like the new Sha don't like us much," Erik said.

"We can't fight them all. We need to get out of here with the Marshal and his people. They know this place better than us and how the Sha will react," Roska said.

Rugrat nodded. "Best plan we've got."

"Wanted to see the realms a bit. Didn't plan on getting caught up in a coup. Great first day in the Violet Sky Realm." Erik's laugh was filled with venom.

Harrod pulled a rug out of the way, ripping it free from the ground, revealing a formation in the middle of the room and tossed it to the side.

"This teleportation formation will take us to the ground," Esther said.

"We can hide in the city under the forest."

"It's filled with monsters," Edmond hissed.

"Better dumb monsters than smart people that want us dead," Robert said.

Edmond clicked his tongue and checked his pistol.

"Half of yours, half of ours." Roska stepped forward.

The Sha shifted, looking at the Alvan group.

"You thinking about turning on us?" Edmond growled.

"What do you mean?" Kameela asked, talking over him.

"She means that five guards and Rugrat go down with three of you. Then the last two go with the rest of our guards and me," Erik said. His skin itched badly, eager to draw in the surrounding elements and charge the enemy.

"Fine," Kameela said. "Esther, Edmond, Robert, you go first."

"Davos, get that door rigged," Roska said, walking into the circle with Rugrat and half of the special team, joining the others from the Sha side.

Davos took out a magical trap spell scroll and fixed it on the door.

The first group disappeared.

"Second group!" Kameela yelled.

They all got inside the formation. Erik pointed his rifle at the ground behind three others. Tully was behind him, leading the half-team. Something clicked in the bookshelf and then they were outside. Most of the mana lights were off, and the Sha Fleet hung above the trees, their running lights creating silhouettes in the night sky.

"Move it," Tully hissed. They ran after the other group.

"There's an entrance here," Kameela said.

"Ah shit, I'm getting too old for this," Rugrat said.

They reached the entrance, a stone building covered in the roots of several trees growing over it as it jutted out of the ground at an angle.

Rob led the way, his blade leaving light afterimages as he cut the roots clear of a window and climbed into the darkness beyond.

Others followed him.

Erik activated his night vision as he reached the window. The interior of the building was a series of broken floors, roots spreading throughout. The interior had rotted away a long time ago. Pools of stagnant water dotted the angled building.

They climbed down the roots and broken walls to a floor that was more intact and took the stone stairs down to the ground.

They stepped out of the building. An apocalyptic cityscape greeted them.

Erik looked up. Some fifty meters above, roots weaved together between the highest buildings to create the ground that they had been flying over, and the ceiling above the city.

Yang Zan hissed and fired into the darkness, hitting something that bled phosphorescent green.

"Ka'tell!" Edmond said.

Cannon fire boomed overhead. "Shit, they must have broken into the library," Esther said as they started to run.

The ceiling shook and then broke open in places, raining tree remains on the city below.

"Keep running! All around security!" Roska said, tearing a Detect Life spell scroll that spread out over the area.

A tree crashed into a building, through two floors. Branches illuminated their barriers as they hit with stunning impact.

Rugrat fired into a Ka'tell, giving Erik a close-up look as it hissed and screeched from the burning round. It looked like a mix between a panther, a viper, and the shadows.

It shot away. Erik swore it became mist before the round in its side exploded, coating the world in green gore.

"Move it!" Erik yelled.

They ran deeper into the remains of the city as the ship continued to fire from above, sending sections of forest crashing into the underground city.

"Will you piss off?" Erik grunted as he fired at another Ka'tell.

The ground erupted underneath one of the special team members and snapped around them to form a pod before it started to retract underground.

George let out a roar, slicing out with his paw. It cut through the underside of the pod, leaving deep grooves in the ground. The pod shattered as the team member within cast a spell.

A screech sounded in the distance.

"Stop using your spells!" Edmond yelled. "Elemental attacks only!"

"The hell are you talking about?" Robert yelled back, killing another Ka'tell. It was only a matter of time before another appeared.

"Everything in the Violet Sky Realm is attracted to mana."

"So what?" Robert said.

"Just trust me!" Edmond looked at the Alvans.

"Melee!" Roska yelled.

Erik pulled hammers from his storage ring. The others drew melee weapons, storing their mana-railguns.

Egbert took out a necklace and hung it around himself, creating a powerful suction as he drew in the minimal surrounding mana, removing any trace of their presence.

"This way," Kameela said.

They ran through the crumbling remains of the city, debris from the forest ceiling above raining down, hitting buildings, and sending stone and tree flying.

Roska grabbed Erik as a section of roof fell, smashing into where Erik would have stepped.

"Thanks." *If I had a domain, I would have seen it. Fuck.*

They ran for several minutes, hiding in a half-broken building.

"Something is coming," Kameela said.

A rustling noise filled the street as a pod grabbed onto the ground. Another appeared, its teeth clamping around a building, dragging something attached to its vines.

Everyone stiffened as Rugrat aimed at it.

Smaller pods appeared, tasting the air, and then grabbing onto the buildings and pulling its main body—a massive maw with a beet-like body—leaving a wet trail on the ground.

A Ka'tell jumped from a building for a pod. Another pod's vines stretched out, trying to catch the Ka'tell. Its snake like appendages fought them off as it got its teeth at the base of the pod and tore it clean, fleeing with its prize as the maw let out a roar. Pods grabbed rubble and hurled it after the Ka'tell.

Something shone above. Piercers thudded into the ground, striking the shambling creature.

Its screech hurt even through their helmets. The Piercers pinned it to the ground. Their grey aprons fell over the monstrosity, covering it in acid.

The creature lashed out with its pods. A pod was cut off, but it regrew in a matter of seconds and attacked the Piercer that had taken away its old pod mouth.

Dozens more of the Piercers fell, stabbing into the creature.

Even its monstrous regenerative abilities couldn't save it.

"Come on, let's get out of here while they're distracted."

"Make sure to watch the ceilings and the floor," Roska said.

They slid out of the ruin, moving between cover. The barrage returned in earnest, causing the creatures of the undercity to hiss, screech, and roar in defiance.

"Getting the cardio in today!" Erik yelled as they gave up cover for speed as a cannon shot pierced the ceiling above, crashing into the ground and exploding, destroying buildings that had survived the passage of time. Sections of the city collapsed, raining down on the group as they ran through the broken buildings.

He noticed shadowy beings, but they returned to the darkness as quickly as they appeared.

Louis reloaded his pistol as he looked over *Le Glaive's* command deck.

"The last of the loyalists have been secured," Captain Kline Adamus said.

Louis couldn't read his expression. *Did he feel anything killing his own cousin?*

Louis cleared his throat. "Very well. As agreed, I will take command of *Le Glaive*. Samara will take command of the *Aquilion*. The rest of you should return to your ships." He looked at the other captains.

"Sir!" They saluted him, and he returned it as they left the bridge.

He turned to face Richard Gerrard, a nephew that would be his second-in-command. "What is the situation with the Marshal?" He cleared his throat.

"Not sure if he is alive or dead. After the bombardment there were some mana signatures, but they went quiet. We could send people down there, but the creatures in the Under City have been riled up."

Louis gritted his teeth. *Our people will get torn apart by them.*

"We tore up the city. No one or Violet Realm creature would have survived that," Gerrard assured him.

Louis rubbed his storage rings. "He's a coward, running from battle. We'll set off on our pre-planned route toward the Treasure Hall."

"Yes, sir."

"Prepare to move in an hour." Louis turned. Crafters worked on the bridge consoles, repairing them and cleaning away the blood.

The area where the sect leaders and elders had sat was blackened and twisted by the explosions. The map table was warped and broken, leaking mana. The bodies had been looted and spells applied to remove them quickly. A clean line ran through the ceiling, walls, and floor where the skeleton's barrier had protected the retreating group.

Those Alvans are a tricky pawn on the board.

He moved through the broken doors to the private quarters and meeting rooms behind the command throne, the same ones Edmond and the Alvans had escaped through.

Guards were posted within the rooms. Louis nodded to them, eyeing their blue and white broaches that marked them as fellow conspirators.

He stepped into the bathroom and washed his face.

He pressed a towel to his face, thinking about his next moves. *Milo will secure the clans while I need to come back with the greatest rewards possible to cement our future and bring the clans onto our side.* He wasn't worried about the Marshal escaping the Violet Sky Realm if he was alive. The transition points were surrounded by strong beasts that would be a challenge to someone from the Ninth Realm.

He looked into the mirror but saw only Markus' body as life fled his body.

Louis shook. He gritted his teeth, turning his head to the side.

I can't focus on that. This is what I signed up for. I agreed to this and orchestrated it. I have to see it through now. For my kids' future and the children of the rest of the Sha, we will forge a future together.

A snarl spread across his face as he glared at his reflection. "Do the fucking job."

He hit the counter, feeling the pain in his knuckles for a few fading seconds as he pulled his uniform tight and turned toward the door.

Three months and we'll return as victors on the winds of change.

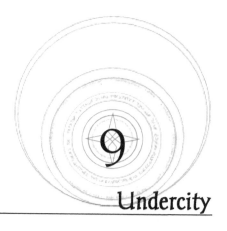

9

Undercity

Erik turned Roderick's arm around. The pod teeth had hooked into his skin and injected venom into his body.

"Poison body?" Erik asked softly. They had stopped using formations and spells to keep from attracting attention.

Roderick nodded.

Erik pulled out Wraith's Touch and a knife and glanced at him.

Roderick grunted, looking away, and nodded.

Erik rubbed the salve around the angry wound, holding himself back from using a clean spell. He poured alcohol on the blade and cut into Roderick's arm, removing skin, infected fat, and muscle, working blind without his organic scan.

He worked quickly, before Roderick's body could neutralize the salve, cutting away the infected tissues. He passed the blade to Nymeria, who cleaned it and handed him the healing powder. He sprinkled some on the wound and then stored it.

The injury was already closing, pushing out yellow Earth-based poison. The blood bubbled, settling down after a few seconds.

Erik continued to check Roderick, treating the infected spots. He used Wraith's Touch as Nymeria passed him his cleaned blade and continued his work, cutting out three more sections in his legs and one in his neck.

He patted Roderick on the side once done. "Good to go."

"Thanks, boss."

Nymeria returned his sterilized blade to him.

"Thanks, I'm gonna find Rugrat."

Erik put the blade into his belt pouch and grabbed the old first-generation automatic rifle. Unlike the newer versions, it didn't rely on formations and spells to function.

He looked around. They were in some burned-out ruin. Here and there, parts of the walls had collapsed.

The Special Team members peeked through windows, or were stuffing some quick food in their faces under their sniper sheets. Formations had been sewn in to remove any sign of their presence.

Erik moved out of the rest area. Each footstep sounded like a saw being dragged across stone as he walked over the dust-covered floor, avoiding piles of rubble and roots.

He reached Tully, who was peeking through a hole in the wall, watching the street. She raised her head in greeting and pointed over her shoulder with her thumb.

Erik patted her on the armor and headed in that direction, keeping low, carrying his rifle in-line with the floor.

Egbert sat on a broken set of stairs in the middle of the house. Erik felt the shifting winds, elements, and mana being drawn toward him, removing their passive mana signatures. He sat against the wall, one leg up on the step, a bow lying along the other as he went back to reading his book.

Erik nodded. *One plus about being mana crippled. Don't have to worry about leaking mana.* He shook his head and kept moving, passing team members. He saw Esther, sans helmet, wearing her cuirass festooned with pistols.

Should get her a helmet.

He spotted Rugrat through a broken part of the roof on the second floor with Big Momma.

Erik peered into the next room where Roska, Edmond, and Kameela were planning their next move under an extra-large sniper sheet.

Harrod sat on a chair in an adjoining room, looking through a broken section of wall. Robert chewed on something, looking through a space where a window had once been. He noticed Erik's approach and raised his head, turning back to his watch.

Erik looked at the sheet and at the hole above him, whistling. Rugrat glanced over and held his hand in an okay sign.

Erik hopped onto a section of broken wall and jumped up onto the second floor. He sank with his landing, deadening any sound. He paused, getting down and inching up on Rugrat's side, away from the hole he was using to look out on the rubble and building outlines that carried into the distance.

"How are they?" Rugrat asked.

"Few scrapes here and there, a broken bone, sprains and cuts. Only Roderick needed my help. Poison was being a pain."

"Roska still canoodling under her sniper sheet with the Marshal?" Rugrat rested his chin on his left hand, the right tapping the selector as he kept scanning.

"Yeah, guess they're still trying to figure out our next moves."

"You see the look on his face when she stepped forward to do the planning?"

"Kameela about near kicked him through a wall."

"Heh, yeah, she did. She's got some fire."

"You sure you're not interested?"

"Brother, those two have got something burning for one another. I ain't interested in getting between them."

Erik felt the pin pricks of pain in his chest. He shifted to reduce it to a dull ache, trying to ignore the itching that replaced the pain. "How are you doing?"

"Not bad, chilling in some lost city, working on my shtank with airships above that want to kill us, and the natural wildlife all around us looking for a snack. Fucking oorah, brother."

"Oorah," Erik muttered. "Not like you haven't dealt with this shit before. Leaving the Army to join the Marines, what kind of backwards slide move was that?"

"You were a medic, short, and missing more than a few brain cells. Thought I'd up the count." Erik snorted and coughed, the tight skin on his neck pulling, causing him to shift onto a piece of shrapnel.

"You good?" Rugrat asked.

"Yeah, just some dust. You?"

"Just trying to ignore the shards. Thankfully, my mana core is pulling in my mana so it's not leaking all over the place, but, shit, I'm getting tired. Two days of ducking and running. This body is only human."

"I can take watch if you want to get some sleep."

"You aren't superman either, my dude."

"I'm dragging in elements. Keeps my body going. Kind of nice here without mana. for me. Less for my core to pull in to tear up my channels again," Erik said.

"Yeah, but we both know how the elements resonate with the shrapnel and fucking suck."

"Embrace the suck."

Rugrat grunted.

They fell silent. Rugrat kept watching the street.

"Sorry, man," Erik said.

"What for?"

"For getting you into this shit."

"Dude, as much as I love you, fuck you. I'm a grown adult last time I checked, and I made decisions that led to this. So shut the hell up." Rugrat lifted his helmet, giving him a you dickhead look, and pulled the helmet back down.

Erik smiled and checked his helmet. "Across eight worlds and a sub-realm, huh?"

"Eight? We've only been to seven realms. I think the Eighth was somewhere in the Seventh."

"Earth, genius."

"Ah, yeah, guess that counts."

Erik heard someone shifting below. He looked down the hole. Egbert was on the stairs, pointing at him.

He saw Roska fall into a crouch. He waved to her as she bounded up the stairs, silent as a cat as she moved with her rifle.

"Looks like we have news." Erik moved back from Rugrat and leaned against the back wall, away from the windows and openings. She settled down next to him. "What's the word on high?"

"Dujardin wants to go back up to the surface. He only has maps for topside. Get some reference points and we can figure out where we are in relation to his plans. Most of the transition points are a no-go, but he knows one that should be unprotected so we can get a ride out of here. I'd prefer to move to a secure position, get somewhere defensible, and then head up when it's safe." She sighed.

"Having troubles with our friends?"

"I can see why they wanted to kick him out. Dude's bullheaded as fuck. Has his own plan and there are no variations he'll accept. Kameela is the only one who can get him to listen. Might've been looking down on me because it wasn't one of you two?"

"He led us into a fucking ambush," Rugrat's voice carried back to them.

Erik shrugged and Roska sighed.

"Yeah, remember someone saying that this was supposed to be an easy job. Just sit on the airship and look scary. Now we've got fucking sentient nails falling out of the ceiling and the plants are trying to eat us."

"Not ideal."

"No, not ideal. How are you two?"

Erik opened his mouth, breathing in, feeling the building pain and aches. "Alive."

"The pain?"

"We're good," Erik forced.

Roska paused and shook her head. "Just don't do something stupid that'll get you killed. My ass is on the line here."

Erik grimaced. "No stupid shit. Agreed."

"Thanks." She sighed and leaned her helmet back against the wall.

"So, what is the plan?"

"We find a position to hold up in that isn't all broken walls. Get our bearings and then head toward this transition point."

"Well, we've got three months. Good thing they started the coup early on," Rugrat said.

Erik just stared at the back of his friend's head.

"Small blessings," Roska said.

Rugrat clicked his tongue, silencing them both as he went to glass.

Erik moved forward, laying down to push up next to him.

Roska sat up and raised her rifle on her leg, using the scope to look through the wall.

The Undercity was quiet, the stagnant air hiding its deadly occupants.

Erik looked through his scope at what Rugrat saw.

Three giants, a good ten feet tall, walked out onto the street. They looked human except for the fact that one had red skin, the other green, and the third was blue. Tails swept over the ground behind them. Each had magnificent horns that extended from their skulls. They wore pants made from lizard skin, cloaks made from Piercers, and hoisted spears tipped with their penetrators.

One held a shield made from the shambling pod creature.

Their eyes shone in the darkness as they looked around. On their backs and hips, pod hooks carried their kills: Ka'tell and various other beasts. They openly walked through the street two hundred meters away. *Either they're idiots or confident enough to deal with the threats of the Undercity.*

They passed on, crossing the street. Erik was about to speak when more of the same creatures of different colors, shorter than the trio at the front, moved into view. There were about ten giants that created the caravan. About twenty or thirty beasts in similar appearance, colored green, blue, red, black, or yellow moved inside the giants' perimeter. They cawed and hissed at one another, headbutting each other with their small horns.

They were as large as two horses, with a tail that extended behind them, making them look like horned Komodo dragons. They shifted their entire body when walking. One tried to nip one of the demi-human's food hanging from his back. The yellow demi-human grunted, stone covering their arm as they batted away the beast casually, sending it sprawling on its side.

The other beasts nipped at their fallen fellow's belly. It hissed and attacked them back, smacking them with his tail like a whip, with a crack that broke the silence.

They pulled together as a screeching howl carried through the Undercity from above.

A black giant let out a whooping hiss, lightning wrapping around his spear as he launched it into the sky.

It struck a falling piercer as red giants called fire along their spears.

Their colors connected to the element they controlled as their weapons cut down the falling Piercers. They howled, gathering power in their antlers and mouths that reached out into the sky above.

The beasts inside the perimeter reared up, using their tails to stabilize themselves and released elemental attacks from their mouths.

The Piercers stopped falling as the convoy yelled up into the ceiling. There was no reply as they pushed and shoved others away to collect their kills. Several beasts fought over the Piercer bodies, tearing them apart in the struggle. They recovered spears and pulled out monster cores, which were rapidly consumed.

One of the leading trio of demi-humans, red in color, raised his bloody sphere and growled at them all.

Thirty or so pulled together into their group, carrying their spoils or fighting over them as they disappeared into the broken city.

No one spoke for some time after they left.

"Well, let's try to not piss *them* off," Rugrat said.

"The sooner we find somewhere to hold up, the better." Roska moved for the stairs. "Ten minutes and we're moving out."

"Yes, boss," Rugrat said.

She headed downstairs to tell the others as Erik and Rugrat kept watching the road.

A bat-like creature landed on the ground. Its bones and skin shifted, transforming into a mix between a white hairless chipmunk with green lines, a constant smile, bulbous doggy-eyes, and butterfly-wing ears.

"Cute-looking bugger."

It opened its too-big mouth and scooped up a forgotten scrap of meat.

Overly large centipedes of white and green bunched together as they crawled out of the sewer system and transformed into the same creature. In a few seconds, the empty street was filled with the transforming creatures, feeding on the scraps left by the convoy.

Either not getting a share or finding nothing left, they kept their form, running along the ground, or turned centipede and dove into the sewers, or took flight as their ears grew into wings along their bodies that thinned.

They scattered in every direction, searching for food and following the convoy.

One landed on nearby rubble and turned into a centipede as it wrapped around the pillar. Turning back to its regular form, it ran forward, pausing every so often to study the area.

Erik grew quiet as others spread out with it, heading for the building.

A creature leapt up and turned into a bat, letting out a shriek that cut through the city.

Others took up the call as they hid in the rubble while they moved closer to the house.

"We're moving!" Roska yelled.

"Guess that one saw us." Erik and Rugrat jumped up and dropped through the hole in the floor. The Special Team and Edmond's team were already in motion.

They hustled out of the ruin and spread out down the street. The little bastards cried out and chased them with the same screeching howl they'd used when the Piercers had dropped from the sky.

"I'm picking up the group of demi-humans and their descendants. They're turning toward us," Egbert said as they ran across the street. He pulled out an arrow with a mana stone head. He paused, drawing back the bow and fired, launching it down the street.

The clamor turned as the small beasts ran, flew, and slithered in the direction of the mana stone. The city started to shift as creatures sensed the mana stone, declaring their rights to it.

The teams kept running, diving through buildings and down streets while checking the ground and the sky.

Erik panted inside his helmet, expecting a penetrator to drop at any second. He scanned the area, grunting as stone hit him, blowing him to the side.

An armored mole with a mouth large enough to eat a pig whole crunched through the ground like a rising ship on stormy waves.

The creature shrugged off their attacks and smashed its foot on the ground, cracks appearing in the road, turning into waterspouts. It arrived in the midst of their group. A team member hauled Erik to the side and away from the beast.

Nymiria flashed forward between the pillars of water that were arcing towards them. She kicked the creature, making the attacks falter, punching it, and wrenching the creature's mouth open with her feet and arms.

"On your right!" Osmo threw a grenade into the creature's mouth. Nymira jumped away as the creature swallowed. It let out a roar, gathering power before it exploded from within.

The creature slumped and died. There was no tombstone.

How the hell is it still alive? There was no way it could survive that.

They must've run for nearly an hour before they found a wasteland in the middle of the city. There were signs of old fighting. Score marks on the ground ran through the streets. There were burn marks from fire, and the ground had been pulled up in different areas in spears.

The blood and bodies were gone, but a battle had shaped this land. There was only one building that had been largely unaffected, a tower that reached up into the roots above.

Erik spotted a ring and amulet on the ground near the epicenter of the destruction. He grabbed them, shoving them into a pocket, and ran for the building with the others. Harrod watched backward as others moved through the tower. He heard fighting on the upper floors as creatures within the building fled and ran away in the path of new inhabitants.

The tower was laid out in a square. There were six rooms on the first floor. A foyer as one walked in, four empty rooms at each corner, and a set of stairs at the rear of the building that led higher.

The building was scarred and showed its age, but it was also made of three-inch-thick compressed stone.

Erik glanced out of the door as the last team members piled in and started to barricade it.

He headed for the stairs, but Tully grabbed his shoulder.

"What?" he growled, throwing her hand off.

"Doing my job, sir." She planted her feet, staring at him.

Rugrat stood off to her side with three guards.

Harrod passed, frowning.

Erik turned his burning glare to the ground and walked past her to where Rugrat stood, noticing Davos and Jo behind him.

Fuck. He kicked a piece of rubble, kicking it only a few feet. He moved to a wall.

Body is taxed to hell with the dungeon core's shards. It's taking me months to heal, and big fucking whoop, I can't use healing spells even if I wanted to. Fucking waste of a healing potion, Erik, you idiot.

He gritted his teeth, wanting to smack himself as he pulled out a healing potion and drank it.

He breathed through the pain, the healing potion stitching him back together as he gripped the barrel of his rifle, his breaths slow and forced as he looked at the ceiling.

Tully had left at some point and returned.

"Building is secure. The Sha group are heading up top to see where the hell we are."

Kameela blinked against the light, her goggles adjusting to it as she stepped out with her rifle. Harrod and Edmond fanned out to her sides. The Alvans moved their own group out to cover the area.

The tower rose out of the ground, poking up through a wooded area. Kameela and the Alvans climbed out of the windows.

An Alvan shot a creature that looked the same as the vines that had twined together to create trees and link an overarching jungle cover.

A beast ran out of its burrow. Kameela fired. Her round shot stopped it before it cleared its hole.

She could taste and smell the powder through her headdress. She tossed the rifle into her storage ring and had another rifle in her hands before the creature rested its head on the ground for the last time. She was tempted to shoot it again, but remembered that creatures in the sub-realm didn't show tombstones.

The other creatures hid or ran from the noise.

They waited several seconds before lowering their weapons.

"Up you go, Edmond, Harrod."

Harrod helped Edmond up, and the Alvans sent up people through the trees with him.

They'd barely been up there a second, just long enough for Edmond to check the map updated, before he dropped down again.

They hurried back to the top of the stone tower jutting out of the ground, covered by the vine-trees.

Darkness greeted her once again as they passed the Alvan guards and stepped deeper into the tower. They descended to an empty floor. Edmond sat at a broken table, studying his map with Kameela.

"So, where are we?" Roska asked, pulling off her helmet and walking to the table.

Edmond coughed and put his map away before she could see its markings. Kameela frowned. *What is he doing?*

"We're supposed to work *together*." Roska rested her hand on her weapon grip, tension spiking as the Alvans subtly moved their backs to walls and held their weapons a little higher.

"Why are you talking for your leaders? Why are you so interested in *my* maps?"

"You got something you need to say?"

"We had an agreement when we came in here. Now we need a new one—one to get us out of here."

Roska laughed. It grew as she shook her head, moving her forearm to rest on top of her buttstock. She could flick up her rifle in a second.

Adrenaline surged through Kameela's veins. *What are you doing, you idiot?*

Edmond smiled, his eyes dead as his hands rested on a matchlock.

"Let's get something clear here, Dujardin."

Edmond dropped the smile.

"I have one mission: get Erik and Rugrat back home, safe and sound. Anything that stops me in that will find itself face down in a shallow grave. Play your games with your sects and clans. You're not part of the Empire. I don't know you, don't care for you much. Says something when all the captains of your elite fleet turn on you, doesn't it? Honestly, that's your problem. Mine is I'm stuck in this shithole with you. So, I don't care if you keep your map, don't care if you fucking jerk off while balancing on your head. You get us to that transition point, and we're good. I'll do a contract right here and now."

"Contracts won't work here. We're not in the Ten Realms," the skeleton, Egbert, said as he walked into the room. "Also, probably why we don't see tombstones on dead creatures, and we're not getting experience from killing them. Harrod?"

"That's correct." The big man nodded.

"In the Ten Realms, contracts bind us. Out here they don't. If they install a new Marshal of the Sha before you return, then they are just fine and can do as they want. It also explains how they could turn against you in here," Egbert said.

Edmond's hand tightened on his pistol.

Egbert laughed lightly and opened his hands. "Children these days. Roska, ease up. I could kill them in a second."

"Here is the agreement, and since we're not in the Ten Realms, we'll have to do something strange; we'll have to *trust* one another. Novel concept, isn't it? You can keep hold of your map if you can guide us to a transition point that will get us out of here—the one you were talking about that shouldn't be guarded as much because it's in the Undercity. We will work together to keep each other safe in our travels. Once we are back in the Seventh Realm, we can each go our separate ways, or even together." Egbert's jovial tone turned serious. "Either we stick together and get the hell out of this place, or we can save the sub-realm from having to kill us themselves."

He looked at the Sha members. Kameela wanted nothing more than to smack that thoughtful expression off Edmond's face with her buttstock.

"Very well. Compasses won't work in here, so we have to work off the maps. We can rest up and head out when we are ready. The transition point is a week's travel in that direction." Edmond pointed off into the distance. "This is the Violet Sky Realm, so any travel is bound to take two or three times that amount of time. Tell your lords that I do not appreciate being looked down upon and being forced to talk to their guard captain and familiar."

Roska clenched her jaw.

Egbert bowed. "I will convey your words. I would also say, never talk down to our lords again. They have done more for us than you could ever know. They might not be the most eloquent, or fashionable, or even the cleanest of lords, but they are ours and you should respect that."

Edmond nodded. "I understand."

"Good." Egbert turned and indicated to the Special Team members. They left the room, leaving Harrod, Kameela, and Edmond.

Kameela waved Harrod to the doorway. He stood there, acting as guard as Edmond activated a sound cancellation formation.

Edmond continued to study his map. "We'll have to watch them closely. As he said, there are no contract—" Her slap cocked his head right around to the other side.

He jumped back, stunned, and hurt deeper than a slap ever could.

"Edmond Dujardin, what a petty little man you have become," she spat, her pointed finger and the fire in her eyes a stronger weapon than any rifle. "They put their lives on the line for us and you're playing power games?" She snatched the map from his hands, zooming it out.

"Kameela."

"Just what I thought. What happened to you?" She snorted and threw the map back at him. It was like she was seeing him for the first time. *Who are you? Where's my Eddie?* It hurt so.

"I became the Marshal. Someone had to." He gritted his teeth.

"Had to? There were dozens of others that could have done it. You said you would pass control to a mixed council to blend the clans together!"

"That was before."

"Before Bartan was killed? That was twenty years ago, Edmond! You never wanted any of this. You never wanted the role of Marshal. You hated the petty power games, but here we are and you're playing them yet again."

"I'm trying to protect us! Can't you see that?" Edmond yelled.

"You're isolating the *only* people we can rely on?" Kameela yelled back. "We are all you have right now. They were right about one thing. You are *not* the Marshal of the Sha anymore. You're just a man, a gun hand."

She saw him grinding his teeth, the seething rage under his skin.

"Why do you care so much about a position you didn't care about?" She shook her head. "I thought you were the same person you were when we were just a party in the Third Realm. But maybe it was just me that remained the same."

"Kameela," Edmond said, his face sinking.

A sad smile rose on her face as she looked away. "It was foolish of me. When we were trapped down here, hiding in the ruins, I was scared, but excited. The weight of the Sha was gone. We could be a party again. I guess we know now why you couldn't pass the Eighth Realm Trial. How focused have you been on doing tasks for others, for running their external wheels instead of taking your own path and pushing that instead?"

She turned and walked away.

"I didn't lie, Kameela," Edmond said.

She turned back to him.

"There is a transition point under the Treasure Hall. The beasts will focus on the Hall instead of the transition point, so when we get there, we can split away from the Alvans. It is risky, but we'll need whatever we find in the Treasure Hall to protect ourselves for when the Sha come after us."

Kameela's heart twisted at his words.

He shifted his feet and cocked his head to the side, his finery in shambles. "When Bartan died, I couldn't turn over my position to someone else. He was killed taking an attack meant for me. That much is true. What I never told anyone else was that the wound was inflicted by a Sha weapon. The attack came from behind, using gunpower, instead of from where the assassins were attacking us from."

"The assassins?"

Edmond shook his head. "They didn't even know they were attacking a Sha convoy. They thought we were rich merchants."

"Then you mean..."

"A Sha killed Bartan. How could I turn power over to someone else when I didn't know if it was the person that had him killed? I could only trust the people that didn't want power. I had to try to weaken them and figure out who it was. I could only trust you and my teammates." He waved to Harrod, who continued to watch the door. "You didn't want power; you wanted adventure. I was the war leader of the Sha. Bartan was supposed to rule in peace. How much peace have we found since founding the Sha? And now... Well, now it will crumble and collapse. I am a man with the secrets of the Sha, and you are all my closest allies. Even if we make it out of here, our lives are in danger."

"That means you should leave the power games behind."

"The world is not that black and white, Kameela.

Her thoughts and emotions were a jumbled mess.

"That is why we need to disrupt Louis' plans as much as possible and we have to make sure that the Alvans know we're in charge."

She saw it then, how he shifted and tilted the scales of relationships. "It's all an equation to you, gain and loss."

"That is how the Ten Realms work."

Kameela turned away from him, her eyes shaking as she left the room. She wished he would call out to her, that he would run up to grab her arm, but he let her leave. It hurt, just how much she felt his words were *right*.

She closed her eyes outside the door, thinking of the time they had shared after a job, laughing in bars, walking to the next job. When relationships weren't weighed against one another, when emotions ruled, and logic was a distant second or third.

"You okay?" Esther asked. She must've been waiting for her to finish talking to Edmond.

"Yeah, just tired." Kameela smiled, realizing where she was.

"Okay," Esther said.

"He's in there." Kameela gestured to the room.

Harrod followed her.

She found Robert sitting in a room, watching the streets.

"Alvans aren't too happy with the state of things," he said into the room, not turning around.

"I doubt they would be." Kameela moved closer to him. They sat on chairs.

"You think there is something odd about their lords?" Robert pitched his voice low.

"You noticed as well," Harrod said.

"What do you mean?" Kameela asked.

"When we were in that last place, Erik needed to jump on a wall to get enough power to get up to the second floor. He's supposed to be strong as hell physically, right?"

"Yes."

"And they have both been in the rear with all of their guards around them."

"They are lords of Alva," Kameela said.

"Yes, who took down airships, if the information from the lower realms is correct. Yet now they stay meekly in the back?"

"Does nothing for us to think about their condition. All we need to care about is getting out of this place and back to the Realms."

"What about when we do?" Robert turned his head over.

"Then we can figure out our next steps from there." She stood.

"Where are you going?" Harrod asked.

"To try to build bridges."

"I'll come with you."

Kameela halted Harrod with a hand on his shoulder. "No, you get some rest. You have been awake longer than all of us and I don't think we will have much rest in our future." She headed for the door. "Robert, make sure he doesn't waste it by messing around in his notebooks."

Harrod clicked his tongue.

"You heard her." Robert said.

Kameela went down the stairs, passing Alvans watching out of different windows. Some leaned against walls, checking their weapons or getting some food and drink into them.

"Where is Roska?" she asked one of them.

"Second floor, in a meeting."

"Thank you."

She headed downward again. There were several floors that were empty of all living creatures. *Maybe bringing Harrod would have been nice.* She kept a hand on her pistol as she walked down the stairs.

Alvans greeted her as she passed below. A guard standing outside of the room knocked on the door as she approached and opened the door.

Egbert was reading a book, chortling to himself. The fire wolf was on one side, sleeping next to the fire imp who snored and hiccupped with his open mouth, splayed out on the other side, his belly rising, falling and jolting with his throaty breaths.

The doors opened. Erik, Rugrat, another female Alvan, and Roska were inside, their helmets on a table they had found.

"Kameela?" Roska bit out the word.

"I wanted to apologize for how Edmond reacted, he's..." *No longer the person I knew.* "Got a lot to deal with right now."

"We're all dealing with a situation we weren't expecting," Roska said, but her words softened.

Kameela walked into the room. "I wanted to offer what information I know. Those transforming creatures that screech and howl, they are called Chimora. They usually work in roaming groups. They eat the leftovers from fights, and they use the Earth element to transform. The demi-humans are called Rin. Their beast forms are called Behir. They specialize in one element. The creature that captured your person in a pod and was killed by the Piercers, they're called Jorken." She waited as the second woman in the room wrote down the names into a notebook.

"You might have noticed that tombstones don't appear over the dead creatures, and you don't get experience here? The tombstones only happen to people and creatures that are from the Ten Realms. When we return to the Ten Realms, you will get experience for the creatures you've killed."

"What about quests?" Rugrat asked.

"If you have a quest to complete, it should still register. Say you were to increase your elemental cultivation. Yeah, that should be fine. You would just drag in a lot of the surrounding elements to complete the changes ignited by the completion of the quest."

Rugrat nodded.

Kameela thought of extending her senses to them but held herself back. It was seen as highly rude and could break her hope of forming closer ties.

She didn't miss the shadow that passed over their faces at the mention of elemental cultivation.

Should I tell them about the Treasure Hall?

"Anything else we should know?" Roska asked.

"That is all I know right now." Kameela smiled.

"Thank you for letting us know. Either Rugrat or myself will attend meetings with Edmond in the future, but I think it would be good if you two kept a clear line of communication. We can only rely on ourselves here," Erik said.

"Understood. Also, I would suggest that if your people have time that they focus on tempering their bodies. The Violet Sky Realm is dense in elemental energy, and it will increase how quickly they recover from fatigue. Cultivating one's body here will be dozens of times faster than in the Seventh Realm."

"Thank you for your advice," Erik said.

Kameela bowed her head and left.

At least they seem reasonable compared to Edmond. A spark of anger burned in her eyes as she turned toward the stairs and began her climb back up. Already, she was keeping his secret about their destination.

Erik leaned against a pile of rubble. After the meeting and Kameela's information they had split up and everyone had gone to ground.

George had padded into the room and slept against Rugrat on a sleeping pad, his gear and boots next to his head as he held Big Momma from his chest down between his legs.

Davin walked into the room, smacking his lips, and rubbing his face. He looked at Erik with his big eyes.

Erik reached into his dump pouch, finding the amulet and ring he had picked up outside the building. He activated the storage formation in the bag, but the ring and the amulet wouldn't go inside. *Storage items?*

He pulled out a small meat pie and tossed it to Davin. He unhinged his jaw, catching the morsel and closed his eyes, chewing.

"Shpank you!" Davin said, heading over to curl up next to George.

"Don't talk with your mouth full." Erik shook his head and pulled out the two storage devices.

The ring was simple, inset with emeralds. The amulet was as big as a pocket watch and had formations carved into it. He would need to check, but it looked like it increased the power of attack spells.

He turned the amulet around. Looking closer, he could see that a simple storage ring had been placed into the center just like part of a formation.

He checked inside the emerald ring first. There were a few mana stones, a collection of weapons, and some bloodied sets of armor that showed signs of how their wearers had died.

Chimora corpses in their original form were in various stages of eating. There were dozens of high-grade variant monster cores of different elemental energies. Plants had been tossed in as well.

Doesn't look like they were an alchemist. The ingredients were tossed about haphazardly and weren't stored properly. Being in a storage device had saved them, but the harvesting was poor.

Several worn and half-repaired formations were close at hand.

A collection of bodies and items from the sub-realm were the only other things of note.

The monster cores would help the Special Team temper their bodies. They would need to be purified more than a monster core from the Ten Realms, but variant cores were a rare treasure and were always of use to body cultivators.

Erik turned to the amulet, and the hidden storage ring.

Inside, things were a bit more ordered. Powerful weapons and a few spell scrolls lay ready for use. It had few remaining alchemical concoctions and empty pill containers and potion bottles.

Is that...? Erik looked at the rune card. It looked like a large bookmark, but was carved with dense formations and runic lines.

Erik continued searching, finding a few sets of armor and clothes all the same size that must have been for the previous owner. There were also dozens of bookshelves filled with books, and tools used to turn Piercer skin into pages.

Writing tools and a book made with Piercer skin had been shoved into the amulet hurriedly with bedding, a lamp, and the remains of a meal.

Erik noticed a map and pulled it out of the handmade book.

The map showed a large section of the underground city. Erik combined it with his own map, expanding his understanding of the area.

I'll make sure the others get a copy when they wake up. He slipped the maps into different storage rings, his personal one and the hidden one in his boot.

He checked the book and opened it. It was more a collection of pages that had been roughly sewn together. Erik had to take care to not let the pages fall out.

"The journal of Lezaar Pipallis."

"I'm trapped, that much is clear to me. The rune card stopped glowing several weeks ago. Long enough for me to make these pages. I really should have invested in a few books to write in instead of spending my time reading up on magical tomes. At least I know enough to pull these pages together so I might have something to write on. I guess this all started when we found the rune card on a One-Star mission. We didn't know what it was for a long time. Emi was able to figure it out. We figured that we would sneak into the Violet Sky Realm. Get some loot. And then return to the Ten Realms and sell the rune card to the highest bidder as a retirement gift."

Erik kept reading. The One-Star party of heroes had travelled to the transition point in the Ten Realms by foot and gained access to the sub-realm. When they arrived in the undercity, they were attacked almost immediately. As they fought, other creatures were attracted by their mana-based attacks.

They lost two of their friends there, running away from the beasts and sealing their mana. They had tried to survive in the undercity, losing party members to the monsters that had claimed the city.

There were several sketches of the different animals, how they interacted, and even information on their habits.

"Chimora, are tenacious little beasts, but their greatest weakness is food. We cooked some Ka'tell meat (Best to add some leaf of Oril some salt and blackstone for flavoring)." Erik checked the ring again, finding cooked meat, spices, and herbs.

"They just appeared, roaming in their broods as they do. We fled as soon as we heard their screeching. They fell silent when they reached our camp, eating what was left of our meal. A few days later, they started howling again. We threw out some meat, and they grew silent. They warned us of creatures in the area, allowing us to avoid or kill them. Always, we left an offering to the Chimora. It was only when an armored mole, a favorite predator of the Chimora, ate into the ranks that they fled. While they are annoying little shits, they can save your life.

"After killing a flowering Jorken, we made an incredible discovery. As

Jorken grow, they gain more pods, and flowers that attack with various elemental properties. They can release blasts of lighting, flame, a hail of stone, and a poisonous smoke. After killing the beast, we opened its single flower to find beast cores in the stem. It appears that they consume a creature, using their body to sustain themselves and their core to turn the pod into a flower. We found another flowering Jorken and threw a mana stone shard at the beast. Piercers fell in droves, killing the Jorken, and most of them died in the process. We stored the mana stone shard and collected their materials. It was a fine harvest. We had food and cores for weeks."

The story went on, talking about how the group was whittled down until only Lezaar was left alive. He took up making pages from Piercers to create a journal. *He had no one to talk to and everything wanted to kill him.* Erik sighed and shook his head. He survived for a year before he was the only one left.

Suddenly, the writing changed, becoming erratic and larger and Erik needed more time to decipher it.

"I found a library! It must have been one of the academies from before the Violet Sky Realm collapsed! I read to my heart's content! There were entire bookshelves on body cultivation. I will take them all with me. Though, the most interesting books were on the purpose of the Violet Sky Realm and the Ten Realms. They were built to train us, to create fighters against a group called the Ravagers, or the Devourers, or the Devourers are the leaders of the Ravagers. I must read more!"

Erik sat forward as he kept reading.

"A group of Blandshlagg's appeared the other night. They are a group of hound-looking creatures. Their head is a series of tentacles that taste the air as their stomachs open in a mouth. Their evolved versions looked like hunched, headless people with worms sprouting from their necks and a mouth on their stomach.

"They hunted a group of Chimora that brought a group of Rin and Behir looking. I had to escape. I ran into an area I haven't been in before. The area looked flattened, leaving only hills behind, and the elements were so thick they were choking. I nearly headed in deeper when one of the hills moved.

"The hills were covered in dragons! Different broods controlled different areas. Several were along the path of demi-human. They were gathered around a massive building, sleeping and cultivating the elements. It must be some grand elemental gathering formation! Rin as large as the Academy tower in Calite rested there. Flowering Jorken huddled together with tens of budding flowers. The dragon that woke up lowered its head. Lightning crackled between its silver antlers and blinded me. When I could see again, the creatures that had been fighting were killed.

"Dragonlings raced out from their nests to claim the prizes as the dragon shifted its head back under the rubble and continued its cultivating."

Erik flipped to the next page.

"I have spent the last week moving between hideouts and away from what I'll call the beast lair. When I've had time, I've been reading the books from the library. There are records on the purpose of this station. Thousands of people passed through here during the War for Ascension. It was built by the Elves and Gnomes. They allied with one another to fight the Ravagers who sought to cultivate the elements and mana without care. This was the station where they gathered, working together, launching attacks on other planets.

"There were ten planets under their protection, and there was fighting on every planet. The Gnome and Elven leaders became Ascendants, who were extremely powerful. They worked together and created the Ten Realms, bound the realms together with magic and the elements. They drew in the elements and created mana. Gnomes and Elves were transformed into their image and imprinted with their teachings. Passing through the Ten Realms, they held on. Then the Gnome and Elf Ascendants disappeared. The Gnome and Elf races were long-lived, but they didn't reproduce that fast. Then, it seems that humans started appearing in the Realms. No mana, no elements, but they remained in the image of the forebears, able to use both and reinforce the ten realms."

Erik looked up as Egbert walked into the room.

"What are you reading?" he asked.

"I need Roska—right now, or whoever isn't asleep and on watch." Erik got up, cradling the book.

"What's gotten into you?"

"This... this book... it... the Ten Realms..." Erik scanned through the page. "It was built to train us, to make us stronger."

"Well, I don't know about that."

"Just get everyone. I'll be in the meeting room." Erik kept reading as he walked toward the room. Egbert shrugged and walked off.

Erik put the book on the table, continuing to read through Lezaar's findings. He pulled out the bookshelves, finding the books that had been referenced and opened them in front of him. Team members arrived, with Davos and Egbert being the last two.

"Egbert, record everything in these books." Erik waved to the table and stepped away.

Egbert pulled out books and formation plates, making sure no mana leaked out.

"This place, the Violet Realm is a station, a way point between planets, or realms. It was created by the Gnomes and the Elves who allied with one another to protect their worlds. Gnomes used technology and the Elves could cast high level magic and had an incredible ability to separate mana from the elements. Between them, they were able to raise several powerful people to the level of Devourer, translated: a really scary powerful motherfucker.

"They established the Ten Realms as we know it. These way stations were used to launch attacks on the other realms, realms controlled by their enemy, the Ravagers, creatures that focus on utilizing the power of the elements. Seems that they come from worlds that have thin or no mana at all. The Violet Sky Realm was the scene of a great battle between the Elves and Gnomes against the Ravager monsters. The Elves and Gnomes retreated back to the Ten Realms. They were losing a great number of their stations and didn't have the numbers to hold them anymore."

The team members looked at one another.

"So, what does that mean?" Davos asked.

"I'm not really sure. I've always thought that the Ten Realms had to be made. It is too orderly once you look at the core of it. We know that there were Gnomes at one time through Alva. Clearly, there were more of them than just the group that made the city. Lezaar thinks that the Ten Realms was designed to train people to fight the Ravagers."

"Lezaar?" Davos asked

"He's uhh, well he was a guy that was here previously and wrote that book." Erik pointed at it. Egbert was flipping through the pages, creating a breeze.

"What are you doing?" Erik asked

"Reading." Egbert picked up another book and began flipping through it as well.

"You can read that fast?"

"Yeah, just don't like to do it with fun books, you know? Ruins it if you finish it all in a few seconds." He snapped closed the book in his hands. "These books agree with what you're saying. This is a mustering point to gather forces to support attacks on other realms. It was overwhelmed, and the Gnomes and Elves retreated."

"So, if there are Elves and Gnomes in the Ten Realms, why haven't we seen them? And who or what are these Ravagers?"

"Seems to be creatures that harvest the elements to increase their overall power. Without mana, they go through alterations and mutations that make them stronger but also leave them deformed," Egbert said.

"This information will be crucial to Alva. We always wondered about the origin and the history of the Ten Realms. This is the origin of everything," Erik said.

"It doesn't change our current position much. But the diagrams and the information on the beasts down here will be of great help." Egbert went back to where Erik had been reading, reviewing the beast diagrams and notes. "I will make copies of the books. We can share them out between everyone."

Then we will only need one of us to make it back alive to get the information to Alva.

Erik nodded.

"That's our new mission. Egbert, keep going through the books and see what else you can learn."

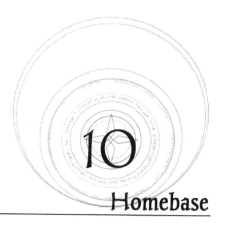

10

Homebase

"Council leader." Storbon coughed as Delilah looked out the air force's hangars into the Alvan Empire.

She smiled to herself, suppressing it as she looked back with an innocent expression, lowering her spyglass. "Is there a problem, Major?" It was hard to keep her expression, seeing the hardened Major's flush.

Some distinctly non-work-related thoughts flashed through her mind.

"Please mind your footing, I don't much want to have to jump down the mountain after you."

"Oh, well, I'd feel safe if it was the Major catching me." She looked over the empire and raised her spyglass again, biting her lip behind her arm.

She followed the growing black line that spread from King's Hill along the main trade route to the growing trading outposts and on to the inner and outer cities, linking the entire empire together.

"What do you think of the rail system, Storbon?" she asked.

"Honestly?"

"When have I enjoyed being lied to?"

"I don't get it. We have carriages that travel quickly and a teleportation network so people can move through the empire freely."

"The carriages are expensive to make and are unreliable. The teleportation network is impressive and quick, but it requires mana stones or monster cores for people to use it. They are not inexpensive. The rail network takes some time to lay down and costs more up front, but it can run off ambient mana, wood, and coal, making it much cheaper to produce and run. It is reliable, can move much more than the carriages, and it can keep running through the day and night. What do people use to mark their wealth in the First Realm?"

He sunk into thought. "Land you own, the number of beasts that you have."

"Exactly. Horses and beasts of burden, or those that can produce products, are highly valued. It costs a lot to maintain a rideable mount. That's why most of the First Realm kingdoms only have riding beasts for the knights and well-supplied mercenaries. The trains will be everyone's horses and they will only need to pay for them when they need to travel. It will connect the farming communities to the cities, decreasing shipping costs and times, allowing the farmers to supply the cities and the cities to supply the technology the farmers need."

"That makes sense. I forgot how they deal in terms of coppers and silvers, and with gold being rare..." He looked at his own gear. "This would be worth more than a knight could make in several lifetimes."

"Right. Our biggest problem right now is that most people in the Alvan Empire are simple farmers or traders. There are many people from the higher realms that want to move into the empire. We need to strengthen our people in a way that inspires their growth instead of expecting handouts."

"It sounds complicated."

"Best to think of it as a service. We provide a service for them that they repay in taxes and fees with a common look toward their betterment. We're all in this together and we have to support those that would fall behind."

Delilah lowered her glass, falling silent, looking over it all. There was still so much to do. *We did all of this and there is so much to be done in the future.*

"Council leader," Kanoa said in his deep voice.

She smiled and bowed to the man who saluted her. The big Hawaiian smiled and lowered his hand. Assistants flanked him on either side.

"How have you been, brigadier general?" she asked as she walked with him, heading into the hangar.

Kestrels were loading up and heading out on patrol. Waiting Sparrows and Kestrels were tended in their aviaries, thankfully behind sound canceling formations.

"Busy, as we all are." He grinned. "Training was ramped up as well as breeding for our different aerial beasties. The new weapons we introduced in our last engagement have matured, giving us missiles, stronger bombs, and railguns. It has been an adjustment, but our people have done well. Patrols and scouting have become our main missions. And finding Special Teams and Close Protection Details in *interesting* places." He raised an eyebrow to Storbon.

"We seem to get lost in the strangest places, near enemy compounds and sect cities." The two men smiled at one another.

"So, the aerial technology has matured?"

"In a way that scares me as much as it's brilliant. Miss Delfina Lucero is an amazing woman."

Delilah snuck a glance out of the corner of her eye.

"Yes, quite. More of you Earthers."

"Bah, you think that we're the only ones with wild ideas? Lucero might have great ideas, but the Terrible Trio gave breath to destruction in a way that shakes my bones." His smile went against his words.

With enough teachers in different disciplines, Qin, Taran, Delfina, and Julilah had turned fully toward increasing Alva's combat abilities through Qin and Julilah's formations, Taran's smithing, and Delfina's extensive mechanical background from Earth.

The teleportation formation left them in a non-descript hallway.

"We have to walk from here." He led the way, passing patrols, soldiers jogging through the mountainous labyrinth.

Windows opened up to landing bays, training areas and testing areas.

"How has the transition been, bringing all the development into the mountain?" Delilah asked.

"Changing anything is a pain, but people seem to have got used to it. It has made things easier in terms of security. The warship docks on the water floor are under construction. The speed that we can build and destroy would make people on Earth's head's spin." Kanoa grinned.

"I'm stunned by it myself. I just okayed an expansion of the city, with the population gain we need more room." Delilah shook her head. "I never thought that Alva would seem *small*."

Kanoa let out a deep rumbling laugh as they turned a corner to face a checkpoint. It was built like a bunker into the four-person-wide corridor. A switchback doorway, two slits on either side.

Their mirth chilled as they walked through the hundred-meter killzone to the slits.

"Identification medallions?" A soldier's voice relayed through the corridor.

Delilah pressed hers to a medallion formation in the wall. Kanoa following afterwards.

"Thank you, have a good day."

Kanoa led the way through the switch-back, past two murder holes before they went through the bunkers door, passing down through the straight corridor and out the other side.

"I know that we talked about increased security measures." Delilah trailed off.

"Better safe than sorry when we control the strongest known weapon systems. There are many groups that would love to get their hands on our tech or people." Kanoa's words were soft, but they made Delilah's chest tighten.

Two more check points and they reached a hallway filled with crafter types in military uniforms moving from one room to the next. They parted ahead of Delilah and Kanoa.

"Medallions." A close protection detail soldier asked as they reached a door no one was walking into.

Delilah and Kanoa presented the medallions.

"Thank you," He nodded to the other soldier. They opened the door, revealing what looked like a mix between a science lab and wood workshop. One large bay window looking down on a massive workspace, desks lining the walls and set up as stations throughout the space.

"Eyo." Taran smiled from where he stood with Qin, Julilah, and Delfina. Around them, different items were covered in sheets to hide the projects underneath.

"Morning," Delilah said. The door closed and sealed behind Kanoa, a sound canceling formation activating. "So, I hear that you've completed the designs for our warships?"

"I hope you brought your credit card." Delfina pulled a sheet off a model.

Swept back Lambda wings met with a boxy body, large nozzles on one end and turrets dotting the spine and belly of the craft.

"What is that?"

"That is the dream, our air-carrier prototype." Delfina said.

"Two internal flight decks for landing and launching craft, they are on different floors so even if one is taken out the other can continue to operate. Lighter armaments primarily for defense instead of offensive operations."

"What are those?" Delilah pointed to the nozzles sticking out the rear of the craft.

"Rocket engines. They take combustible compounds, mix them together, and blast them out the back. Allowing the craft to move without formation support, saving us on mana drain." Julilah said.

"Okay, walk me through this," Delilah said.

Taran cleared his throat. "Warships in the ten realms are little more than movable fortresses, heavy, power hungry and mana dependent. The Sha had an edge with their massive sails. Utilizing wings and rocket engines our ships will fly, not merely float, pushed on mana formations. Our warships will be much faster and less power hungry."

"With the wings we couldn't have a belt of cannons like the Sha and other ten realms warships. So we used turrets like that used on Earth warships to the spines and belly's of the craft's main body. With the defense of Alva, our missiles proved themselves, with some tweaks we've improved on their design to create more reliable ship launched versions." Qin said.

"With less mana intensive weapons and flight systems, we have more power to dedicate to mana barriers. Though building these warships is going to take a pile of materials. Most can be mass produced thankfully." Delfina shrugged and grimaced, moving her head side to side.

Delilah focused on the aircraft carrier, its sharp lines, imaging it cruising through the skies, her heart shuddered, in fear, in excitement. Everyone was looking at them and military might was a sure way to keep people focused on other problems.

"While they are expensive, with these designs we can use weaker dungeon cores to support our ships." Julilah hurried to say in the lull of conversation.

Delilah favored her with a smile. "Small mercies, and these other models?" she waved at the other sheet covered tables.

They pulled off the covers.

Delfina cleared her throat on the right side of the room. "This is our corvette design. Built for speed, light armaments with a small crew and the ability to drop bombs and with four missile tubes. Intended to be scouts, get ground forces into the fight with internal teleportation formations, or support kestrel and sparrow wings." She turned to Julilah.

"The frigate. We have turned these into missile haulers. They're around seventy-five meters long and forty wide. A little slower than the corvettes. We're talking about five times faster than the current airships. Can drop bombs, launch twenty missiles, medium sized turrets."

Qin cleared her throat. "The Destroyer is a multi-purpose warship. A mix of medium and heavy turrets with two wings of kestrels and four wings of sparrows, it hosts a heavy missile payload, barriers nearly four times stronger than the frigate's armor."

"The cruiser is a killer. Super heavy triple gun turrets. The largest we've made. Largest missile load of any ship." Taran's deep voice was solemn his eyes flicking from the model to Delilah. Armor twice as strong as the Destroyers, mana barriers based off of Alva's own ground based designs. The only thing more armored is the carrier in certain places. Its meant to tear ships apart from kilometers away, or in knife fighting range."

Silence settled across the room. Delilah's eyes passing over the warships, her mind filled with them cutting through the sky.

"In several years, they'll pay for themselves making mana stones," Taran said.

"You mean decades," Delilah said wryly. "Begin construction immediately, focus on the ships we need to defend Alva first."

"That would be some of the corvettes, a few cruisers, frigates and Destroyers." Kanoa said.

"See to it, everyone is looking at us and we need to show our strength." Delilah let out a sigh. "Now you've squeezed the coffers dry, I have to attend a meeting of the Alvan heads, as I so love talking about harvest rotas and trade route contracts. Good work everyone." She smiled at them. "Your work here gives our military the weapons they need to defend our empire and provide security for our people."

"Just one small formation in an array," Julilah said.

Delilah spared another look at the models.

"Aren't we all." She pressed a smile together and headed out of the room.

Milo accepted the tea from the maid with a smile, she served Maria beside him and departed, sealing the doors behind her as a sound canceling formation activated.

"By now it should be done," Lord Abe Velten, Milo's father-in-law, said, sitting in one of his family estates' living room. Maria smiled, sitting next to Milo, biting her lower lip before she hid it behind her teacup.

"I wish that we could communicate with those inside the sub-realm. We placed our trust in Louis Gerard and the others, but now it is time for us to do our part." Milo drank from his cup, trying to keep the eagerness out of his voice as he glanced at Maria and then refocused on Abe.

I have missed you. All of this planning has been too long and too far apart. Milo thought.

"Caution is our greatest ally," Abe said, stroking his finely trimmed beard and mustache.

Milo coughed away his immediate words.

"Slowly, we shift opinion in our favor without the input of my sister or the recently deceased Marshal. Once Louis returns, we will succeed Dujardin and take control over the clans." Milo paused in thought. "I am scared that, upon returning, Louis Gerard will have the popular opinion on his side. We must take measures to protect against this."

"We hold all of his family's defense contracts. If he goes against us, the losses from the contracts will be extreme," Maria said.

"Of course, but he is a man of passions as much as he doesn't want to show it. He leads with his heart and once he is set on a path, it is hard to dissuade him," Milo said.

"You are correct. The less chaos there is in you assuming power, the better. If there is a fight for succession, then it will only weaken us and create greater issues in the future. Others will use it to get more concessions at the very least," Abe said.

Milo sighed.

"Do not worry, Milo. We have waited years to bring about this change. Now, we are just weeks away. We must remain strong. How go your preparations?"

"Two cruisers, three destroyers, five freighters, and fifteen corvettes have allied themselves with us. The recent fighting and the Violet Sky Realm fleet took a lot of our resources. We have moved ammunition to the loyal ships so they are fully stocked if any complications arise."

They were meant to be a defensive force to ward off others who might make trouble as they were putting the Sha Clans in order. *I hope that they are only used for defense.* He wasn't so naïve to think that if there was a force that rebelled in the clans, that they would just defend against external threats.

"Your ally among the crafters is very resourceful," Abe said.

"I will reveal who they are once this is complete. They pride themselves on their secrecy."

"We all have our hidden cards," Maria said.

"We are all united in our cause. Without that backstabbing murderer leading us, the Sha Clans can finally grow and become the clan my father hoped to create," Milo said.

"Your father was a visionary and a man with great ambition. I see that flame has remained strong within you." Abe smiled.

Milo bowed his head. "Thank you, father-in-law."

"So, what are our next moves?" Maria asked.

"Strengthen our position, make sure that our fighting forces are ready to defend our holdings, and start to approach friendly traders to sell the items we have stored up over the years. Mana stones and resources are a great bandage for any political wound." Abe laughed.

A knock at the door interrupted them.

Abe frowned, cast a wind spell on the door, and turned off the sound canceling formation inlaid into the table beside him.

The door opened to reveal one of his secretaries.

The man marched in quickly, ducking into a half bow, holding out a report folder. "There has been a change with the Black Phoenix Clan."

Milo's stomach gripped as he rose with the others.

Abe strode forward and took the report. "Speak."

"They are under attack by a united force of smaller sects from the lower realms. They can only call on a few airships. But they have focused on attacking the Black Phoenix shipyard locations."

"Desperation against the Phoenix Clan?" Milo asked.

"No, they are showing their allegiance. Each of them has roots in the lower realms. They want to become allies with the Alvans. They must be using this attack to show that they are on the Alvan's side and gain recognition. For one nation in the First Realm to create such a stir…" Abe fell quiet and waved the secretary away.

He ducked in his bow and quickly retreated, closing the door behind him.

Abe activated the formation table again.

"It seems that you will have to move up the plan to claim Alva. They are still just a minor nation in the First Realm. Now that they don't have their two lords anymore, their position will become tentative. There are sure to be others that will want to take up the position of Lord of Alva."

"Are you sure you don't want to keep them as an ally? They are such a small force."

"A small force that is capable of making gunpowder and weapons that use it. We need to secure power over them to make sure that they do as we say. There is a reason that they have not claimed any of the cities in the lower realms. They are too weak to do so. Otherwise, why would they just take resources and establish recruiting halls?"

"I have heard that they are rather popular," Maria said.

"A thing of interest. They had some power in the Fourth Realm. Of course, weaklings in the higher realms would be interested in going to the lower realms to gain position. Neither West nor Rodrigeuz have a family, to our knowledge. Without a clan, one is groundless and without allies. Family is everything. You can't trust others that are not in your family unless you have binding contracts, and there are ways around them."

"Where is Mother?" Milo asked one of the servants as he walked the halls of his estate with Maria.

"She is in the conservatory." The servant bowed.

"Thank you," Milo said.

"It has been a long day; I will freshen up and meet you for dinner afterwards?" Maria asked, her hand resting in the crook of his elbow.

"Certainly, my love." Milo smiled and kissed her.

She kissed him back, wrapping her arms around him. They looked at one another breathlessly. She stared deep into his eyes. "I missed you."

"I missed you, too." Milo smiled.

"Tell your mother I said hello." She released her hands.

Milo wanted to ask her to join him, but he saw the pain in Lily's eyes when she was around his mother. Saddened by being in her presence, he knew she was scared how she would react if he was to die.

They had been childhood friends and when their marriage was announced by their fathers. Milo had been nervous at first, but their friendship had turned to affection.

He squeezed her to him, and she returned the embrace.

"Be safe with all of this," she whispered.

"You're the one doing all the leg work." He held her lower back, separating as *business* distracted them from finer uses of their time. She traced out the design of his shirt on his chest.

"I know. You and father have done so much, working so very hard. It is the right thing to do. Justice must be served. But I don't want to lose you. Promise me that if we have to, we'll flee this place. I don't care if we have to rebuild our lives as long as we have our lives." She gripped onto his shirt, the playful veneer turning into something focused.

He traced the worry lines on her face, cursing himself for their presence. "Everything will be fine. We are doing what is right. We can set things to how they were supposed to be, get the clans to work together instead of fighting one another."

Maria pressed her lips together into a smile and kissed him. "Just be safe."

"This is the Ten Realms. It's only through our strength that we can bring around change."

"I wish that wasn't the case," Maria said.

He kissed her and released his hold. "Go and get cleaned up. I'll see you once I've seen mother."

"Okay."

She held onto his hand till the last second as they parted.

Milo continued walking through the estate, passing through echoing rooms. The conservatory was bright, filled with flowering plants with a mix of subtle scents.

He walked to where his mother sat. She stared blankly at an array of roses.

"Mother." Milo pushed his smile into his words as he knelt next to her, holding her hands. They remained cold, seemingly devoid of life.

She had declined into this state after the death of his father, barely eating or drinking, spending her time staring off into space, caring not what happened in the world around her.

"Mother, finally things are moving. I am sorry that I have not seen you these past months, but I had to make sure that everything was in place." Milo bowed his head. He took a breath as he felt tears well up in his eyes.

He looked at her, tears running down his face.

"Mother, finally, that murderer will be brought to justice. I didn't want to say more because it might shock you, but I cannot hold on to the lie any longer. Father was killed from behind with a Sha weapon."

He swore he felt her hands twitch, but he couldn't find any traces of emotion or clarity in her vision.

"It wasn't the assassins that went after the Marshal. No, the Marshal didn't want to lose his power. He orchestrated it and used a hidden weapon up his sleeve to kill father. Then he blamed it on the assassins and killed them to silence his actions. He killed a man he called brother without a second of regret." He bowed his head as he rubbed the back of his mother's hands with his thumbs. "I have worked all of these years since his death, never forgetting his actions for one minute. I intend to bring him to justice. In the Violet Sky Realm, where the Ten Realms hold power no longer, they will remove his tyranny, and we will end the division between the clans. We will bring peace and grow together. I will carry out father's wishes to see a united Sha Clan as he hoped for before he was betrayed."

Zala Leblanc furrowed her brows, her lip shaking for a half second before it disappeared.

Milo looked up from her hands to find her blank expression.

"Mother, do not worry. Father will rest easy now. We will develop the clans properly."

He had hoped to see something more in her expression, but she kept looking at the roses. He sighed, standing and released her hands. Hhe kissed her on the cheek.

"Maria sends her love. She has just returned. I hope you have a nice day." He pulled out a blanket and put it around her shoulders. "Make sure you don't get a chill."

He rubbed her shoulder, grimacing before leaving the conservatory.

"There has been no change." Ranko's voice projected into Stassov's ear by her sound transmission device.

Stassov bared her teeth. "Go through it again."

"When we arrived, the ships were firing into the ground, collapsing sections of the forest and opening up the undercity. They angered the beasts underneath and slaughtered them. They searched the area under their ship, returned some time later, and left."

"For what reason?"

"I cannot be sure, Captain," Ranko said.

Stassov bit the inside of her cheek. "And since then, they have been going between different points of interest?"

"That's correct."

There must have been some prize.

"Also, Captain, we lost seven people." Ranko ground his teeth.

"Lost them, how?"

"The ground is much deadlier than the air. There are many powerful creatures and we cannot use our true power to fight them."

Stassov hated losing clan members to the sub-realm, but she had her mission and it seemed that the Sha had their own internal issues.

We won't get another opportunity like this.

"I will send you replacements. Make sure you continue to follow the Sha."

"Yes, Captain." She cut the channel and called Commander Chmilenko.

11

Undercity Critters

Four days quickly passed in the undercity as the special team and Edmond's party rested and upgraded their gear to fit the situation.

"Stealth and mana gathering formations," Erik said, checking the formation stack and attaching it to the harness on his leg, much like a drop-leg holster.

"The less we have to fight, the better. We have a lot of ground to cover and little time in which to do it," Egbert said. He wore Alvan Army caster robes and armor, with stacks on either leg and a stack backpack, allowing him to carry four stack formations within.

He pulled on a helmet, the fire of his eyes illuminating the visor from behind.

Erik checked his rifle, seating a magazine into it and pulling on the cocking handle. He looked around the room. George wore his battle armor, and Davin held a mage's staff of blood-red chipped obsidian that glowed faintly, warming the surrounding area. Rugrat checked his rifle and looked over.

"Well, let's do this."

They grouped up with the others and moved to the front of the tower. All of them had Piercer blood on them to ward off the dropping creatures.

Esther and a special team member ran across to a half-broken tower, watching the area. The next group ran past them to another point further on.

So it went, with them making a line across the broken area in the direction that Edmond had pointed out.

Erik ran with Egbert, racing past the groups and into the denser building cover, bypassing roaming Chimora.

Kameela spotted a Jorken hiding underneath a broken building, its pods spread out just below the ground. There was only a slight disturbance where the vine had passed to show where the pods were hidden, waiting for a victim.

They circled through several broken buildings and continued onward.

They were crossing a main street in twos when a group of Chimora noticed them.

The special team members threw out meat and kept up their progress. The Chimora went quiet as they fought over the scraps.

They'd be cute if their screams didn't mean death.

Roska signalled back as they all ducked into buildings.

Erik had his rifle up as he leaned against a broken wall inside the building. Egbert was beside him, peering over.

A growl cut down the street, followed by others.

A group of Rin with their weapons at the ready loped down the road, looking around. The smaller demi-humans and their Benir descendants followed behind.

One jostled another, crashing into another building, causing it to collapse. It shook free of the building, and they continued running in the direction of the Chimora.

They grew distant, and Erik relaxed and started pushing forward again.

Wait, they have their own Chimora following.

The screeches rang out, and the Rin roared from behind.

"Shit." Erik and Egbert moved to the front of the building.

"Engage them!"

Erik looked down the street. The Benir were trying to turn, smashing into the buildings on either side.

The team opened fire with their rifles and threw grenades into the creatures.

They died instantly, blocking the other Benir and Rin.

A Rin jumped over a Benir and was hit with multiple rounds. It was pushed back. Faint wounds showed on its body before two grenades went off beside the Rin, smashing them through a building and out of view.

Formation-less guns are too weak down here.

"Aussie, peel-back!" Roska yelled.

Those at the rear turned and ran toward the front, passing others, then the second last, then the third.

They retreated up the street as a red Rin jumped onto a wall and landed on the street. He hit the ground, gouts of flame shooting through the broken street and cracking the buildings on either side.

George roared, sending a blast of fire back in his direction and halted the progress of the cracks as more Rin used the buildings to climb over the trapped Benir.

They shrugged off the incoming fire. It slowed them but didn't stop them. The grenades were the only thing to leave lasting damage.

George's attack struck the fiery Rin, defeating his fire-coated spear. Rugrat's rifle fired, piercing the eye of a yellow Rin, making its head snap backwards.

"Aim for the eyes. Their skin is hardened!" Rugrat yelled.

"Last man!" A team member ran past Erik, hitting him on the shoulder.

One Mississippi, two Mississippi, three Mississippi.

Erik felt the heat of George's passing fire attacks melting stone as he fired at the eyes of the Rin, who were covering their faces with raised arms. Kameela's rifle thundered, taking out another Rin. More fell under the weight of fire.

"Go!"

Erik grabbed Egbert, turning and running as fast as possible, letting him go as they ran down the street.

Erik slapped the next man on the shoulder, shooting past him. "Last man!"

He ran on to the next. "Second last man!"

The Rin pushed forward under the attacks.

"Hit them with an arrow, Egbert!" Roska ordered.

Egbert grabbed an arrow, notched it, and fired it. The mana stone was larger than before.

The mana stone shot down the road, making the Rin lower their arms. It pierced one Rin and stuck into another behind them.

The mana was drawn into their body.

The other Rin roared and ran forward to attack the teams.

"Looks like they're smart enough to know where it came from!" Erik ran past George and on to the rest of the team keeping the road clear.

"The Piercers aren't!"

Erik glanced back to see Piercers smash into the Rin. They fell in the dozens. The distracted Chimora ate the fallen Benir and didn't make a noise as the leading Green Rin was nailed to the ground. The Piercers fell like a heavy rain, crashing into buildings and using their waving walk to get close to the Rin, absorbing the mana stone.

The Piercers hit the ground where the last group was shooting from, spraying them in dust as their aprons covered the ground.

They shot point blank into the Piercer's head, killing the creature.

"Last two, pull back! Double time it!" Roska yelled. "Harrod, blow it!"

Harrod yelled and threw a black spear. It stabbed into the ground, showing a silver line at the neck.

They pulled back as fast as possible, the Rin fighting off the Piercers.

The spear detonated the powder within, directed partially by the remaining buildings, right into the Rin's teeth and chased the teams as they ran. The building collapsed into the road; dust covered everything.

"Groups of four, keep moving! We need to get clear of this area," Roska said.

They ran in groups, covering one another but moving as fast as possible to put distance between themselves and the Rin.

Chimora screeched all around the area, converging on the street. Other creatures moved in to defend their territory or were drawn in out of interest.

Erik looked at the team ahead, checking the passing buildings. A minotaur ran out of several buildings, slowing to a stop between Erik's group and Roska's.

Tully yelled, turning and hurling a spear.

The minotaur raised its head to roar, but only a gurgle came out as it collapsed to the ground.

Erik and the others picked up speed, following Tully, who stored the spear and the minotaur.

They kept running, tossing out scraps that interested the Chimoras and diverted their attention.

A winged beast dove out of nowhere, grabbing onto Esther. She fired her pistols into the creature's underbelly. It shook her, trying to stop her, but her attacks didn't pause. *Dammit, goddamn useless.*

Davin jumped into the air with George, gaining on the creature, their fire attacks startling the creature as it released Esther, increasing its speed as it shot away.

George caught Esther and brought her back to the ground. They had no time to wait.

Erik panted under his helmet, his shrapnel pain a constant companion.

They found several warehouse looking buildings. Harrod and Davos scouted them before they piled into one.

Erik found Rugrat leaning against George.

Erik pulled off his helmet. Rugrat's teeth were stained red, and he was panting.

"Shit, man." Erik made to move him into the seat.

"Just give me a potion," Rugrat wheezed, pushing into George to stay standing.

Erik gritted his teeth and pulled out a needle. He stabbed it into Rugrat's shoulder and injected it.

Rugrat let out a shuddering breath as the potion went to work.

Erik drank a stamina potion in a few gulps, gasping as he wiped his mouth on the back of his arm.

"Well, this is a fine fucking mess," Rugrat said, recovering.

"Might be getting too old for this shit."

"Hah, yeah."

They recovered before Erik reached out to Rugrat.

"Come on. They'll want to plan out what we do next."

"More of the same, I'd guess." Rugrat accepted his hand and stood upright. He rinsed out his mouth, clearing it of blood.

Edmond, Roska, Davos, and Kameela had claimed a corner of the warehouse for their meeting.

"About time," Edmond muttered, loud enough to carry through the space. "We need to push in that direction." Edmond pointed out of the building.

"We need some time to gather our strength before we do another run. Every time we go out there, we run into some big bad," Roska said.

"Time to rest? Aren't you the famous Alvans, able to do anything? My team is ready to go right now."

"No, we agree that taking a rest would be for the best. We have been running most of the day. Every time we've paused, some damn Chimora found us, or we were ambushed by different creatures. Just a few hours."

"I agree. We have a long way to go. We can't push ourselves all out in one shot," Erik said.

"I've always heard tales of your body tempering. Guess there's a difference between rumors and reality." Edmond sighed and nodded.

Erik's fist tightened against his legs, imagining dragging him across the table and delivering a few quick punches.

"Very well. We need to move as soon as possible. The Transition Point won't remain open for forever. If we miss it, we'll be trapped here until the next time the realm opens, or we're killed by the local inhabitants." Edmond left the corner.

Kameela gave them a tight smile and followed.

"I can see why people turned on his ass," Davos muttered.

Roska shot him a look but didn't say anything. Erik pulled out his map and put it on the floor. They crouched around it. Davos glanced around to make sure they weren't being watched.

Erik pointed at their marker and orientated the map. He drew a line from where they were to where the Marshal had pointed.

Rugrat pinched his fingers together and scrolled over the map, widening his fingers as he searched. "Beast Fields." He mumbled the name and zoomed out again. He raised his eyebrow and traced a circle from where the beast fields appeared to the direction they were heading in.

He traced their path along their current line and tapped a location in the middle of the map. Roska crossed her arms as Erik bit the back of his lip, standing and shrugging.

If it is in a circle, then we're heading right into the damn heart of it.

What other option did they have at this point?

Rugrat pointed in the direction Edmond had gone and tapped the map.

The trio shared a look, sighing and nodding their heads. If it came down to it, they had one goal. To get home. If Edmond was leading them into a death trap, they'd need his map to find a way out of the realm.

Sudden and repeated explosions sounded in the distance, stirring the city.

Erik stuffed the map into his storage ring, catching up with the others looking out of breaks in the warehouse.

A section of the roof caved in, the light streaming through the forest canopy made Erik curse. His vantage didn't let him see much, but he saw aerial beasts sweeping down.

Another group from the Realms?

More aerial beasts dropped from above. They settled down. A few seconds later, metal plates covered in formations dropped down to the ground. As they settled, the beasts that had been hiding and watching boiled out of their hiding places.

The mages and fighters unleashed their attacks. The mana drove the inhabitants wild.

"Prepare to move in five minutes," Roska said.

"Got it." They wouldn't get a better opening.

Another section of the city was hammered from above, torn away by the airships dropping their forces into the city.

Erik pulled his helmet down as everyone rushed to finish up their tasks. *We'll rest at the next place.*

They rested in some random building. Maybe it had been a store or a house, or a crafter's workshop. Time wore away ownership.

Erik coughed, trying to keep it quiet, feeling tired from the constant running. He took out a pill and swallowed it with a gulp of water. Everyone was feeling the effects of elemental poisoning. They all had high levels of body tempering, but tempering one's body had to be done in order or it would negatively affect them.

Even the damn elements are trying to kill us.

It had been a week since they left the warehouses. They had been on the run constantly. The airships had been fighting for two days and two nights, riling up the inhabitants in the undercity. Even if they were not interested in the beings throwing out mana all over the place like a flare in the darkness, creatures leaving their territory led to other beasts trying to expand their own hunting grounds.

The undercity was well and truly riled up. The fighting had increased over the days as airships moved above, striking at the locations with the greatest treasures. Positions that had been dominated for centuries by the strongest beasts in the area were now laid bare.

Erik felt the wood element being pushed out of his body, allowing him to relax. The Water element was still there, tempering his body, a constant pain that only added to the throb from the dungeon core shards.

Background pain. Erik sighed, closing his eyes then batting them open to not let sleep in.

He shook himself and forced a few breaths out. Moving his hand, he felt the weight of the air, the Fire, Earth and Metal elements, a hint of the Water element. It was like putting his hand in water, feeling the warmth and chill, the currents and pull.

He could identify each element through touch now. He reached out and pulled on the Earth element. Dirt and stone appeared in his hand. It acted like magnets. One just had to find the right polarization, or element in this case, and then increase power to it, and the external elements would be attracted or dispersed. Each acted in a different way. Earth element was the most comfortable for Erik to work with. When it combined, it created dirt and then stone.

He gathered the Metal element. His hair started to rise with the charge and small sparks formed in his hand. He dispersed it and gathered Fire. The heat shimmered in his hand, becoming harder the more he compressed, the element getting excited, rebelling, then becoming a small dancing flame.

Erik dispersed it again. He breathed and picked up some broken stones.

He focused on the image in his mind. Looking at the stones, he watched the elements shift to his command, moving the stones themselves, fusing them together, dust coming off in places.

Erik raised his helmet and blew on his hand. The dust floated away, revealing gray, black, and white stone pyramids. Erik looked closer. The pyramids showed lines of blocks. Erik tilted his hand, and the pyramids fell apart, a series of small bricks.

He wiped his hand, hearing the wind whistling through the buildings, cooling with the lack of movement and adrenaline in his veins.

Erik drew some Fire element into his body, warming himself.

Lee's lessons feel like a lifetime ago.

Erik played with the elements on his fingers, keeping his elemental draw down. In a place as abundant as the undercity in elements, he'd gained a boost to how long he could last. His ability to sense elements had been stretched as they couldn't rely on mana anymore. They'd all had to change their training to adapt.

Just need to project it. I'm missing that part. I can gather, integrate, and manifest, but projecting is beyond me.

The wind seemed to be getting closer. Something pulled at the corner of his mind when a roar came from down the street.

Everyone was on their feet in seconds, weapons ready as a pile of debris fell away from the beast that had been concealed in the city's remains.

Erik looked up at the six-legged, two-winged nightmare above. Its mouth had been stained red with blood and its eyes were like captured lightning. Light grays fading into black and silver stripes ran down its body, its wings almost a blinding cascade of metallic feathers. Its body was as large as a house, its head the size of a car. *It's a fucking dragon.*

It fanned out its neck as it roared. Its tail lashed out like a whip, creating a silver blade that carved through the city like a train through snow.

Its tail pierced a Rin, unleashing a wave of lighting that cut through several others before it breathed lightning as someone might breathe out normally.

"Move it!" Roska said.

They boiled out of the house as the Rin and the Berin attacked the dragon, summoning stone and metal spears or calling down a hellish rain upon it.

The teams moved in their groups, elemental senses stretched to their limit to make sure they didn't run into other beasts that might be ahead of their head-first dash.

Erik glanced back as the dragon threw a Berin in the air, crushing it in a series of tosses before swallowing it whole.

Blood stained its scales and feathers. Its eyelids blinked. Erik swore it stopped on the ground as it let out a roar and jumped into the air.

Not even the Piercers thought about interrupting the beast's feast and stayed hidden above.

The dragon disappeared into the sky.

"Is it following us?" Rugrat asked as Erik clambered over a pile of rubble, jumping over the other side as the rest of the teams scanned and ran.

"I fucking hope not!" Robert yelled.

"I hate this goddamn place," Esther said.

"So much for a relaxing adventure to recount the old days," Kameela said dryly.

There was a screech from above, followed by lightning crashing through a broken house and an unfortunate three-story building raining debris on Egbert's barrier. Everyone flinched and kept running.

The team fired at the dragon as it flew over them. It roared in pain and its wings threw dust clear as it climbed again.

Rugrat fired *The Beast*. He would have been knocked off his feet if not for Davos catching him.

The dragon roared with the hit, his tail gathering lighting as it struck out with a *clap*. Lightning like a scythe cut through several houses, filling the street with more dust. They weathered the hits from the collapsing building and broke through.

"It's coming around!" Tully's rising voice made Erik turn, seeing the dragon coming up right behind them.

"Rugrat, do it!" Roska yelled.

Rugrat wrapped the sling along his arm, as Davos braced him against a building.

"Don't get too excited," Rugrat muttered.

Lightning shot out of the dragon's mouth and tore down the street, shredding stone and buildings, creating a wave of broken stone.

Rugrat fired.

The elements and the little mana in the area were sucked in, the force clearing an area around him.

The round struck the dragon in the mouth, whipping it around to the side. Half of its jaw blew off. The dragon flapped its wings and dove away as Piercers fell from above, trying to reclaim the skies as their hunting ground.

The badly wounded dragon could no longer use its breath and lashed out with claws and its tail as if half-blind.

Erik noticed Rugrat sneak a healing and stamina pill. The force on his weakened body was too much for it to handle. Adding in little sleep and the constant fighting, it was surprising he was still on his feet.

"Let's keep going." Edmond said.

They agreed and pushed on. Being in the undercity for so long, they had adapted to the regular stresses and looked for constant places to rest, reading the area with elemental senses.

It took them several hours before they found another place to rest.

"Well, I guess dragons aren't morning creatures," Davos said.

Erik groaned as the others let out notes of complaint with a collective eye roll.

"Come on, that was a good one!"

Erik found a section of wall, falling against it and sitting down.

He couldn't help but think of the dragon's breath. There had been no casting time, no spell, just flame. The attack didn't hold any of the mana that spells might. *A true insta-cast.* Many people had looked into how they could decrease the time it took to cast a spell. There were many tricks, but it always required time to cast a spell. This had been nearly immediate.

Erik thought about the dragon's actions, how it had projected lighting through its surroundings.

The lightning came from inside. It breathed out with every attack.

He couldn't help but think back to the Fire element moving through Lee's body when he punched, and recalled the sensation of the elements drawing toward the dragon, then its projection out.

It was spitting. Erik's eyes opened. "He was drawing in the elements to his lungs and gathering it in a funnel around him to increase the power of any aligned elemental attack."

Maybe he used his elemental domain, drew in the Metal element. Then, when he snapped out his tail, the lightning gained direction and followed the path of the tail.

"No, it was almost as if he was throwing lightning. He manifested it in his tail and on it, but when he sent it out as a ranged attack, he had to build up the lightning again." Erik bit the inside of his lip, falling into thought, connecting what the dragon had done with Lee's lesson.

Anjea Gerard shifted in her seat as the carriage passed through the King's Hill guards.

Pieter Velten smirked, looking out at the passing city with mild interest. "Are they armed that well?"

Anjea checked the formations on the carriage were active. "If the reports from the fighting are anything to go on, yes."

"I do not understand why the elders of our clan are so worried. They are just a group in the First Realm. They haven't even reclaimed their city in the Fourth Realm and merely recruit in the higher realms." He snorted.

"Pieter." Anjea's voice commanded his attention. "It would be wise to not look at the Alvans in simple terms. They have hundreds of thousands of sect fighters from the Fourth to the Seventh Realm working under their command, and an army that should be around two hundred thousand strong." She frowned. "Have you read the reports on the Black Phoenix Clan?"

"Yes. Several clans are using the opportunity with their ships away to attack their positions."

"They are trying to gain the attention and favor of Alva. The worst thing you could do is underestimate them. We can shoot once every four seconds if we have our rifles reloaded. They can shoot multiple rounds in a second and reload in as long as it takes us to change rifles." Anjea looked out at the city beyond.

"They don't have any airships, though."

"That we know of." Her soft words lay heavy in the carriage.

"But why would they only keep one city? Vuzgal was a trade hub for the entire realm."

"They would have to break up their force into two groups instead of concentrating them in one area. Also, they can go anywhere in the Ten Realms through their totems."

Pieter bit his lower lip in thought.

I hope the clan leader is right about this. She had spent several weeks reading every piece of information related to the Alvans.

Pieter ran his jeweled fingers through his hair. "Is it true what people say about their manufacturing capability?"

"They have built places—factories—that churn out items as long as they are fed resources. It allows unskilled workers to create items of the Journeyman grade."

"And this is what is supplying our gunpowder?"

"Yes, the Alvan traders, they have a far reach across the realms. Getting access to those routes and their agreements could help the clans in the lower realms." Pieter's mouth curled upwards.

"That is dependent on how they react," Anjea said.

"When they find out their lords have died, they will seek another force to protect them. We have seen it happen countless times. If they do not have strong leaders, they will collapse."

"I don't think it will go that smoothly." Anjea watched outside the carriage as they moved through King's Hill.

Police were out walking the street. Alvan military marched to and from their camps and the city defenses.

It feels like we're in a city from the Fourth Realm, not the First.

They drove up the maintained and planned streets to the Lord's castle, going through two more inspections before they reached the actual castle. There had been outer walls around the castle district hosting military and administration offices, but the buildings, while strong, were out in the open.

They have half windows at the base. Anjea looked at the high windows at the base of the buildings. A shiver ran down her spine as she stepped out of the carriage.

"Well, this is rather nice," Pieter said, admiring the flower beds and trees that grew alongside the buildings. People sat on benches for their breaks, hurried between buildings or out of the castle's gates to head into the city.

"Please come in. Lord Aditya is waiting for you," a man said, standing ready next to the carriage.

He guided Anjea and Pieter with four guards through the castle. The temperature warmed up against the spring temperatures. *Formations.*

They walked through the castle, passing offices. Every room was a hive of activity.

The man guided them to a door flanked by two guards. They nodded to the guide.

"There is a seating area for your guards to wait." The man gestured to a side room.

"Thank you," Anjea said. She shot a look at their guards who moved to the alcove.

The castle guards opened the door for her and Pieter.

"I don't care how much they're willing to buy the land for; it's a flood plain. Were you able to get the plans for the new river?" A man's voice exited the room.

Anjea found chairs facing a fireplace in front of her. To her left was a wall of books, a large desk with chairs and a smaller desk to its left. A map table lay behind the couches and the chairs facing the desk. A glance showed Anjea it was a map of the Alvan Empire. Beside it a bulky man, an ex-fighter by his stature, leaned on the map table.

"We have guests," the other occupant, his secretary, said.

Lord Aditya nodded, and she headed to the smaller desk, jotting down notes as he turned to Pieter and Anjea. "Ah, sorry about that. Try to squeeze out every minute of every day." Aditya grinned and held out his hand, shaking theirs.

Anjea bowed when taking his hand, but Pieter simply smiled.

"Shall we take a seat?" Aditya gestured to the couches.

He sat in one of the armchairs near the fireplace while they sat on the couch.

"So, I hear that you want to increase the amount of gunpowder we supply, and you're interested in purchasing weapons from us too?"

"That is correct." Pieter sat forward.

Aditya pulled out two sheets and passed them over.

Anjea looked at them. They showed the prices for increased gunpowder and the per unit cost of the repeaters and their bolts as well as Journeyman level armor and simple helmets. The prices for rations, healing potions and all manner of concoctions and smaller items, including farming equipment, were also listed.

"These are the items that Alva is able to produce currently. I would suggest that you meet with the Trader's Guild as well. The empire makes a lot of simple items, but the Guild has more specialized items. They will also be open to negotiations on price. We only have set prices and our gear goes up to the Journeyman grade, while they have items in the Expert Grade."

Anjea looked at the list of supplies.

"With the changes to the Black Phoenix Clan, you must be relieved. Soon, your main rival will disappear and you will gain a new time of peace." Aditya shook his head and sighed. "War is such a waste."

Pieter cleared his throat. "Yes, fighting can lead to such problems."

"I heard that the Black Phoenix Clan members that surrendered have been turned over to Alva?" Anjea said.

"Yes," Aditya sat up, his eyes narrowing. "They serve out sentences for their crimes. They will have hard labor and work in their future. But they will be fed, housed, and taught new skills so that they have a path in the future to use their skills to help rather than hinder."

"They are your slaves," Pieter said.

"That is what others might call it. But we make sure that they are well treated, their health needs are seen to, and we try to teach them. They carry out tasks to help the empire grow, but if you want to see their conditions, you can check out their camps," Aditya said.

"I heard that a lot of your allies are giving you people that surrendered," Anjea said.

"It is a sad reality of the Ten Realms. If you can't make money off a person by selling them, then they will usually become a slave. The agreement we have with our allies allows them to pass their prisoners over. Then we pass them through a trial. Many are just pressed into service. They didn't want to fight and have committed no illegal acts. Many of them are relocated and set free. Those who committed crimes are put to work and re-educated. They work alongside others who are not prisoners, but get paid for their work."

Pieter and Anjea looked at one another.

"Those that are serving their sentences out are under our care. We will not trade or sell them to anyone." Aditya's voice grew harder.

"We understand," Anjea said.

Aditya nodded.

"I see that you do not have firearms for sale here."

"We have to look to our own needs first and, as you know, there is no problem with having an edge."

"What if we increased the amount of powder that we need by ten times? When could you deliver?" Anjea asked.

"Evernight?" Aditya turned to his secretary.

"Yes?"

"Ten times the amount of powder we send to the Sha, how long to get that prepared?"

She shuffled through papers on her desk and then checked a cabinet. Pulling out a folder, she compared a sheet against it.

"We could start delivering in two months," she said. "And it would take three months to ramp up to that level. Our current powder production has already been earmarked."

That would put it after the Violet Sky Realm closes.

She looked at Pieter.

"We were also interested in some formation work," he said.

"While we have the formations on those sheets, most are simple things like heating and cooling units, fridges, water pumps and washing machines. If you are looking for custom formations, then the Trader's Guild would again be a great help. Or you could go to the Mission Hall. Though those might be best for one-off formations. Crafters from all over, and even from the Alvan Academies, take the jobs that are posted there. They require the materials and plans while you can just purchase them from the traders associated with the Trader's Guild."

"What about entrance into the guild?" Pieter asked.

"Certainly." Aditya pulled out another sheet and passed it to Pieter.

He studied the sheet quickly.

"We were hoping that we might get entrance to Alva as well," Anjea asked.

"Access is restricted. There is only so much room within the capital." Aditya's eyes darkened, the room chilling with his impassive expression. "And the last Sha group wasn't so respectful of our rules. It was a good thing Lord West was nearby or we might have a very *different* problem."

Anjea and Pieter looked at one another.

"It seems that it might not be well known. Your messengers tried to *race* within the city, and they knocked a carriage out of the way that could have injured or killed those on the sidewalk. They showed little remorse for their actions. We were hoping they would get a punishment worth their actions."

"Let me apologize for their actions," Anjea said.

Aditya waved off her words.

"While we live for peace and like to be left alone, know that those men would have joined the Black Phoenix Clan prisoners if they had hurt one Alvan and our agreement would be null and void."

And look at what happened to the Black Phoenix Clan. Anjea looked back at the list of items. They were simple, but everyone could use them. *And each comes with a non-aggression pact.* Anjea had looked through the agreement. If any of the people from Alva made it back to the Ten Realms, the contract stipulated that fifty percent of their mana stones and dungeon cores would shift to Alva's care. *It would gut us.*

The atmosphere recovered as Pieter discussed particulars and they left before Aditya's next meeting, heading to an inn.

"So, what do you think of Aditya?" Anjea asked.

"Smart, simple and bullheaded. He is no merchant," Pieter scoffed. "He is likable enough. It will take a lot of work to integrate ourselves with the people in King's Hill and the Alvan Empire. We need to become a part of the fabric of this place in a few short weeks before the sub-realm closes. What did you think of him?"

"He has formed his mana core and tempered his body with the Fire element and is tempering himself with the Earth element."

"How does that match against our people?"

"Our elite forces in the Seventh Realm have the same body cultivation, but they are working on their Solid Cores or have achieved a mana heart. Levels mean little compared to the changes one can create with cultivation." Anjea paused.

"And?" Pieter looked at her.

"And..." Anjea turned the word in her mouth. "I wonder how they look at the Eighth Realm."

"You think they would challenge the test?"

"How many have tried in the Clans? How many have made it to the Ninth Realm? There are very few. Most are unable to find the reason they fight for their lives. Though there is no denying the strength that comes with unlocking one's will." Anjea thought back to demonstrations she had seen by people that had passed the Eighth Realm Trial. *Control and direction.* They came back sure of their path and with power to support them.

"The Ninth Realm is a place of outcasts. Tenth Imperium mutts." Pieter said.

"But you can't deny how strong they are. Aditya has power compared to our elites. He could make it into the Seventh Realm with ease. How many other Alvans are there in Alva with the same level of cultivation and the levels they need to get to the Eighth Realm. What if they were to get just one person into Avegaaren? Hell, how many heroes do they have in their ranks?"

Pieter chewed on his cheek but remained silent.

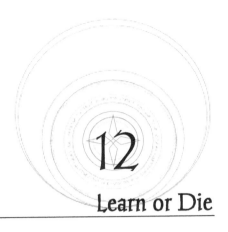

12

Learn or Die

Erik tilted his head to the side. A Chimora screeched out on the left flank.

The two teams worked as one now. Two-thirds shifted around to face whatever had alerted the Chimora while the rest covered their backs in case the screeching holler drew any other creatures.

A baying grunt rose from beyond the street, followed by several charging feet.

Minotaurs.

"Push on," Roska ordered.

Silently, they filtered down the road, checking as they went.

Erik threw out some scrap meat. Working with the Chimora had turned out to be a beneficial relationship. They got scraps, and the team gained an alarm system that didn't rile too many of the creatures.

The minotaurs weren't the smartest, but they moved in packs and hunted Chimora primarily, hearing them call out and hunting them down by bulldozing through buildings or chasing. It gave the teams time to move away before they started fighting one another or smashing other things.

They snuck through the buildings, then moved into the under-warren, the guts of the city where all the sewers ran.

The Chimora chittered to one another below, communicating in their odd way. They were one of the few races that didn't openly kill their own unless they were starving.

"Devils," Esther warned, up front on point. They were somewhat humanoid, short, and dumb, but smarter than most other creatures and vicious, using their victims' bodies as decorations and warnings to those entering their territory.

They moved up cautiously, watching every nook and cranny. The Chimora wouldn't be nearly as helpful here, eating up the scraps left on the Devils' totems and scattered around their domain.

The Alvans and Sha disarmed traps as they went, the Devil's favorite past-time. Bones on a string here, hidden spikes, the same glue-like substance they stuck creatures to the wall with.

A thin fog grew as they pressed forward. A poisonous cloud created by the Devils.

They reached more totems, marking the other side of the Devil's territory. Their steps lightened as they moved on Edmond's heading.

Erik heard a snap in the distance, a breaking twig.

No, please no.

A group of Chimora screeched; one of the totems turned into a trap for the little beasts.

Cackling noises filled the sewers. The teams moved as quickly as possible.

"Set charges behind us, one minute," Roska said to the rear team.

They pushed on, hearing the Devils wake from their slumbers and gather to where the Chimora had died.

Several Devils ran into the point team. Their formation-silenced rounds and guns made the barest of flashes as they removed the oncoming threat.

They increased their pace.

"They're starting to look this way," Nymira said from the rear.

They picked up the pace, moving into a half-jog as Devils let out squeaking growls that constituted a language between them before they started to sound closer.

Erik ran past the ones that had run into the point team. Yellow and red were the only two colors the devils took on, poison leaking from the pores of the yellow Devil in death, coloring the surrounding fog. They had horns on their heads, hooves for feet and wicked tails behind them. Knick-knacks covered their bodies and small sharp wicked blades sat on their belts.

The Devils' war cries grew at the rear. Then the charges went off one after another, rushing back in the direction they had come from, blowing apart the sewers and dropping part of the undercity on top of them.

George led them forward, guiding them to an exit, a crater in a road.

They pushed out of the sewers. The smells that might have offended them weeks ago now just par for the course.

They fanned out around the entrance, tossing out a few scraps unconsciously. One team member scanned the skies, the others checking the street and ground.

Erik clicked his tongue to Tully, who had become his team member, pointing at what might have been the remains of a cart, just another piece of rubble. But Erik saw the unnatural line leading to it, a sign that there was a Jorken pod there.

He smelled through his mask, finding the air sickly sweet.

"Must be a flowering Jorken nearby," Erik said to the team.

"More of the damn things as we get closer," Tully said on a private chat.

"We're nearly there. I'm interested in seeing what this place is like."

"Great views, apparently dragons, and all the man-eating flowers you could want. Fucking paradise," Rugrat grumbled.

Erik snorted, agreeing. But they had no choice. Edmond thought he had a way out. *And right now, that's our only option.*

"Looks like there's a group of buildings a few blocks up on the right. We'll head there, see if it's clear, and set up," Roska said, pointing to the building.

They moved to the building in groups. The first group cleared out the first floor and moving up to the second. The next checked the bottom floor and placed traps of their own at any entrances.

"All right, get settled in."

The team filed into the house, finding positions to watch the area. They had houses on either side, a courtyard around the back, and a road out front with houses crushed together and showing different states of damage.

Erik set up formations. Other people spread out to cover the entrances. Everyone had their job down and well practiced.

People checked their gear, replacing anything they had used. They cleaned their guns the old-fashioned way to save mana.

They were well rehearsed as they ate and drank at the same time they worked on their gear.

Erik moved up to the second floor, pulling out his map, checking it. They'd added some more information as they'd skirted around different areas filled with undercity creatures that wouldn't take too kindly to their presence.

He found his heading and moved around the building, settling in front of a window that looked across the courtyard. He stored his map and took out his binoculars, zooming in through a broken building to the city beyond. The area had seen more fighting than most places.

He saw it in the distance, the massive metal-looking dome that sprouted from the ground. He checked where they had come through a hole in the interior wall.

Just as we thought.

Roska entered the room. Erik passed her the binos and pointed in the direction of the dome.

She checked it and grimaced, passing them back.

Erik grunted in agreement. He used a sound canceling field and checked his rifle. The mana gathering formations on their armor allowed them to shoot their weapons and use formations on their guns without alerting the mana-sensitive residents of the undercity. It meant that their weapons could damage what they were fighting.

Silence formations on everything, though. They had silence formations on their armor to quiet their movements, on their guns so they wouldn't make noise, and they were using silence spells on their rounds so the targets they shot wouldn't make a sound.

Erik unloaded, checking his rifle. Roska used a cleaning spell on it and Erik lubed it up, drinking from his water reservoir before reloading the rifle.

It wasn't long before Kameela and Edmond arrived.

"Rugrat is watching the street that we came from to make sure that there isn't anything following us," Roska said and took a drink from her canteen. Erik passed her jerky, and she nodded in thanks.

"Good, we should rest here for a bit then continue on. We should be almost at the transition point," Edmond said.

"About this transition point. I think it's time for some more answers," Erik said.

"Still trying to gain leverage?"

"Is it before or after the dragons and all the nasty ass beasts in our way?" Roska asked.

Edmond closed his mouth, clearing his throat. "I don't know what you mean."

"Edmond, just tell them. They could have killed us at any time or not watched our backs and we would have died down here," Kameela said in a tired voice.

Edmond's face twisted.

"I'm guessing that the transition point is inside that big silver-looking dome in the center?" Erik held out his binos and pointed through a break in the wall.

Edmond took them and looked to where he had indicated.

"It is called the Treasure Hall by many. It is the heart of the Violet Sky Realm. Everything leads to it. From my information, people that use mana can't get close to it because it will wake the creatures and they'll launch a vicious counterattack." Edmond lowered the binos and looked at them. "We will claim fifty percent of the spoils within the Hall."

"Screw the damn spoils. Is there really a transition point in there? And how the hell do we get past all of *them*?" Erik growled.

"There is a transition point inside, and we just need to do what we have been doing already. Think of what we have been doing to get to this point as training. It should be easier to cross to the Treasure Hall, actually."

"Easier! One dragon attacked us, and we nearly turned into Christmas lights. We only wounded it," Roska said.

"All the creatures around the hall are cultivating. They are nearly unconscious. They'll wake up to disturbances of mana, but they are so focused on cultivating that they don't care otherwise. We sneak through, get to the Treasure Hall, use explosives to gain entry, then mana to power up the vault doors to get inside," Edmond said.

"You just said that mana sets these things off," Erik growled

"Yes, but the doors are deeper inside the Treasure Hall, and they need mana to work. That's one of the reasons the creatures are outside the hall instead of inside it."

Kameela scoffed and shook her head.

"Alva will take eighty percent, and we will take the most direct path to the transition point. Have you any information on the layout inside that place?" Erik said.

"Forty is the highest I can go." Edmond gritted his teeth.

"If we gave up our share, would you consider us joining Alva? It seems that we don't have a home anymore," Kameela interrupted.

"Kameela," Edmond growled.

"We can think about it. We aren't recruiters. But we'll give you a fair shot," Erik said.

"You should make it in," Roska assured her.

"Now, we were talking about the inside of this place, Edmond," Erik pressed.

Edmond grimaced, rubbing a hand over his face. His beard had become rugged and there was more dirt than makeup on his skin. "At the peak of the facility, there is a command center that controls this sub-realm. In the bottom, transition points back to the ten realms. There are several. Even if one doesn't work, there will be others. There are also storerooms throughout, crafting facilities and—"

"We have those back in Alva. We don't need to get sidetracked to find some trinkets," Erik cut him off. "Roska, what are you thinking?"

"Well, there won't be any stopping once we get out there. That place looks big, but we'll have blown our cover. We should get moving and quick. Hit the transition points. Gonna have to do it in one run. We don't know if there will be creatures chasing our asses or not."

"Rest up, get everyone ready, and then go for it in one go."

"Yup," Roska said.

In all of that, Rugrat and I are the weakest link. Damn this body.

Erik looked at the hall in the distance. "That makes sense. Make sure that everyone uses up their monster cores. Might as well make the most of our time and be as ready as possible for what's coming. We have what, five days until we're closed off? We'll move in three."

"You got it, boss."

Roska headed out of the room with Kameela. Erik held out his hand in a give motion. Edmond put the binos into his hand and turned to leave.

"Seems that the Ten Realms changed you, or maybe it was just being a noble back in France."

Edmond laughed. "I wasn't much special, a son that wouldn't inherit anything, a man that thought joining the army would lead to adventure, pretty women, station." Edmond snorted. "Instead, I ended up in this place. I made friends. I was a decent person. No. I think it was when Bartan died that everything changed."

Edmond walked out of the room with hunched shoulders.

Erik remained on watch. He sat in his chair, his rifle across his legs, scanning the street. A Glider beast silently passed through the air. It banked and ran across the buildings without a sound.

It kind of looks like it's inhaling air, but its body doesn't expand.

He heard the shuffle of feet and saw Esther walking up.

"Couldn't sleep?" Erik asked as she approached.

"Too much on my mind." She pulled out a chair from her storage ring.

They sat in silence. There were sounds of fighting in the distance for a split second, but it faded as soon as it arrived. Erik and Esther didn't flinch.

"I'm sorry about my uncle. He's... well..." She sighed, smacking her thigh. "A lot has happened in the last couple of weeks."

"You could say that." Erik caught the flicker of the glider again.

Esther shuddered.

"Sorry, they interest me. It's odd how they look like they're breathing in but don't expand and they're constantly banking and scanning the ground."

"Just be happy that you're on the ground and not being hauled up by one of them. Also, they have gills under their stomachs."

"Huh? So the air is going through them? Wonder if they use it to stay aloft, or decrease their noise maybe? Does that even make sense?" Erik frowned, caught up in his own thoughts.

Esther laughed and pulled out her canteen. "Anyone tell you that you aren't a typical lord?"

"Pfft, you think I want to be one of them, thinking of schemes and ploys and working alliances and the cost of grain? Do you know how much those rounds cost?" Erik smirked. Somehow, Delilah's voice seemed to overlay his words. "Nah, that's not for me. Thankfully, there are a lot of people supporting Rugrat and I. Really, we aren't the leaders of Alva. Just figureheads."

"Are you sure it's wise to tell me that?" Esther said.

Erik shrugged. "We won't get anywhere if we don't trust one another. While they might disagree, Rugrat and I know the truth. We wouldn't be where we are without them." Erik smiled.

"I guess that is the difference between you," Esther mumbled.

"Wait, hold on to that," Erik said, sitting up as the Glider flapped its wings, coming to settle on a mound of debris in the distance several floors high.

Erik looked through his binoculars as the Glider bobbed its head and opened its mouth. *Something* was pouring out of its mouth. Erik pulled on his helmet and looked at the Glider, switching the formations to pick up mana.

Nothing. Elements?

Erik switched to the next formation; a gasp escaped him as a *potion* fell from the Gliders mouth. *Could only be a potion with that kind of elemental signature.* Erik sat back and then leaned forward further, studying the beast through his binoculars again. He scanned the area quickly. Esther had her hand on her pistol, ready for a fight.

"Sorry, nothing to be alarmed about, just. I think..." Erik trailed off. *It must have been sweeping through the air to gather the elements it needed to create a potion within its body. From the faint elemental signatures, it must have young up there. Feeding them elemental potions.* No, that was incorrect. The Glider's spit was the potion. The collected elements combined with it, increasing its elemental properties, turning it into a training potion.

"She was right. Damn. Alchemy is the combination of elements into a substantial form." Erik sat back in his chair, scanning his arcs.

"Alchemy?" Esther said.

"Delilah, my student, did this lecture about how elements affect concoctions. She theorized that concoctions are a blend of mana and elements in a substantial form balanced out for our bodies to accept them instead of being destroyed by them. It makes sense with the mana cultivation pills, the things that have the most mana, and the least impurities pulled together into a concoction and entering your body. Though healing pills, maybe they're like healing spells, requiring a lot of Water, Earth, and Wood elements combined with mana?"

"What are you talking about?"

"Oh right, I guess pure mana theory isn't taught outside of Alva, just buying spells and using them." Erik scratched his head. "Basically, it has to do with alchemy on a really small degree and building it up from there. I guess that the chemistry of the ingredients interacting might be enhanced by the elements in the concoction and be affected by the elements in the surrounding environment of the person taking the concoction."

Erik wanted to race to tell Delilah. Instead, his world came crashing down as he recalled her expression after the lecture. His stomach turned in on itself. *I ambushed her. She wanted to show off what she had learned. She mentioned me, proud of her theory, and I didn't even congratulate her. I just ambushed her. I wanted her to give me permission to go to the Eighth Realm. I manipulated her.* He leaned forward on his knees, pulling off his helmet and looking at the street beyond.

How many people did I hurt being an asshole?

Erik cleared his throat. "Sorry, alchemy things." He gave Esther a smile. "You said something about difference?"

"Oh, well, you Alvans work together to support one another. The Sha used to be like that, but as more people joined and the clans remained clans, they started working against one another. With the Black Phoenix Clan having to take a step back, there was no external threat, and the clans turned on Edmond. You lost your cultivation, didn't you?"

Erik sat up, looking at her.

"I'm not asking you to confirm, and really it's none of my business, but something is wrong with you and Rugrat. Instead of isolating you and driving on like others would, your entire team is working together. You value one another's inputs, no matter how weak or strong they are. That's rare. I never thought such a place could exist in the Ten Realms. But Alva is a real community. You support one another, no matter what, while the Sha Clans just look for benefits." She shrugged. "It's rather sad. I studied how the Willful Institute fell. Their inner strife, which might have been stoked by *certain* parties, weakened them before the battle even started. They brought themselves together through external conflict and inner threats. Using their riches, they would have covered over their wounds continuing on as if there were no issues."

"Bigger isn't always better; sometimes you need fewer people to do more," Erik said.

"A few strong fighters that can work together will always be stronger than a strong but divided force," Esther looked to the doorway. "I think that is why my aunts and uncles didn't leave the Sha when they should have. They cared deeply for my mother and father and Uncle Edmond. They were one hell of a team in their prime."

"Bartan, that was your father, wasn't it?" Erik asked, remembering Edmond's words.

"Yes, why?"

"What happened to him? Sorry if you don't want to talk about it."

"Ah, no, it's fine. If you were back in the realms, you could find out from any information broker. My father died defending Uncle Edmond. They were attacked by bandits who thought they were a trade convoy. A lucky shot hit my father before they knew what was happening." Esther curled her knees up.

"I'm sorry to hear that."

"It's in the past." Esther put on a smile and looked out of the window, starlight striking the silver of the Treasure Hall dome, lighting her face in white. "Though Mother, she made it through the funeral, she and Uncle Edmond grieved together. It was too much to lose my father. They were almost inseparable. She became numb to the world. Thankfully, we had my uncles and Aunt Kameela. Milo distanced himself from everyone and went cold towards Uncle Edmond. Now he can't talk to him. I know Uncle Edmond can be a bit *strong* and while others don't see it, he has always tried to do what he thinks is best."

Erik nodded, keeping his comments to himself. *Sometimes doing what we think is best only hurts those who care about us the most.* His thoughts turned towards Alva, to his friends and those who cared for him, and whom he had steam rolled, ignoring their comments, carrying on his own path. Trying to prove them all wrong instead of accepting their help.

I have to make it back if only to apologize to them.

"We're all just idiots trying to make the best decisions we can."

Esther let out a dry laugh. "Some decisions are worse than others."

Erik grunted. They spent the rest of Erik's watch talking about a lot of nothing, just seeking companionship, and to bitch about the world.

Robert had a smirk on his face when he arrived to take over the watch. Erik and Esther headed for their own sleeping areas.

Erik found George cultivating a Fire variant elemental core.

He opened an eye as he approached.

"Congratulations on passing the Eighth Realm Trial, bud." Erik smiled and patted his back.

George softened, his mouth pulling into a doggy-grin.

Erik laughed and scratched behind his head.

"Sorry it took me so long to say that. I was being an ass."

George nudged his arm with his nose as if to say he understood.

Erik gave him some more scratches. He passed others cultivating elemental cores. Some of the team were sleeping in the corner. Rugrat was cradling his rifle again.

Erik got out his sleeping gear. *Kind of nice to need sleep again. Just wish that it hadn't happened while we're in a deadly undercity where everything wants to kill us.*

The second day passed without much change. Thankfully, everyone knew the use of packing extra supplies, even if not necessary, so there was plenty of food and water. Those that weren't on watch spent most of their time cultivating.

Erik gave lectures on tempering their bodies and created concoctions to assist them. A few were able to have breakthroughs.

Some were finally able to finish tempering with Metal, reaching the same stage as Erik. He smiled and congratulated them as they continued to gain their strength. On the third day, things continued, but most were working on the tips that Erik had provided, and they had all the concoctions they would need.

On the night of the third day, Erik had nothing to do.

He listened to the odd calls of the city like wind passing through the streets. He had become used to the strange sounds of the undercity.

I didn't finish Lezaar's journal.

He pulled out the book and sat in the corner, flipping to where he had stopped. Lezaar had fled the Dragon Fields and headed into the areas where there were fewer creatures. *I can't think what that must have been like, all alone in here, watching all your friends die.*

Erik gritted his teeth and continued reading.

"It feels like several creatures have been watching me for the last couple of days. I changed locations a few times. I found a new tower; this one reaches the forest above. I took some time going up to feel the mana lights upon me. I had to take my time; the light burned my eyes. This is a nice place. I will try staying here for some time.

"I was right. I am being followed. I kept thinking it was just the wind I was hearing, but there is no wind in this hell! I saw them today, damn Rin. Some must've survived the dragon's attack. They seem to have gathered allies and are surrounding my tower.

"The Rin are calling to one another. Their talk sounds like wind through the city, but they're coordinating with one another. My exit to the surface has been blocked as well. I'm trapped here. They have tracked me over weeks."

Erik leaned forward.

"They have turned to using roars and growling. They are so close. Ah, it was a good run. I refuse to die like a rat in a barn. This will be my last entry. I was hoping to read more about this place. We were so foolish to think we could snatch a few rewards from under the sects' noses. At least I will be seeing my party soon enough."

The book ended. Erik felt a chill, remembering the scene in front of the building, the destruction around the tower and signs of a fierce battle with only Lezaar's amulet and ring remaining.

He frowned; something tickled the back of his mind.

Erik shrugged and headed to check on the people on watch. He found Davos watching the courtyard.

"Damn weird noises here. That wind sounds freaky," Davos said.

Lightning ran down Erik's spine as the hairs on the back of his head raised. "When did you start hearing it?"

"I don't know. Been around for a while. It's just wind."

"Davos, tell me, do you *feel* any wind?"

"No, but…" Davos fell silent as Erik focused. The sound of wind started and died in one area, then appeared in the next, and the next in a counter clockwise direction, and they were *close.*

"Shit!" Erik said as Davos grabbed his rifle.

Erik activated his sound transmission device. "I have reason to believe that we are currently surrounded by Rin. They have a long-range way of communicating with one another and it sounds like wind in the distance. These noises are happening all around us and they're getting closer."

"Everyone, grab your gear. We're moving out in ten," Roska said.

Not even Edmond said anything. Those that were cultivating or sleeping were roused and readied.

Erik pulled on the remaining pieces of his gear and headed downstairs. He checked his storage ring and the extra mana stones and stack formations he'd prepared.

Everyone got organized, finding their partners and moving to the first floor.

"Okay, let's move," Roska said.

Four by four, they moved in the direction of the Dragon Fields.

They checked the streets as they passed, keeping up the pace, tossing out scraps and Undercity meat. It would lure the Chimora. While they were great alarms, they didn't want any noise while they were in the Dragon Fields.

Erik was in the second group, trailing behind, when Roska engaged the Rin. Their silent weapons lit up the street as they fired on the group of Rin and Berin walking down the street.

One let out a sound like a roaring tempest.

Erik heard the rising roars on either side as the Rin rushed into the hail of attacks. There had to be four Rin and five Berin.

They unleashed their mouth and horn attacks, hitting people in the lead group, breaking barriers, and throwing them back. Esther struck the street, skipping and hitting a wall.

Erik and his group moved up on their right flank, adding in their fire. Two Berin were killed, but the rest were still coming.

Damn this undercity!

"Melee, arrowhead, drive through!" Roska yelled as the third and last group combined with the other two.

They drew their weapons and pushed forward.

The Rin unleashed their attacks, imbuing them with elements.

Erik grabbed his hammers, feeling woefully unprepared.

Davos deflected a spear from Erik. As Erik called on the power of his body, he felt the shrapnel stabbing through him. The pain fueled his strike, hitting the Rin in the side, lifting him up with the sound of broken ribs.

Davos' blade, imbued with fire, hissed as it stabbed through the Rin's trap and burned through its body, leaving it smoking and unmoving.

A Rin threw a spear a half second before Erik's hammer hit him.

Davos grunted with the impact of the spear, stumbling into Erik, who grabbed him with his now free hand.

Erik called upon the power of the elements, twisting them as he released lightning from his hand. It ballooned from finger-thin to the size of a fist, punching through the Rin.

Erik coughed and stepped backward. Someone behind him supported him and pulled him to the side. Erik held onto Davos, who was groaning.

His vision cleared as he looked around.

Yang Zen had taken his position. The team used elemental attacks, releasing the forces of nature with each blow, tearing through the Rin attacks.

Careful to not use any mana.

They had punched through.

"All right, everyone aboard," Egbert said, jumping onto George's back as Davin flew above, watching the skies.

Erik moved close. A suction force fell over him as he entered the beast storage crate on Egbert's hip.

He put Davos down and pulled out revival needles, stabbing one into his own leg and another into Davos. The spear had pierced through the right side of Davos' chest and gone through the back of his shoulder.

Others entered the beast storage crates, wounded from the teams.

"Osmo, I need your help," Erik called to a nearby team member. He lowered Davos to the ground and pulled out medical gloves. He tore Davo's IFAK from his back, pulling out a revival potion and stabbing it in Davos' right pec above the spear.

"Tell me what you need," Osmo said.

Harrod appeared inside the storage ring, carrying an unconscious Esther. "Erik!" he yelled, running over.

Erik pulled out a mana stone and put it on the ground. *This is going to suck.*

"Assess her," Erik yelled at the nearby team members. They rushed to help as he used organic scan on Davos.

Erik took out a potion, poured in a powder, and shook it with his thumb on the lid. "You! Hold him. Jin, be ready to pull out the spear."

The team members moved to obey.

"Pull it."

Jin pulled it out in one vicious motion.

Davos gasped and curled. The others held him down as Erik angled his thumb. The potion and powder came out in a spray like foam. It quickly coated the inside of the wound and filled out. Erik could see Davos' body starting to repair itself.

"Jin, get an IV line in. Add in a shot of grade two revival potion. Get him on his side, Donnie," Erik said to the man holding Davos down. "Watch his breathing. He's gonna have shit in his lungs. Use mana spells to drain it out but keep him breathing."

Erik pulled out a salve and put it under Davos' lip.

"That will keep him under." Erik put it next to Donny.

"Osmo!" Erik turned. "How's she doing?"

"Nasty wound. Elemental poisoning is spreading! Cracked skull and spine. Her upper chest collapsed. Heart's under external pressure," Osmo yelled as he worked.

Erik gritted his teeth, forcing back the blood as he called the power of the mana stone through the embedded shrapnel that burned through his skin. Erik's elemental domain spread out of his body.

I missed that.

Erik reached out, summoning the elements out of Esther and Davos' body, using the elements he could control to drag the others out.

He panted and sweated, blinking to get past the light-headedness. His latest meal of water and jerky threatened to make an appearance. He forced it down.

"That should deal with the poisoning. Relieve the pressure on the brain. Drain the blood. Get a revival potion in through her left shoulder. That will get into her heart quicker and up to her head. Get her armor off and check for internal bleeds."

Nymiria moved to assist him as Harrod hovered nearby, the giant man's face pale and slack.

Erik looked around wildly.

"Rugrat!" He caught his eye and looked at Harrod.

Rugrat moved over to him.

"Come on, Harrod, let's get you over here."

"But—"

"She's in the best damn care in the Ten Realms. All of them are better medics than I ever was, and Erik is an Expert healer, nearly Master. He's got them."

Rugrat pulled him away from Erik and Esther. "Come on, get your gear prepared. Don't know when we'll get called out there."

"I—" Harrod started to turn back and Rugrat grabbed him by the head, looking into his eyes.

"This is their fight. You would get in the way. Let them do what they're trained for," Rugrat said.

Harrod hissed.

Tully stumbled in, bloody as she carried a team member. "Team Two, you're up!"

Team Two stood up and exited the Beast Crate. Harrod looked over, his fists tightening. Rugrat caught him by the bicep.

"Don't do anything stupid. Esther needs you," Rugrat said.

He nodded tightly, gripping his iron gauntlets and left the Beast Storage crate.

Rugrat looked at where he had disappeared. He turned his attention to Erik and the others working on the wounded. Tully dropped off the bloody soldier and left again.

Erik's teeth were gritted in pain. Rugrat saw the mana stone on the ground crumbling as his eyes shone. *He's drawing on the power of the dungeon core. He's fighting for them all.*

Rugrat crouched out of the way, watching the team members working on the wounded.

Roska stumbled in, missing an arm. Rugrat steadied her as she poured a potion on her arm. "Let me get you to the healers."

"No, just need—" She gasped, using a healing spell. Her arm weaved back together, and she drew out a sword. "Thanks."

She left.

How bad is the fighting to make her lose an arm? I didn't think we'd have to fight once we broke out from the Rin! Are they fighting dragons out there?

Rugrat's stomach somersaulted as his body filled with energy.

The wounded were being stabilized. If death wanted to claim them, they would have to *fight* Erik to claim them.

Kameela came in, holding her torn stomach, using her rifle like a crutch. She dropped to a knee. Erik sent out a healing spell and threw out powder that covered her wound. She staggered to her feet, grunting, storing her rifle, and pulling out a loaded one then headed out.

Damn this all. Rugrat crouched back down, feeling tears burning in his eyes, the bubbling rage, the shame. *I'm sorry Dad, I'm sorry, Antonio, I'm not strong enough.*

"I just wanted to be closer to you. I wanted to do you proud, Dad. I just wanted to be closer to you both." Fiery tears blurred his vision as a screen appeared, and something shifted inside his body. He cried out, falling backwards as his body burned from within.

Quest Completed: Why do you fight?
You fight to be closer with your father and brother.
Rewards:
Reformation of Will Entrance to the Ninth Realm once you reach level 80

The dungeon core fragments in his skin dissolved and spread through his body as a familiar golden energy, soothing mana, and elemental energy.

It swept through his body, healing him. The flood of energy increased his cultivation and surged towards his mana and elemental cores. It felt like something *unlocked* in his brain. His senses spread out through his body and the immediate area.

Damn, like messing around with the radio dial and getting it just *right.*

Everything came into focus, his mind racing through memories. Joining the Marines. Those inner moments when he was at his weakest but a half-step away from giving up. How he'd drawn strength from knowing his father and brother had been through the same thing and made it through.

Dad, Antonio. A peaceful smile filled his face as his mana cultivation continued to rise, breaking through a barrier that seemed to end at his skin. He reached out and his power, his *will,* spread out into the ten realms, resonating as if something had been out of place but had clicked back together perfectly.

His mana core shifted, and changed. Five new veins, as thin as a piece of thread, connected to his arteries.

Rugrat let out a shocked breath as sparse mana and a torrent of elements continued to run through his body. He shivered. Like water upon fresh fields his cells vibrated with power, washing away their fatigue and flourishing. He examined his shattered body. Before, he had guided his mana, but now he *controlled* it.

He reached inward, feeling his will strengthen his actions, aligning with purpose as his body changed at his direction. He had studied the damage he'd received hundreds of times, both with others and by himself; he knew the way things were meant to be. Now, he remembered everything they had said, and changed his body, adding in his own alterations.

He altered mana pathways, maximizing their efficiency. It was as if he had a regular rifle and, after shooting it for years, was applying customizations to fit it perfectly to his shooting style.

Rugrat grimaced as he paused, the changes causing pain. He felt like a balloon that had reached its limits., *My body is too weak for all these changes. I don't have enough energy.*

He pulled out beast cores and pills to increase his tempering and threw them into his mouth.

He controlled his elemental core completely and drove the elements through his body. Pain like rough clothes over sunburn came, increasing in intensity every second, but mana washed through him, healing him. Rugrat infused his will into his body, increasing its strength, forcing it into his elemental core, turning it into a tool.

He had all the power he needed within his body, but now he could *use* it with an incredible degree of control.

He felt himself break through. The Earth element flowed through his body like broken levees, charging his elemental core.

Rugrat grunted, pulling it under control and tempering his body further. He threw in more pills and monster cores.

He yelled as his body completely tempered with the Earth Element.

Regenerative power flooded his body as his control over the Earth Element reached the point where it was akin to a familiar rifle in his hands.

He used the power of his body to sustain the changes. Rugrat opened his eyes, awakening to his power. His Mana and Elemental domains overlapped one another. Insights into his power pooled in his mind, but he didn't have time to write them down or think on them.

He pulled out the Beast, checking the rifle.

"Rugrat?" Erik yelled from where he was.

"I got my why," Rugrat said, looking at Erik. "I've got some high standards to meet."

Rugrat pulled his helmet on and exited the beast storage crate.

The city had been smashed around them. Flowering Jorken were attacking with their pods and flowers. Rin ran after them.

Ran right into them. Rugrat could see the Dragon Fields in the distance.

Edmond danced through the Jorken. His sword cut off one flower, and he fired his pistol, knocking a pod away from a team member.

Egbert was on George's back, making sure that none of the mana made it out of his domain.

Rugrat grasped the mana, using his will to draw it to himself, creating a mana void in the area.

"Got some things to learn." Rugrat ran and jumped. Earth rose from the ground to meet him.

A pod shot out toward him. A blade of mana appeared, splitting the pod with its own force.

Lee was right. Control beats power every time.

He also realized that he had been looking down on Erik for focusing on tempering his body. Now he could feel the strength through his body. It was more than any workout could do. The Earth energy was like an inexhaustible spring running through him.

Mana wasn't simply a tool anymore. Like the elements infused with his will, it was a *part* of him and an extension of himself.

His domain wrapped around him as he dodged between the pods and flowers using the elements and spells to enhance himself. His control was such that any mana wasted in his spells was dragged back into his mana gates before it could escape.

It took incredible control, and he missed one pod that reached out for him.

Mana blades pierced through the pod, shredding it. Spell formations appeared in front of Rugrat. Chains shot out, pinning the vines out of the way as he fired the Beast through the opening they created.

The round struck the heart of the Jorken, spreading green blood across the ground behind it.

Rugrat waved his storage ring, storing it away.

He turned, using his domain to locate Rin, and fired the Beast.

His reactions and strength had shot up to another level. The mana running through his brain made it seem like the world was moving through molasses as he rode the recoil from one shot to the next.

Pressure spread through his body, and he released his will, feeling drained even with his new body.

Seven Rin dropped to the ground.

Rugrat fired and killed two more. The teams used the space to charge the remaining Rin, ending four Rin and their eight Berin as fast as their blades could move.

Rugrat turned, reloading his rifle as the last Jorken drop to the ground.

Edmond stored the Jorken he and his team had killed.

"More will come soon," Davin said.

"Get the reinforcements stored. We'll run for it," Roska said. "Boss, you good?" She used a private channel.

"Same as I was before, maybe a bit stronger." Rugrat looked at her. "We need to move."

She nodded in her helmet.

"If you could guide us? Your domain is the largest."

"Can do." Edmond and Kameela remained outside with George, Egbert, Davin, Roska, and Rugrat. The rest stored themselves in the beast storage crate.

They took off at a run.

Rugrat felt like he had been blind before, having relied on his eyes this entire time. Using his domain was a newfound freedom.

"Move to the right a bit. There's a Chimora moving past," he warned Kameela, who jumped on the right side of a wall as a Chimora flew past in bat form, diving towards the ground.

They moved like silent wraiths through the city. Davin flew; Egbert and George loped alongside Rugrat.

Elemental power was unleashed behind them, the aftershocks reaching Rugrat.

"Looks like the Rin just ran into those Minotaurs we passed," Egbert said.

They paused. Mana light poured down from above, shining off the silver dome and covering the dusty ruins. It was hard to see the creatures sleeping below, buried under buildings, dust, and debris. They had become part of the landscape.

Holy shit. Rugrat could see all of them. Their elements stained the area as they drew in mana. It was only a small stream between them all, but little of it passed beyond the edge of the beasts.

"Everyone, seal your mana gates. Even a small disturbance could set them off. Kameela, go in the storage crate. We need to keep people to a minimum." Edmond's voice had changed, looking to Roska.

"No, Edmond—"

"Yell at me later. Getting out of here is our priority." Edmond's expression and tone cut off her words.

"George, Davin, you go in as well," Roska said.

They disappeared into the beast storage device.

"And then there were four," Rugrat muttered.

"Let's get on with it." Edmond breathed in and stepped forward.

Rugrat grabbed onto his sleeve. "Let me go first." He pointed to the sleeping Chimora under a piece of rubble.

Edmond shuddered, slowly moving his foot back.

"Might be a good idea," he whispered even while using his sound transmission device.

"Step where I step."

Rugrat led the way. His footprints were thankfully clear in the dust. He pushed forward in a quick walk.

As he advanced, the creatures increased in size and lethality. Rugrat forced himself to breathe through his nose, focusing totally on the path.

"Seems the Rin are devious bastards, but they're not suicidal," Egbert said.

Rugrat glanced back to see a swelling group of bloodied Rin staring at them from the edge of the Dragon Fields.

A Chimora called out in a different direction. Rugrat crouched low, looking around as they all paused.

The Rin scattered at the noise.

A dragon, smaller than the one Rugrat had shot, shifted in its slumber, scratched itself, and went back to sleep.

Rugrat could tell the creature wasn't really asleep by the mana it was drawing in.

The Chimora's cries died out and Rugrat kept moving. He slipped on some debris and Edmond grabbed his arm to stabilize him.

Rugrat nodded his thanks, righted himself, and kept moving.

He got a good look at the dragons, not letting his gaze stay on them long, scared they might sense his eyes falling on them.

They were massive, with bodies as big as a semi-truck and trailer and heads the size of golf carts. Some snorted fire Others had antlers crackling with lightning. They came in all different shapes. Most had scales but some had feathers.

Groups of dragons with similar appearances kept together. They got bigger and fewer in number as they got closer to the dome.

Rugrat continued leading, getting half a kilometer from the dome.

A few hundred meters on Rugrat's left a dragon reared out of the ground. A dozen smaller versions of her brood stood with her.

They looked liked an Armadillo lizard's grown-up and beefed-up older cousins. Dark brown and sand colored spiked, interlacing scales ran down its body to give it a horned appearance. It didn't have horns but had a spiked shin and four claws that tore through stone as if it was sand.

Their tails created a dust cloud as a thinner dragon with mottled green, yellow, and purple spots raised its green wings. Black smoke that melted the ground spread from under its wings and drool dripped from its mouth, burning through stone like it was sugar.

Rugrat saw smaller versions around the mottled dragon blinking in interest but not moving.

The armored dragon flapped its wings, throwing dust off several other dragons. Some shifted, and a few opened their eyes, looking at the entertainment.

The poisons dragon expelled a stream of black flame with a sickly green core.

The Earth dragon breathed back with a yellow Earth flame. The shockwave of the two dragon breaths clapped like thunder running through the undercity.

Rugrat looked at the nearest dragon.

"Come on," he said, moving slowly and surely as the Earth dragon's brood screeched and attacked the Poison dragon, a deviant Wood dragon.

The dragon clawed at them, poison fingers cutting down two of them. It waved its wings, getting airborne. The Earth dragon fought to match it but was much heavier.

The Poison dragon's tail cut through the ground, hitting the Earth dragon's head. Its attack went wide as the Poison dragon's breath carved a black line in its armored scales, melting through them as green lines traced the Earth dragon's flames.

A hundred meters from the dome, broken sections allowed Rugrat to see inside. Massive supports arched together to create the outer opening. The dome wasn't perfect anymore, time having worn away most of its shine. Sections had fallen beyond the pillars. Doors led to a large tower that fused with the dome above.

Rugrat's eyes were drawn to motion, and he unconsciously looked to his right. *Nope, nope, nope, nope!*

A blue eye the size of Rugrat opened, blinking away the vestiges of sleep. The dragon turned its head, a mix of bright blues, shimmering metallic silver, and light devouring black.

Oh fuck, fuck, fuck. Fuckiity, fuckington, fuck!

Rugrat sped up, leaving a dust trail with the rest following him as the dragon eye focused.

Rugrat felt it inhale, trying to pull the air from his own lungs and creating a breeze that tugged at his clothes as they passed the dragon and ran across the open ground towards the arches.

"Fan out!" Roska yelled.

"Incoming!" Egbert yelled.

Rugrat looked back to see the dragon snap out at Egbert, who dodged just as it breathed out a mix of lightning and water that turned an eye-watering neon blue.

It crashed into Egbert's barrier, then into his stack formation barrier, weakening it some before it blasted through. Rugrat infused mana into his body. He called the ground to him using a pillar and a wind spell to send himself to the side. He glided through the sky as the plasma stream struck the ground, releasing heat, dancing sparks of lightning, and leaving a melted scar through the stone.

Roska and Edmond used spells to dodge the attack. Roska pulled off her stealth stacks and slapped new formations onto her legs.

They ran past the outer dome arches and across the open ground before the tower.

Egbert raised another barrier, replacing the barrier formation on his leg.

"They're waking up!" Rugrat yelled. The fields were in movement as nearby dragons and other beasts raised their heads at the commotion.

"Door!" Edmond yelled. He pulled out a small cannon and fired. It dented the doors inward before exploding, opening a hole.

The plasma-breathing dragon smacked its hand against the ground. Cracks that radiated blue light ran through the ground.

"Underground!" Egbert yelled.

They dodged as the cracks diverged and exploded upwards, releasing pillars of lightning.

Egbert flew in the opening he'd made. Edmond ran in behind him.

Roska turned at the door, throwing out a smoke grenade.

It covered the area rapidly. The smoke shifted as George pulled his wings in and grew smaller. Egbert jumped off into the door and George squeezed through behind him, crashing into things unseen.

Rugrat ran through the opening, grabbing Roska and pulling her inside the dome.

It was set out like another miniature city, more orderly than the city beyond and in better condition, but time had not been kind.

They ran through a building that could have been a transplanted skyscraper from Earth. They found themselves in a hallway, broken from disuse. George burst out of the room he'd crashed into. Edmond and Davin were ranging up the hallway, pushing inside.

Rugrat released Roska. Pumping their legs, Rugrat could feel the coming dragon breath on his back. The unlight hallway brightened with telltale blue.

"Into the rooms!" Edmond yelled, catching a door frame, kicking in a door, and running inside.

Rugrat jumped over rubble, condensing elements under his feet to turn mid-air and enter the same room as Edmond. He went through the door and passed the wall beyond as the dragon's breath passed along the hallway.

Rugrat was punched forward, smashing through two walls, and tossed out into an open area. Plasma burned through the hole he'd created in the wall, melting it and the floor behind Rugrat.

The skyscraper they had been in shuddered and shook, tilting it seemed to collapse forward in slow motion.

Rugrat could smell his burning clothes and feeling the burning heat on his limbs. When he came to a stop, he grabbed his rifle, grunted, and levered himself to kneel. His back was a mass of pain, but his Earth-tempered body sewed his flesh and muscle back together.

The ground jumped as the skyscraper crashed into the ground.

"Sound off!" Rugrat yelled, checking the area with his rifle, coughing on the smell of burnt clothes, skin, and other materials on his back.

"Roska here," she hissed.

"Egbert here with George."

"Edmond here. Davin is with me," he said.

Rugrat turned to see him and the fire Imp. "Davin and Edmond are with me. Egbert, did you go to the right or left?"

"On the left. I see Roska now."

"We're going to have to move deeper into the dome to find a way for us all to meet up again," Roska said.

Rugrat looked around. He appeared to be in a large gathering area. Plants had claimed most of it, growing wherever they could find purchase. A roar thundered through the buildings, shaking Rugrat's bones.

"Okay, move towards the center. Now!" Roska said.

"Change to stealth if you can," Edmond offered.

"What he said," Roska agreed.

Rugrat started running, casting stealth spells. He moved silently towards the center of the tower. The buildings opened, allowing him to see up dozens of floors. Catwalks strung overhead, some broken, the debris across the ground.

The dragon's second breath tore through the skyscraper, covering it in sickly blue flames that caused stone to explode.

Light shone through a broken section of the dome.

Looks like a second city in here.

It was in much better condition than the rest of the undercity and looked similar to Cronen City.

After a few minutes of running, Rugrat caught sight of Davin and Edmond.

"Looks like the dragon lost interest in us. I hope so, at least," Roska said as Rugrat, Edmond and Davin grouped together.

"Edmond, you got a bearing on this transition point?"

"It should be located in the middle of the Dome. I'm not sure what floor, but we can go up floor by floor."

"All right, sounds like a plan. Everyone, check your gear. I know I need to replace my back plate."

Rugrat, Edmond and Davin moved into what might have been a store in a lost lifetime. Rugrat pulled off his carrier, finding the plate melted, and the material burnt off in places.

"Dragons." Edmond shook his head, watching the doorway as Davin stood on the counter.

Rugrat stripped his shirt off, pulling on a fresh one and a backup carrier. He stored the rest away. His pants were burned around his calves and his boots were slightly melted. *Take too long to change them.* He checked his legs. they had recovered, showing fresh pink flesh.

"Another day in the office." Rugrat pulled his helmet back onto his head.

Erik coughed blood into the crook of his arm, sewing up Davos's side.

He moved to the next patient. Each had been stabilized. There were five critical wounded with injuries that would have killed a normal human. Those with non-life-threatening wounds were healing themselves, regrowing lost limbs. Once they had their stamina back, it only took them a few minutes to do so.

Erik checked on Esther; she was the worst. She didn't have the body tempering of the Special Team members and was riddled with injuries.

Harrod, Kameela, and even the frivolous Robert were grouped together nearby, watching everything Erik and the medics did.

Erik checked on his other patients. They'd used physical means such as stitches and bindings where they could to let their bodies heal naturally with less of a toll, allowing them to focus on the worst injuries.

Good, all stable.

Erik looked around, seeing everyone not wounded or working on them gripping their weapons tight.

Each were fine warriors, but not knowing what was happening outside was its own kind of pressure.

"Why isn't she waking up?" Kameela asked.

"I've used a concoction to keep her unconscious. I don't want her to wake and move around with this kind of wound. I'm scared she might have a seizure, so I've used a potion that essentially paralyzes her muscles." Erik coughed. It rolled on as Yang Zan supported him with a hand on his back.

"You're in worse shape than the walking wounded," he whispered in Erik's ear, and used a discreet healing spell on him.

"Still standing," Erik joked.

Yang Zan took a deep breath and sighed, not moving away.

"We are using stamina and healing potions on her. We've fused her ribs together, but they need time to heal. They shouldn't puncture a lung or cause other complications." She was secured with splints and bandages, holding her in place. A neck brace supported her neck.

"Why are your people all better?" Robert growled.

"My people have a higher body tempering. Esther has a Mana heart and Earth tempering. While that will help speed up her recovery because of her increased stamina regeneration, she has only got the basic tempering," Erik muttered.

"Basic tempering?"

"She tempered till she got the first notification instead of completely tempering her body."

"There's more beyond it?" Harrod raised his head.

"Yeah." Most of the Special Teams had the same tempering, but they'd gained the titles as well as the quest completion, raising them to a whole different stage. It was like comparing someone that swam for their high school and an Olympic swimmer. They were both swimmers but in different leagues.

Egbert flashed into existence.

"We're inside the dome, but we've been split up. Everyone without tasks, stealth formations and gather outside. Everyone is fine. We were attacked by a dragon, but it didn't follow us."

He disappeared again.

Erik turned to Yang Zan, using his sound transmission device. "You head out, I'll watch things here."

"Okay, just no more dungeon lord stuff."

"You got it, Doc," Erik said.

Yang Zan held out a Revival needle.

Erik sighed and took it, jabbing it into his leg.

Yang Zan checked him as the others disappeared from the storage crate.

"Your fragments have shifted and are moving deeper into your body. You can't keep exerting yourself like this or they'll pierce your vital organs."

"Rest and recuperation for me. Don't worry, I've done this job before without spells."

Yang Zan studied him.

"I won't do any stupid shit. I'll stay in here unless you need me," Erik said.

Yang Zan patted him on the shoulder.

"Stop worrying about me. I'll play nice."

"Okay." Yang Zan shook his head and then disappeared from the beast crate.

Robert remained. "A mage won't be much use out there other than attracting attention." He gave a weak smile. It faded as he cupped his hands, looking at Esther.

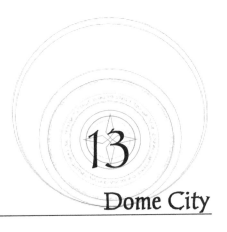

13
Dome City

Rugrat scanned the area around him, moving deeper toward the center. The closer he got to the center of the dome, the greater signs of fighting. Buildings that had been pocked with spell marks had been carved into with attack spells.

Some were leveled or showed lines as if they had been cut with swords wider than a man was tall.

Must've been one hell of a fight. Maybe the Ravagers and Devourers against the Gnomes and Elves?

"I thought there would be more beasts in here," Edmond said.

"That dragon didn't follow us in either."

They reached a doorway. Rugrat and Davin fanned out as Edmond gripped the door and hauled it open. He stepped to the side as Rugrat looked beyond, through the hallway and flickering lights.

"Homey," Rugrat said, moving forward.

"Did you ever think that you would be doing this again?" Edmond asked.

"I hoped that I would." Rugrat grimaced in his helmet. *What if Erik never passes the test?* "Never been one for parties and sitting around doing paperwork."

Edmond snorted. "You're right there."

They moved down the corridor.

"You know, how the dragon didn't come in here makes me think about the fire floor," Davin said thoughtfully. "The creatures fight in their own areas to get better locations and get stronger. A few challenged me when I was first trapped down there, but after a few tests, they stopped trying to pick a fight with me, staying away. They would try every so often, but most of them gave up and gave me room after."

Rugrat stilled his steps. "You think there's something stronger in here?"

"There are signs of fighting all over the place, and there are lots of openings in the dome. I guess there could be?" Davin strained the last word and looked to the ceiling as if looking at the apex of the dome.

He let out a nervous laugh at Rugrat and Edmond's looks.

"I'm sure I'm just imagining things. Something that could scare dragons. Wwhat could do that?" He rubbed the back of his head.

Rugrat and Edmond shared a look and kept walking.

"You couldn't have picked another transition point?" Rugrat growled.

"I didn't think the dragons would pick a fight in the middle of us crossing the field, or that the Rin would ambush us."

"No plan survives contact with the enemy."

They continued to advance, reaching another door. Edmond opened it and they slipped through. Light shone through the building.

Climbing over debris, they came to the edge of the building. A honeycomb of underground areas had been opened in a spherical blast that had eaten part of the building. The large, open area was easily three hundred meters across and surrounded a pillar reaching up towards the peak of the dome.

"Fighting must have been bad here," Edmond said.

Rugrat nodded, looking at the pock marked city.

What the hell kind of person could have cast these attacks? The crater looked like someone had scooped out a perfect sphere out of reality itself. It must have been three hundred meters across.

Rugrat used a small Inorganic Scan through his foot. *And this place is built from Sky grade materials.* "What you think did it?"

"I'm not sure, but they must be as strong as those freaks in the Ninth Realm," Edmond said.

"You been to the Ninth?"

"No, but I've seen a few of those that have. They're on another level." Edmond turned his head to Rugrat. "In their eyes, anyone below the Ninth Realm is dirt."

Edmond moved through the building. Rugrat followed as the buildings and destruction guided them further away from their people.

Louis Gerard wiped the sweat from his forehead. The smell of gunpowder was thick with his group as they ran down the streets of the undercity.

He knew the undercity was a deadly place, but it had surprised even him. Four days ago, they had been gathering resources at a nearby location when Louis and two hundred fighters had headed toward the Treasure Hall.

He wondered if he should have taken Fredrick's advice to stay with the rest of the fleet. *I can't take command of the fleet and kill the Marshal, then put off my responsibilities. I would be no better than him.*

Louis waved his hand, scattering his people into the broken buildings as they looked out at the dome.

"Dragons," one fighter whispered.

A roar carried in the distance as several dragons pawed the ground, growling at the dome. Another dragon guarded its prey, an armored dragon, whipping its tail at those that approached.

They should be far enough away.

"They won't notice us if we go between those flowering plants to get to the dome. Make sure you don't use your mana."

Louis waited for his orders to be passed back. They had already lost thirty of their members, Sha Elites with the best rifles and gear the Sha had.

He looked at them all in their helmets and fine armor, now stained black and grey with powder and dust, scratched from use.

They look like real fighters now.

Louis stepped up and pushed forward. The rest followed him as they stayed low, moving between debris and entering the area filled with flowers.

They followed Louis, weaving through the plants.

Louis saw a flower twitch. He stared at it, but it didn't move anymore.

The fighters passed him, the last entering the flower-filled area.

The dragons seemed to settle down. One smacked another with his tail. The snap rung out, shifting a yellow flower.

Pollen drifted free and touched a fighter.

The fighter screamed as the pollen started to petrify her skin, dissolving into dust. She used spells to try and get the pollen away from her.

The flowers twitched.

Louis looked forward as the ground erupted under one fighter, a pod snapping shut around his screams as he fired at his feet.

Louis felt the bloom of mana as it seemed like *everything* woke up in the area.

"Run!"

They dashed through the deadly fields, the ground erupting and snatching fighters, dragging them underground.

Dragons moved closer to their border with the plants. Some got a bit too close and vines whipped out, leaving bloody scars on the dragon's hide as they tore free and retreated.

Elemental attacks struck fighters before pods snatched them up.

Louis fired at a flower looking at him. The flower reeled back, and Louis kept running. He stored his rifle and fired a pistol, running through the powder's smoke. The fighters were running all-out as creatures woke up and started charging into the flowers, fighting one another to reach them.

The flowers started attacking them back.

Louis made it under the arches along with a few dozen of his people. They ran through a break in the dome's wall, entering a large open area filled with buildings and catwalks.

"That way!" Louis yelled, pointing at a nearby building. They turned; another fighter was hit by a blast of flame that disintegrated the upper half of their body.

Elemental attacks followed them into the building. Louis ran through a door, smashing it open and through several rooms before he slowed as the attacks dropped off.

He pulled out his sound transmission device. "Head for the center!" He turned and ran for the center of the dome.

They tore out of the building and ran across the ground, vaulting broken catwalks, eyes wide for creatures.

The first fighter to the next building used a throw charge. It blew up, hitting the door, blasting it open, clearing it for him to run through the smoke.

The rest ran inside. Louis stopped at the door, glancing back. *I don't see anything following us. The flowers must be stuck in place.*

He grimaced at the two dozen or so fighters crossing the open area the last of his group.

He could still hear the creatures roaring at one another and the sounds of fighting through the opening in the dome.

Though he was surprised. They could move, but nothing dared to enter the dome.

Must be some kind of restrictive formation?

Aziri's hand twitched, disturbing the dust that had piled up over the centuries. He raised his head with feline grace, the glow in the room reflecting off his slick scales—a deep blue that only gave a hint of the color. His eyes opened bright yellow, his double eyelids blinking away the time. His tail swept behind him, clearing dust off the faintly glowing formation beneath him.

"It appears we have guests." The words hissed with his forked tongue.

He stood upon thick legs, built for power, his demi-human body more lizard than human.

Cracking noises came from his body as he breathed in the thin mana of the room and the elements. His body glowed with power. Around his formation circle lay dust-covered books and bodies in various stages of dissection. There were beasts, Rin, and dragonlings. Various demi-humans as well as elegant Elves and squat gnomes, but several human bodies were the main attraction. The bodies were shaded blue, held together with his elemental power.

He reached out with his perception, sensing the elements of Earth and Water passing through the tower, through the fog and through the ground.

The beasts that had been raging around his domain settled and lowered themselves in submission. He found signs of mana as he spread out his range.

His perception searched through the buildings, finding no sign that any beasts had made it inside.

"More bodies will help me understand their cultivation." He stepped forward; the formation brightened without him drawing mana from it directly.

He walked out of the room through broken doors and pulled on a cloak, the tired runes glowing with power as he stepped out of his cultivation chamber.

He passed through several rooms that showed signs of heavy fighting and reached a corridor, a doorway the floor on the other side having been destroyed.

He looked at the light from several broken mana lights a hundred meters above that illuminated the shaft that the round building he resided in rested.

The building was slanted, several of the lower floors pierced by a monument in the ground.

Broken catwalks lay above as Aziri stepped out into the void. Water materialized into a water carpet. He spiralled down the earthen spike that impaled the command center.

I remember when a beam as thick as a Karanti Ravager illuminated this place.

He flew down several floors, passing broken debris and catwalks. With a small motion of a finger the doors three stories tall opened.

One door weighing several tons was ripped free, passing Aziri.

Seems I must learn how to use my newfound strength. Alas, there is little to use it on in this prison.

A sneer ran along his face as he flew through the doors, entering hallways, signs of fighting positions stained with the reminders of battle.

"What was that?" Rugrat froze, feeling something pass through him, and looked around for the source.

"I don't know, but it felt like the Earth element," Edmond said.

"Almost felt like a scan," Rugrat said.

"Maybe a defense of the dome?"

"I hope so. Let's find that transition point, and quickly." Rugrat checked that his stealth formations were still active.

Most of the doors were sealed inside the tower. It was a honeycomb structure of rooms, their functions lost to time.

Fighting had destroyed rooms and broken the tower in different ways.

"This must be the main tower," Edmond said.

"So, the transition points should be at the bottom?"

"In here somewhere." Edmond used his sound transmission device. "We should go in our own directions and look for it. It should be a black and white with a blue formation and green runes. There might be defenses around them."

"Sound off if you find anything. I'll have everyone break up into groups of two to widen our search," Roska said.

"Anything else?" Rugrat asked.

"There will be a podium in the middle of the formation that will accept a rune card. There should be five transition points in the tower about fifty meters in."

"How big is this thing?" Harrod asked.

"Nearly a kilometer tall and two hundred meters across," Edmond said.

"Let's get searching. The sooner we can get out of here, the better," Roska said.

Rugrat, Davin and Edmond pushed into the tower more.

"I should have brought my climbing gear," Rugrat muttered, slinging his rifle as they tried to find a way around. The tower had been partially destroyed, collapsing several floors.

"Did you know that this place was a training area for people to temper their bodies," Edmond said.

"Temper their bodies?"

"Yeah, people believe that this place was used to raise beasts for their cores, that they revolted, and it caused this place to be lost. There hasn't been anyone strong enough to take it back, so the beasts control it, and we get limited returns."

"So, humans were just using this place to temper their bodies. Seems like a lot."

"There are plenty of ruins and cities from previous generations that we use today. The Seventh Realm is practically littered with them."

"Uh huh, I was wondering why this place looked similar to some of the cities I've seen before," Rugrat said. *Did they lose the information about the Gnomes and Elves, or has it been suppressed?*

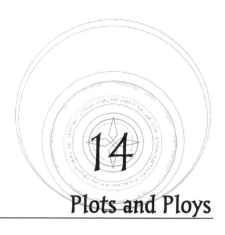

14

Plots and Ploys

They're still cruising toward the next resource point," Ranko reported.

Stassov frowned and pushed out of her chair, walking to the map.

"Where have they been so far?" she asked the person manning the table.

He marked out the different locations. "They were in this area nearly a week ago."

She studied the map, looking at different markers and locations. *What am I not seeing?* She pinched the bridge of her nose as the map manager put down some more markers. They didn't reveal anything other than a confusing pattern. "This would waste mana stones. The fact that it is so erratic, something is wrong. What am I not seeing?" She leaned on the table.

"What resources did they collect at these locations?"

The map attendant pulled out a list.

"They took Greania Fruit from this location, and Roaili Flowers from here. Here, they killed beasts."

Stassov took the list from his hands and started to read from it.

She frowned. A pen of flame appeared in her hand, leaving black marks under different resources. *These aren't related to any of the other items they gathered.* The Sha gathered alchemical ingredients, reinforced woods they could use on their ships, and hunted for variant beast cores of the Earth and Metal elements.

She noted their positions and looked at the map. She flicked away the other markers, leaving five markers in a rough circle.

"The Treasure Hall? They wouldn't..." She trailed off in thought. *They don't require mana to fight if they use their rifles.* "They might get through the city with their rifles, but there are beasts surrounding the dome. The ships went around the Treasure Hall but never went to it." She used her sound transmission device to get Ranko. "Was there anything strange at any of the sites? Did you see any people leaving the Sha and heading for the Treasure Hall?"

Ranko paused for a few minutes. "We didn't see anyone moving in the forest, though at the location where the Roaili flowers were from, they were out of sight and blasted a hole into the undercity itself. It raised hell for some time. We thought they might be trying to get the beast cores from the area."

"They could have used the cover to get a group into the undercity and push towards the Treasure Hall." She gripped the side of the map table. "Ranko, let me know if there is any change in their movements." Stassov felt the ship shudder as another barrage fired down into the undercity. Commander Chmilenko's actions were simple. The creatures in the undercity loved mana, so he had set a trap and was using the Warships to kill any beasts below, gathering a massive harvest of monster cores.

Natalya moved closer, examining the map close to Stassov.

"Get me the commander," Stassov said.

Her sound transmission device vibrated a few moments later.

She activated it.

"Do you have something on the Sha for me, Captain?" Chmilenko asked.

"I reviewed all the places they went to. There are several locations that have special resources that should not interest the Sha. All of them are located around the Treasure Hall. I think they have sent people into the Hall. Even if they haven't, they are now circling the hall. If we attack them from one side, we can force them into the range of the Treasure Hall's beasts."

"Going for the Treasure Hall? That's brazen even for the Marshal. How confident are you that we can ambush them?" He paid no attention to the possibilities.

"I think we have a good shot. I believe that they are heading for the Yellow Weeping Tree Forest. It is close to the Treasure Hall and falls inside their pattern. They have been harvesting rare woods across the sub-realm."

"Looking to make up for their losses and add a few warships to their fleets." Chmilenko fell silent. "Very well. We will clear things up here and move within the hour. Drive them into the range of the Treasure Hall and then move to leave the sub-realm.

Sha walked out of the teleportation pad in ranks. Louis hid his sigh as the reinforcements climbed.

An officer ran up. "We haven't found any supplies in the Eastern area, sir. Everything of use looks like it was looted or has been destroyed with time. We have found storage rings, though, that contain resources."

"Gather up all the storage rings you can find. Reinforce the area, but be ready to move. Any groups that go out, make sure that they have teleportation formations so they can return to the ships right away."

"Yes, Admiral." The man saluted and walked away before Louis could countermand him.

"The next group is about to head out, sir," Louis's guard said, one of his cousins. He nodded, catching sight of the cousin that had killed Markus. He turned away, unable to look at him. Seeing him was like a punch to the gut.

"Okay, we'll join them in heading deeper, there are just storage rings out here." *I hope that we can find pills and other consumables that would be worth it. The greater the rewards we bring back, the easier it should be to ease the transition to Milo.*

Louis raised his head, realizing he had sunk into his thoughts. Since Markus' death, he was slow to share what he was thinking with others.

He looked at the group of fighters arrayed in rows, a hundred strong and fresh from the warships.

"Captain, let's head out," he said to the leader.

"Yes, sir." He saluted with his sword and gave orders to his people. They quickly spread out and headed toward the center of the tower.

They fanned through the area; more Sha were arriving every minute.

Louis moved with the first group. They arrived in the open area between the outer buildings and the central tower that reached up to the center of the dome littered with the signs of fighting, the heart of the Treasure Hall.

The group stayed in the outer building. Louis looked at the building, relief filling him. *Even if it is only trinkets, then they are sure to be useful from a group that could build something like this.*

He looked behind him. Not one of the beasts from outside the dome had appeared. They had all stopped outside.

I shouldn't question our good fortune.

They moved across the open ground, finding storage rings and valuables on the ground. Half of the force guarded while the others looted.

"Looks like they've been sucked dry of mana. There is nothing left on the formations. Must have just been the time," the captain reported, holding out an armband.

"Can we charge them?"

"Some of them maybe. Others might break. Even if they are useless, the metal will make up for it."

"How do you mean?"

"The metal is Celestial Grade."

Louis stared at the piece of iron in his hand and at the pieces dotted across the ground. There were dozens. *Maybe the storage rings haven't been looted.*

They worked up through the tower. Where the fiercest fighting had taken place, there were usually more discarded items.

"Hold," a guard said, stopping everyone in their tracks. He turned his head, looking toward a broken room.

Louis walked over quietly to him, the others waiting.

"There's someone out there." The guard pointed beyond the broken room. There was a small area to crawl through.

"Alright, you two get a rope around his waist." Louis patted the guard's shoulder. "Scout the room. You run into trouble, you pull the rope twice, or reach as far as you can go, and we'll haul you backward."

"Yes, sir."

The two guards secured a rope around his waist.

The guard got down on his knees, moving to the small opening and crawled through, disappearing out of view, his rope following him.

He stilled at the edge before slowly crawling backwards. Only when he was back from the edge did he use his sound transmission device. "Sir, I think I see the Marshal down there with that Fire Imp and Lord Rodriguez."

Louis stopped himself from running to the edge. He got on his knees and moved toward the scouts, shooting a look at the guards who made a noise.

He got onto his belly as he got closer, looking over the damage. They were several floors up now. A section of the building had turned into a courtyard of rubble in past fighting. There were several collapsed floors. The guard pointed at a floor opened by the destruction.

Louis cast a spell on his eyes, allowing him to zoom in on the movement.

Lord Rodriguez had slung his large rifle over, pulling Edmond up to the next level. The imp came from deeper in the building, flapping his wings lazily. They talked and then headed deeper into the tower, following him.

That bastard! The others must have died and they're the only three left. How the hell had they survived this long. He didn't care. He had an opportunity to get rid of them. He checked what floor they were on and the direction they were going and studied his map, although it was incomplete.

It would have to be enough.

He backed up, using his sound transmission device.

"The tyrant is out there. He is with an Alvan Lord and a Fire Imp. They are four floors below us. We will move with all haste to reach them and make sure that we end them once and for all. They must have looted the storage areas, which is why we couldn't find anything."

"Yes, sir."

They moved quickly and quietly through the building, dropping four floors and working around the debris ahead of where Louis had seen the trio.

The lead guard held up a hand, stopping them all. He pointed to the corner and made a turning motion.

They moved down a corridor flanked by cultivation rooms and reached the end of the hallway. The guard peeked past the corner. He ducked low and moved out quietly.

They moved out to a counter; beyond it, the building had been destroyed. It was nearly pitch black except for some flickering mana lights. Everyone was using a night vision spell or formation.

Across the section that had been destroyed, Louis heard stone crack and fall. The trio were walking on the other side of the opening in the building, a third of the way across.

They moved into position, using the corridor and the remains of what must have been a lobby.

Louis' sound transmission device went off and he answered it.

"Sir, we're being attacked at the first teleportation formation. It's tearing through our people. We're evacuating! Oh, oh, what the hell *is that?*"

Louis cut the transmission. *The others weren't dead—they were flanking his people!*

"Fire!" Louis yelled, turning and firing his pistol.

Their rifles filled the space with smoke as they shattered the dead silence.

Roska and her team fanned out as they reached a reinforced door. Nymiria used scan on it and then pushed it.

"Locked with mana."

"You sense anything inside?"

"Nope."

"Rob." Roska gestured to the panel next to the door with her chin.

George shifted his wings, watching one corridor, Egbert watching the other.

"As the lady requires." Rob sketched a quick bow, always the charmer. He pressed his hand against the panel. It lit up with his mana, lighting the runes on the door. It shuddered and started opening with the sound of scraping stone.

Roska and Nymiria examined the open room with their raised rifles. There was nothing inside but a formation with a raised pedestal.

"Clear," Roska called and moved to the entrance. She lowered her rifle and used her sound transmission device. "This is Roska. We have a transition point. Move toward my position at your best speed."

"Team Two acknowledges. Moving to you," Rugrat said.

"Team Three on our way," Tully said.

Roska waved to Nymiria to start setting up a defensive position. The surrounding area was set up like the defenses around a totem. The Transition Hall was in the middle, sealed with a large door, with a ringed defensive structure around it, facing outward.

The outer defenses had been largely destroyed. A series of half-standing walls and rubble remained where they had fallen.

Roska flicked stone away from the doors to the transition point with her foot, looking through the open hole to the open area beyond. Several corridors terminated at the transition point.

George watched the area as Egbert, Nymiria, and Roska piled the rubble to create defensive structures.

At some point, it had just become a natural reaction.

Roska paused at a section of wall four times as tall as she was. Her eyes narrowed. *What is that noise?* She heard cracks in the distance. She threw the block and grabbed her rifle.

"We're under contact! Ambush!" Rugrat yelled.

Roska stilled, listening.

"Muskets. That has to be Sha," Edmond growled.

"We're pinned here. Getting shot at from across an opening!"

Roska checked her map. "Egbert, you hold here. Tully, bring your people to the transition point and hold it. My team will move to support Team Two. We'll break off contact and head back here. Prep charges to blow the transition point so we don't have anyone following us!"

Roska and Nymiria jogged toward the sounds of fighting. Robert ran with them as George loped ahead, leading the way.

They ran through the halls, pounding on the stone as the sounds of fighting drew closer. George barreled through a half-closed door. His body started to change, his armor moving with him.

Robert gave Roska a wide-eyed expression as George finished transforming into a demi-human. Roska burst through the door, breaking it off its hinges. George hit another door at the other end of the room, Roska right behind him as the scene opened up. To the left, Rugrat and Edmond hid behind a wall that was slowly being destroyed. Davin was running and flapping between cover behind them, firing out fire balls.

Straight ahead there was a broken section, creating a chasm between them and the shooters on the other side hiding behind cover, working in groups to fire and then reload their muskets.

George roared. A cone of blue flame shot out from in front of him, doubling in size with the external elements as he punched out with his hands, fireballs crossing the opening. Roska braced herself and fired at the Sha, killing two as the breath smashed into the side of the building. The building shook with the impact, knocking several feet of floor from the edge.

Nymiria and Roska fired at targets moving through the destruction. Their own mages counterattacked George's fireballs and tried to form barriers.

"Earth Spike!"

Spikes shot out of the ground and through the area around the Sha, forcing more of their mages to deal with the attacks.

Roska released her seals, allowing her mana to circulate freely.

Rugrat was able to get his head up, firing into the building the Sha were in. He got off three rounds that destroyed the half-barrier that had been thrown up. His third round exploded, blowing out that section.

The Sha activated spell scrolls and several spell formations appeared, blasting out attack spells. Rugrat's stack formation barrier took several hits before being depleted. Edmond's life saving artifacts broke, defeating some of the other attacks before Rugrat's artifacts activated, being broken in the process.

Rugrat pulled out his machine gun, hosing the enemy position.

Edmond turned the corner of his defense. Moving toward Roska's team, he fired his pistols, dropping them into his storage ring.

He paused next to another set of defenses. His hands blurred as he was covered in gun smoke. His rounds looked like they had eyes as they sought out those peeking around the Sha defenses.

"Moving!" Rugrat turned and ran past him.

He jumped a broken wall and found a half-wall for cover, bracing his machine gun and firing.

"Covering!"

"Reloading!" Roska yelled. She dropped her magazine, storing it and pulling out a fresh one from her storage ring, slapping it into place and hitting the forward bolt release, firing.

"Back in!"

Then the wall on her left exploded.

"You're with me. We'll move around and flank," Louis said, seeing Edmond pinned behind the short wall. The little imp was dancing around, shooting back fireballs, but the mages easily dealt with that.

Louis shoved off the wall and the ten soldiers he had picked moved with him.

They threaded through the rooms, his guards with their swords and pistols raised and ready.

He reached the end of the destruction and they turned. The world lit up as a blue breath of flame spewed across the open area to his left, hitting the rooms he had just left.

"Counterattack!" the captain yelled through the communication channel. Louis could faintly hear his yelling as new weapons cracked out from the direction of the flame. Louis increased his pace, feeling the impacts. The building shook as stone was dislodged and dust rained down from the attacks.

Louis and his group reached the other side of the chasm. The guards drew him back. The fighters set their charges with their hissing fuses.

The wall exploded, and the fighters rushed out.

Their rifles cracked in a volley, a second following the first, then a third as they fired in two lines, five standing and five kneeling, changing to new loaded rifles in between.

Louis ran out.

Rounds tore through several Sha before the others dropped or ran for cover.

They have better long-range weapons, but they're from the lower realms.

"Charge them! Get under the range of their weapons! *Montjoie Saint Denis!*" Louis yelled. Only realizing afterwards that he had used Edmond's battle cry.

Some took heart and yelled, charging out. Louis and his guards pushed to the left flank.

He saw Edmond turn just a few meters away. He was using a pillar to protect himself from the Sha shooting across, but he was open from the side.

He fired, killing one of Louis's guards.

Louis swung his sword at the man, holding his pistol up and at the ready. Edmond's sword swung out, meeting his.

"Seems you can do your dirty work yourself! Hah!" Edmond laughed, his neck cording to strangle out the noise as he went on the attack. Louis turned with his blade, using the flat to guide the point of Edmond's sword to the side.

He brought his pistol up to bear, only to have it turned against his body by Edmond's dagger.

"So short minded, Louis!" Edmond hissed. Their weapons danced, their training, strength, and reactions pitted against one another.

"Short minded! Says the Tyrant that drove us into the ground. Scared that in giving up your power, someone might try you for your crimes?"

"I have done many things, but none that I wouldn't do again. Tell me, did you kill Bartan, or was it one of your people?" Edmond's eyes flashed as he sped up.

"I killed him? Coming from the murderer's mouth!" Louis yelled. "You killed him to remain in power. Milo told me everything!"

Edmond stumbled.

Louis pushed his blade wide and cut back to open Edmond's stomach, only to find air as Edmond turned his blade lightly and jabbed.

Louis pivoted, putting him off balance. He used a wind spell to shove himself backward, gaining his footing and space.

"A lie from a man that is unable to look past his own clan, unable to work for *all!* Taking Tiberius's mad ravings and using them as truths!"

"You slander my father-in-law! You treated him as your dog, but he served with distinction! At least I trusted in someone. Bartan was your brother, and you killed him from behind to remain master and commander!"

"You betrayed your oath. You betrayed *us!*" Edmond surged forward as iron clashed once again.

I need help. Louis looked at his people, who were pinned down by the two women around Robert. He picked out Roska.

Lord Rodriguez was hidden through a wall from his position.

"Us? No, I think it was just you. And betrayed? I set things right!"

Iron rang out as their blades clashed. No breath for words for several seconds of buzzing iron, trying to tear the life from one another.

"How can one feel betrayed when you have treated us as if we are one step away from turning on you? Keep us divided and fighting over the scraps and holding all the power to make us do your bidding! Trying to cover up the murder! By now, all the Sha will know the truth. You are a tyrant!"

"A tyrant, a murderer, you have many names for me, boy! All lies you've made up," Edmond growled, his attack cutting Louis' arm. "Pull your head out of your ass! This is the Ten Realms! What action did I undertake that did not think of the Sha first? Which action did I not take to make sure that the Clans would not consume one another? Fighting at one another's throats! What rule did I lay down saying that a clan could specialize in only one area? Was that me? No! You fools!" Edmond's veins bulged.

Louis fought off his barrage of attacks, pushed backwards. Turning to his left, he lined up his shot.

"I gave you the path, but it was your stubborn, mule-headed clan leaders that sought power over unity!"

"You sealed our weapons, sealed us off from others."

"Yes, I did. I didn't want you to die in battles for someone else."

"For you!"

"All that fight volunteer to fight for the Sha Clans." Edmond backed off, mirthless laughter spilling from his lips, shifting his weapons. "Clans, ah, now I see it. I see that I was a fool. I should have left you to yourselves. So, tell me, who told Milo I murdered his father because the only thing I seek from the Sha is revenge for my brother!"

"You sit upon a seat of lies."

"And you should question those that tell you truths," Edmond spat.

Louis raised his pistol, aiming at Roska.

Edmond dove sideways, taking the shot in the chest. He had no remaining defensive artifacts. The round caught him and tossed him backward.

Louis stared at him, his face pinching together in disbelief. "Edmond!"

A chain shot out from where Lord Rodriguez was. It grabbed Edmond and hauled him backward. Grenades hit the ground around the Sha and Louis.

Louis's mind was a mess as a guard tackled him into cover just seconds before the grenades went off.

"They're withdrawing!" the captain yelled as the weight of fire wavered. Louis moved, but the guard only groaned. Louis shifted him, finding him peppered with shrapnel.

He drew out a loaded pistol as the fire mage unleashed another barrage of attacks. Sha fighters shot at them, but Louis knew they were gone.

"Group up on me. We'll deal with the wounded and move on!"

Louis got to his knees, watching for them turning back around, his head spinning from what Edmond had said.

He was many things, but Edmond didn't lie to me, not once. Louis wanted to throw those words away, to think them a lie, but that would only hurt more. *Even if he did kill Bartan, am I any better?*

Markus' face appeared in his thoughts.

"Sir, we're ready to head out," a guard said.

Louis looked at the four remaining fighters. Others looped around to meet them.

"Come on, we'll slow them down for the others to catch up."

He got to his feet and started after the Alvans and Edmond's old team.

They caught sight of them down the hall and fired. They hit one of the armored Alvans in the back, tossing them forward. They skidded onto their side, coming up and firing, making the Sha dive for cover.

"Davin, get him back to Erik!"

Louis saw the fire Imp grow, turning into a Demon, picking up Edmond and running.

How much did they hide?

Erik checked on his patients. They were recovering nicely. He'd kept them out of it, knowing they'd want to jump right back into the fight instead of letting themselves heal. He had a few shots of stamina potion to kick start them if things changed.

Egbert jumped into the beast storage device. "Wounded coming in!" he yelled, and then disappeared again.

Erik checked the area he had prepared for them.

Davin, in his Demonic-looking form, arrived carrying Edmond. His chest armor had crumpled in. Erik checked for an exit wound out the back of his armor but didn't see anything.

The man was pale as death, coughing and spluttering. A lesser man would have died.

"Put him down there." Erik gestured at the table he'd set up.

"He saved Roska. Dove in front of the shot," Davin growled, putting him down gently.

Erik tore off his armor. It had dented inward. He used his white gloves and found blood on Edmond's back with his pat check.

"I've got him now. You can get back out there," Erik said. He didn't know what to make of his words. Edmond and Roska had butted heads constantly. If there was one person that Erik was sure Edmond wanted to die, it was Roska. Diving for the shot was out of character.

"The hell did you do that for?" Erik muttered as he studied the wound. It had gone through his lower ribs, up through his insides and out his mid-back near his spine.

"It's my why," Marshal coughed, sputtering with a mad bloody smile.

Erik gave him a Revival needle around the wound, prepping another. *Keep him talking and awake.*

Edmond seemed happy to oblige. "You must have tried the Trial to go to the Eighth Realm. Figure out your why." Erik hit him with another needle and pulled out an IV insertion kit, prepping his arm.

"Yeah, I did." Erik cleared the area, moving with quick precise movements of one that had gone through the process all too many times before.

"Why do you fight? A great question for someone that has a reason to fight. Not much of a reason if you don't want to fight."

"What do you mean?" Erik tapped down the needle and got the stamina and healing potion flowing. *Sorry, Yang Zan.* He used his Medical Scan through his dungeon core.

"You have to fight for something to reach the Ninth Realm. See, if your why is to support others from behind, that's not really a fight. That's just dying by inches, swarmed by others."

He coughed and Erik saw the shards of bone and metal inside his body, as well as the elemental poisoning. He took out a powder and threw it over the wound, making Edmond hiss.

Edmond pulled out a rune card and passed it to Erik. "You'll be needing this."

"Cheers." Erik put it to the side.

"I brought the Sha together, hoping to help the clans, provide security to them all and my people. I was made the leader of it all. I wanted the groups to work together, but they kept on fighting one another." Pain, deeper than his wounds, rang out in his words. "I tried to control everything, tried to draw it all together. I pushed my friends away, those that I called family. The woman I love, I never once told her those words, scared that she would be targeted for being with me."

Erik pulled out the shards from inside Edmond's body.

Edmond grunted in pain.

He gave up on his life, hoping to give better lives to others. What the hell did I give up to join the army? A comfortable, secure life? "All done. So, what made you start fighting for others? When you first got together with your team?" Erik asked.

Edmond was going empty-eyed.

"Hey, come on there, Dujardin. No sleeping on the job!"

Erik gritted his teeth at the cavity inside Edmond.

"I, uhh, well, I just wanted to belong somewhere. I wanted to have people that would care for m*eee*." Power surged through Edmond as he grunted in pain.

"Well, shit!" Erik yelled, remembering the changes he had seen in Rugrat. "Uhh, okay, use your power on yourself. Focus on your body and how it was. Here, let me guide you."

Edmond let out a mix between a scream and a grunt.

Erik took out more potions and powders.

"Okay, follow what I do," Erik said. He started to heal Edmond and felt the power within him follow what he was doing, sowing back in his internal organs, and moving outwards.

Edmond slumped on the table.

Erik checked his heartbeat. It was weak but stable. He poured Stamina potions into Edmond's body, bringing him back up. The worst of his wounds were dealt with.

Erik sighed and kept working on Edmond. His body was healing at an accelerated pace compared to before.

He pressed his lips together. *When I came to the Ten Realms, I had Rugrat beside me. Now there are all these people standing with me, supporting me that I hurt, that I attacked. For trying to help me.*

Erik worked on Edmond, stitching up the last of his wounds.

I'm just glad that I didn't turn out like my parents.

Nymiria stumbled into the storage crate on a twisted leg.

"What happened?" Erik asked, finishing up his work.

"The Sha pinned down Team One. Their reinforcements just showed up." Nymiria grunted. She'd been hit in the leg.

Erik moved to her, putting it in place and fusing the bone, turning her paper-white through the pain.

"They've got nearly a hundred with them. Team Two is hurrying, but they're too far away and we need his rune card." She gestured at Edmond with her chin.

Erik remembered the card on the ground. He grabbed it. "Watch the place for me, will you?"

He pulled his helmet on, grabbing his rifle and exited the beast storage crate, looking around wildly. Egbert fired spells over the ancient broken defenses outside of the transition point hall. They were all hiding behind the low walls and pillars that broke up the approach.

Unfortunately, the debris also gave the Sha cover to advance towards the hall.

Erik dropped down next to the wall, rounds hitting it.

"Erik!" Egbert ducked down.

"You'll need this," Erik held out the rune card.

"Got it." Egbert tucked it into his robe.

"Coming in!" Tully yelled as her group came in from the flank opposite the Sha.

Roska seemed to have been waiting for this and used several spell scrolls, forcing the Sha to find cover.

Egbert stood back up as Rugrat and Davin added their attacks.

Erik raised his rifle, firing at the Sha positions.

Tully's team ducked, weaving between cover to the transition hall. A team member was hit. Osmo grabbed them and dragged them through the broken outer walls, towards the transition point.

"Peel back!" Roska yelled.

Rugrat released his spells, hosing the area with his machine gun.

Erik turned and ran with them toward the hall. Impacts hit the broken defensive walls. Beyond the transition point, the doors lay open, showing the softly glowing formation's runes.

Erik staggered as the ground softened to swamp mud. He didn't have time to cry out as stone shot up from the ground, wrapping around his body like a snake, lashing his arms to his side as he stopped mid-stride.

Silence snapped through the hall as Erik turned his head. It was the only thing free from the cocoon.

What the hell kind of spell is this?

Others were trapped and struggling in cocoons, too.

Erik used the dungeon core shards to try and create spells, but the stone drained their energy.

Mana won't work against it. Harrod and Roska strained against the stone, unable to break free even with their strength.

Erik turned his head, dread in his bones as a demi-human walked down the hall. The lizard demi-human had blood on its hands, maw, and clothes.

"I thought I sensed mana over here," the creature hissed, reaching out a hand. A Sha, bound in stone, shot over to the demi-human. It held out its hand, grabbing them by the neck. "How delicious."

His head enlarged as he bit off the man's head.

Erik could feel the heavy Earth elements within the stone leaching through his pores. It hadn't been made with mana or spells, but through manipulating the elements themselves.

He remembered Lee Perrin's words, and instead of calling on the elements, he tried to use them. He reached out to the stone prison with his Earth element, holding an image in his mind and opened a cavity for his index finger.

The stone shifted away from his finger slowly but surely.

I can do it! He looked at the others and gritted his teeth, catching sight of Rugrat.

The demi-human reached out and grabbed another Sha fighter. Her cocoon shifted closer and peeled open. Water looped around her hands and legs, binding her as she struggled.

The beast inhaled; a stream of purple, gold and one multi-colored were pulled from her body.

She screamed as her body hollowed out then turned to dust, reminding Erik of what happened when they collected a tombstone.

Why do you fight? Why don't you want to die? Why do you go out and fight when you don't need to? Do you like fighting? Why did you leave a comfortable life behind for this? He tried to not focus on the demi-human walking around the outside of the transition pad.

Erik felt a tug in his mind. His thoughts pulled in the direction of his words. *I joined the army because I wanted to see people as people, not just money. I didn't want to have my medical abilities twisted into profit.* "I wanted to fight for people's lives, be with them in their time of need." *I did it because I didn't want to end up like my parents.*

Erik didn't feel excited, but his mind cleared. His thoughts lightened by degrees. The sensation didn't wash through him, but it felt as if he had just come out of the black, his tunnel vision expanding to take in the rest of the world.

"I fight to not be like my parents," Erik frowned, confused by his own words, but feeling that they were right somehow.

Quest Completed: Why do you fight?
You fight to not be like your parents. To help others rather than profit.
Rewards:
Reformation of Will
Entrance to the Ninth Realm once you reach level 80

Erik felt as if a barrier had been broken, as if his mind had been united with his body. It was no longer some disassociated thing that it had been all his life, something that he had existed within a part of.

He could feel the dungeon core shards dissolving into his body, revitalizing him.

Quest: Mana Cultivation 3
The path to cultivating one's mana is not easy. To stand at the top, one must forge their own path forward.
Requirements:
Reach Liquid Mana Core
Rewards:
+40 to Mana
+40 to Mana Regeneration
+500,000,000 EXP

Quest: Bloodline Cultivation 2
The power of the body comes from the purity of the bloodline.
Requirements:
Form a Sky Grade Elemental Core with 3 elements
Rewards:
Sky Grade Bloodline
+10,000,000,000 EXP

Quest: Mana Cultivation 3
The path to cultivating one's mana is not easy. To stand at the top, one must forge their own path forward.
Requirements:
Reach Liquid Mana Core
Rewards:
+40 to Mana +40 to Mana Regeneration +500,000,000 EXP

Quest: Bloodline Cultivation 2
The power of the body comes from the purity of the bloodline.
Requirements:
Form a Sky Grade Elemental Core with 3 elements
Rewards:
Sky Grade Bloodline +10,000,000,000 EXP

123,023,379,747/128,249,000,000 EXP till you reach Level 86

More than that, his world gained color. His mana domain stretched out with his elemental domain. It was as if he had been looking at it all wrong before. His world filled with the color of the elements.

A shadow passed Erik. He looked up to see a lizard demi-human glide to the transition point entrance on a carpet of water.

The creature was *dense* with Water and Earth elements, drawing those elements to himself through mutual attraction instead of conscious effort

"Finally, I can escape this prison." The creature looked at the transition point.

Erik called upon the Earth element, reaching to the stone around him and through the floor to those nearby.

"Too tall for gnomes. Manufactured mana system. Must be the new humans. So much easier to draw from than Gnomes or Elves."

Erik watched the Earth elements move to the creature, creating stairs as he stepped down toward the transition point.

The demi-human tilted his head in an inhuman manner, staring at Nymiria, who was closest.

Erik tried to use spells, but they fizzled out, entering the stone, and only strengthening the bind. He reached out to the stone encasing him instead, trying to exert his control, remembering what Lee Perrin had taught him. *Resonate with it like a tuning fork. You are part of it, and it is part of you.*

He thought of how he created hammers from the ground, that resonance that he *knew* he could create a hammer. He recalled how the dragons used elements naturally.

Erik sent a surge of lightning through his body, shattering the stone prison around him.

He extended his hand, feeling the Earth elements still under his command before he *pulled*.

They exploded, freeing his allies. Rugrat unleashed chains from his feet, smashing through more cocoons as he fired on the beast.

It closed its mouth with a snap; water elements congealed into spears. Erik called upon fire, his strongest element, and punched out, using One Finger Beats Fist to create a lance of flame that broke through several spears, turning them into steam.

Alvans unleashed their mana, making the air shimmer like summer heat.

The defense walls shattered, spells striking the creature's skin.

"You dare to attack me! Aziri the Devourer!" He dodged rounds. Blades of water shot out of the sky around him.

Erik drew upon his Fire element, blasting it out to stop some of Aziri's attacks.

Others cast spells, but by the time they, did Aziri had moved already. Erik hissed as he and others were struck by the water blade rain from behind.

I should have seen that!

"Push him out of the way and move for the transition point!" Roska yelled.

She cast a burst spell, hitting Aziri in the side. Several rounds hit the beast. The wounds healed in mere seconds.

Erik felt the surge of power through the ground like snakes underground rippling out according to Aziri's will. Stone spears shot out of the ground.

Erik blocked several with his own Earth element, but he wasn't strong enough. He used the butt of his rifle to smash another nearby.

Someone screamed out, hit with the attacks.

Aziri stepped forward, but the ground under his feet shoved him to the side, next to Tully.

Rugrat's mana chain grabbed her and hauled her toward the transition point.

Harrod let out a yell and charged forward. "Come on, you bastard!"

"Harrod!" Kameela yelled as Harrod smashed into Aziri.

His gauntlets and armor glowed with power, his fist meeting the creature's, creating a shockwave that shook the defensive structure. The blow was stronger than any that Erik could have landed.

Aziri turned with the blow, his tail whipping out and hitting Harrod through the defensive wall.

Erik threaded poison into his rounds, hitting Aziri with several. Green wisps of smoke rose from where the rounds hit, his skin darkening as his body healed around the rounds.

"Last man!"

Erik felt a tap on his shoulder.

"Five Mississippi," Erik counted under his breath as Aziri was driven to the side under the weight of attacks.

They tore open spell scrolls; Aziri threw up defenses and continued attacking.

A spear skewered a special team member.

Erik's count reached zero as he ran for the transition point. They had a firing line arrayed against Aziri.

Egbert reached out with his spells, pulling the wounded into his beast storage crate.

Erik felt the water needles appear above. He pulled on his Fire element creating a sheet of heat, pouring mana into it, expanding it several times.

It hissed as the water darts turned to steam.

Erik missed the pillar of water that stabbed out of a nearby wall. He turned his plates into it and was tossed to the side.

He hit the ground and rolled. Spells shot over him as Aziri reached over. "Those who gain their will are so much tastier!"

Erik felt water curl around him. He reinforced his body with just metal and water. His skin took on a metallic sheen as he reached out and drew the Fire element behind Aziri.

The air turned into a wild flame, hitting Aziri in the back. It wasn't powerful, a half-formed attack, but it created a sheet of flame several meters wide.

Azizi hissed as smoke boiled off his skin. He punched out. Stone gathered around his hand before he released it. It struck Erik in the chest, cracking his armor and his metal enhanced ribs. Erik hit a wall as the stone fist melded to his armor and grew around him, trying to secure him to the wall.

Erik fought Aziri's attack as Aziri fended off the attacks of a dozen Special Team members. He seemed to get annoyed and ran into the fray. Erik sensed him pulling in the Water element, speeding up his movements and making him hard to catch as the Earth element flowed to protect his vitals from attacks and aid his own kicks and punches.

Erik tore off the stone that encased him. He released flame, stone, and metal to divert attacks and break them before they appeared. He could see them spread from under Aziri as he fought.

It took all of Erik's concentration to just stop them, fighting several others and moving at the same time.

Roska was hit with water blades and Walkins sunk into the ground before a stone spear stabbed through his neck.

"Everyone not on the skirmish line, pull back!"

The ground underneath Aziri shoved him to the side as he threw out his hands. Thin spears of water grew in size and speed as they cut through the air while he stomped his foot. A pillar as thick as a man sharpened into a point and stabbed out of the ground along with several spikes.

"He's sending Earth spells through the ground!" Erik yelled as he ran past the line of team members across the entrance of the main door. He grabbed a wounded team member, throwing them on his shoulder as he ran for the pad.

They used their own spells and Earth element mastery to fight off his attacks. Aziri jumped into the air and the ground attacks stopped. Water materialized under his feet. The Sha he passed escaping from their prisons screamed as his mere presence dehydrated whatever was closest to him, turning them to dust as he devoured their power and drew the water from their very bodies.

Erik extended his hand, reaching for the lightning in his elemental core and releasing it *through* his mana channels. It ran through his body like a charging horse, his will the guiding the rider. Lightning shot out of his hand, resonated with the heavy metal elements in the air, growing from fist sized lighting to man-sized, obliterating a water spear, striking the water around Aziri and running through his body.

Aziri was hit, tossed aside, giving Erik time to turn and run. He called upon his elements, infusing them into his body and the area around him. He shot through the main door, past the special team as they ducked back away from the earth spears that stabbed through the entrance.

They ran for the transition point. The team had lined up outside the inner hall in a skirmish line. Erik ran past them, leaving them to their job, creating another skirmish line. With the others already on the transition pad, Egbert fed it energy from his mana stones.

There was the sound of shooting and an explosion that sent dust into the transition hall. The skirmish line outside ran back to the transition point.

"You won't leave!" Aziri grabbed Osmo at the rear, crushing Osmo's neck, sucking his energy then tossing him away.

Aziri was about to reach the transition point, his body glowing with a dusty yellow and a deep dark blue.

"A tasty one!" Aziri dropped through the ground,

"Egbert!" Erik yelled as Azari shot out of the ground, his mouth opening as he reached for Egbert.

"Have a taste!" A spell formation snapped in front of Egbert and blasted into Aziri's open mouth. His body lit up from within, bursting through him as if a sun had been born in his stomach.

Erik could see the outline of his body and how rapidly he drew in the mana, bleeding off the effect of the spell as he was sent flying backward, crashing into the Sha fighters who were still trapped in their cocoons.

"Aziri didn't say you could leave!" The beast was missing parts of his body, and its jaw was half broken, making it sound like a drunkard, but already healing as it rushed the transition point. They fired their rifles into the creature, stripping meat from its bones as the undercity and transition point disappeared.

15

Bittersweet Revelation

L ouis had never seen such a monster before. The beast smashed through several cocoons, freeing some and killing most.

"Aziri didn't say you could leave!" It jumped for the transition point as the Sha used spells to free one another.

Louis was broken free by his cousin, the one who had killed Markus.

He threw down a teleport pad and activated it.

An explosion rocked the interior of the defensive structure, breaking the outer walls. The Sha crouched as they readied their teleportation pads.

A roar shook the very building as the rubble shifted. The beast was like a whirlpool, drawing in elements and mana from the air.

Water shot down as Louis felt a shove from behind. He looked back to see his cousin pierced with dozens of raindrops turned water spears. The teleportation formation activated, and he found himself aboard *Le Glaive*.

What the hell was that demi-human?

Louis looked at the pad; no one else came through.

He snarled as people mobbed him with healing concoctions. "Get out of my way!"

He turned, forcing his way through them, and heading for the bridge. His mind flicked to that beast, to Edmond's words. He wasn't sure what he felt, seeing the Marshal sacrifice his life to protect someone that he hadn't known for more than a few weeks. He pulled out his sound transmission device as the ship rocked.

Alarms went off as people rushed to their battle stations.

"Fredrick!" Louis yelled.

"You've got some timing. We're under attack from the Black Phoenix Clan. They must've—"

"Pull back all the Sha in the Treasure Hall now! Have the fleet move to the nearest transition point immediately! Full power to engines!"

The ship rocked with hits, the floor vibrating from the impacts.

"It's only the Black Phoenix Clan. If we run—"

"I don't care about them. We need to get the hell out of here. Now!" Louis contacted the other captains. "We need to leave the Violet Sky Realm right now."

"We need to deal with the Black Phoenix Clan, we can't let this kind of—"

"Shut up, Kline! There's something in the Treasure Hall that is stronger than anything I have ever seen. We were like children in front of it. Even with a warship, I don't think we could defeat it. We need to go before that thing decides to leave its home."

Kline clicked his tongue.

"We will take more damage like this," Fredrick said.

"I don't care what damage we take. Get us the hell out of here."

Louis stormed through the ship toward the command center.

He reached the bridge to see the fleet was in its diamond formation, one to either side, forward and rear of *Le Glaive.*

"They came in from the forest. They're trying to push us in the direction of the Treasure Hall."

"They're powering a Phoenix Breath!"

"Shift the barrier to compensate!" Louis yelled.

The frigate opened its armored plates before belching out a beam of destruction. The elemental makeup of the Violet Sky Realm tinted the attack, changing some of its properties as it struck the mana barrier, leaving an angry scar across its surface.

The ship's formations dimmed under the light, their cannons trading fire with the Black Phoenix's.

"Tell me if you see anything odd from the direction of the Treasure Hall. Do we have a location to jump to?"

"No, sir. All of our grounding points have been destroyed."

Louis hit the table. Without those points, they would be jumping blind. It would be hard to tell where they would end up.

They prepared for this and have the weight of ships on their side. The Sha Ships were heading away from the Treasure Hall, but the Black Phoenix Clan were on them and holding the advantage, raining destruction on their barriers.

"Another frigate is preparing their main cannon."

"What's that?" one of the sensor officers said, barely audible in the shouting of the bridge.

"What do you see?" Louis moved to them.

"Strange readings from the Treasure Hall and approaching quickly."

"What kind of readings?"

"We have visual, but it's hard to keep up. It looks like the ground is being torn up."

A roar shook the air as Louis looked through the windows, utilizing a far range spell on his eyes. A wyvern with yellow and blue colorations grew in size as it approached.

They had to get out of there as quickly as possible but had no points to teleport... Wait. "Can we use the teleportation pads in the Treasure Hall to jump to? There's more than one transition point down there," he asked across the bridge. It grew silent, everyone looking at the helm-team, who in turn looked at the helmswoman.

"It should." She grimaced.

"Teleport us to them *now!*"

"Attack coming from right flank!"

The barrier shuddered with the breath attack. Sheets of rain crashed against the barriers of both fleets as spears of stone shot out of the ground, striking the airship from below, the attacks draining the barriers. Aziri was around twenty meters long and just as wide.

He must've been holding back in the Hall.

"Ten seconds!"

"Fleet Mana barrier is down!" The hits made the ship shudder as they kept moving.

"Don't fire on him!" Louis yelled.

Aziri roared as Black Phoenix Mana cannons fired. He weaved through their fire, moving higher.

Louis held onto the consoles around him as Aziri reached the first Black Phoenix Clan frigate. He pulled his wings in and breathed out a stream of sapphire that burst the Black Phoenix barrier, coloring it before his head poked through, carving into the armor of the ship and through the intervening decks.

The beast showed signs of his previous battle as the ship fell towards the ground. The beast breathed in, drawing in golden, purple, and multi-colored light, expediting his healing process as the Black Phoenix Clan's formation collapsed. He turned to charge another warship.

Le Glaive shuddered as the fleet appeared above the Treasure Hall.

"Find us a transition point and get us the hell out of here," Louis said.

He looked around, the pale faces and stillness filling the bridge.

"Do it now!"

That pulled them back into motion. Louis breathed out as he looked at the sensor screen, seeing under the fleet.

The rubble around the Treasure Hall shifted. Bodies as long as a corvette shook free of centuries old debris and dust, turning their hungry eyes skyward.

Roars tore free from their throats as small hills covered in flowers twitched and attacked the barriers above. Dragons and their broods shivered and wafted their wings, lifting them upwards.

"Barriers underneath! All cannons, fire!" Louis yelled.

Cannons rotated to their new targets and fired, striking the dragons and Jorken as they decorated the barriers.

Le Glaive shook with enemy attacks once more.

"Find that damn transition point! And keep an eye out for Aziri," Louis barked.

The dragons' breaths carved into their barriers.

A group of sickly-looking dragons, smaller than their brethren, passed through the *Tourville's* barrier, several dropping down below, dead.

One grabbed the side of the ship, only to have several cannons go off at point blank in its body.

Half a dozen others of all sizes clawed their way into the ship, leaking noxious gasses from their mouths. One smashed the ship with their tail, skewing the entire ship and breaking its barrier.

A dragon shoved its head into the hole it had made in the top of the ship and breathed its poison inside. Smoke poured out from several floors of the ship, blowing out of cannon ports.

Louis shuddered as the ship bent and warped, and as the wood rotted and the metals melted.

"We found it!" the woman manning the helm said excitedly.

"Louis! Louis, I need help!" Boudet's voice filled the bridge.

"Transition us as soon as we can!" Louis yelled. "Pass the order!"

The *Aquilion* bucked as it was hit head-on by several dragons, losing its armor plating. *Le Glaive* shuddered, telling Louis their barrier was gone as hits struck their armor.

Several silver and blue dragons screeched as lightning ran down their bodies before reaching their opening mouths. Their attacks broke the *Amazone's* barriers and raked her sides, melting and warping iron.

Méduse gained the attention of several dragons, their fiery breath melting armor and setting fire to the timbers underneath through sheer heat.

They circled, their tails smashing into the side of the ship, tearing armor asunder and spilling gunnery teams.

"Transition!"

Le Glaive disappeared in a flash of light and reappeared near a city perched in the northern mountains of the Seventh Realm.

The ships appeared one after another, damage across their hulls.

Several dragons and dragonlings looked around, releasing their attacks. A dragon roared and jumped free of the warship. Dragonlings followed it as it headed for the city.

"Clear the ships of dragons and teleport to Purkesh," Louis said.

The weapons opened fire on the much-reduced dragon numbers. The *Tourville* didn't appear even as they finished off the last dragon. Louis stumbled back, looking at Marshal *Edmond's* throne. He grimaced as he sat down in it.

For the first time in what felt like years, the wind howled, the biting cold across the mountains tearing the breath from Erik's lungs. Team members fanned out, checking the area.

Roska supported Kameela, blood staining her clothes, her own and Harrod's.

Erik blinked and then shook his head as the golden experience rose like a cloud, entering the bodies of everyone as they paused for a half second. They grunted as their bodies glowed; mana, elements and *experience* flooded their senses.

Erik pushed off his notifications, scanning the remote mountains they found themselves on.

A flying beast screeched in anger at their presence.

George roared in his demi-human form, making the regal flying beast squawk like a drowned chicken as it eagerly fled the mountain top.

Erik welcomed the flow of mana and elements permeating the Seventh Realm.

"Egbert, find us some shelter," Roska said. "No time to relax just because we're in the Realms."

They found a cave, the Special Team clearing out any critters found within. The wounded were laid out along the cave wall. Yang Zan was pulled from the beast Storage Crate as they worked on them.

Erik worked on getting in IVs. He used his domain to see through the bodies of his patients, calling upon the Earth element directly to increase their stamina while he used healing spells in conjunction with Water and Wood to assist.

He didn't have time for further thought. It was a mad dash to save lives.

It was nearly an hour later before he rested, the patients having stabilized. Erik looked around; their numbers were four less than what they had left Alva with. Nymiria had been saved from her wounds, but she had lost most of her left side. Erik had never seen anything like it. It was as if her body had been broken down, torn apart, leaving only ash in places. Thankfully, it hadn't burned through her vital organs or her brain.

Erik sat back, drinking from his canteen blankly. He opened his notifications and checked his stat sheet.

Skill: Alchemy
Level: 107 (Master)
Able to identify 3 effects of the ingredient.
Ingredients are 10% more potent.
When creating concoctions mana regeneration increases by 40%
Upon advancing into the Master level of Alchemy, you will be rewarded with one randomly selected item related to this skill.

You have received the *Elemental and mana alchemy interactions* book +10,000,000,000 EXP

Skill: Throwables
Level: 58 (Journeyman)
Your throws gain 5% power
Stamina used for throwing is decreased by 15%

Skill: Healer

Level: 121 (Master)

You are a Master on the human body and the arts of repairing it. Healing spells now cost 20% less Mana and Stamina. Patient's stamina is used an additional 30% less.

Skill: Stealth

Level: 95 (Expert)

When in stealth, your senses are sharpened by 10%

Movements are 25% quieter

Upon advancing into the Expert level of Stealth, you will be rewarded with one randomly selected item related to this skill.

You have received *lock picking tools*
+100,000,000 EXP

Quest Completed: Purpose

There are many secrets and half-truths about the Ten Realms. Why does it exist? What is it for? Separate the myths and legends from lies and truth.

Requirements:

Reach the Eighth Realm

Join the Ten Realms Mission Hall

Become at least a one-star level hero.

Rewards:

The Ten Realms stands as the last bastion against the Ravagers and Devourers of the Shattered Realms. The home of the Elves and Gnomes at first, it now hosts Humans the most populous race.

The Ten Realms- serves one purpose. To train people strong enough to drive back the shattered races.

You are invited to join the Academy Avegaaren.

+1,000,000,000 EXP

You have reached Level 104

When you sleep next, you will be able to increase your attributes by: 110 points.

587,162,136,144,775/1,168,160,000,000,000,000,000 EXP till you reach

Level 105

"Roska wants to see you. She's planning our trip back," Egbert said.

Erik looked up to see his robe was in tatters and part of his face and ribs had dissolved. His head twitched to the side.

"You going to be okay?" Erik asked. He knew that Egbert's knowledge and personality were engraved onto his body.

"Ah, just a little bit of damage. The girls have a copy of my runes in Alva, they—" He twitched again to the side and back again. "Uh, what was I saying? Sorry, just need to get my runes re-carved." He lurched and backed up.

"No worries. Take a seat and work to repair yourself," Erik said, hiding his worry.

"Ah, I think that would be a good idea. Dungeon core has the plans, will lay in the runes and repair—" He shuddered. Erik helped him sit. "Me... Oh, twitchy. Hello."

Egbert lurched uncontrollably a few times before he settled down. Mana flowed through his mana gathering formations and into his dungeon core, his skeleton regrowing and formations chasing afterwards.

It was several hours later when Erik was able to get some rest and add in his new attribute points.

He was heavily geared towards mana with his cultivation breakthrough.

When I enhance myself with elements I'm much stronger physically.

He worked to try and balance himself out a bit more and fix where he was lagging, dropping a full seventy points into stamina, ten into Agility and thirty into Strength.

Name: Erik West	
Level: 104	
Race: Human-?	
Titles:	
From the Grave III	
Blessed By Mana	
Dungeon Master IV	
Reverse Alchemist	
Poison Body	
Fire Body	
Earth Soul	
Mana Reborn V	

Wandering Hero *Metal Mind, Metal Body* *Sky Grade Bloodline*	
Strength: (Base 90) +88	1958
Agility: (Base 83) +120	1218
Stamina: (Base 93) +105	3267
Mana: (Base 317) +134	4700
Mana Regeneration (Base 340) +71	264.04/s
Stamina Regeneration: (Base 162) +99	59.52/s

Yang Zan had just finished checking Edmond. Kameela sat inside the beast storage ring with Robert, Esther, and Edmond. She was the only one to come away without injuries.

Edmond was awake but resting as Robert slept and Esther was still being kept unconscious. Erik had explained what he had done and what his motivation was.

"What were you thinking, acting the way you were?" Kameela hissed, wrapped up in an extra thick coat.

"One of the fastest ways people bond is to have a common enemy. I thought…" He trailed off under her glare.

"Finish it, Edmond Dujardin."

"I thought that you and the others could bond with the Alvans over your anger with me, integrate the groups better so that you might be able to join them and gain protection from the Sha."

"And you thought to carry out this plan without consulting what *we* wanted?"

"Kameela…" He moved to grab her hands, but she flinched away. It dug deep, seeing that anger in her eyes. "Everything I did, I did to help you."

"Help us? I want to believe you, but these last weeks you have acted like a different person. How am I supposed to know who you are if you don't tell me? How can I trust you when you would so easily manipulate me or the others?"

"We are a team. We make it out together," Edmond said.

Kameela looked away. "I don't think we have been a team since Bartan's death. I wish that we were, but I've been blind." Tears ran down her face as she forced out her words. "Robert, Harrod, and I have always been a team, but you left us."

"Kameela." Edmond felt that his world was tearing worse than ever losing the Sha. "I love you."

She stilled with his words. "I've wanted to hear those words for nearly two centuries." She looked back, the pain burying itself like a blade in his stomach, punching the air out of his lungs. "And I loved you, but I'm not sure I can love someone I don't trust. I'll see you at the meeting."

She disappeared from the beast storage crate, and Edmond took a deep breath, closing his eyes against the hot tears that ran down his face. He rubbed them clear and sniffed, blinking to try and bring them under control.

He got up from his cot and walked away from the others. Standing, he left the beast storage crate, finding himself in a cave.

He glanced at a team member who nodded to the back.

Edmond walked to the end of the cave where Erik, Roska, and Kameela were talking.

"If you will take us," Kameela said, "Harrod, Esther, Robert and myself will come with you. We don't know what the situation will be with the Sha, and we don't have a place there anymore."

Roska glanced up and Kameela went quiet as Edmond approached with a pressed smile. He brought himself up to standing and bowed as much as his wounds would allow, getting a cough from Erik as he stared daggers at him. Edmond slowly returned to standing.

"I am sorry for the way I have acted in the past, being a pompous ass. I wanted to make sure that the people I cared about would become close to you and have somewhere to go after all of this."

Erik nodded. Roska held out her hand.

Edmond took it.

"You saved my life and fought for the lives of my people every step of the way. I can't say that I didn't want to smack you a few times. Just don't be such a dickhead."

"I'll take it under advisement." Edmond gave her a slight smile.

"Then the next thing we need to do is head back to Alva," Erik said.

Edmond swallowed his words, scared of what might have happened in their absence, the bite of betrayal all too recent.

"We spotted a city about a day's walk away. We'll head there, use the totem, and go to the Alvan Empire. From there, everyone can do as they want," Erik said.

The meeting broke up shortly after that. Edmond found somewhere quiet to sit. The mood was sobering, friends lost too recently, but there was more to do before they could grieve.

Edmond sighed, pulling out a jacket and pulling it around his shoulders. He sat against the wall, watching all, but not seeing anything as he lost himself in his thoughts. He cast his mind back to when he started the Sha with his team, bringing others together to support one another, binding them into one whole. *Optimistic idiots.* He smiled, raising his knee, and grabbing a rock, resting his arm on his knee, and turning the rock.

Where did it go wrong? When Bartan was murdered...

He breathed in, remembering the crazed action of those few minutes, how Bartan had looked up at him, gasping.

"From behind, protect the others." The words of a ghost sounded in his ears as fresh and jagged as the day he heard them.

I became dictatorial in my rule. I forced others to do as I wanted. I wished for the best, and I forced them to do as I wanted.

He felt tired, as if the years had suddenly caught up with him, hollowed him out from the inside. The craziest thing was that he craved to be back in that position of power. He wanted to protect others, to do a job that he trusted few others to do.

He looked at the stone in his hand. There were no meetings for him to run to. There was just one task ahead of him and then he could leave it all behind.

For the first time in a long time, he felt like he was moving forward, not being held back by powers beyond his control. He could make changes. That frustration and anger burned at the roadblocks and problems that had been thrown in his face to stall him and lead to furious inaction.

Now that all lay behind him. Given the choice to go back to leading everyone again, he didn't want to anymore.

He held the stone in his hand. *I need to talk to Milo, find out who has been feeding him lies.*

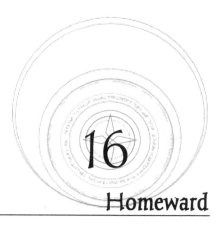

16

Homeward

Delilah drank a stamina potion as she and the council members assembled. Glosil, Jia Feng and Elan were present.

"Approximately one hour ago we were notified that the contract with the Sha has been broken. We received half of their dungeon cores and mana stones," Elan said. "I've contacted everyone concerned, and we notified our guilds. All work with the Sha has ceased and my people are working to make sure that everyone near or working with them are safe."

Glosil cleared his throat. "We apprehended all Sha personnel inside the Alvan Empire with minimal issue."

"Do we have any information from the Sha, or from the Violet Sky Realm?" Delilah asked.

"Nothing from the realm, but I have reports of the Sha fleet appearing near a Seventh Realm city. Their ships were badly damaged, and they were being attacked by *dragons*. There were four ships instead of five. Since then, they have returned to Purkesh," Elan said.

"And no communication from Special Team One or Erik and Rugrat?" Elan shook his head.

Delilah gritted her teeth. *I shouldn't have let them go there under the command of another group. What was I thinking?*

"Commander Glosil, options?"

"All dungeon cores are being moved to ship-building locations to speed up production. I have brought the Tiger Corps up to full readiness. All Totem guards have been notified. I suggest that we send Special Team Four through the Eighth Realm Trial with the mana stones. That should help those that can get into the Ninth Realm to descend again to assist. I suggest we move to the defensive. We can work with our allies to host our forces. In three days, we will move the Tiger Corps into the Seventh Realm, ready to strike at Purkesh."

"I would suggest caution and patience. Also, we shouldn't forget our allies would be happy to support our efforts," Jia Feng advised.

"Elan, do you want to contact them, grill them for information?" Delilah said.

"Do we want to be aggressive or interested?" Elan asked.

"Interested, with the threat that we will tear them down if they have betrayed our trust." Delilah snarled.

"Then I would suggest that we ask Elise to talk to them. She has more trading contacts, and she can apply pressure with her association as a council member."

Delilah worked her jaw and let out a heavy breath. "Make it—"

"Hey everyone, you're up late."

"Egbert?" Delilah looked upward.

"The one, the only, the fabulous. Ah, hello. Oh, sorry, just a little glitch there. Uhh, we're back? I'm going to send Edmond and his team to King's Hill. The rest of us are—"

"Egbert?"

"Sorry, just teleporting into the city."

"Teleport us to King's Hill. To wherever you are," Delilah said.

"Okay!"

White light surrounded them all as Glosil pulled out a rifle and Elan circulated his mana.

Kameela blinked as they arrived on a teleport pad inside Alva. Alvans looked over as soldiers ran forward. Kameela reached for her weapon as the soldiers split up, pulling out stretchers and checking on the wounded.

"Looks like the council is coming," Egbert said. There was a flash of light beside them, and several tired looking people appeared.

Kameela recognized the leader of the Alvan military, Commander Glosil, with his rifle ready standing next to Director Silaz, Academy Head Jia Feng and Council Leader Delilah, and several guards.

Kameela looked at Edmond, who frowned, rubbing his storage ring, ready to draw.

Delilah ran from the group and hugged Erik, nearly toppling him over.

"Oof! Trying to flatten me!" He laughed as she quickly checked him and moved to Rugrat.

"You know how much Momma Rodriguez would hit me if you two were hurt?" She sniffed as she kept looking over Rugrat.

Rugrat smiled and pulled her into a hug. She let out a shuddering breath as others looked over.

"Elan, if you could have someone debrief our friends here. They are our guests. They have fought alongside us and risked their lives for us. The Sha had a coup against Edmond, and now Louis Gerard is in power over them," Erik said.

"I will see to it somewhere more private."

"Egbert, take us to the council chamber. Send Elan and his guards with our Sha friends to one of the military camps."

"Erik," Edmond started.

"You will be looked after and cared for; you have my word. You are under Alva's protection now. Elan, inform them of what is happening with the Sha as long as it isn't operational information."

"Yes, my lord. It is good to see you all back." Elan bowed and gave a tired smile.

"Your bodies," Delilah said, stepping back from Rugrat and holding his arms, studying him for possibly the fifth time.

Kameela turned away from their reunion. White light surrounded her as Edmond, Rob, and the rest of her group appeared at another teleportation pad with Elan Silaz and his four guards.

Alvan military members stood guard, weapons raised.

"Password?"

"We grow together," Elan said.

The rifles lowered.

"Can you get me somewhere to host my guests away from prying eyes?" Elan asked.

"Certainly, Director, if you give us a few minutes to make some preparations?"

"We have the time." Elan smiled and turned back to Kameela and the others.

"Welcome to the Alvan Empire. Don't worry, you are under the protection of Lords West and Rodriguez. No harm will come to you."

"That isn't all that comforting. What about Harrod and Esther? They are still healing," Kameela asked.

"Neither Erik nor Yang Zan or any special team member will let anyone under their care come to harm. That's part of the code that all healers take."

Kameela reached out a hand, silencing Edmond. "Thank you for your hospitality."

"Sorry it's not much right now." Elan bowed his head.

"The quarters have been prepared for you," the soldier said, and pulled out cloaks for them.

They donned them and followed the soldier through a series of tunnels and up to a barracks with simple beds, and a bathroom and showering areas.

"There will be a guard posted outside. Tomorrow we'll go over everything," Elan said from the doorway. He bowed down to his waist. "Thank you for fighting alongside our people and being true allies. I hope you sleep well." Elan's voice held a gravitas to it as he turned and left.

Kameela looked at Rob and Edmond.

"I think I was wrong," Edmond said.

"About what?" Kameela scoffed.

"Alva is more like a family, a true community, than any sect."

Kameela thought of how Delilah had run to them, checking them over. How Glosil had clapped Roska on the back, his face darkening as he realized that they weren't all there.

Edmond sat down on a cot, letting out a sigh as he closed his eyes.

Kameela felt the energy draining from her as fatigue set in.

"You two sleep. I'll take first watch."

"Thanks, Rob."

"No, you sleep first; you were badly injured."

"You got a round through your chest."

"Yes, but I reversed all of that."

"Sleep, Edmond," Robert said.

"Ah, fine."

Kameela smiled slightly, remembering the old days as sleep took her.

Erik came downstairs to the smell of food and the sound of talking.

"You didn't need to do all of this," he said, looking at the feast spread across the kitchen table.

"You two are skinny as rakes. Need to fill you out again!" Momma Rodriguez waved a spatula, turning her scrambled eggs.

"Thank you, Momma," Erik said.

She put her cheek out and Erik kissed it.

"Ah, that's better! No more moping around?" she said.

"No," Erik said, turning his eyes to the other occupant. Delilah smiled as she pulled down plates.

"Delilah, could I talk to you?" Erik pointed to the other room.

"Sure." She wiped her hands down on a cloth and followed him into the dining room.

Erik took in a deep breath, looking down at the floor. "I'm sorry about being such a friggin' asshole. About what I did at your presentation, that is. I was out of order."

Delilah made to talk, but he waved her off.

"I was a prick. Your theory was brilliant. Pills act not only as a chemical reaction but an elemental one, creating the core of a concoction, the effect that it will have, then combining it with plants, mana and elements to increase those effects as variables. Just brilliant! I shouldn't have gone to your lecture to use it to get onto the team going into the Eighth Realm. That was callous and out of line."

Erik looked at Delilah. "Can you accept my apology and me being an ass when I should have supported you? And my thanks for helping me and Rugrat when we're being idiots."

"Well, you'll always be idiots, and thank you for apologizing. It did hurt, but it worked out in the end."

"Yes, but it working out in the end doesn't mean I should hurt the people that are doing their damndest to help me."

"Well, I'm sorry we were stifling you. We got overprotective. In trying to help you both, we were keeping you caged up here and unable to do anything," Delilah said.

Erik opened his mouth and nodded. "Thank you." Erik sighed, feeling the weight shed from his shoulders. "Oh, and also, I found out some information on your theory. There were these birds in the undercity that harvested elements from the air. Then they returned to their nests and gave it to their young like a potion."

"A pure elemental potion?"

"I guess. If you were to find a formula of ingredients that would just absorb the elements, then they could do so and create a kind of tempering concoction of pure elements. Though you'd need to match it with a healing concoction as well."

"Those are much more complicated. We could increase the time that one tempers their body. Then they could heal passively from a series of small doses."

"Or you have the healers working with them. That way, you only have to make one less complicated concoction. If you have to make a tempering concoction, they get complicated with the tempering and healing effects working together."

"Lots of chances for it to go wrong," Delilah agreed, holding her chin in thought.

"Well, I've got a greater control over the elements. What about we do some experimenting when you have some free time?"

"Thankfully, things have calmed down." Delilah frowned. "What happened up there?"

Erik gave her a quick version of what had happened.

"They should be weakened after losing their dungeon cores and mana stones. The Black Phoenix Clan will make use of that."

"Maybe they would have a few months ago. The Black Phoenix Clan has been under attack ever since their ships left for the Violet Sky Realm, and only three of them made it back from the realm. That leaves them with just twelve fighting capable warships."

Erik shook his head. "That deals with one problem, I guess."

Rugrat made it to the bottom of the stairs, wearing shorts and sandals. "Morning. My damn tattoos disappeared again," he complained, scratching his chest.

Delilah blushed and looked away.

"Come on, time for breakfast. Jimmy, where's your shirt? Did you put deodorant on?" Momma Rodriguez said, coming out with two plates.

Delilah and Erik moved to help her.

"Sorry, Ma!" Rugrat's feet pounded on the stairs, heading back up.

Louis stared at the Sha compound over Purkesh. Several ships had crashed into the buildings below. Smoke trailed into the sky and there were flashes of fighting in different areas.

"Louis, this is Abe Velten. It's good to see you," the man said through his sound transmission device.

"What happened?"

"The contract with the Alvans was broken upon their return to the Ten Realms. As part of the terms, we lost several dungeon cores and thousands of mana stones." Abe's voice darkened. "We told everyone that Marshal turned on the Alvans, and had Milo take up position as Marshal. Then the Alvans told us that their people had made it back and Edmond Dujardin and his team helped to save their people. Now the Sha are riled up and groups are fighting one another across the realms, saying they are loyalists to one side or the other or using the confusion to settle old debts. It's a mess." The fight went out of his voice. "What happened in there?"

"Everything was going well until the Alvans and Edmond's team escaped into the undercity. "For weeks they traversed the undercity. They must have looted the place. We found it empty. We ran into them and fought them, but then a demi-human unlike anything I've seen in the Ten Realms cut through them and attacked our ships. We barely escaped with our lives."

"What about the loot?" Abe's voice tightened.

"We got a lot of loot from the realm by visiting different locations. Enough to build some ships." *Which we won't need now.* "And we found storage rings that are filled with all kinds of items from the sect that originally occupied the Violet Sky Realm."

"That is better than nothing. We need to do everything we can to placate the clans and gain people on our side."

"We were in the right. We took out the murderer and the clans that were bleeding us dry!" Louis snarled.

"Be that as it may, it was a coup. There are people loyal to the Marshal, and many had dealings with those other clans and sects. Their interests have now gone up in smoke. Go and get some rest and make sure that your ships are manned and repairs are underway. We don't know if someone will try to take advantage of us in our weakened state."

Louis sighed. "Very well."

"Good to have you back, Louis."

"It's good to be back, Abe, even if it is a mess."

The fleet descended toward the shipyards. Several corvettes patrolled the area aggressively, while Louis saw corvettes piled atop a cruiser coming in across the city.

Louis went through the final checks. The crews started to disembark, anxious to see their families.

Louis teleported to his clan's compound with several guards.

Clan members stood around, looking for their loved ones. A path opened for Louis as his guards escorted him to his home.

The guards were on alert at the gates, opening them just wide enough to admit one person at a time.

He moved through to his house, his protection detail turning to just two people.

"Louis!" Selma cried. The children turned from their lessons and ran towards him. The eldest had tears in her eyes. It seemed she had realized what he was doing. They hugged him and asked him a stream of questions. He looked at his wife, who stood back from them, clasping her hands and chewing on her lips.

"Go back to your lessons. Your father will be here when you are done. Go on now!" Selma said.

The children said their goodbyes and headed back as Louis looked at Selma.

She put a hand to his chest, breathing. "I'm glad you're alive." She moved past him and beckoned for him to follow.

Louis felt his shoulders tighten with his gut.

She walked into his office, moving to the windows. Louis closed the door behind him.

"Selma." He walked forward as she activated the sound canceling field, turning, and crossing her arms.

"What the *hell* were you thinking?"

"I was doing what is best for our future and the future of our children."

"Did what was best for us? We are a half-step away from civil war and my husband, the man who tried to kill our last leader, didn't think to tell me of his plans."

"Everything moved so quickly."

"I guess it must be hard to tell us that you were staging a coup. Though easier to tell our guards and the clan elders?" she yelled.

Louis gritted his teeth and looked away.

"Do you think that I'm an idiot, that I would go around telling everyone? Look, my husband? Yeah, he's going to kill the *Marshal!* I thought I married a smart man. Why in the realms did you *try* to kill him?"

"He is a tyrant; he was using the clans as his own pawns. With the restrictions, it wouldn't be long until our people could do nothing more. All of our defense contracts are down. We cannot support our own training."

"Our own training? Anyone that joins as a Sha fighter has their training paid for!"

"Yes, but only for the basic gear, and the basic gear isn't enough!"

"So you wanted more gear for them?"

"I want our children to do whatever they want, to become crafters or traders if they want to!"

"And you think that killing the man that kept everything running smoothly was the way to go?"

"He was a murderer, Selma!"

"Who did he kill?" Her eyes thinned.

Louis looked away. It was these moments he knew that, while she was the mother of his children, she was also the daughter of one of the Sha's greatest warriors, previous protector of the Marshal himself. She knew the realities of the Ten Realms.

"He killed Bartan Leblanc."

"His *brother?*" Selma seemed unbalanced.

"I was shocked too. I didn't believe it at first, but Milo told me..."

Selma's face was rapidly whitening. "You fool. You blind fool." She held her hair and turned toward the window, stricken.

"I know it is a lot to take in." Louis moved toward her.

She turned on him, her face regaining color. "I know that Bartan was murdered! Do you forget who my father was? Head of the Marshal's protection detail. When he was dying, he told me during one of his episodes that Bartan was killed by a Sha, but it wasn't the Marshal."

"Wait," Louis was brought up short.

"You idiot." She hit his chest. "You talk about the clan this, the battle that, but did you pay no attention to what was happening? The Marshal was the only one keeping everyone together. Who said our children can't do what they want? How many exchanges did we have with the clan and sect leaders that you *murdered,* that you were bound to protect and you *killed?*"

"We will pull the Sha back together," Louis said.

"Pull them back together? The Marshal is *alive,* and you attacked the *Alvans.* Do you know what is happening to the Black Phoenix Clan?"

"They lost most of their cities to an alliance working against them."

"An alliance that wants the Alvan's support. Do you know what they call the Alvans? The lords of the Earth Realms. You wanted to give our children opportunities. Well, you just gave them a title." She stumbled against the window, her lost eyes finding his. "The children of Louis Gerard, the man who *tried* to murder the Marshal and the Emperors of Alva, lords of the Earth Realms. Betrayer of trust and murderer of allies."

"Selma," Louis pleaded.

Her eyes hardened as something deep, dark, and protective came from within her. "The situation is cast. There is nothing for it. We need to deal with what we have. What was your agreement with the other clans? Wwhich ones are on our side and which will be against us? What are you prepared to do against those that riot? What about the crafters and supplies? can we keep them on our side? And your backup plan if this fails?"

Selma drew herself up. Louis felt like a ship among the elemental storms. She must have seen the look in his eyes.

"You are my husband and I still love you, but you are a thick-headed idiot. You have placed our entire family, your clan, in jeopardy. What are your plans?"

Louis started to go through his plans as she tore them apart, adding to them and refining them.

"Where is Markus? Surely, he would have added greater detail," Selma said, slumping into a chair.

Louis dropped his head.

"Louis?"

"Markus died. He was loyal to the Marshal."

She sat up, staring at him, the question just behind her tongue.

"One of the guards came in and Markus... and then..." Louis saw the scene in his mind play over again. He didn't know how many times it had done so in the intervening weeks.

"And this guard, he can attest?"

"He died in the fighting."

"You need to put that information out to the clans before someone twists it like they did with Bartan's death."

Harrod and Esther joined the rest of the group the next day, tired but healed from their wounds.

"You wouldn't believe their medical facilities," Esther said as she sat down.

Kameela helped Harrod to a bed. The big guy was still tired from his healing. The bed squeaked under his weight as he fell asleep.

"What do you think about staying here?" Kameela asked.

Esther looked at Edmond, who raised his hands and sat back in his chair.

"I'd like to, but Mother and Milo. I know he can be a prick at times, but he does what he can for the Sha and he's my brother. Are we sure that he's leading the Sha now?"

"I believe so." Edmond ran a hand through his hair. "When I was fighting with Louis, he said that I had killed your father, stabbed him in the back. That's too precise to be made up. He must have gotten the information from Tiberius, his father-in-law, or from Selma's father. He was half-mad by the time he died. He must've twisted it and spread the rumor."

"You think Louis would do that?" Harrod asked.

"He staged a coup, and I never thought he would do that. Are we sure we know what he is capable of?"

"You think that he killed...?" Esther trailed off.

"So, we still have no idea of who the murderer is, but we think that Louis is using Milo," Robert said.

"Correct, but I made an oath to Bartan to protect his family and I do not break my oaths." Edmond stood. A knock came from the door before it opened, revealing Erik and a lady.

"Edmond, this is Melissa Bouchard. She is from Paris. She learned that you are from France and wanted to talk to you." Erik waved her forward as Edmond cleared his throat. He had missed France for so long, recreated a version here in the ten realms. He opened his mouth but didn't know where to start.

"*Monisour* Dujardin," Bouchard bowed her head.

Edmond cleared his throat and bowed back to her. "*Madame*, it would be a pleasure to talk to you about—" He paused, realizing that France was no longer home, bringing another stab as he no longer had a home. "France." He pushed out a smile.

"If you'd like to take a walk, there are a few hundred years to go through." She smiled.

"Please," Edmond raised an open hand and moved to follow her.

The next day came, and they were allowed to leave the camp, having answered all of Elan's questions.

"So, we're free to go, just like that?" Robert asked as they left the camp's gates.

"You heard what they said. They don't think that we had any part in attacking the Alvans and that we acted in good conscience," Harrod said, much better than even the day before.

"Are you sure about this?" Esther asked.

"I think that it would be best to go as soon as possible. The longer we wait, the more time they have to gain control over the situation and lock down Purkesh. What do you all think?" Edmond asked.

"That's a pleasant change. I think you got through to him, Kameela." Robert grinned.

Kameela shook her head.

"I think you're right." She looked at Esther, who nodded.

"Never been one for the planning. Sounds like a plan at least."

"All right, off to the Seventh Realm we go," Robert said.

17
Removing the Mask

Milo's sigh seemed to release the stress and strain that rested upon his shoulders.

His guards closed the doors behind him, peeking into his home to check for intruders.

He walked deeper into the house. It seemed emptier than ever as he strode toward his office. He walked in to see his mother sitting in front of the fireplace in her chair, warming herself by the fire.

"Good afternoon, Mother," he said, walking over to her and kneeling by her chair. His smile slipped with the news from earlier. Esther was with Edmond. It was not known if she was alive or dead and they were with the Alvans.

He gripped his fist. *I knew that he had put restrictions on the contracts to make them binding. I did not think they would be so severe.* The loss of their dungeon cores had been a great blow, but the contracts went further, putting mana stones and stores of resources on the line as collateral. The loss of so many resources so quickly had nearly bankrupted them.

"Running an empire on the leftovers of storage rings," he snorted and rose, rubbing his mother's shoulder.

He looked around the room for a minute.

"I just need to talk to a friend, Mother. Don't worry, you know him."

Milo made sure the door was secure, activating his formations and the teleportation pad.

He thought he heard a noise, but when he looked, the curtains had just shifted.

It'd be easier living in one of the smaller houses. So much room here to make one paranoid.

The teleportation pad glowed and Crox flashed into existence.

Crox paused, looking at his mother's chair.

"Zala?"

"Yes, Mother is just warming up by the fireplace," Milo said.

"Milo, what did I tell you?"

"That others shouldn't know of our cooperation, but that was when we were working against that murderer. Now he is gone."

"He is in Alva; he is not *gone*." Crox cleared his throat and ran a hand through his hair. "Sorry, just so much has happened. Even a young man like you looks tired."

"Ah, heavy is the head that wears the crown. How are things with the crafters, Master?"

They moved to the windows with Milo pouring drinks.

"They are leery. It has gotten out how little we have in the way of materials remaining. Is Velten able to do anything about getting us more?"

Milo heard a click from the wall. He turned to see the wall open, and Esther walk out, standing between them and the teleportation pad.

"Esther!" He almost ran to her, but saw the others coming through the open section of the wall.

"Have you come to join us now that you've seen the truth?" His expression died halfway through as Edmond walked out of the opening.

"Milo, Zala, Crox." Edmond frowned at the crafter.

"Marshal." Crox returned the look with an upturned eyebrow.

"What the hell is *he* doing here? He murdered our father, Esther! I know it's a lot to take in, but he killed him and then called us nephew and niece! Called our father brother!"

Milo wasn't well-versed in the arts of body cultivation, but he had a decent mana cultivation compared to most in the Seventh Realm. He circulated his mana.

"Louis has been lying to you," Edmond growled. "Old Tiberius was there the day that your father died. The only people who know how he died are Tiberius, your mother, the murderer, and myself. Tiberius must have told his daughter the truth, and she told her husband. He used it as a lie to gain others' support."

Milo frowned and shook his head, gripping his fists tighter, readying a fire spell in his mind.

"Don't think that you can confuse me with your games! It wasn't Louis who told me about my father's death."

Edmond's eyes widened.

"Then who?"

A dry laugh came from beside the fireplace.

"It was me, *Edmond*," Master Crox said, a tube poking out from the underside of his arm as he stood behind Zala, stroking her hair, the barrel just inches from her head.

"Crox," Harrod growled.

"Don't think about doing anything to my mother." Esther aimed at the man.

"Master, what are you...?" Milo half-turned, stumbling over his words, thinking it a ruse. His mana circulations stopped as he saw Crox's hidden weapon.

"You idiot boy! You're the one that put me in this situation. I'm just changing the dynamic. Away from the teleportation pad now. We don't want anything to happen to *another* Leblanc. They do die so messily." He half hauled up Zala to her feet, holding her so the barrel was pressed to her ribs, keeping all of them facing towards him.

"Now, if you could all move toward the desk, I'd rather like to be on my way. Milo, even as an idiot, you're a disappointment. Just like your father. Edmond saw what I was doing and protected your father from me in those last moments," Crox spat, looking at Edmond. "It was *you* who was supposed to die."

"You bastard," Esther said as Edmond remained unnaturally still.

"Y-you, but you told me..." Milo shuddered. "Then everything I've done..."

"A most masterful coup. You might be an idiot in most areas, but you're a fine tool for breaking apart the Sha Clans. Ah, to a most brilliant civil war. I do hope you enjoy the innocent blood on your hands." Crox laughed as he edged toward the teleportation pad, everyone moving away from him. "And I thank you for removing my contract. Once you usurped Edmond, my clauses lifted, and I became a free agent. I was hoping you would have more resources to help me with. A shame really."

Milo let out a cold breath as mana fluctuated in the room.

"Zala, no!" Edmond yelled.

The weapon went off in an explosion.

"Mother!" He and Esther yelled at the same time, running forward, stopping stunned by the sight of their mother standing there, her eyes clear as glass as any signs of weakness were washed away. Her barrier returned to normal as she turned to the screams left behind by the deafening shot.

Crox's fine suit was a bloodied mess. The arm that had held the hidden weapon was pulped, ending at his elbow. The side of his body was one gaping wound as he screamed like a stuck pig, curling around his wound as he calmed.

"So, you're the pitiful creature who killed my Bartan, and then used my son as your weapon," Zala said, stunning everyone but Edmond. "I bet that hurts. Won't be enough to kill a snake like you."

She pulled out a contract and placed it against his side.

The contract flashed with light as Ten Realms light entered his body.

A slave contract.

"Did you kill my husband?"

"Yes."

"What were your plans?"

"To use Milo to stage a coup to free me of my bonds as a Sha crafter. To gain fame among the other crafters that I was denied. Having Milo fund all of my developments."

"Was this all your plan?"

"Some."

"Who were your accomplices?"

"Milo, Maria, Abe Velten, Louis Gerard—"

"Write it down," She gave him pen and paper and he started writing.

"Mother," Esther said.

Zala turned as Kameela, Robert, and Harrod moved past her, aiming at Crox, eyeing her out of the corner of her eye.

"Oh, Esther," Zala said, holding her close and hugging her. "I am sorry for everything." Tears sprang to her eyes, a different woman from the one questioning Crox.

"What?" Milo asked. Everyone seemed to have forgotten him.

"After your father died, we didn't know who the murderer was. We knew they were high up and had the means to hide everything from us. We also knew that Edmond needed someone to listen and learn everything about the clans. See who was loyal and who wasn't. It was messy. I took it on. With the cover of being grief stricken, I was able to carry out my work discreetly." She looked at Milo, patting Esther on the back, and walked towards Milo.

Milo took a shuddering step backward, his foot catching on the floor, and she stopped, looking at her hands. "I-I cared for you. I sat beside you and talked to you about *everything* and not once did you smile or laugh or even talk to me," he said, his vision blurring.

"Milo," Edmond said.

"You stay away from me!" Milo shot out a fist of flame at Edmond, backing away further, spitting as he wiped his eyes.

"Milo," Zala cried out, stepping forward.

"Y-you knew the truth. You kept it from me." *What have I done?* Guilt tore through him.

"You betrayed me with your *secrets.*"

"Brother," Esther said.

"Brother, son, nephew, fuck off! Should I just call myself a puppet and dance on your fucking string?"

Zala flinched as if hit with a physical blow. Edmond closed his eyes, wincing as he tightened his expression.

"What you did was by your own hand. You are an adult now."

Milo tore off the symbol of Marshal, backing up and throwing it at him. "You placed this on me. You may not be a murderer, but you are a *liar,* a man that *uses* others for his own gain!"

"Milo Emmanuel Leblanc!" Zala filled her voice with power.

"Shut up!" Milo roared, his voice filling the room as he pulled a pistol. "Get out! Get out of my *home!*"

"Come with us. We can protect you," Kameela said.

"Protect me from what? A man that uses you for his own gains and a mother that uses the loss of your father to hide herself? A sister that doesn't trust me? I have family and I see *none* of them here." His voice dripped with anger, with venom. "Leave now before I do something we'll all regret." Milo drew himself up, regaining his composure, the anger, the hate, turning stone and solid, fueling him.

Harrod made to grab Crox.

"Leave him! I have many questions to ask my dear *master.*"

"What are you going to do, lad?" Robert asked.

Milo's head swam. *What can I do? The Sha Clans have been shattered. I have to tell everyone what happened, or I will just be another liar. That will open us up to external and internal attacks.* His thoughts turned to Maria, to Abe

Velten, who had taken him in as a true family member and helped him through this all. He realized that it wasn't as hard to answer.

"I'll do what I have always done: protect my family. Now, *leave.*" He brought his pistol back to full cock.

The group looked at him. It was clear they had more to say, but he was too angry to trust himself and he didn't know if he had anything more to tell them.

They left through the door.

"Do you want to know what we will do?" Edmond asked, the last one at the hidden entrance in the wall.

"How do I know if I can trust you? And I know what you will do. Mother has been your spy. She knows what groups are loyal and which ones are not. You will gather them together and you will become Marshal again and you will try to take all this back."

"I did think that, but I don't want to be Marshal again."

"Like I should believe you. No matter what, you will not find me here. This place holds nothing for me now."

"Mi—" Milo fired into the wall, withdrawing another pistol as Edmond's barrier colored with the force of the passing round shot.

"*Leave.*" Milo hissed, no longer wishing to be mocked by him.

Edmond pressed his lips together, eyes filled with unshed tears as he swallowed and left, closing the door behind him with a click of finality.

Milo pressed a formation on his robes.

In minutes, his guards burst through the doors, finding him and the bleeding Crox.

"Secure him and bring me a seer projection stone. I want this recorded and sent to every Sha member throughout the Ten Realms." He took out his sound transmission device and contacted the Veltens and Louis Gerard. "I have found out some disturbing information. Louis, you should prepare your ships and Abe, you should get everyone aboard them. Maria, we have already talked about our plans if we must flee. I believe that time is upon us."

Louis looked down at Purkesh. The fleet didn't know if it was Sha anymore, or just another traveling group of airships.

The bridge was silent, still covered with the signs of battle like the compound below the bridge was silent. He wasn't sure if that was better or worse than the opening riots.

"The rebel fleet is moving into battle formation."

"Keep them on our left side. If they attack, we'll be sure to reply. Send a message. We have all lost enough today." Louis looked as if he had aged a decade, slumped in his commander chair.

Milo had sent a broadcast to all the Sha Clans. The message was simple. Milo had been deceived. He thought that he was going against the man who had killed his father in cold blood to remain the leader of the clans. Edmond Dujardin might have become a tyrant, but he was no murderer. Milo apologized to every Sha member, telling them that the foundations of the Sha Clans were broken and disjointed. Instead of trying to fix the clans, he extended an invitation to join the Sha. One group, one sect that would work together.

Louis looked out at the edge of the compound to where carriages waited. Recruiters from different sects and clans were there, scouting out the talent that was leaving the Sha and everything it entailed behind.

Others were invading the compound as peacefully as possible, claiming the land in the name of their group.

Clans loyal to Edmond had joined with him, gathering ships under his banner. They had been open with their intentions. They were heading to the lower realms to support the Alvans, their staunch allies.

Selma's hand rested on Louis's shoulder and squeezed.

He took comfort, placing his hand atop hers.

"One day at a time," she said.

They had uprooted everyone in their clan, sending them to secure locations with the lack of space aboard the ships they controlled.

When we get there, wherever there is, then I'll step down. I just want to live comfortably with my family.

18

Bitter Lessons

E rik was resting at home, letting the world go by as he ran through his stats again.

It was several hours later when Erik was able to get some rest and add in his new attribute points.

He was heavily geared towards mana with his cultivation breakthrough.

When I enhance myself with elements I'm much stronger physically.

He worked to try and balance himself out a bit more and fix where he was lagging, dropping a full seventy points into stamina, ten into Agility and thirty into Strength.

Name: Erik West	
Level: 104	
Race: Human-?	
Titles:	
From the Grave III	
Blessed By Mana	
Dungeon Master IV	
Reverse Alchemist	
Poison Body	
Fire Body	

Earth Soul	
Mana Reborn V	
Wandering Hero	
Metal Mind, Metal Body	
Sky Grade Bloodline	
Strength: (Base 90) +88	1958
Agility: (Base 83) +120	1218
Stamina: (Base 93) +105	3267
Mana: (Base 317) +134	4700
Mana Regeneration (Base 340) +71	264.04/s
Stamina Regeneration: (Base 162) +99	59.52/s

484,841,267/547,148,000 EXP till you reach Level 78

A knock came from the front door, pulling him from his thoughts. He opened it to Delilah and her protection detail.

"Ready?"

"Yup." He walked outside, putting his head back into the house. "Momma R, we're heading out now. See you later!"

"Stay safe!" she called from the back of the house.

He closed the door and indicated for Delilah to carry on.

The dungeon living floor had continued to grow. Pillars reached out to support the ceiling above and the floors below. Structures had risen around the columns, turning them into large apartment buildings.

"This city keeps changing faster and faster," Erik said as they walked.

"Ah, just part of the times," Delilah said as they walked through the streets. People bobbed their heads in greeting at their passing.

They weaved through, reaching the academy, talking about small matters.

"So how is the family?"

"They're all okay. Father is interested in settling a farm out in the empire. He has been working the land with some of the other farmers in exchange. The conditions aren't as controllable, but there's more opportunity, and he misses the open sky."

"Will the rest of your family go?"

"No, my brother is heading to the Fifth Realm to set up a chain of Sky Reaching Restaurants. The others are happy to stay here. Not sure what they will do in the future." Delilah shrugged.

"This grew a bit." Erik looked at the academy. The original buildings were the same, but the newer buildings dwarfed and surrounded them.

"Just a little." She chuckled.

They entered the alchemy labs, getting a room for their own use.

"So, to start, we'll work with just the potion and add in the elements afterwards. I can show you what I have learned already. Then we can try making potions with increased elemental density in the room, then making them with elements." Delilah led the way down the hall, passing other alchemists, reaching the door to their alchemy room.

Erik opened the door for her.

"And we are using the Grand healing potion."

"It is rather basic, and the ingredients lean towards Fire, Earth and minimal Water elements."

The room was set up with a prep and concocting area, widely spaced out and formation-enhanced to assist the alchemist.

"Was it only yesterday we were working with just cauldrons and a few formations to help?" Erik shook his head.

"Do you want to make the potion or me?" Delilah asked.

"Been some time since I've done a concoction. Would you mind?"

"Not at all. I've already prepared the ingredients."

Erik pulled out his cauldron, a gift from the Academy. "Well, let's get to it then. Damn, it feels good to do some alchemy again."

Iron Will Cauldron
Weight: 28.9 kg
Durability: 1000/1000
Innate Effect: Increase efficacy by 20%.
Enchantment: Decrease mana flame cost by 15%
Enchantment: Temperature control
Requirements:
Mana, magical or formation flames
Expert-grade Alchemist

"Cauldron is like nine-in-one," Erik said.

"Eight secondary crucibles around the main crucible in the middle. Nice! You could have one as hot as the Fire floor and the other as cold as the mountains in the north. Makes it easier to juggle between ingredients.

Shouldn't be too hard."

Erik placed the cauldron on the concoction formations. Hooks attached to the bottom of the cauldron as he put sockets into the formation pad, changing its kind of enchantments.

He drew the Fire element in the room, chilling it as it gathered around the cauldron. He formed the Fire elements and injected his mana. Beasts of flame appeared around the cauldron, quickly warming it.

Erik's mana and elemental domain allowed him to see throughout the cauldron as he removed any elements from the cauldron.

Satisfied, he reviewed the formula once again.

"All right, let's get started. Utteka root and Yuris bulb?"

Delilah handed him the ingredients, already prepared into a powder and a liquid. As he poured in the powder, a beast of flame rose out of the cauldron, the powder falling into its belly before it drifted off to the compartments in the cauldron. The animals looked like they were carved from liquid flame, showing detailed feathers and fur that had been mere sketches before.

He poured in different ingredients; the cauldron was a hive of activity before he closed the lid. The creatures moved in accordance with his commands, refining the ingredients, combining them.

They moved from one crucible to another, the beasts combining into new beasts.

Then there were just three beasts remaining.

They exited their separate crucibles, consuming one another until they turned into a large bear covered in fiery runes.

The liquids gave off a pungent odor as the last impurities were boiled off.

Delilah passed Erik a series of vials. He opened the cauldron, and the bear rose as if from slumber. It opened its mouth, the potion pouring out into the vials.

With the last drop, Erik dismissed the flames and the beasts.

"All right, now for part two." Delilah took the potions to the workbench, placing it atop a formation. She took out one potion at a time and activated the formation. The deep red and neon blue with black glitter potions changed color under the formation's effects.

She went through four potions that turned different colors before the potion started to glow.

"Just need to get the elements required right," Delilah said.

The potion turned green in an instant.

"And not too many elements or they're ruined." She did it again and then passed over an untouched potion and an enhanced one.

Erik checked them both with his Reverse Alchemist. "It increased its quality by nearly an entire level," he said.

"Right! Now we have to see if you can introduce more elements and mana into the concoction as it's being made, and see what the effect would be. I think that it should make the potion even stronger!" Delilah was nearly buzzing with excitement.

Erik studied the elements being pushed into the potions, remembering their quantities before he sat back in front of the cauldron.

He finished concocting the potion, and portioned it into the different crucibles, giving him nine chances, and started introducing elements into the cauldron.

The first turned yellow and then purple rapidly.

"Too much metal," Erik muttered, letting the flames burn it away and purify as he moved to the second potion. And so it went.

"Uhh, we'll try it again," Erik said several minutes later, realizing he had no more potion to test with. He saw Delilah's face fall out the corner of his eye.

"Good thing we've got plenty of ingredients." He grinned and pulled out a bag, raising the corners of her mouth upward.

"If I had listened to your lessons more..." Erik looked away. *Maybe Nymiria or some of the others might have made it home.*

Lee patted him on the shoulder. "You have stepped on the right path. Since you entered the Ten Realms, you've focused on increasing your power through whatever means possible. Body tempering, mana cultivation, all of it to get an edge. Most people take years or decades, sometimes centuries, and you did it in weeks or months. You are bound to have missed a few things along the way."

"Please, teach me," Erik said.

"I will teach you what I can, but for you to develop your talents, the Ninth Realm would be the best place to go."

"Trying to get rid of me already?" Erik grinned.

Lee shook his head. "No, nothing like that. Your cultivation is higher than mine. I have studied and learned much, but like you, I worked on increasing my levels and now I'm taking time to integrate what I learned. In the Ninth Realm, there is the Academy of Avegaaren. Most just call it the

Academy. I was unable to enter the Academy in my current state, but you and Rugrat should be able to. The Academy was built by the Tenth Imperium to raise fighters against the shattered realms and to battle in the Tenth Realm."

"Why couldn't you enter?"

Lee sighed. "You might have noticed that my cultivation is rather low, but my level is a bit high?"

Erik nodded.

"When I joined the Ten Realms, much like you and Rugrat, I looked to game the system. I did everything I could to maximize the amount of experience I gained. It allowed me to ascend rapidly through the realms. I took on every craft that I could, learned it to my limit, and jumped to the next. Then I took on fighting in every way I could think. Consuming monster cores and elixirs, I got to the Eighth Realm, passed the trial, and entered the Ninth Realm. I had tempered my foundations and just formed my mana core at that point. Mostly because of the environments that I had been in with higher mana densities." Lee cleared his throat.

"When I got to the Ninth Realm, I learned how off-balance I was. The Ninth Realm is filled with those that have talent. I had achieved the levels I needed, but I didn't have nearly enough depth. I learned what I could, spent everything that I had to gain information. I cultivated my mana until I ran out of funds and managed to form my solid mana core. I was a teacher back on Earth, and while I hadn't gained a great depth of knowledge in one area, I had a great array of knowledge. So I headed back down to the lower realms and started teaching." Lee scratched his head.

"if Rugrat and I get into this Academy, why is it so important?"

"You can join the Academy as a free agent, but you have to defeat someone in the Academy for their position. Then, as long as you remain undefeated, you can make use of their facilities. They have knowledge of tempering with Wood and with Water. More than that, they have practical classes to train you on how to use your elements, mana and fighting techniques."

"What's the catch?"

"The Tenth Imperium uses it as a place to recruit people from. They will constantly be looking for a way to hook you into their group." Lee pursed his lips-frowning.

"Anything else?"

"The Tenth Realm. I don't know what kind of place it is, but I don't think that it's like any of the lower realms. From what I can gather, I think the

Tenth Realm is a war zone."

"A warzone at the peak of the realms?"

"There is a lot we don't know about the Ten Realms."

Erik thought about the information they had recovered from the Violet Sky Realm. "A place to train the generations to come."

Erik and Rugrat sat on the back porch of the house, nursing beers as they looked up at the Alvan's night-time sky.

"I'm glad we didn't try to hold on to controlling Alva and all this." Rugrat gestured with his bottle.

"Think we would have turned out like Edmond?"

"Don't know how we would have turned out, but we're not meant to rule. We have our skills and our desires, but ruling isn't one of them, at least not personally."

"I agree with you there." Erik thought on his why. "Yeah, we could have easily got into every nook and cranny, trying to make it the best possible instead of helping, we would have been trying to turn everyone into a soldier. A peg to fit in a hole."

"We'd get caught up in the past victories and defeats. Delilah always stuns me." Rugrat drank from his beer. "We get great wins, or we lose, and she just rolls on, learning from it and not focusing on it. I'd focus on what happened too much, for sure. She just adjusts and keeps driving forward."

"It'd feel like we were in a swamp unable to do anything, used to getting things done right away, but she can wait weeks, months or even years for something to come to fruition. That's a skill," Erik agreed, drinking from his beer.

"Well, now that we've passed the Eighth Realm and gained the ability to manipulate our mana, elements, and body directly, I think we should take some time to figure out how to use it all," Rugrat said.

"I spoke to Lee about that earlier."

"Ninth Realm?"

"Yeah, how did you...?"

"I swung 'round to talk to him, too. I was an ass, frustrated and pissed off. Thought he was looking down on me, but he was just looking out for me. Got to work on my spells and casting, stop relying on large costly spells and focus on smaller less mana-intensive ones. Get out the most effect from my mana pool. I'm too used to having a large mana pool and waste it on spells that I juice up with mana."

"Same here."

"Well, seems like there is plenty to learn in this Ninth Realm academy. Should pay them a visit soon."

"Might take us some time to learn what we want."

"Time well spent." Rugrat held out a bracelet. "I reduced the usable amount of my mana pool. Teaches me how to cast spells more efficiently."

"Kind of like weights for your cultivation. All right, I'm in," Erik said.

"Gonna suck. Back to school, dude."

"What's that saying? The more you learn, the more you know you don't know."

"You trying to give me a headache with your tongue twister?"

Erik shook his head and held out his beer. "To the fallen."

"To the fallen," Rugrat echoed, tapping his bottle. They hit them on the deck and drank. Lost in their own thoughts and memories.

19

Another Invitation

"**O**ld Hei, good to see you again." Erik walked into the meeting room, glancing at the person sitting beside him, their cloak's hood covering their features. The clothes reminded Erik of the sensory sheets that the army used to hide and that he had used for months in the undercity. It was finely made without a spare stitch; elegant without being gaudy.

Rugrat walked in behind Erik.

"Thank you for meeting with me. You might have been wondering why no one from the Mission Hall came down with me the last time and why I acted a little *weird* about the whole thing. Well, honestly, that's because of certain mitigating circumstances." Old Hei turned to indicate to the hooded man.

"Four-Star Heroes are rare within the Ten Realms and there are only a handful of them that are still alive," the hooded man said. "It is not so simple to just give someone their emblem, but when we were ready to do so, you went off to a sub-realm and gained your will. Most interesting."

Erik frowned at the man's perceptive words. "What does the Mission Hall want from us?"

"The Mission Hall was created to bring out the very best that the people of the Ten Realms have." The man reached up and pulled his hood down.

His skin had a sheen to it, as if it were marble with a green patina that increased the sharpness of his amused features: his nose, his cheekbones and jaw, his ears.

"Elf," Rugrat said.

"Seems that you know something about my people."

"Worked with the Gnomes to create the Ten Realms. Mind telling us just what for?"

"Oh, very interesting. You've got some information before the fall, it seems. Still, I should introduce myself. I am Arlen Reylar, administrator of the Tenth Imperium. These are your Four-Star medallions." He took out the intricate emblems that seemed to weigh down the mana around them and slid them across the table to Erik and Rugrat.

They grabbed them as Arlen sat back in his seat.

"And I want to ask you if you would be interested in joining the Tenth Imperium."

"No."

"No, thanks," Rugrat agreed as he turned the medallion and pocketed it, treating it just like another bauble.

"You know those emblems are particularly useful."

"Eh, something for the formation monkeys to have a look at. Seems it's made of Celestial Iron, at the very least." Rugrat grinned.

"We just started getting Sky Iron and you want Celestial Iron. Won't be long before you'll want Divine Iron," Erik muttered. "And don't go melting that down just because you want some Celestial Iron to play with."

"Imagine how the Beast would be with Divine Iron."

"You didn't hear a thing I said, did you?" Erik shook his head. "And if you made it all out of Divine Iron, it wouldn't be the Beast anymore! It would just be based on the Beast."

"Just have to change out the barrel, the chamber, the housing and receiver. I think the trigger will be the same."

Arlen coughed.

"Something else?" Erik asked.

"Are you sure you are not interested? You could keep your position here. There would be nothing more required of you. You would get resources and information beyond what even the largest sects in the Seventh Realm could provide."

"We're all good. We can figure out things just fine. Might take us longer," Rugrat said.

"We could make it easier for you to enter Avegaaren."

"Do we have to be a member of the Imperium to join the academy?" Erik asked.

"Well no, but..."

"Then thank you, but no thanks. We can do it ourselves. We've got plenty of people supporting and helping us."

"They really are as stubborn as you reported." Arlen smiled at Old Hei, who just grinned and shrugged. "Well then, I look forward to hearing about your admittance to Avegaaren. You've given me a new hope for the coming generations."

Arlen nodded his head and left the room.

Old Hei sighed and melted into his chair.

"So, who is he?"

"He's like my boss's master's boss's boss's grandmaster's boss." Old Hei sighed again. "He practically runs the Tenth Imperium, which is to say he runs every Association, Avegaaren, and the Tenth Realm."

"Oh, so no big deal."

Old Hei scoffed. "Yeah, something like that. I told them that you wouldn't join someone else."

"Is all of that why they took so long to give us our emblems?"

"Well, becoming a Four-Star Hero isn't something they hand out all the time. They were doing a thorough investigation into you."

"Interesting how they only gave it to us when we were healed," Rugrat muttered.

"They didn't know about that, and I think they were more interested in if you would pass the Eighth Realm Trial. There aren't any Four-Star Heroes that haven't passed that test."

"Are they all...?"

"Tenth Imperium? Yeah, all of them joined. Be right to say that they're power houses in their own right. The ones that are still alive."

"What do you mean?"

"The Tenth Realm, up there, even Four-Star Heroes find their lives in danger."

Erik and Rugrat glanced at one another.

"More unknowns," Rugrat said.

Erik nodded and turned back to Old Hei.

"There's something that Delilah and I want to show you."

"Don't worry. I have metal to pound on somewhere." Rugrat smiled.

"Well lead on!" Old Hei said, getting out of his seat with speed that belied his appearance.

"Egbert!"

They appeared in an alchemy room where Delilah was going over reports. She jumped in her chair, holding her hand to her heart.

"Damn it all to hell." She calmed herself, flushing. "Sorry, Old Hei, Erik." She shuffled her papers away.

Erik and Delilah worked together, creating a Grand Healing potion as Old Hei observed, marking down notes.

They set it to the side and Erik used his elements to concentrate the potions, increasing their efficacy before Old Hei's eyes. They'd practiced to perfection.

Delilah pulled one of the element-enhanced potions and passed it to Old Hei.

"It is almost like casting a spell, making the basic form from the ingredients. They then draw in the external elements, which increases the amount of mana that is added as well. This cycle continues several times, increasing the overall potency of the concoction several times," Erik said.

"While you can do this with making certain pills, it is easier to control the elements and, in a way, inject them into the potion, but it requires precise control," Delilah said.

"And you can look at that as being hard or easy. If an alchemist who has a good command over the elements is to enhance their own concoctions, it should be rather easy and much stronger. If they don't have control over the elements and mana to a high degree, then the balance of power will be thrown off and the potion or pill could easily become useless," Erik said.

"And mass-produced concoctions become easier, since the formula and the methods should not be changing. Using formations or other ways to induce elements and mana into the concoction will increase their level without too much issue."

"So you are saying what? That you could produce Journeyman level concoctions in higher quantities?"

"We're saying we could produce Journeyman concoctions and use elemental and mana enhancement to take them to Expert level and increase the potency of all pills by several levels."

"Because you are not worrying about the efficacy of the pill so much, people don't have to worry about the pill throughout the formation stage, just in the concentration and purification stages at the end." Old Hei stroked his beard.

"That could increase the number of concoctions created by an order of magnitude. What about experience?"

"One will only earn experience if they go into the concentration stages right from the formation stage. If they take out the pill, then they will get experience connected to the level of the capsule retrieved. Even if they enhance it later on, they will not gain more experience," Delilah said.

"Well, you are always coming up with new ideas." Old Hei smiled and swirled the potion in his hand.

Epilogue

Aziri waited impatiently as the man whimpered, injecting his mana into the door. It clicked and opened ahead of Aziri. He breathed in the musty air deeply, a smile spreading across his face as he looked at the Transition Point and the podium in its center.

"Y-you..." The Sha man whimpered, keeping his head lowered, not looking at the bodies that lie around the Transition Point.

Aziri turned to the man and opened his mouth.

The man screamed as Aziri drained him in a matter of seconds.

Aziri pulled out a rune card from his robe and the body of the Sha man collapsed into dust. He walked through and the dust scattered beneath his feet.

The floors shook as he stepped onto the formation and placed the card on the transition point podium.

His smile widened as light flashed around him and the Violet Sky Realm disappeared. Mana swirled around him as he stepped forward, the ground shook again as Dragon after dragon appeared behind him.

They let out roars, mana spreading through their bodies. Aziri drank in deep, power swelling and pouring into him.

Alva's Intelligence Department Director Elan Silaz, put down the information book he was about to absorb with the knock at his door.

The door opened allowing Aureus, one of his agents inside.

"Sorry sir for interrupting you."

"I asked you to report back as soon as you finished clearing out that Willful Institute backup site."

"It was as we suspected, though things didn't exactly go to plan."

Elan sat up, his face hardening, they had lost so many people losing more was like a knife to the heart.

"When we go there, the fighters that were hiding there were dead. Instead we found a man half alive in the midst of them. It looks like he got there before us and killed his way through them."

"By himself?"

"Yes."

Elan raised a eyebrow.

"He was laughing through his wounds, said his name was Sage, Sage Nightshade, looked at our weapons and said they were awfully familiar. We got him stabilized and healed up. Said he comes from Earth too and that he has a deal for us." Aureus waited for Elan's signal to go on. "He said that his best friend was killed by the bastards, ambushed on the road. He set his life's purpose to hunting them down and getting back to Earth. He said he knows where all the rest of the Willful Institute are hiding, he just wants us to promise him if we find a way back he gets a ride and that he is part of the teams that hunt down the Willful Institute."

"Is his information valid?"

"He gave us two locations. I checked them, they're both legit, Commander Glosil is preparing forces to attack both locations as we speak."

"How did he get this information?"

"After his friend died, he went around basically killing fighters from the Willful Institute. He learned how they worked, operated as a kind of assassin. Seems like when we found him, he'd taken on a group that was just too strong for him. These other places he knows he wouldn't be able to kill on his own."

"Taking on the whole Willful Institute on his own," Elan shook his head as his words trailed off.

"They killed his best friend, known him since they were kids, did nearly everything together. He wants to go home to tell his wife, to give her closure and to fulfill a promise to his fiancée. He's been working for years hunting them down."

"And any traces of the Institute?"

"These were the last, we've torn them out from the root."

Elan let out a sigh that came from his core.

"The Willful Institute defeated. I never thought I would see the day. Years ago I sent Domonos to join their ranks, a giant that I couldn't see the knee of. Now just another broken group." Elan shook his head.

"The future is not set." Aureus said.

Elan snorted. "Too true."

Trouble in Kushan

"Good trip, Eli'keen?" Beatrice asked as she helped him out of his cloak, taking it to a hanging rack.

"Interesting," Eli'keen pulled his hair back away from his pointed ears, taking the time to look through the windows of the Imperium's administrative tower and over the vast lands of Avegaaren Academy and its supporting cities.

Beatrice moved behind him.

"I made a little stop along the way." He pulled out a paper bag that smelled of sugars, fruit, and dough, winking as she accepted them with both hands and a chortle.

"And no doubt raided poor Lou of all his treats!" She put it away into her storage ring.

Eli'keen smiled, his eyes crinkling with even his advanced years. "So, tell me, what happened while I was away." He walked to his desk.

"The Imperium Head has gone missing again. He left a note saying he had gone training." There was a note of wry humor in her voice.

"That explains the pile." He turned to the growing paper tower on his desk. "He only controls the strongest force in the Ten Realms, surely there would be enough things to keep him tied down in one spot," Eli'keen muttered while Beatrice's smiled chewing on her treat.

Eli'keen had nothing to say to her expression.

"I met with the two from the first realm."

"The ones that earned four star hero medallions?"

Eli'keen nodded.

"What were they like?"

"Brash, powerful, untrained, determined—interesting."

Beatrice raised an eyebrow, opening her mouth to speak as her sound transmission bracelet illuminated. She listened intently, her face shifting to cold professionalism.

"A low-level Devourer has appeared in the Seventh Realm with a brood of Dragons, heading towards Lystenor. It had been renamed Kushan by the humans."

"How is there a Devourer in the Seventh Realm?"

"Rumors are that it came from one of the old defensive outposts. Renamed the Violet Sky Realm. A number of powerful seventh realm sects just returned."

Eli'keen sucked in a breath. "Send a team to remove the threat, we cannot have Devourers appearing in the lower realms. The tenth realm is under enough pressure with our limited forces."

"Yes, Deputy Head."

"We received a message ten minutes ago from an alliance member in the Seventh Realm. They reported Dragons heading past their territory, looks like they are heading for the mountain city Kushan."

Commander Glosil nodded to Pan Kun, heading into the meeting room.

"Now we're all here I'll begin. First, congratulations Lieutenant General Chonglu on your new position. We might be needing your assistance sooner rather than later," Director Elan Silza said as they found their seats. Elan turned to Erik and Rugrat sitting behind Delilah.

"You are not the only ones to leave the Violet Sky Realm. A brood of Dragons was reported to the North of Kushan. They match the description of the Dragons you encountered there. Leading them is a demi-human that seems to manipulate water and stone."

"Sounds like Aziri alright," Rugrat said.

"I was hoping he'd stay in his little prison. He won't be easy, let alone those dragons." Erik breathed out through his nose.

"Kushan is led by Lord Ziyaad al-Saade, part of the alliance and they have requested assistance." Council leader Delilah looked at Glosil. "What are our options?"

"At the very least send up a company to assist. We would need to send one of the Lieutenant General's if we want to control the battlefield. Kushan is a series of pillar like mountains that have been carved and interconnected into a super-city. It would be best to defeat these dragons before they reach the mountain range, to reduce the possibility of friendly fire. I would suggest sending Sparrows to assist, utilize the transport on-site and also utilize the upgraded rail cannons. We get stuck into the mountains, we deal with the outer defense."

"We are the leading party of this alliance and this is a clear attack on an allied city, we must show our support here," Delilah said.

"If we leave it up to them, they'll just start to fight between the sects, try and get the most amount of support," Erik said.

"So, we need to go with an overwhelming force that will allow us to take command. What about the airships we are building?" Delilah asked.

Glosil looked at Lieutenant General Chonglu commanding the newly formed Crow Corps.

"The warships are untested currently, we are still assembling the crews to man them. Edmond Dujardin and Esther Leblanc have been instrumental, but everything is untried and tested. I have only just assumed command, myself and my people need training."

"Edmond turned over the airships under his command, several corvettes, four Frieghters and two Cruisers." Glosil cleared his throat and sat forward.

"We can free up the Tiger Corps to assist. Take the combat mages and artillerists from the Crow Corps as support, should give us another fifteen thousand, bringing us to eighty thousand in strength." Glosil checked his watch. "We have just six hours before they arrive at Kushan. We will need to move quickly to establish control and get our forces into position and our allies."

"I believe that is a solid plan," She looked to Erik and Rugrat.

"Agreed," Erik said while Rugrat nodded.

"I'll leave it in your hands commander Glosil."

"Thank you," Glosil nodded his head as the room stood and broke apart.

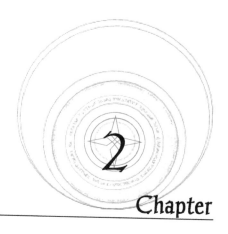

2

Chapter

Erik pinched the bridge of his nose at the noise in the meeting room, several dozen men and women from various factions from within the city, from allied sects and clans, talked over one another.

The muscles in Lieutenant General Yui's jaw buldged with his clenched teeth.

"We must shore up the defenses in the Western mountains. These beasts are interested in mana, and all our crafting facilities are there, it is sure to attract them," Ziyaad al-Saade, the lord of Kushan city was one of the loudest. "The area has limited defenses, it will be a great blow to lose it. We can defend there and push them into the teeth of our defenses."

"We should move the warships forward from the mountains, meet them in the open air and throw them back!" A man with wild black hair and several piercings but wearing the finest of gems and silks hit his armrest.

And so it continued, with everyone vying for a different defensive plan.

Erik cleared his throat, getting no response in the room.

He clapped his hands. *Jeez worse than four-year-olds fighting over sugar-filled cereal.*

"Yo, *shut up!*" His words shocked them into silence, he quirked his eyebrow seeing the half-formed rebuttals that died upon the leaders lips. *Might makes right here.*

"They are attracted to mana stones like crazy, they'll go for any warships with little care for themselves. We will carry out the plan proposed by Lieutenant General Yui. We don't have time to mess around, they will be here within four hours. We know that they are generally coming from the north so we will focus our defenses in that direction."

"The defenses in the north are the most developed, we must shore up our weakest in the Western crafter regions." Sl-Saade said. "Ravagers are not stupid."

"We have fought them before and we know what they're going for and we know the direction of their approach. Lieutenant General Yui will fill you in on our plans for defense."

Erik turned, dismissing any other dissenters or others with their own plans.

"Alright, this is the plan," Yui said as the doors closed behind Erik and Rugrat.

Erik looked at Rugrat, surrounded by their Special Teams. Because of Alva's power they would do as he said, at least close to it. With their honor, they would have to break up the meeting instead of debating every little thing.

"It's nice being the strongest," Rugrat said. "Maybe fortune is favoring us."

"Welcome to the Ten Realms, fortune favors the strong. I used to hate that saying, now, being the one on top, or at least taken seriously, it has a nice ring."

They exited the estate where the meetings were being held, outside was a hive of activity. The mountain rose up like a pillar to the sky, the inside had been hollowed out to create buildings along the outside, a spiralling road that curled around the hollowed center where lifts reached to the peak of the mountain and down into the magma base.

An elevator whisked them upwards. Fighters moved out of totems inside the mountain, marching up the main road or taking the elevators as well.

"Looks like our stop," Gong Jin said.

They headed between the buildings, instead of great mountains that rose into a peak, the mountains of Kushan had been worn down into straight pillars that rose up into the sky. Below lay magma fields thick with elements and mana as the pillars viewed one of the Seventh Realm's deserts before piercing through the low-lying clouds.

Bridges hung between the mountains with buildings hanging from their suspension. Flying beasts and small ships that used mana stones instead of dungeon cores at their heart connected the incredible city.

At the center a mountain had been carved with incredible skill showing an impassive figure sitting and cultivating mana.

"I wonder if there are any more Elves around like that Eli'keen," Erik spoke against the wind, turning his eyes from the statues to the warships that were docked beside the different mountains, transporting people and materials.

People worked to reinforce their homes as best as possible as ranged fighters, mages and Alvan Artillerists took over towers, courtyards and every open piece of land they could see clearly from.

"Has to be. Weird that there aren't Elves in the lower realms. Alva was made by gnomes. Probably a story there. I don't think the nobles are going to be too happy with us." He snorted and motioned at the artillery team stabbing in the Rail cannon's massive spades digging into the grass.

"When that thing fires, it's going to leave a nice groove in their lawn, that's for sure." Erik smirked. With spells and formations, the mountains hidden defenses were revealed and adding in their allies, armor, and weapons with visible speed.

"Make room!" A woman called out, Erik and Rugrat moved to the side as a group of soldiers appeared on the street and moved past to their positions.

"We've got the location of your standby position if you want to follow me," Gong Jin said.

"Lead on," Rugrat said. "Just what I like, being in the rear with the gear."

Erik's smile soured into a frown. "Fucking Aziri," He couldn't forget how *helpless* they had been in front of him.

"There were only fifteen of us last time."

"And Gerard's people."

"Still, we have thousands of people to back us up and this time we're playing from the home advantage not him."

"Back in the Violet Sky Realm, he didn't have access to mana and he was able to hold us back with just his control over the elements."

"Well, just have to see how good he is with a rail cannon in his face." Rugrat said.

Erik grunted. *No sense in worrying about it now.*

"Dragons spotted!" The communications officer sent a thrill down Yui's spine a moment of pure calm as everyone looked to him, silence, like a vacuum just about to take over the room, making his words clear to all.

"Make ready, have all units finish their final preparations and move to their standby positions immediately. Only people in the streets should be our fighters."

The room's volume rose as the projected map, something akin to a 'holographic' Erik had called it, showing everything.

"Do we know the Dragon types yet? Identifying features?" he asked his assistant.

"We have beast masters working on that currently, a mix, each based off of an elemental constitution."

So, no. Yui looked at the mountains that were in a rough circle shape, to the south were the three fleets, Edmond's was to the southeast, Sha turned Alvan hopefuls. Other allied craft and the small fleet of Kushan.

Facing thousands of dragons.

Mages were still running around trying to protect as much of their home as possible.

Demi-humans from the city called for the dragon's surrender in hopes that they were intelligent to know what they meant and not completely dominated by Aziri.

"There are three groups of Dragons." The communications officer circled the groups.

Yui traced where they were going.

"The fleets, they must want the mana stones powering them. Have Edmond move his fleet to the Allied fleet in the south. See if the Dragons alter their course."

Five minutes later he had his answer.

"Well the fleets are now our bait. Lord Al-Saade, I think it best that we combine our fleets so they can operate as one." He turned to the lord off to the side.

"The Western side is where all of our crafting is located and the most mana stones in the city, if these beasts are as you say, they will push to those western mountains. We have to protect them."

"I have my orders sir," Yui said.

Al-Saade's brows pinched together, looking pained. "I understand, it is as your Lord West said. Very well my fleet will work under Edmond Dujardin."

"Thank you." Yui nodded to his communications officer who started sending the orders.

He watched the fleets reposition themselves to the direct south of the mountains.

That will force them to come through the mountain range to get them, let us rake them with everything we have.

"They have made it inside our extreme range."

Come on further.

They continued to fly forward, as he started to get some scale for the beasts, some which were as big as a frigate, all scales, tooth and claws.

He watched as they broke the firing line.

"Fire!"

He heard the rumbling of weapons, the rush of mana as spells discharged and spell scrolls activated.

Attacks rose up from the mountain pillars, the Dragons attacked with their own elements, destroying attacks. The broods fell apart under the attacks, the weakest unable to defend, thinning their ranks.

Event
The city of Kushan **is under attack! Pick a side!**
Defend *Kushan*
Attack *Kushan*

Rail cannons fired flak shot, trying to tear wings and drop the gigantic beasts. Spells hit their scales but they flew on, losing tens through their advance but they had thousands, they must have cleared out the Violet Sky's Under City.

The peaceful clouds were shattered, clearing the skies around Kushan.

Dragons banked heading to the Western side of the mountains and unleashed their attacks.

Their breaths struck the barriers with streams of pure elemental fury.

"Get those barriers reinforced now, they're like paper lanterns!" Yui yelled.

"The elemental attacks are burning through them faster than mana attacks," Al- Saade was drowned out by a spell breaking the barrier and hitting somewhere on the mountain the command center had been set up.

"Machine guns are up, combat mages are attacking." Yui's ever-present communications officer said.

The attacks nearly tripled, targeting was tighter than before as Dragons started to fall from the sky. The quick mana boats raced to move mages around to support the Western side.

Dammit, should have listened to Al Saade, the Ravagers are going right for the Western mountains.

The Dragons raked the mountain with their attacks, their speed allowing them to pass through the barrier in seconds as they unleashed destruction on the Western Mountains, the younger Dragons roared and dove crashing through buildings with their bodies, picking up towers with their claws and hurling them down into the magma flows beneath the mountain pillars.

Others breathed flame, through openings in buildings, causing it to explode out with the attack.

"Move forces to reinforce the Western pillars."

They'd lost a third of their broods on the way to the city, now half of them focused on destroying the western mountains the other half continued to charge over the mountains, losing more of their numbers, but passing over the pillars too fast for a group to get more than a few hits while they breathed destruction upon the city's pillars.

A cloud that was drifting towards the city instead of away from it like the others twisted into a spiral and shot forward, turning into a lance of water. It crashed into a barrier, darkening it to the point of nearly breaking before the attack ran out.

The clouds were gathering again, but inside a person could be seen.

"Aziri, we've got him, tell the teams." Yui looked at what he had been aiming at, seeing the boats moving reinforcements to the Western district.

Every Kestrel, mage and soldier that could target the Dragons opened fire.

The dragons diverted to attack the barges carrying defenders.

"Have Storgaard raise the fleet, draw the Dragon's attention, launch Sparrows."

He flicked back to Aziri, he flew around the sky, attacks coming close to him were destroyed by his clouds, turning into whips dozens of meters long.

He remembered Erik's advice. 'We cannot let him set foot in the city, with direct contact with two elements he will be hell.'

The Dragons were splitting into different groups, attacking the city randomly now, losing their previous cohesion.

Edmond Dujardin, former Marshal of the Sha and now leader of the Alvan Airships, looked through the bridge's windows, as they cleared the tops of the city's spires.

The defender's spells intersected with elemental attacks, one hitting dragons and sky, the other tearing through buildings and darkening barriers.

"All cannons are ready to fire." Esther stood at his side as his second in command.

"Full broadside, all ships, don't hit the cities, dragons only, get their attention on us and not the assault teams."

"All batteries confirm."

Edmond glanced over to the reclaimed Black Phoenix Clan ship, now under the command of Heidi Storgaard of the Grey Peak Sect and staunch ally of Alva.

How the world changes.

"Fire!" Heidi's order was relayed directly to the cannon teams as mana cannons and Sha's gunpowder cannons fired after one another.

Dragons were raked by the incoming fire, their anger flared as some turned towards the fleet, away from Aziri.

"Come on, focus on us over here with the mana stones, you don't need to care about him, he's strong sure he can deal with all the attacks himself. Over here, nice mana stones for you," Edmond muttered, holding onto the bannister.

The combined fleet continued to fire, adding to the spells and attacks from below, Dragons fell from the sky, crashing into pillars, buildings or the magma flows below. Some broke off and fled, but the strongest opened their mouths towards the fleet.

"Brace!" Edmond yelled as dragon breath from a hundred different throats crashed into the airship's barriers.

"They're away from the city!" Esther said.

"Fire missiles."

They hurled out the side of the warship, in a flare of blue flame.

Edmond spared a glance for those fighting Aziri, he had turned the cloud into his personal weapon it compressed into tentacles and expanded out into shields of ice, several dozen appendages waging war against thirty or so fast mana craft. Cultivators with enough control over mana dodged and zipped through the sky, ambient mana supporting them.

A missile was struck by a dragon's breath. Nearly a meter long packed with Sky mana stone, explosives and stack formations the wave of explosions tore into even the strongest Dragons that had been able to shrug off most of the damage through the power of their body.

Others intersected with the dragons.

A wave of explosions propagating through the Dragon ranks.

Chunks of the Dragon formation were gone, but they pushed on.

"Here they come," Edmond said, the clouds from the missiles clearing as the first Dragons made it through, flying through mana barriers they crashed into the ship line with enough force to shift the warships, taking out one Corvette as the crew fought to keep her aloft as a dragon's claws raked the ship and it bisected the ship with a stream of Plasma.

Mages and Cannons fired at the Dragons where they could.

Edmond felt his cruiser being hurled to the side, the multi-ton behemoth, a toy to the kings and queens of the sky.

"Right the ship, keep us level!" Edmond yelled as Sha rifles and Alvan machine guns opened up on the three medium sized dragons that had attacked the ship.

One swiped their claw at the ship, white wind blades cut deep into the ship's armor, raking the cannon decks.

A mounted rail cannon fired into the Dragon from the side at almost point blank range, the crew moving with their Ten Realms speed, the cannon seemed as if it was automatic, shredding the Dragon's wings, cutting up their side. The Dragon wailed in pain and confusion, blasted with attacks it fell from the side of the ship and tumbled down, spells and shot following after it as a second Dragon wailed releasing a dragon breath of wind at the railgun emplacement, tearing through it and boring a hole into the deck of the Cruiser.

Roska fired at Aziri. With all the experts they had, they were just able to pin him in place while his attacks were deft agile and sneaky. *He has gotten stronger, I can sense more mana in his attacks.*

A tentacle, nearly a wisp of water ballooned to the size of a man and cut through a mana boat.

People were thrown free as Roska focused fire on the tentacle.

It broke into water, but it had done its damage.

"The other formation holders are nearly all in place, I will need a few seconds," Egbert said in her ear.

More experts jumped from their ships, using formations or their abilities to stay in mid-air.

"That's it!"

Formations on everyone's backs released from them, and floated in mid air, lines shot out to one another, creating a multi-faceted sphere with Aziri at its center. Runes and spell circles appeared around the formations reinforcing the ice like sheets that created the enclosure.

The formations activated, drawing power from inside the sphere, the clouds around Aziri thinned, leaving only globes of water as the elements and mana were drawn out of the area within by the formations.

Roska fired on Aziri with others that had ranged weapons.

He swirled and dodged around, the worst attacks missing him.

"He's chanting something," Egbert warned.

"Keep shooting, he could be going for a spell!"

"You have some dragons inbound to you," Yui Silaz reported.

Roska glanced back, seeing five of the largest dragons, new scales showing where they had been wounded by the city's defenses.

Attacks raked them from behind but they ignored them.

A spell appeared outside the sphere, exploding into diamond-ice daggers.

Experts cried out as they were blasted from the sky, several formations breaking as the others glowed brighter to make up for their loss.

"Recalibrating."

Aziri was slowing, wounds appearing on his skin and his robes unable to protect him much longer.

A roar from behind made Roska feel the hairs on the back of her neck raise up.

"Die you bastard!"

She felt twin fluctuations, not as powerful as Aziri's but strong enough to be made out in the chaos.

Aziri snarled, his body expanding as he dropped.

"Bind him!" Roska yelled, spell scrolls were torn by those without ranged weapons, chains appeared within the sphere, wrapping around Aziri's limbs, binding him as he expanded, returning to his Dragon form.

The chains started to snap, the wounds no longer small scratches as poisons and effects stacked upon one another, entering his body.

Roska heard the fighting going on behind her as Sparrows attacked the remaining Dragons with the support of Erik and Rugrat.

A dragon breath raked the sphere, cutting several formations apart and creating a hole in the experts as they dodged the attack.

Roska could feel the fighting tilt out of their hands. They were fighting against forces way beyond their ability.

A spell formation appeared around the base of one of the mountain pillars.

"He's casting another spell!" Fighters from the city focused on the spell.

"We need to contain him!" Roska yelled.

"This is our city, not yours!" One of the defenders yelled.

The spell completed, the formation turned and linked together before smashing into the pillar and tightening, cracks ran through the mountain.

Fighters from the city broke rank, turning back to protect their home.

"We need you!" Roska yelled as three containment formations broke from the pressure, the pillars of elements they had drained before, turning into threads.

"Watch out!" Erik yelled.

Roska sensed the attack, dodging to the side of the Lightning attack that burned through her vision, relying on her domain she dodged the Dragon, the lightning spreading like a net through the formations as the heavily wounded Dragon smashed into the ice panes, cracking the sphere, elements and mana rushed back in as the formations failed and Aziri roared, stretching out to his full length, breaking free of the restraining chains.

A flap of his wings tilted Roska and she had to use spells and elements to right herself against the force.

Dragons roared, greeting their master.

They redoubled their attacks and those that had begun to fly away turned back.

The four other dragons flew around Aziri as he surged forwards.

"Use everything!" Erik yelled, releasing several missiles from his storage ring. George and Davin unleashed their fire attacks, Rugrat riding on George's back as he fired his rifle continuously.

Roska tore the spell scrolls attached to her harness, chaining spells together against Aziri.

Whips of water appeared around Aziri as he used spells of water at distance. *We need to kill him before he can spellcast.*

His whips took out mana boats, whittling down their elites.

He surged forward towards the city as a humming noise filled the air.

Aziri was smashed backwards, crashing into a mountain, pinned there by a silver spear that seemed to draw the very elements from his body, hues of metallic blue and yellow, wrapping around it.

"Get the smaller Ravagers!" A man's voice boomed through the sky as Roska looked at the five-person group charging up from the city.

Their armor was stronger than anything she had seen before and they all manipulated the mana around them to fly with ease.

Stone broke around Aziri turning into spears that shot back at the group.

They dodged and stepped on the spears as if they were a garden path, closing with him as he lashed out with water whips, grabbing the spear with both of his lower legs and tearing it from his body.

The spear hummed, pulling free and shooting into the lead man's hand.

Roska looked at the Dragons that the group had passed, turning on them.

She yelled as she fired on the Dragons, casting spells on her attacks, leaving Aziri in the hands of the new group.

They chained their attacks together against Aziri, supporting one another, like they had done this a dozen times before.

One slashed with their sword, a mana blade cutting away Aziri's wing, another sending an arrow into his side as a third used a technique or maybe ability with their sword, creating a wall that hit Aziri's jaw redirecting a dragon's breath of twisted earth and water upwards giving the spear user an opening to slash Aziri's stomach and the archer to stitch up his side with arrows.

All along a mage remained at the rear, watching over them and commanding the four others into a dance. It reminded Roska of the bands, orchestras she had sometimes seen when on recon missions or attending high end events as a protection detail, one part flowing in with the rest.

They whittled down Aziri leaving him no way of escape as the remaining experts vented their attacks on the Dragons. Rugrat released two missiles, hitting the Lightning spewing Dragon to the side as Alvan rounds impacted and exploded, the damage too much for the beast as it rolled and spun, twisting away before smashing into the cracked ground below, leaving a crater that broke the nearby lava flow, the red-hot material pouring down the side of the crater around the beast.

With the tombstone experience flooded into the experts.

A second Dragon was hit with a combination spell, piercing through its wing and back, coming out of its chest.

A third used a burst of fire element, calling out, as she made a run for it, other fire dragons calling back as the brood ran from their battles to try and catch up with their matriarch.

Roska recovered from the rush of massive experience when she was hit with a wave several times stronger than both Dragons combined together.

The Dragons roared in panic, and fear, disengaging and flying away from the city in every direction.

She turned to see Aziri's head disappear into the storage ring of the shield user, the sword user flicking her sword clean, on the other side of Aziri's neck.

The tide of battle turned as the defenders hunted down the Dragons as they tried to flee.

"Gather the wounded, get them back to the city," Erik yelled, securing another wounded falling from the sky in his beast storage crate.

Event
You have successfully defended Kushan.
Rewards:
850,000,000,000 EXP
+15% defensive bonus to Kushan defenders.

Erik pressed his thumb on the man's leg, making him groan between his teeth in pain as Erik fused the bone and then healed the artery.

He released the pressure from his thumb carefully, seeing through the man's body.

"Good to go."

The man looked up at the ceiling, breathing heavily as he'd just gone from life threatening injury to healed in seconds.

Erik turned away, using a cleaning spell, finding three people waiting for him, the spear user, the sword user and the shield user.

"What can I help you with?" Erik asked, looking at his next patient, *thankfully most are walking wounded with their cultivations.*

"We hear you are running this show, you knew that thing out there," The spear user growled.

"Aziri, Devourer I think, that's what some people call him, he was in the sub-realm Violet Sky Realm, must have got out." Erik said.

"Fucking sects going where they have no business, you know what you could have done letting a Devourer out in the lower realms?" The spear cracked the ground.

"Not like I gave him an invitation to come here."

"You might as well have."

"Syd, he doesn't know he's not from the Associations or the Imperium."

"Just wants to lord over the other weaklings instead of fighting for his freedom, just accepts it." The spear user Syd looked like he was working up spit when the archer cleared his throat.

"All Devourers and Ravagers are to be reported to the Mission Hall as soon as possible, if not the Mission Hall then one of the Associations. Thankfully the City head Al-Saade did so that we could come and assist."

"And now you've come for your rewards?" Erik raised an eyebrow. "Go talk to Al-Saade, he is the one that called you here. I have wounded to see to."

"At least he had the presence of mind to call us, if you had called us sooner then you would have less to heal."

"Who the fuck are you anyway?" Erik crossed his arms.

"You from some backwater realm? How the hell are you leading this all?" Syd said, none of the others disagreeing.

"You sects and associations like to keep all the information to yourselves. Yeah you could say I'm from a backwater, Earth."

"Just cause you're from the Earth realm is no excuse," The sword user admonished.

"No, Earth earth, home of the humans."

The three frowned and looked at one another.

"So got no idea who the fuck you are, where you're from, guessing by the talk of Associations and Mission Hall, must be from that Imperium Eli'keen was talking about?"

"Watch your tone talking about the Assistant Head," The archer threatened.

Erik rubbed his face.

"Thanks for your help, Al-Saade will know how to help you. See you around and don't worry we'll see if we can't bother you in the future about these minor issues."

Syd stepped forward, his power flaring. Erik hid his surprise. *He is about as strong as me in terms of power. Though he defeated Aziri so easily.*

Several special team members stepped out of where they were waiting, ready.

"We can't help people that are blind to the truth." The sword user said.

"Fucking lower realm idiots."

"Have a nice day too," Erik's chest tightened seeing the wounded laid out in the courtyard. *Could I have prevented this from happening? We had no idea that Aziri was at the heart of the Treasure Hall.*

Erik focused on his task, pushing away his errant thoughts.

Author's Note

Thank you for your support and taking the time to read **The Eighth Realm**.

The Ten Realms will continue in **The Ninth Realm.**

As a self-published author I live for reviews! If you've enjoyed The Seventh Realm, please leave a **review**!

Do you want to join a community of fans that love talking about Michael's books?

We've created this Facebook group for you to discuss the books, hear from Michael, participate in contests and enjoy the worlds that Michael has created. You can join using the QR code below.

Thank you for your continued support. You can check out my other books, what I'm working on, and upcoming releases with the QR code below.

Don't forget to leave a review if you enjoyed the book.

Thanks again for reading ☺